THE RUTLAND CONNECTION

THE RUTLAND
CONNECTION

Michael Dane

The Book Guild Ltd

First published in Great Britain in 2023 by
The Book Guild Ltd
Unit E2 Airfield Business Park,
Harrison Road, Market Harborough,
Leicestershire. LE16 7UL
Tel: 0116 2792299
www.bookguild.co.uk
Email: info@bookguild.co.uk
Twitter: @bookguild

This work is entirely fictitious and bears no resemblance to any persons living or dead.

Typeset in 11pt Adobe Garamond Pro

Printed and bound in Great Britain by 4edge Limited

ISBN 978 1915853 462

British Library Cataloguing in Publication Data.
A catalogue record for this book is available from the British Library.

For Fina

THE INVESTIGATORS

Branch 11

Assistant Chief Investigation Officer – Alan Matthew Hawkins

Nottingham A – The Bravo Golfs
Bravo Golf 1 – Howard Gideon Spencer – SIO, Nottingham A
Bravo Golf 2 – Andrea Cordelia Woodman
Bravo Golf 3 – Julia Hayes
Bravo Golf 4 – Francis Daniel McBride OBE
Bravo Golf 5 – Kevin David Cleary
Bravo Golf 6 – Gillian Esther Murray
Bravo Golf 7 – Gerry June Day
Bravo Golf 8 – Carl Mark Sanders
Bravo Golf 9 – Christopher Simon 'Monster' Bolton
Bravo Golf 10 – Joseph Michael Lake
Bravo Golf 11 – Nicholas Stuart Harper
Bravo Golf 12 – Mark William Hardy
Bravo Golf 13 – Stephen William Bradford

The Other Office

Tommy Stone
Sid Baker
Jack Norton

The Targets

Tango 4 – Stephen Lewis 'Maxi' Pettigrew

Tango 5 – John Edward 'JP' Pyke

Tango 6 – Donna Cynthia Pettigrew

Tango 7 – Leanne Macpherson

Tango 8 – Gary 'Gazza' Phillip Barham

Tango 9 – Diane Lisa Bartholomew

Tango 11 – Shane Patrick Hartney

Tango 20 – Stanley Pieter Maas

Tango 30 – The Brigadier, aka Lefty, aka Peter/Pieter

PROLOGUE

Amsterdam 1996

At eight thirty-five, hopefully for the last time, John Pyke heard the twin keys being turned in his cell door. He and Stanley Maas had been incarcerated on the same day and now, nine months later, they were being released on the same day. The prison officer came in carrying two cardboard boxes. He gave the small one to the Englishman and the larger one to the Dutchman. "Be ready in forty-five minutes," said the officer. Pyke had picked up just enough Dutch to understand.

From the small box he retrieved the clothes that he had been wearing on the day of his arrest: a football shirt, a pair of jeans, underwear and socks, and a pair of white trainers upon which the blood had faded into a rust-brown stain.

The Dutchman's box contained the suit he had been wearing at his trial, a silk shirt, Italian loafers and an ostentatious gold Rolex. Maas took his time dressing. Making a good impression on his exit was important. He wanted to exude power and confidence. He wanted to pick up where he had left off as a leading distributor of synthetic drugs, recreational pharmaceuticals, he called them, in South Holland. (He would have called it the Netherlands. People from Tilburg are fussy about such things.) He recognised that this would be no easy task. His absence had created a gap in the market that he knew others had been only too willing and too quick to fill. Dealing with that issue was his second priority. Dealing with those who had failed him, or in one particular case betrayed him, leading to his imprisonment, was his first priority. Some people were going to be taught a lesson. Some people were going to be hurt.

Pyke too had plans. His spell in prison had given him an opportunity to take stock of his life and to review the achievements and the accomplishments of the previous twenty-eight years. In truth, they hadn't amounted to much. He had a couple of children that he almost never saw. He lived, or at least he had lived, in a small semi-detached house on Lincoln's Ermine estate that his current girlfriend (again, he wasn't wholly sure that the present tense was appropriate) had sort of inherited from her grandmother.

Somewhere under the stairs at his parents' house, also on the Ermine, were a few boxing trophies, a last legacy of the brief time when he 'could have been a contender'. But, like his teachers, his parents and his various ex-partners, his coach had eventually accepted that Pyke just didn't have the will, the sticking power or, above all, the discipline to make it in the fight game. He had the talent alright and more than enough aggression. He just wasn't prepared to do the work, make the weight, give up the booze and the weed.

But things were going to be different now. Pyke was on his way. He had received an education and learnt a trade. He was making his way in the world. And paradoxically it was his fondness for alcohol and violence that he had to thank for it all.

At his many appearances at Lincoln Magistrates' Court Pyke had usually been described as a petty criminal, occasionally as an habitual criminal and only once as a career criminal. In his trial in Amsterdam, the case had been moved there at the request of the British Consul, he had been described as a violent anti-social individual. Pyke would tell his friends that he had been persecuted for being an English football fan and that all he had really done was move some furniture. However, the furniture concerned had been two chairs and a small table, and Pyke had moved them through the plate-glass window of a bar on the Stationsplein in Eindhoven the day that PSV knocked Leeds United out of the UEFA Cup. The resisting arrest and the possession of a knuckleduster were additional aggravating factors. But without that incident Pyke wouldn't have met Stanley Maas in Bijlmerbajes. And Maas wouldn't have become his friend, his tutor, his mentor and eventually, he hoped, his business partner.

Maas definitely did not see his imprisonment as a fortunate event. He was angry, chiefly at himself. He had found himself in Bijlmerbajes as a result of misjudging the reliability of some of his business associates. Valuable lessons had been learned, bitter lessons, lessons about loyalty, discipline and adherence to protocols. There was a right way and a wrong way to conduct a business like Maas's. He had had plenty of time to reflect upon that and he would not be repeating the mistakes that he had made in the past. In an odd way his tutoring of Pyke had crystalised things in his own mind. He had grown fond of the Englishman and, perhaps, if he took on board what he had been taught he might one day represent a worthwhile business opportunity.

The two men, who had been dressed identically for nine months but now represented different ends of the sartorial spectrum, travelled down together in the prisoners' elevator. On the ground floor another prison officer was holding a clipboard. The formalities took only a few seconds and then the main door opened. The two were free men again. On the pavement outside Maas and Pyke shook hands.

"When you are ready, Johann, call for me at the Superkruiken Bar in Tilburg. We will do business together. We will become very rich."

And Maas walked across the pavement to the large BMW, the rear door of which was being held open by a man in his early twenties, so similar in appearance to Maas that it could only have been his son, Sebastiaan. In the back of the BMW were two young women who, very likely, were not blood relations and certainly not dressed for the weather, which was unseasonably chilly for July. The BMW drew smoothly away and Pyke was left on the pavement clutching a carrier bag and a travel warrant from the consulate.

ONE

Nottingham 1997

The trouble with super-cool, top-secret locations, mused Lake as he plodded up Clarendon Street, *is that in order to be top-secret they are seldom ever cool.* A genuine top-secret location needs to be dull, inobtrusive, the sort of place you could walk past every day and never notice. Yep. His new office fitted the bill. 13–15 Clarendon Street was as anonymous a building as one could imagine. Once a pair of Edwardian semis – or Victorian, Lake wasn't a student of architectural history – it was now the sort of place that tends to be used as the offices of small firms of accountants. It looked like there ought to be gold lettering in the window reading, 'Scrimshaw & Balderdash – Solicitors and Commissioners for Oaths'. Anyway, it was Lake's new office and if it was anything like his last one there would probably be plenty of oaths. It was probably 'No Smoking'. Government buildings tended to be in 1997, even top-secret ones. Lake examined the cigarette in his hand. Too long to throw away just yet. And in any event, he wanted a minute or two to prepare himself. He took a drag.

Lake was thirty but precocious. In terms of cynicism and world-weariness he could pass for forty-five or fifty. He had been an investigator for six years, spending all of that time in London. There were nearly a thousand investigators in London. Nottingham had perhaps two dozen. But the job was the job. Investigators were investigators. How different could it be?

There was a handful of cars parked in front of the building. Official cars. Government cars. You could tell by the number plates, if you knew what you were looking for. Also outside was a silver Jaguar XK8 with a red leather interior. That was not a government car. At least not the sort that was left parked outside the office. Lake took one last puff, cast his butt into the gutter and headed for the door. It was as anonymous as the rest of the building. There was a small intercom entry system. One button only. No name listed. Lake took a deep breath, let out a shallow sigh and, mentally and emotionally shrugging, he pushed the button.

"Hello."

"Joe Lake. I'm starting here today. Nottingham A."

"Hang on!"

A few seconds later the door was opened by a young man wearing the unofficial uniform of a Customs and Excise investigator: jeans, trainers, polo shirt. He was younger than most, though. Maybe twenty-four or -five. The same age that Lake had been when he started. Lake fished out his identity card and badge.

"It's alright. You're expected. I'm Nick, Nick Harper."

Lake entered. He was in a small passageway. Again, if you knew what you were looking for the signs were there that this was a government office. There's something about the carpet, the shade of beige paint on the walls, the health and safety notices, and the smell of bureaucracy, underfunding and neglect. But to identify that this was an investigation office required you to use your ears. Behind a door to his right Lake heard someone swearing at a photocopier. The stream of profanity – fluent, unceasing and utterly obscene – being punctuated by the sounds of some percussive engineering and ending with a serious of prophesies about the short-term health prospects of variously the manufacturer, the government procurement department and whoever had jammed it last time was unmistakeably investigation. Behind another door was the sound of two (or was it three?) people arguing over whose turn it was to make the tea. The casual profanity flowed like a verbal sauce bearnaise – no, earthier than that, less sophisticated. It flowed like chip shop gravy. Yep. Just like his old office.

"I suppose you'd better start by meeting the SIO. Like I said, you're expected," said Harper. He turned and headed for the stairs. Lake followed.

"Rest room," said Harper, nodding at a partially open door on his left on the first floor. "And this is Howard's office."

In front of them was a door. It was closed. It bore a sign that read, 'Howard Spencer MA (Oxon) – Senior Investigation Officer – Nottingham A – Knock and Wait'.

Lake raised an eyebrow. SIOs' doors didn't usually contain details of academic qualifications. Most SIOs had none. And they didn't normally include an instruction to knock and wait. They were either open or you waited until they were. Knocking on a closed SIO's door was a hazardous business. You could expect a stapler or some similar piece of office equipment to be thrown at your head if you entered.

Nick shrugged in a faintly apologetic way. "I'm in the attic. Probably see you later." He paused for a second. "I think we might be working together actually. My manager is Frank McBride."

"Frank McBride! The Frank McBride?"

Nick looked blank.

"Angry Scotsman? About a hundred years old? Smokes a pipe?"

Nick nodded. His face wore a puzzled expression. He must be very new if he didn't know who Frank McBride was. Anyone who had been in the job for more than five minutes knew Francis Daniel McBride OBE, by reputation if you were lucky, personally if you weren't. Because Frank McBride was a legend. For lots of reasons. Some of them good. He had been in investigation since, well, nobody knew exactly, a long time anyway. First officer to go long-term undercover, part of operations that were still talked about twenty years later. Promoted, demoted and promoted again so many times that even he had probably lost count. He had won ten gold medals at the Grumpy Bastard Olympics and came dead last in the 'suffering fools gladly' event. What the hell was he doing in Nottingham, the smallest and lowest-profile office in the whole of Customs' National Investigation Service?

*

Lake turned again to the door. As instructed, he knocked and waited, but not for very long.

"Enter!"

Generally, there were two types of SIOs. The first were men, or occasionally women, who had come up the hard way and now spent their mornings wrestling with the crossword and their afternoons in the pub. They usually had only the sketchiest idea what their teams were doing and very seldom knew why, or sometimes even where.

And then there were the bad ones. The bad ones were out to impress. Not to lead, to manage, to encourage – to impress. And not the poor sods working for them, of course – the senior management. The people who prowled Whitehall attending nonsense meetings, wearing their old school ties and spending ninety per cent of their lives ensuring that they were well placed to garner maximum credit where it was available and a million miles from any blame or responsibility when it wasn't. Lake thought he knew into which category Spencer fell. It was nine o'clock on a Monday morning and he wasn't even visibly hungover.

"Welcome on board, Joseph."

He must have said more, but Lake wasn't listening; he was appraising Spencer. Was that an old school tie? Certainly possible.

And those cufflinks. Oxbridge college? The accent was definitely upper class. Was that a tailored suit? Lake couldn't tell. But if it was it was certainly consistent with the overall impression. Oh dear.

He could tell from the tone of the words, to which he was paying almost no attention, that it was time to switch on in case he had to make some sort of reply.

"You've been assigned to the drugs team."

Lake already knew this.

"Your call sign is Bravo Golf Ten. You will report to Frank McBride, Bravo Golf Four. You'll be working with Nick Harper. Good chap but brand new. He'll learn a great deal from Frank, of course, but I'd like you to take him under your wing. Frank's a splendid fellow. Tons of experience, but I run a thoroughly modern team here. Thoroughly modern. You'll let me know if there's anything you need, won't you? Or anything you feel I ought to know?"

Apparently no reply was required after all.

"Well, you had better go and introduce yourself. You're in the attic. Top of the stairs. Can't miss it. And please let Frank know that I'd appreciate a few moments of his time if he wouldn't mind."

And thus, Lake was dismissed. And Spencer had never thought to ask him why he, a thirty-year-old investigator, had chosen to leave London and move to the smallest and most obscure office in the land. Lake wondered whether he had bothered to ask McBride either. Perhaps he didn't care.

At least it had spared Lake from choosing between his two prepared answers. The first was a tightly reasoned and well-rehearsed story about seeking new challenges, developing his career and more obvious bullshit. Although having met the man he wondered whether it would have been obvious to Spencer. The second answer was a great deal more straightforward. Lake was in Nottingham because his wife, Bella, didn't want to raise children in London. She dreamed of wholesome family Sundays, cycling through country lanes, waving at passing steam trains and stopping for tea at thatched cottages. And what Bella wanted she tended to get. She had already begun house-hunting amidst the villages of the Vale of Belvoir. She was poring over Ofsted reports and buying books about home baking.

The first person that Lake saw in the attic was not Frank McBride or even Nick Harper. It was Monster. Monster, on formal occasions Chris Bolton, had been on Lake's surveillance course many years earlier and was the only person in Nottingham NIS that Lake knew. It took him a moment or two to recognise him. Monster had always been a big lad, hence the moniker. He had played rugby to a fairly high standard back when the game was one hundred per cent amateur. Now he was enormous.

"Eh up me duck!"

"Do you really say that up here?"

"Not really. Well, not often. At least not all the time."

"Am I in the right place?"

"You are. The Tartan Terror's on the fire escape." He nodded towards the back of the room where a fire door, in contravention of all regulations, was propped open and led to the fire escape. Immediately outside a group of Apaches was sending a long and complicated message by way of smoke signals. Either that or McBride was lighting his pipe.

"I'll let you make your introductions." With that Monster left, or, more accurately, fled. Lake heard him scurrying down the stairs. It would have been hard not to. People weighing almost twenty stone seldom move like Fred Astaire. Nick Harper entered from the fire escape, emerging through a cloud of tobacco smoke like a boy band taking the stage through too much dry ice. He saw Lake and he too headed for the exit with unseemly haste.

Lake understood the power of first impressions. He had planned that the first impression that he would convey to his new guvnor was something along the lines of, "I have been around the block, I know what I'm doing. Leave me alone and we'll get along fine." But this was Frank McBride. He didn't have a game plan for

Frank McBride. No-one did. He headed for the fire escape.

There was a small landing or balcony directly outside the door. On it, no doubt in breach of even more regulations, was a garden chair, and on the garden chair was Frank McBride. Lake had seen him once or twice in the corridors of Custom House in London's Lower Thames Street and a few more times in the local pubs. People would point him out in hushed and slightly awed tones, a bit like you would point out a famous footballer, or entertainer, or murderer. Now that he was close Lake would estimate his age as being somewhere between fifty and Methuselah. He had a full head of snow-white hair with a beard to match. He looked like a lighthouse keeper from an episode of *Scooby-Doo*. The knot of his tie was somewhere near the second button of his shirt. The tie itself was a plain bottle green, not one of those 'Friend of the FBI' or French Brigade Criminelle ties that some liked to use as an indicator of their seniority and experience. McBride really had nothing to prove on that front.

"Ay oop me dook," said McBride.

"I don't think they really say that here."

"You'd be surprised. Have you met our esteemed SIO, Mr Spencer?"

"I have. I take it that's his Jag out front."

"Of course. Did he ask you to spy on me?"

"Of course. And to guard young Nicholas from your malign influence and evil ways. What the hell is he doing here anyway?"

McBride shrugged. "Don't know. Blue blood of some sort, probably destined for the Foreign Office and got out of the lift on the wrong floor. He's never worked in investigation. Won't be here long with any luck."

"He wants to see you, by the way."

McBride gave no sign that he had heard. "That's your desk. Good bunch of lads here, mostly. Team pub is the Limelight. Senior management mostly leave us alone. Anything else you need to know?"

"How do you take your tea?"

McBride grinned. "Coffee. No milk. No sugar. No rum. No gunpowder. My mug's on that desk."

Lake glanced over his shoulder. The attic had three desks. One looked empty and unused. That was presumably his. Back to back with that was a second desk, presumably Nick Harper's, and abutting them both was a desk upon which was a colourful mug, red, yellow and purple with a red three-pointed star motif on it. Lake knew what that signified. Presumably McBride did. He wondered if anyone else in the office did. He picked up the mug and headed for the door, humming softly: *Avanti Popolo...*

*

McBride knew that he was a legend. Or rather, he knew that many people considered him a legend, and mostly that was a bad thing. Some people resented his status because they thought that they had similar legend-like characteristics that deserved more attention. Some people resented that anyone at all might be considered a legend. Others, who had once been junior to McBride, and in one or two cases even a little in awe of him, had risen through the ranks and some of them resented that they had once looked up to him. For half of these people he was an object of resentment, for the other half an actual target. McBride didn't care.

McBride was more concerned about the young and impressionable, like Harper and, to a lesser extent, Lake, who might look on him as some sort of eminence gris, a source of all truth and wisdom. McBride knew he wasn't that. He was a good investigator – okay, let's not fall into the trap of false modesty, he was very good. But he had enough self-knowledge to understand that the reason he was good was because he had been doing this job a very, very long time.

When he was young and foolish the job had meant too much to him. That cost him his first marriage: working three quarters of the time and boozing for most of the rest. The job, the lifestyle was more addictive than any drug (which was ironic if you thought about it – McBride tried not to). He told himself that he didn't have a choice, but the truth was that he didn't want to go home. Home meant reality, and dirty nappies, and responsibilities. Worst of all it meant serious conversations with Janice. Conversations about school reports and summer holiday destinations. He didn't exactly encourage her to throw him out, but he certainly didn't do anything to stop it.

Perhaps the marriage wouldn't have lasted anyway. They had been very young, and they certainly weren't ready to be parents. Janice had done her best. And McBride had made it as difficult for her as possible. He wasn't proud of it. He hadn't been much of a parent to Michelle when she was growing up. The weekly visits became three and then two each month. As she grew, he understood less and less about her life, and played an ever-smaller part in it. He was at least trying to make up for that now.

If he had been a different type of person McBride might have blamed the fact that he had had no father himself. He had been killed in action a couple of months before McBride had been born. Sniper's bullet. At least that's what the letter from the captain had said, but that's what they always said, wasn't it, quick and painless? The truth was probably far worse.

McBride had responded to the divorce by doubling down on all the things that had caused it. A sort of masochistic way of proving to himself that he was happy with the outcome. The hours increased, the beers grew fewer, but only because the whiskies grew more frequent. Then there had been the stint undercover. Six months of living a lie with the ever-present risk of discovery and whatever that might have meant. These days it was all psychometric tests, training at Quantico, Virginia, and a million risk assessments. Quite right too. It was bloody difficult and bloody dangerous. But McBride had been a pioneer. There had been no training and the only qualifications required were a lot of bottle and a willingness to subsume everything to the job. He survived, physically, mentally, emotionally. At least he thought he had, but only just.

After Janice had come Theresa. Theresa had been the love of his life. She had saved him. He cut down on the booze. He transferred to a VAT investigations team, started to work something a bit more like office hours. He got promoted, first to senior officer, then to SIO. People were talking about him as a possible future chief investigation officer. He had been embarrassed when he was nominated for an OBE. His first instinct had been to throw the letter in the bin. "What bloody empire?" he had asked.

Theresa had persuaded him – wanted to go to the palace in a new hat or something, he would grumble. But he had accepted to please her. He would do anything for Theresa. The day that she told him she was expecting was the happiest of his life. The day seven months later was the worst. The unbelievable horror of it! The surgeon emerging from the delivery suite, shaking his head. And they, he, had lost the baby too. It would have been a son.

So, a widower, he accepted a liaison post in Bangkok. That was a mistake. An almost daily round of embassy cocktail parties. Booze everywhere and no well-meaning friend to tell him he'd had enough, that it was time to go home. Nobody to tell him to ignore the supercilious little twerp from the Foreign Office. To ignore the sniping, the snobbery, the incessant political jockeying and backstabbing. No excuses, though! And no regrets. The recall to London, the demotion, the dressing-down from the chief investigation officer, they were all bad, but it was worth it.

Of course, by the time he had got back to London the story was there already, and grossly exaggerated. He had only hit the little twerp twice. And with his fists, not his forehead. And whilst it was true that he had broken his nose and knocked out a couple of teeth, he had not rendered him unconscious. None of that mattered: it all formed part of the Big Bad Frankie McBride legend. He didn't bother to correct it.

These days he would have been given counselling. For grief, for drink. These days he would probably be sent off to some former aristocratic pile to spend a couple of weeks wearing a bathrobe and drinking carrot juice. Instead, McBride was sent to what Customs called 'the Other Office'. No therapist on earth would have prescribed spending twelve hours a day in a room with no windows, but it worked for McBride. He threw himself into his work. Nothing else mattered because he had nothing else. He worked, and he worked. Slowly he rebuilt his career. He was temporarily promoted three times but never substantively promoted. He married again, and that worked for a while, until she ran off with a copper. The saddest part of that was that after a couple of weeks he realised that he didn't care.

Janice had re-married. A nice bloke called Geoff, some sort of engineer. They had moved to Swindon. Michelle went to university. McBride had been so proud, sitting at the back of the great hall with tears in his eyes as his only living relative had graduated. Their relationship had started to re-form that day, and this time McBride had done it properly. Emotional support, financial support, a father of the bride speech. And then had come Maisie, and then Frankie Junior. Tony, his son-in-law, was a good man, a teacher. He had been an attentive husband and a loving father. Pancreatic cancer. Terrible. Dead in less than a year.

And that, that, was why the legend that was Frank McBride was in the smallest office in the National Investigation Service and living in a flat just around the corner from Michelle's house in the Nottingham suburbs. Not that he told anyone, of course. They were investigators. Let them work it out.

TWO

Michael Butcher sat in silence waiting. That is to say that Michael was silent. Around him the Eagle was a bustling humming cauldron of anticipation, relief, disappointment and satisfaction.

Michael continued to wait, his pint untouched. The clock struck one. Michael reached for the glass and picked it up. A small act of self-discipline, waiting for the hour. He took a deep draught. His first as a graduate or his last as a student. The results would be posted at one o'clock, but until he knew them, he was still both a student and a graduate. He was still a carefree young man without commitment and responsibility, and a reluctant worker bee on a slippery slope that led to mortgages and insurance policies and owning his own socket set. Schrodinger's pint. If only he could remain in this limbo forever.

It wasn't fear of the unknown that was making Michael long for this moment to endure. Quite the opposite. He knew exactly what his future held. He was to pursue a career in the law. Not through choice. He had no particular interest in the law and even less in becoming a lawyer. But it was his destiny. His father was a lawyer, and his father and the inns of court and the more reputable firms of Chancery Lane were absolutely littered with Butchers. There were even one or two who had become judges.

It had required all Michael's rhetoric, his charm and his obstinacy to have persuaded his parents, realistically his father, to allow him to study modern European languages. But all that had done was to postpone the day that he would have to attend the College of Law and start learning all about equitable maxims and promissory estoppel. He was dreading it and not because he had set his heart upon some other career or vocation. He had no clear idea of what he wanted to do. He was dreading it because he imagined that with every step he took towards the woolsack he could imagine doors clanging shut, doors of opportunity, doors of excitement, doors of fun. He saw how his father earned his living. He had even spent one awful summer pottering about his office flirting with the secretaries, jamming the photocopier and generally reducing the net efficiency of the firm. His only real contribution had been as a ringer in the cricket team.

Giles hurried in, red-faced. "Results are up!"

Michael glanced at the clock. One minute past one. He must have run all the way from college. "And?"

"And you ought to go and look."

Michael looked at his pint. "Can't you just tell me?"

"I could, but I won't. This studied indifference of yours isn't fooling anyone, you know?"

This was a pity since Michael had spent a good deal of time working on his studied indifference. Possibly Giles was wrong. Perhaps the truth was that his studied indifference was fooling some people, lots of people, possibly everyone in the world except the Hon Giles Templeton. Because Giles wasn't as hopelessly naïve or foolish as he appeared. The difference was that Giles hadn't had to work at masking his intelligence behind a slightly distracted and faintly puzzled persona. Generations of breeding had done it for him. Nine hundred years earlier one of Giles' ancestors had probably been following William the Conqueror about looking slightly vague before absent-mindedly suggesting that it might be worth trying to lure Harold's army down off that hill.

"I assume that the results aren't written in condensation on the window. They will still be there at chucking-out time, won't they?"

"Oh, for God's sake, just go and look at the results, will you? I'll mind your pint."

"It isn't my pint. It's Schrodinger's." Michael rose, took another large gulp and headed for the door. As he reached it he turned. "And it's Abbot," he said. "And a packet of salt and vinegar."

Michael emerged from the pub into a bright June afternoon. The sun was high and the air echoed with the sounds of a thousand camera shutters as a million Japanese tourists gazed in awe at King's College Chapel or browsed the postcards in the tourist shops on Trumpington Street. Weaving between them he entered the main gates of Corpus Christi College and headed for the Junior Common Room. The crowd of keen students, less keen than Giles but a million times keener than Michael, was starting to disperse. He went to the noticeboard. A small ironic smile appeared for half a second. He dismissed it angrily and turned away. He paused. He ought to check on Giles. Rude not to. An upper second. Giles would be happy enough with that. Not that it mattered. Giles was studying, had been studying, land management. His father owned several large estates in northern England and Scotland. He would probably spend the next thirty years trying to outwit ragwort and managing the grouse moors until it was time for his eldest son, the next viscount, to take over.

Michael walked back to the Eagle. It had got a lot busier in the five minutes that he had been gone.

"I said salt and vinegar, you muppet!"

"They didn't have any. So I got you cheese and onion. Well?"

"What? What do you want me to say? We passed."

"Passed? You got a first! First-class honours. Captain of cricket. The world is your lobster!"

"I don't like lobster. And I don't like cheese and onion."

Giles looked chastened.

"I like Abbot, though, cheers!"

Giles brightened.

*

The Range Rover cruised up the A1. Michael was in the back brooding. No, not exactly brooding. He was contemplative. No, not that either. Oh, who are we kidding? He was sulking. The previous day he had told his parents that he had no intention of pursuing a career in the law. It had not been well received. There had been an entirely predictable row including a lecture from his mother on the subject of how much his parents had sacrificed to give him a good education.

His father had taken it even worse than that. He had obviously been schmoozing various law firm partners and heads of chambers, telling them about his bright young son and what a wonderful associate/pupil/gopher he would make. Michael suspected that what really hurt his father was that he wouldn't have a sufficiently impressive answer when his friends asked him what 'Young Michael' was up to. This was probably at the root of his mother's unhappiness too. Who knew what stories she had been telling her bridge club? It was bad enough that his little sister Emma was spending a year working as an au pair in France. "Unpaid skivvy!" had been her mother's verdict. She had been relying on Michael to provide her with bragging material.

Michael had thought the worst had been over yesterday, but his father came back for round two that morning.

"I'm not prepared to have you moping around here under our feet all day. And I'm certainly not paying for a London flat or to fund you going to Tibet and finding yourself alongside all those other aristocratic hippies you call your friends. You need to come up with some serious proposals as to how you are going to pay your way. If all else fails you can intern at my firm. I assume you remember how a photocopier works."

Michael had had a plan. He had intended to announce it at the same time he revealed that he didn't want to be a lawyer. He was going to spend the rest of the summer playing cricket. He had been virtually promised a place in the Sussex second XI. It wasn't exactly Lords, but it would have been a start. Now that was no longer an option.

The irony of it, the brutal, cruel, stupid irony, was that the game had been won. Cambridge, helped by a rather nifty fifty-five that Michael had scored between lunch and tea on the first day, were on the brink. Nine down in the second innings only a pair of tail-end batsmen stood in the way of Michael being the first Cambridge captain to beat Oxford for five years. That was when a truly hopeless number eleven had slashed at a wide delivery outside off stump and Michael, fielding at gully, had taken the ball on the end of the ring and middle fingers of his left hand. Five broken bones! He had been in Paddington Hospital Accident and Emergency when the trophy had been presented. He wasn't in any of the photographs. It wasn't serious. He could still write. He could still drive, ride a bicycle, undo bra straps (he was right-handed), still do anything. Except play cricket.

Now he was, where was he? On the A1, probably. Somewhere near Peterborough. His mother stifling sobs in the front seat. His father driving with a grim expression that seemed to say, "Now look what you have done to your mother."

This was unfair, of course. His mother was crying because she, all of them, were on their way to her mother's funeral. Michael scarcely knew his maternal grandparents. He had only seen them half a dozen times throughout his childhood. His grandmother had been a shy, mousy-haired German woman whom his grandfather had met in Berlin after the war. His grandfather was some sort of military type. Michael liked him but he hadn't been given the chance of developing a proper relationship. If it hadn't seemed so preposterous, he would have said that his mother regarded her father as a bad influence, someone to be kept well away from impressionable young boys. She may have had a point. The last time that he had seen his grandparents, he would have been about thirteen; his grandfather had given him whisky.

"The whole country to pick from. Why did they have to choose to live in the middle of bloody nowhere?" muttered Michael's father.

"Daddy always promised Mummy that when he retired, they would live in a little English village."

"We live in a little English village! But at least we are within range of civilisation. I mean, Rutland! It's not even a real place!"

"Next turning, dear."

*

St Cuthbert's was the sort of fourteenth-century church you see on biscuit tins or jigsaw puzzles. Honey-coloured stone, small belfry, huge oak doors and, even in July, freezing cold. Michael stood at the end of the front pew in the area reserved for 'family'. He half turned, trying to steal a glimpse of the rest of the congregation. He had never seen so much tweed in his life – well, possibly in Giles' wardrobe. There were about two dozen mourners in all, and Michael estimated that he was at least fifty years younger than most of them.

The vicar – Michael assumed it was a vicar, he was not an expert on ecclesiastical titles – was a woman. It gave the whole occasion a distinctly *Vicar of Dibley* vibe. Michael had no idea if his grandmother had been religious, or what her religion might have been. He was pretty sure that there were not many Anglicans in Berlin. But perhaps she had converted. It seemed unlikely. He found it hard to picture his grandfather as some sort of evangelising missionary.

Michael realised as he half listened to some well-meaning and vague platitudes that he knew next to nothing about his grandmother. Katrin she had been called, and she had met Bernard amongst the ruins of Berlin in 1945 or '46. They had spent most of the next thirty or forty years in that extraordinary city. Michael's mother had never spoken about it. She had been educated at boarding school in England since the age of seven and spent most of her holidays with schoolfriends or at the home of a spinster aunt in Sussex. As a small child, raised on Sunday-afternoon war films on television and shared copies of *Battle Picture Library*, Michael had wanted to know what Grandpa had done in the war, but a fear of upsetting his grandmother meant that he had never asked. This didn't seem to be the right time either but, glancing sideways at the tall man leaning slightly on a stick, he wondered if he would ever have another chance.

His grandfather – the other villagers seemed to refer to him as 'Major' – lived in the old vicarage next door to St Cuthbert's. But after the internment the mourners gathered instead in the village's only pub, the Old Volunteer, where the landlord had closed off the dining area to host a small wake. Michael stood on the edge of things clutching a paper plate with a quarter of a scotch egg and a handful of crisps – damp cardboard box flavour, probably. After a while he could stand it no longer. His suit was too warm for July and his tie felt like a noose. At the first opportunity he retreated to the small beer garden, where he lit a cigarette and gazed across the bucolic landscape. After a few minutes he felt a presence beside him.

"Well, Mikey!" His grandfather was the only person who had ever called him that. "I gather that you have decided to turn your back on a career of chiselling and avarice. Good man!"

"My mother would not agree with you."

"No, no, I suppose not." The old man's face signalled that he recognised the truth of that assessment. "So what will you do?"

"Lead England to victory in the Ashes?"

"Not with that paw you won't." His grandfather nodded at his bandaged left hand.

Michael shrugged. There was a long period of silence.

"Were you a major then?"

"For a while." His grandfather looked behind himself slightly furtively. He leaned forward, lowered his voice and winked. "Actually I retired a brigadier, but the chairman of the parish council here was a half-colonel and it would break his heart if he knew I outranked him." He chuckled.

"Your mother has suggested that you stay with me for a little while. I think she's worried that I will get lonely or something. To be honest, I would appreciate a little company, and since you are at a loose end…"

Michael extinguished his cigarette. Technically speaking he had no plans. Or even the vaguest idea of what he was going to do. But if he had been forced to list his options, and you would have had to force him, he doubted that residing in Rutland with a septuagenarian whom he hardly knew would make the top thousand.

"I can't promise you an exciting time but at least I won't nag you about smoking those. Or anything else."

Michael was mentally composing a polite refusal when his father appeared in the pub doorway. He was on his mobile telephone. He was always on his phone, pacing to and fro, looking earnest and fraught. The damn thing seemed to be clamped to his ear twenty-four hours a day, an ever-present necessity without which he could not function, like a pacemaker or some sort of aural colostomy bag. Someone, somewhere was paying three hundred pounds an hour for that frown and those 'hmm hmms'.

Actually, a few weeks with his grandfather in Rutland didn't seem so unappealing.

THREE

The nine men and three women of Nottingham A, Branch 11 (Midlands), Her Majesty's Customs and Excise National Investigation Service were gathered in the rest room. Twelve chairs were set out in three rows facing a whiteboard covered in a sheet. Somebody had covered the small window in the door. Pretty pathetic really. McBride was sitting in the front row humming quietly to himself and waiting for the clock to tick around to eleven o'clock.

"Der der der, duh der de der duh. Der der der, duh de der duh der."

"Joe? Is McBride... is he humming?" asked Monster in the same tone of voice that he might have used when asking if the Queen was rolling a fag.

"He is."

"Oh! Right. Thought so... Do you know why?"

"I do."

"Care to share?"

"We've got a target job. The real thing. Support from the Other Office and everything."

"Nottingham's never had a target job."

"Nottingham's never had McBride."

At the appointed hour Howard Spencer strode into the room. "Good morning, everyone." With a flourish he attempted to sweep the cover from the whiteboard but caught the top corner of the frame, causing it to tilt alarmingly, almost reach the point of no return, pause for a second and then return to its original position with a clatter. Eleven pairs of eyes rolled upwards. McBride was like a statue. An embarrassing introduction like that would have unnerved many people but Spencer's parents had paid many thousands of guineas to ensure that their little boy had received daily intravenous injections of self-assurance and sangfroid at some public school founded in the Middle Ages and still with the same plumbing. He barely broke stride.

"Welcome to the first briefing for Operation Baguette," he announced, indicating the white board upon which in large red letters was written 'Operation Bagration'. He looked quizzically at McBride.

"Had to change it."

Lake suppressed a giggle. Bagration!

"The first briefing for Operation Bagration, which I am pleased to tell you is the first operation run from the Nottingham office to be investigated in conjunction with the team from, err, the Other Office. Frank McBride will be the case officer, assisted by Joseph Lake and by Nicholas Harper. Frank? Would you mind?"

Possibly a professor of linguistics could explain it, or someone with a PhD in sociology, but some people can say 'the Other Office' and sound like they are speaking their first language. And some can't. It just jars, like Prince Charles trying to use rhyming slang or an American saying 'quid'. It just doesn't fit properly in their mouth. It doesn't sound right. Howard Spencer couldn't say 'the Other Office' authentically. In a sane and rational world that ought to be unimportant. But here, in this place, it mattered. He may as well have been wearing a T-shirt that read, 'I am not of you. I am not one of you. And I don't know what I'm doing.'

McBride got slowly to his feet and faced the room. "We're doing a target job. Hard work. Long hours. And we will be based near Lincoln, not in this office. We start in earnest in two weeks. Clear your diaries for six months. Gentlemen, stop shaving, no haircuts. Fill in these forms. I need two passport-size photographs from each of you tomorrow. And keep your mouths shut. Any questions?"

There were none. Spencer appeared slightly disappointed. He resumed his position at the front of the room, but the meeting was already breaking up. McBride handed him a form: 'Permission to be on Ministry of Defence property'.

"I don't suppose that we'll see you very often, but you had better complete this, just in case."

McBride fished his pipe out of his pocket, thrust it in the corner of his mouth and headed for the stairs. Lake and Nick followed. McBride could sense the excitement of the two young men following him up the stairs to the attic. He understood. He empathised. He remembered what it felt like, just.

*

"Der der der duh der de der duh. Der der der duh de der duh der."

If you are familiar with RAF Scampton, and I doubt that you are, it will be because somewhere in the darkest recesses of your memory you might recall that it was from RAF Scampton in May 1943 that nineteen Lancasters took off with the aim of doing some German dams a bit of no good and to provide the less imaginative fans of the England football team with some musical inspiration fifty years later.

By the summer of 1997 Scampton was no longer an operational station. Once home to two thousand, it was now effectively mothballed. The buildings were still there, though. Mess halls, briefing rooms, offices and barracks that echoed with the unseen ghosts of young men who set off on dark nights to be blown to pieces in the skies above Hamburg or Cologne or Berlin. There were hangars too and a small guard post at the main entrance on the A15 a few miles north of Lincoln.

McBride halted by the guard post. He lowered the driver's door window and waved a small card in the general direction of the guard house.

"Six cars, a van and a motorcycle," he said.

The bored-looking security guard, an underpaid employee of some private firm – not a military sentry – nodded. He returned to his little booth and pushed a button. The barrier rose and a small convoy of very ordinary-looking vehicles processed into the base and parked behind what had once been the main administration building where they were invisible from the road.

McBride fished a key from the pocket of his jacket and unlocked a door. He led eleven investigators into a musty, cobwebbed corridor, shuffling his feet through a carpet of paperclips, broken pencils, old newspapers and thick, thick dust.

*

The administration block alone was many times larger than the team needed. It had about twenty rooms of various sizes and it was even beyond the capacity of investigators to expand to fill the space available. There were at least a dozen echoing empty rooms that remained unoccupied. But half a dozen were in use.

There was McBride's office, of course. Once the preserve of Flight Lieutenant GL Whitfield, if the name on the door was to be credited. It now housed a grumpy Scotsman, a desk and an old wooden chair with a leather seat highly polished by the posteriors of heroes past. On a small table next to McBride's desk was a radio with a desk-based microphone like you see in the dispatch offices of minicab firms, which in a way, it was. The desk itself was littered with coffee cups, ashtrays and various buff folders containing who knew what. There was a pipe rack containing three briar pipes, which, to the untrained eye, appeared identical. They weren't. At least so far as McBride was concerned, they each had their own roles, personalities and uses. McBride's pipes were his only reliable allies in the battle that he had been waging on the world for at least thirty years.

Immediately outside McBride's den was what had probably been Flight Lieutenant Whitfield's clerk's office. It was now the tearoom. There was a kettle and a fridge that somebody had bought for ten quid or possibly found in a skip. Above the fridge was pinned a roster outlining milk buying duties and a further handwritten warning as to what fate would befall whoever it was who kept nicking the teaspoons.

On the other side of the corridor was the obs room. Somebody, McBride presumably, had arranged for a camera to be inserted in the streetlight outside a modest little house on a council estate. The camera relayed its captured images via microwave to a mast on the roof of Lincoln VAT office from where it was broadcast to a monitor in the obs room. It was showing a grainy black and white image of an aged Mercedes saloon. In defiance of a thousand health and safety ordinances there was a nest of electric cables and extension leads charging radio batteries, mobile phone batteries and a variety of slightly more exotic pieces of equipment. There were two small desks that were occasionally used by Lake or by Harper.

Next to the obs room was the briefing room. Like all the rooms the ancient and dusty venetian blinds were closed. On the north wall was a collection of photographs of young men wearing the surly, resentful and very slightly resigned expressions that are only ever seen in charge room photographs and the album covers of indie bands. The central photograph was slightly larger than the others and below it was a typewritten note that read 'John Edward PYKE – Tango Five'. Pyke was flanked by photographs of 'Steve 'Maxi' PETTIGREW – Tango Four' and 'Gary BARHAM – Tango Eight'.

There were street maps of Lincoln with the targets' home addresses marked. There were Ordnance Survey maps of the wider region, pictures of various cars. Finally, on the south wall there was a photograph marked 'Stanley Maas – Tango Twenty' and maps of Tilburg, the Netherlands and north-west continental Europe.

The largest room was one that the team had already nicknamed 'Dispersal'. There were a couple of sofas that the Ministry of Defence had forgotten to throw away in 1966 and some more chairs similar to McBride's throne. There was a television, mounted on an old filing cabinet, the key long lost, a video recorder and a selection of VHS cassettes of the type of films popular with investigators: *The Italian Job*, *Kelly's Heroes*, *Battle of Britain*. Not *The Dam Busters*, though. That sort of seemed inappropriate, disrespectful.

McBride's voice sounded from somewhere: "Briefing! Five minutes!"

"Scramble, scramble, scramble!" muttered Monster.

*

McBride strode into the briefing room holding a sheath of papers. His pipe was puffing like a tank engine pulling a heavy load up a steep incline. Lake was starting to learn how to interpret McBride's mood from the smoke signals. This morning's message was business-like but not urgent.

"We've got an intelligence blackout today so there won't be any live intel to respond to," he began, "but there is still plenty to keep us busy." He added a photograph to the north wall.

"Police Constable Stephen Pyke. Collar number 112. Traffic, based at Scunthorpe, so we shouldn't have anything to do with him. Just don't get caught speeding on the M180."

"Brother?"

"Cousin. Right! Some tasks for you all." A business-like puff

25

from the pipe. "Joseph and Nick, check out Lincoln Station and the two Newark stations. I want plot maps with identified places to keep eyeball, take the Mondeo.

"And I want the numbers of any public telephones in the vicinity. Got it? Pick up some timetables. And buy some bloody bog roll!"

Lake and Harper headed for the door.

"Monster and Julia, take the Renault. Check out these cafés. Same drill, plot maps, telephone numbers. Andi, Carl, I want you to take a drive around, look for anything that might be called 'the Windmill' in or around Lincoln."

There was the sound of scraping chairs.

"Kevin, I want the number of every public telephone on the Ermine estate. Gill, the same for the St Giles estate. Mark, city centre."

*

"I suppose all this is new to you, is it, Nick?"

"Well, fairly new."

"Well, normally you'd have to do some course, but we don't have time for that, so you'll just have to pick it up as we go along. Pay attention and it will all become pretty clear, pretty quickly."

Nick nodded. He had been out on surveillance once before, told to sit in the back of the car, say nothing and pay attention. He had found the entire experience utterly bewildering; Even when he could understand what was being said through the crackle of the radio the words themselves made no sense. Were they speaking in code? Or was it just slang and jargon? And the surveillance itself was almost as puzzling. Sometimes they were cruising along at thirty miles an hour and the next they would be tearing down the same road at twice that speed. Then they would stop, he knew not why, and the radio would burst into incomprehensible chatter. It was all a deeply disorientating mystery.

He didn't want to let anybody down, but he didn't want to be the new boy asking stupid questions either.

"So today we're…?"

"Getting to know the lie of the land. Surveillance is easier if you know the territory. You don't need to be right up behind them all the time for a start."

Harper nodded again. He thought that he was probably going to spend a lot of time nodding and so it proved. Lake talked him through basic surveillance technique, radio discipline and a few set routines. He made it all sound so natural, so obvious, so straightforward. But he couldn't help wondering whether it would all be so easy and logical when he was doing it for real.

"Okay, our targets are given codenames. Just so if someone overhears us the security of the operation is not breached. They are all Tango – for target – followed by a number. The numbers are allocated randomly so no clever lawyer can make a big deal out of the fact that their client is Tango Fifteen and therefore a minor player who should be let off. Pyke is Tango Five. So, his car is X-Ray Five, got it?"

Lake was just pausing for breath. The question was rhetorical. "His home is Gold Five, yeah?"

Nick nodded. "Got it," he added, mostly for the sake of a little variety.

"Right! Any questions?"

"Just one. The intelligence blackout?"

Lake shrugged. "It happens, won't be for long, we'll have him hooked up again in a day or two."

This told Nick nothing. It was something to do with the Other Office and he was clearly supposed to understand. He daren't ask.

FOUR

Pyke pulled up outside the small house he shared with Donna on Lincoln's Ermine estate and switched off the ignition of his Mercedes. Glancing at the three-pointed star in the centre of the steering wheel prompted a small smile of satisfaction. The engine continued to run for a second or two and then halted, to be replaced by a plinking sound as the engine block cooled. The small smile disappeared. But, at the end of the day, a Merc was a Merc, even if it was fourteen years old. *This time next year*, he told himself, *it will be a new one. With leather upholstery. And a multi CD player.*

It was exactly a year since he had walked out of Bijlmerbajes and things had gone well. Now he was the head of his own gang. His gang, he admitted to himself, was small. And his gangsters were not of the very highest echelon, but like the ageing Mercedes he considered them to be just the start. In time he would build an organisation like Maas's. In time he would lead not a gang but a network and then an empire!

He was regularly importing and distributing product supplied to him by Maas. It was mostly ecstasy tablets but he was thinking that he might branch out into other forms of amphetamines.

Margins weren't high but he was reinvesting most of his revenue into stock. With each monthly shipment he bought a little more, made a little more profit, bought a little more. He had read about exponential growth, and whilst he couldn't have explained the concept in detail he was fairly certain that this was it and that it was a good thing.

There had not been many English-language books in the Bijlmerbajes library. Pyke was not much of a reader anyway. But one book had left an impression upon him. It was the biography of some business titan of whom Pyke had barely heard. It told a predictable, tedious and probably inaccurate tale of rags to riches, the way such tomes always do. But it also introduced Pyke to some key business principles: investment and return, margins, overheads, operating costs, and profit and loss. And it taught him the importance of cashflow.

Pyke considered himself a businessman. He was, in truth, a mindless thug with a calculator, but he wasn't the first such to suffer from delusions of commerce. Maas had impressed upon Pyke that the distribution and sale of drugs was, above all else, a business. Pyke wanted to explore new markets, increase profitability and drive growth. It would soon be time to renegotiate his purchase price with Maas. He was now buying ten thousand tablets a month. Perhaps next month Maas would be willing to let him have a larger shipment partly on a sale-or-return basis.

But successful businessmen did not live on Lincoln's Ermine estate. They didn't keep their operating cash in the boot of a fourteen-year-old car. Their staff did not comprise a small number of unreliable and careless losers. Every element of his enterprise needed to be upgraded if he was going to move from small-time dealer to a serious player.

Pyke had just returned from a business meeting concerned with cashflow. That is to say that he had just returned from a small garage on the edge of the city. The garage's proprietor, Little Glen, probably didn't understand exponential growth. But he did understand diversification. He fixed cars, he bought and sold stolen goods, and he sold drugs, drugs supplied by Pyke. He was by no means Pyke's most important customer, and he certainly wasn't his best. Little Glen did not understand the importance of cashflow, and Little Glen did not understand the importance of meeting his financial obligations promptly. This is what had necessitated the meeting.

Pyke now reflected on that meeting, which he deemed a success. Little Glen had paid in full, including a little extra as a late payment penalty. In truth the success of this meeting was due to another meeting twenty-four hours earlier. Pyke had arrived at GJ Hayton & Son without an appointment. GJ Hayton Senior, Big Glen, was not on the premises. He hadn't been for four years and wouldn't be for another four, even with good behaviour. Little Glen was alone, turning back the odometer of a Toyota Camry, when Pyke arrived. Little Glen was able to guess the purpose of the visit and decided to let the spanner remain in his hand, just in case.

"Five thousand pounds." Pyke was not really one for small talk.

"Ah, John, yes, I was just going to call you, actually."

"Five thousand pounds."

Little Glen's usual resting state was shifty, but on this occasion, he had turned it up a notch.

"Is it, is it today?"

"Do you have it?"

There's a lot of nonsense talked about body language. Some maintain that a liar will look up and to the right. Others say that the liar will attempt to cover his mouth or the lower half of his face. Little Glen was the type of person who looked at his shoes like a guilty schoolboy. This was a serious error. He should have kept his eyes on Pyke. That way he might have seen the straight left coming. Not that he would have been able to do very much about it. Little Glen was so called because he was named after his father, not because of his size. In fact, most people would have described Little Glen as a heavyweight. But not boxers. Boxers would have described him as a two-legged punch bag. The left caught him just below the right eye and he staggered backwards into the wall behind him. The second punch, this one a right, caught him in the solar plexus and he went down with the breath knocked from his body.

Pyke knelt on his chest. From somewhere he had produced a knife, not a large one, not a machete or even a flick knife, just a small vegetable knife. It looked sharp. Little Glen had an opportunity to satisfy himself on this topic because the blade was half an inch from his eye.

"Five thousand. Tomorrow."

Little Glen wanted to assure Pyke that he would have the money. He wanted to explain that it was just an oversight. But he didn't have the breath. It was all he could to give a tiny nod. Not that he needed to. The terror in his eyes was enough to satisfy Pyke that he would be paid in full the following day.

Pyke had spent the day chasing up his various customers for payment and taking orders for his next delivery. Most of the meetings had been more straightforward than the one with Little Glen. He now had fifty thousand pounds and a brand-new pay-as-you-go, and therefore untraceable, mobile phone. Later he would call the Superkruiken Bar and let them know his new number. A few hours after that somebody in Tilburg, and it seemed to be a different person every time, would tell him Maas's current number. Maas seemed to change his phone every week and sometimes more often than that.

Pyke understood that success was a two-edged sword and that with greater prominence came greater risk. He knew that if his business continued to grow it would only be a matter of time before he came to the notice of the police. Alongside all the other elements of his business he knew that he really needed to upgrade his security. For now, he would have to rely on his own wits.

He exited the car and looked carefully up and down the street, then along the windows of the houses on both sides of the street, looking for twitching curtains or the flash of light reflecting from a tele-photo lens. Maas's home in Tilburg was bristling with CCTV cameras. One day. One day.

He walked to the boot of the car. One last look round. He opened it and removed a navy-blue rucksack secured with two small padlocks, one key, one combination. Ten seconds and a Stanley knife would render this security irrelevant, but that never seemed to occur to Pyke. He hefted it onto his shoulder and, blipping the remote locking over his shoulder, opened the front gate and covered the few yards to the front door in an almost jaunty fashion.

"I'm home!"

"Did you get me my fags?"

Pyke reached into the pocket of his tracksuit top and retrieved two packs of Silk Cut, "Yeah, got 'em, babes." He stuck his head around the kitchen door, where Donna was filling the kettle.

He called Donna his 'missus', although strictly speaking they had no legal or religious bond. They had something much more important than that, though. They had loyalty and trust. She had waited for him for nine months when he was in prison. And remained faithful too. (He had made enquiries – they didn't have *that* much trust.) Her loyalty meant that he had someone and somewhere to come home to. And her little brother, Maxi, had become the first member of his gang.

Pyke trotted upstairs into the spare bedroom. He opened the rucksack and spilled its contents onto the bed. He had counted it once, but he liked to count it again. He liked the feel of it in his fingers, the sound of the gentle riffle. He even liked the smell. Twelve thousand, five hundred pounds. He knelt by the room's only wardrobe and started to remove the shoeboxes, coat hangers and other rubbish from the floor. He used the hook of one of the coat hangers to slip into the tiny hole in the false floor and he prised it open. He took out the carrier bag, opened it and checked its contents, thirty-eight thousand. He added the twelve and put the five hundred in his pocket. He put the false floor back and covered it again with the detritus. It had been Maas's suggestion that he work in the prison carpentry shop. In this, as in so much else, Pyke appreciated the Dutchman's wise counsel.

Pyke trotted downstairs. Donna was now in the front room, smoking. She looked up. He waved the five hundred at her. "Put on something nice. We're going somewhere special."

*

Pyke didn't spar or skip or work the bag anymore. But he still went to the gym. At least he went to the café nearest to the gym. Boxing gyms were full of fit and aggressive young men. Such men were in demand as bouncers for night clubs and bars. And such bouncers were well placed to sell drugs to fun-loving youngsters. These were his bread-and-butter customers and together they could provide Pyke with a modest income. But somewhere in a cell in Bijlmerbajes Pyke had finally found some ambition. A modest income would not satisfy him. He wanted more. He was not content to sell penny packets of pills or powders. He wanted to command a business empire, like Maas's. He didn't, he couldn't, manufacture the product and he certainly didn't want to stand on street corners dealing it. He saw himself as a middleman, a broker. His was a strictly business-to-business operation. No manufacturing. No retail. He wanted to assemble a network for that. Fighters had managers. And those managers knew other managers and those managers had connections. Therefore, he had a wide pool of potential customers. Stanley could supply him with all the product that he could handle. He just needed to move it from A to B. He certainly wasn't going to do that himself. Far too risky! For that he had his associates.

Three of his associates were supposed to be meeting him in the Lindum Café, just around the corner from Monty's Gym. One was late, one was badly hungover and one was his brother-in-law, 'Maxi'. Pyke knew that as a crew they were not absolutely the first division, but they were all he had. At least for now.

"Where's Gazza?" he asked.

He was met with two blank and slightly apologetic looks. They sat in uncomfortable silence as Pyke painstakingly transferred his contacts from his old phone to his new one. A small show of displeasure and of authority. He texted his new number to Stanley. When he was finished, he held his hand out to Maxi. Maxi handed over his phone. Pyke deleted the number for 'JP' in Maxi's contacts and inputted the new number. He then held his hand out to Shane. Shane handed his phone over.

"Battery's dead," he said with a shrug.

"Muppet!"

Pyke looked around. Nobody was within earshot. "Right, Maxi, here's what I want you to do. There's a rucksack under the table. Day after tomorrow I want you to take it to Margate in Kent."

Maxi responded with a blank and uncomprehending expression.

"Margate. Kent? Near where you've been before – look, just buy a road atlas, okay? Be there by noon. Call me when you get there. Understand?"

Maxi nodded.

"Don't open the bag, don't look in it. Understand? And when you phone me don't mention the place. Got it?"

Maxi nodded. It was frustrating that he had to use Maxi only for the money, but he had promised Donna that he would never ask her little brother to carry merchandise. She was very protective. But Maxi was the only one whom he could really trust to follow instructions. Shane – and Gazza, who hadn't even managed to attend the meeting – was not reliable. But what could you do?

"Shane. Day after tomorrow I want you and Gazza to go to Canterbury. Be there at one. I'll call you then you will have my number. You need to be straight, understand?"

"Yeah, yeah, no problem."

Pyke pushed the rucksack towards Maxi with his toe.

*

"*Control, Control, Andi, receive.*" Andi was calling Frank on the radio.

McBride reached for the microphone on his desk and pressed the transmit button. "*Control receiving.*"

"*I think we've found your Windmill. Anything else for us?*"

"*X-Ray Five has moved. Take a quick spin through the city centre, see if you can find it.*"

"*Yes, yes. Andi out.*" The message literally meant, I have received and understood your instructions and am carrying them out, but Andi Woodhead was an experienced radio user; she used her tone to transmit a message more like, "Seriously? You want me to do what?"

Carl turned to Andi. "Somewhere in this city there may or may not be a knackered old Merc."

"Ah, the glamour of target jobs!"

"The thing about target work," McBride had once said in one of his unusually loquacious moments, "is that you spend a lot of time pursuing long shots. But if you persist, eventually or occasionally it might pay off." McBride wasn't the sort to utter tired clichés about tickets and raffles.

Andi thought that there had probably been some wisdom in this bon mot, but cruising an entire city looking for a single car seemed to her to be national lottery odds of success. And then she saw it. She was simultaneously pleased and also slightly resentful that McBride had been right.

"What was that? Down that side street."

She pulled over, and Carl hopped out of the car and walked back towards the junction. As he passed the Lindum Café, he noticed Pyke and Pettigrew, Tangos Five and Four, and an unknown man sitting at a table in the window. Glancing down the side road he saw Pyke's Mercedes, X-Ray Five, parked outside Monty's gym. He crossed the road and walked back. He risked a second glance through the café window. The scene was unchanged. He hopped back into the car.

"He's having a meeting in that café. Pyke, Pettigrew and some bloke I don't know."

"What do they look like?"

"Well, Pettigrew, he's Tango Four, isn't he? He looks like Stan Laurel in a navy-blue Adidas tracksuit. Gormless-looking, with a baseball cap on backwards. White, mid-twenties, clean-shaven, short dark brown hair."

"Why do these losers always were tracksuits?"

"Well, in his case I'd say it's because buttons might be a bit too tricky for him. The other one, the unknown male, he might be even worse. White, fair hair, wispy sort of goatee, early to mid-twenties, sort of cream-coloured Ellesse tracksuit over a black T-shirt with a big green cannabis leaf on it. Oh, and lime-green trainers you could see from space."

"You are kidding!"

"Nope. He's like directly out of central casting. Send me up a dopey-looking scallywag whose IQ matches his shoe size."

Andi was concentrating on the rear-view mirror.

"Pyke's leaving. We'll let him go. We want to get the others to a car… There they go… And here they come. I bet they're heading for that Peugeot."

Parked directly in front of Andi and Carl was a white Peugeot 205 GTi with green rims, a small collection of obscene bumper stickers and an exhaust pipe like the Dartford tunnel. Maxi walked to the passenger side, Shane to the driver's door. He opened it, utterly oblivious to the two officers sitting in a parked car ten feet away. The Peugeot pulled out and roared away.

"Golf, Four One Six, Hotel Echo Whisky."

Carl wrote G416 HEW in his notebook.

"Right, back to Scampton, via the chip shop, I think."

It was about three in the afternoon. Michael Caine was trying to persuade Noel Coward to support his plan for a robbery in Turin when McBride walked into the 'dispersal' room. The smoke signals were of a pattern Lake hadn't seen before.

"Briefing, two minutes!"

When the team walked into the briefing room McBride was adding a picture to the wall.

"Right! Thanks to Andi and Carl we have a new target: Shane Hartney, Tango Eleven, lives in Furness Street. That's now Gold Eleven, White Peugeot 205. Green wheels, you can't miss it. Index Golf, Four One Six, Hotel Echo Whisky. Designated X-Ray Eleven."

McBride surveyed the assembled to make sure that everyone was giving him their full attention.

"I want everyone here oh seven hundred tomorrow. I want all the radios checked and tested. Batteries fully charged. Cars full of fuel. Bring a change of profile. Make sure you have your cuffs and keys."

McBride turned on his heel and a buzz of conversation immediately commenced. If you were to transcribe what was being said you would be using the '?' key a great deal. Nothing was actually said, but Lake had the impression that the team would like to know a little more and that it was his role, his duty, as McBride's senior underling, to make enquiries.

He followed McBride into his little office. He wasn't exactly sure how he was going to raise the subject. If McBride had wanted people to know a little more, or if he wished to share a little insight, or explain what was behind his thinking, he would have said so. *Perhaps*, he thought to himself, *I might risk a slightly elevated eyebrow and see what results.*

McBride was sitting at his desk when Lake came in. He appeared to have dismantled his pipe, there were little pieces lined up in front of him, and was cleaning and re-assembling it. "Care and maintenance," he said without looking up.

"Oh," said Lake.

McBride was running a pipe cleaner through the stem. He frowned and reached for a small set of tools, like a set of lockpicks. He selected one, still frowning, and dug away. A small piece of something brown fell from the end. McBride grunted with satisfaction and reached again for the pipe cleaner.

"Zen," he said. "Everything about smoking a pipe contributes to zen. The smoking, obviously, but the filling, the packing, the lighting, even the cleaning. It's all good for the soul. Less good for the lungs, obviously."

He put a small white filter into the steel shank and then fitted the black plastic stem. He placed it, almost reverently, in the exact centre of his mouth and blew gently. Then he inhaled. He appeared satisfied. On the desk in front of him were three different bowls. McBride selected a smooth, medium brown one with a meerschaum lining and fitted it to the little metal saucer at the top of the shank and screwed it down.

"The Falcon," he said. "The Falcon is a good pipe for the working day because it has interchangeable bowls."

"Oh," said Lake.

"Saves you having to carry two or three pipes when you're expecting a busy day, d'you see?"

"Ah!" said Lake.

He picked up another bowl and, selecting another tool, began to scrape away at the inside. He inverted it and tapped it out onto the racing page of the previous day's paper. McBride's paper. Nobody else read that particular daily. Then he scraped away again, inverted it, tapped it. Finally, he picked up a small cloth and briefly polished the inside of the bowl. He put the bowl, it had a rougher finish than the first, in a small cloth bag. Then he picked up the last bowl; this one was black, or very dark brown at least, and put that in the bag too. Finally, he added the cloth and the set of tools and a few filters that had been on the desk.

"One moment!" McBride could see that Lake thought that the little ceremony was over, and it was safe for him to speak.

From his right-hand jacket pocket, he took a black tobacco pouch. "McLintock's Black Cherry," he said to nobody in particular.

Slowly he started to fill the bowl of the Falcon. When it appeared to be full, he examined it closely. He paused, gave the tiniest of shrugs and then added a further pinch of tobacco. He tamped it down with a thumb that was the colour of a pirate's treasure map. He closed the pouch and returned it to his pocket. From the same pocket he retrieved a box of Swan Vestas.

"Now. What was it you wanted?" The scrape of phosphorous on matchbox.

At that exact moment what Lake most wanted was a pipe. He was absolutely mesmerised.

It didn't matter. McBride had been in investigation teams for over a quarter of a century. He knew why Lake was there.

"The Other Office says there's something happening tomorrow. Not sure what. Best guess is that they are making a run. The picture isn't clear and there are pieces missing, but I think that Pyke will send one or more of his minions south to make a collection. Kent has been mentioned. You look puzzled!"

"That's probably because I am."

"Okay, perhaps I should have told you this before. Pull up a chair. I'll explain."

FIVE

Leighton Parva was not a busy, thriving metropolis. It had ninety-nine residential dwellings; Michael had counted them. The house names reflected echoes of what the village had once been. As well as the old vicarage, his grandfather's home, there was 'the Old Post Office', 'the Old School', 'the Old Reading Rooms' and 'the Old Forge'. Everything in the village was described as old, but actually, it was dead. Where the road forked at the west end of the village there was a war memorial: a grey stone cross atop a three-tiered plinth. There were thousands very similar in villages everywhere. Nine names for the First World War, three for the Second. The Taylor family had lost four sons. The memorial put Michael in mind of the inn sign at the Old Volunteer. On one side there was a picture of a redcoat in a tricorn hat. On the obverse was a young man in First World War khaki. Modelled on a young Taylor, possibly.

There was morning service and evensong on the second Sunday of each month at St Cuthbert's. Michael did not attend. And neither did his grandfather. The Old Volunteer was a pleasant pub serving good beer and slightly expensive food. The landlord seemed to think that the addition of olive oil and balsamic vinegar to just about every dish conferred upon his establishment the status of gastropub and justified a fifty pence uplift. But it was not the sort of jumping hot spot that would normally have won Michael's custom. He managed to lower the average age by about ten years just by crossing the threshold. It still fell considerably even when he visited with his seventy-six-year-old grandfather, which he did on Mondays and Thursdays. There were discounted lunches for pensioners on Monday and a pub quiz on Thursday evenings.

The only other source of entertainment was provided by the village cricket club, which backed onto the old vicarage. Division 2 of the Melton Mowbray and District League was not the highest standard, but Michael watched it all the same. He prowled the boundary from the small wooden pavilion, past the scorers' hut, a bench, a sightscreen, another bench, a pile of grass clippings, a little shed that probably contained some rollers and a lawnmower or two. He might pause here and politely applaud a cover drive or snigger quietly at an amusing mis-field. Beyond the shed was another bench, another sightscreen and then back to the pavilion. The Taylor brothers had probably walked the same track eighty or ninety years earlier.

Beside the scorers' hut was a white plastic garden chair. Michael used to sit there one or two evenings a week and enjoy a spliff whilst he contemplated what his next move ought to be. He was having to ration himself now. The quarter ounce he had brought with him was almost finished and he had yet to tap into the seedy underbelly of Leighton Parva's demi monde and find a dealer. Despite what he had read in the Sunday colour supplements about recreational drug use amongst the middle class, he was not optimistic. Rutland was not Hampstead.

It was life in a low gear, but Michael didn't mind. It wasn't like he was in a hurry to get anywhere. In the late evenings when his grandfather was on his second Macallan the old man would tell him stories of Libya, Tunisia, Salerno and Normandy. Not stories of derring-do, stories of camaraderie, shared hardships and occasionally of loss. The old man had had what people of his generation called 'a good war'. He had emerged with his original quotient of limbs and a collection of medals to be taken out once a year in November. By the time he was Michael's age he'd commanded a troop of tanks and been barred from twenty different Cairo nightspots.

"What were you doing in Berlin all those years?"

"Oh, that? That was mostly desk work. The odd brief moment of excitement."

"What type of desk work?"

"Skulduggery and mischief, mostly." He chuckled. "I miss it, frankly."

*

Stephen 'Maxi' Pettigrew had phoned in sick at a quarter to eight. His supervisor didn't sound wholly convinced, but that couldn't be helped. He checked that his phone was fully charged. He checked that he had a charging cable that he could plug into the cigarette lighter in his car. He checked that he had a road atlas and he checked he had some cash. Maxi was the reliable one. At one minute to eight he left his house, walked down the short garden path and, reaching the pavement, looked left and right. He saw nothing unusual. He crossed the road and opened the driver's door of his Renault 21.

"*Control, Control, Andi.*"

"*Control.*"

"*Tango Four from Gold Four towards X-Ray Four.*"

Nick frowned. So that is Maxi Pettigrew leaving his home and heading for his car.

"*Control. All units standby, standby.*"

Everyone sat up straight. Hands hovered over ignition keys.

"*Tango Four is carrying a black or navy rucksack.*"

Sounded like Andi; presumably she could see all this from wherever she was lurking.

"From Control. We go with him, repeat, we go with him."

Four keys turned. Four engines started.

"From Andi, X-Ray Four is mobile, mobile, mobile, towards you, Gill."

I'm getting the hang of this, thought Nick.

"Received."

Gill Murray held her breath waiting for Maxi's Renault, X-Ray Four, to come into view at the T-junction. It turned left.

"From Gill, X-Ray Four is left, left, left towards you, Monster."

She slowly counted to twenty and then pulled out into traffic.

"From Monster. Monster has eyeball, Monster has eyeball on X-Ray Four."

The cars fell into place behind Maxi's Renault and settled into their roles for the journey, wherever X-Ray Four would take them.

Maxi was relaxed too. He had done this before. There was no law against carrying cash, so he had little to fear. That wasn't strictly true, but Maxi was not a legal scholar. He wasn't any sort of scholar actually. Or any sort of high achiever. School had been a struggle. His employment career had not been rewarding, financially or in any other way. Maxi was not the type of person who sought responsibility and decision-making was not his forte. He really only had one strength. He did as he was told. Armed with explicit and detailed instructions Maxi was reliable. If you asked him to move outside the scope of the specific task that he was assigned he started to flounder quite quickly. But amongst Pyke's crew, he was the star performer.

Maxi had been told to be careful. He looked in his rear-view mirror a little more often than he normally would. But he didn't see anything unusual. By half past eight he had joined the A1 at Newark and was heading south only slightly in excess of the speed limit. By eleven he was over the Thames at Dartford and joining the A2 towards Margate. A few minutes before noon he was parked in a supermarket car park. He got out of the car, took the rucksack from the back seat and went in to use the toilets.

He bought a takeaway coffee and a sandwich from the café, then returned to the car and this time placed the rucksack in the boot. At noon he made his phone call, exactly as instructed.

At the same time Andi phoned Scampton.

"Control."

"Hello, Frank?"

"It's Joe."

"Right. We're in Margate. In a supermarket car park. He's still got the rucksack. He's just sitting in the car. Wait, he's making a phone call."

"Okay, keep us updated."

*

Edwin was also in Margate. He had parked in the car park of a DIY store. When he had finished speaking to Maxi, he too made a phone call. His instructions were very clear. They had not altered since he had received them the day before in the room above the bar in Tilburg.

Fifteen minutes later Maxi drove into the same car park. He completed a full circuit before parking next to a blue, Dutch-registered Audi. He wound down the window and exchanged a few words with the driver. Maxi got out and walked to the rear of his car. Edwin did the same. Both looked about. There was a middle-aged black woman perusing the pot plants displayed near the store entrance; otherwise there was not a soul in sight. They nodded to each other and simultaneously opened the boots of their respective vehicles. Within five seconds both boots were closed again. Both men returned to their drivers' seats. Maxi pulled away almost immediately. Edwin stayed in place. He looked for people racing back to their cars or cars leaving the car park in a hurry. He checked rear-view and door mirrors. Nothing.

Andi's right thumb found the transmit button concealed in the strap of her handbag.

McBride was more than satisfied with the events of the day so far. The team had observed the handover in the car park and noted the number plate of the blue, Dutch-registered Audi. McBride had told them to let the two cars leave unmolested and make their way back to Lincoln in their own time.

"It'll be cash," he told Lake. "I've given the details to the uniformed staff at Dover, Ramsgate and the Channel Tunnel. Our Dutch friend will be subjected to a 'routine' check and if that rucksack is full of cash, and I am almost certain that it will be, it'll be seized."

"But how does that help us?"

"It puts Pyke under pressure. He can't afford to lose that money, and neither can the Dutch. Relations will sour. There will be mistrust. They'll probably have to have a face-to-face meeting to smooth things over."

He smiled, he actually smiled. And then he waved his empty mug at Lake.

When Lake returned five minutes later McBride was on the phone and he looked a good deal less happy. He ended the call, reached for his coffee and then reached for his pipe.

"Damn!"

"Guv?"

"That was the Other Office. There's a second handover, Tango Eleven and probably Eight. Don't know where but I'm guessing Kent. Get the team on the phone, find out where they are."

He took a sip of his coffee. "And don't call me Guv! We're not bloody coppers!"

*

Gazza and Shane should have been on the road by nine, but Shane had had a big night. It was half past before he even stirred and that was only because he received a call from Gazza. He didn't collect Gazza until a quarter past ten and then he had to stop for fuel. Then they had to stop for a McDonald's breakfast. By the time they had reached Peterborough it was gone eleven and clear that they were not going to be in Canterbury by one. Or it would have been clear if either of them properly knew where Canterbury was. They needed a further pit stop to buy a road atlas. By one o'clock, when Pyke phoned, they had only reached Cambridge. He wasn't very pleased.

Gazza and Shane eventually arrived in Canterbury at half past three, just as fifteen miles away at Ramsgate Edwin was being directed into the examination lane by Customs.

Edwin's brother, Marius, was not fazed. He had been assured that his contact was delayed but would be arriving eventually. He decided to put the extra time available to him to good use. Marius was naturally calm, and he had made this run, or one very like it, many times before. He found a small shop that suited his purposes perfectly. It was one of those that sell everything from egg cups to step ladders. Most of the wares are on the pavement outside and crucially the shop assistants are almost always immigrants with a poor standard of English. Marius intended to say as little as possible, but it was likely that the staff would not be able to identify his Dutch accent. And he made sure to park around the corner so that his Dutch-registered Volvo would not be noticed.

Had he genuinely been in the market for a good quality sports holdall he might have been a little disappointed with the range available. But he was not. He was concerned only with capacity and that the bag should be as unremarkable and as forgettable as possible. He found a navy-blue bag with no distinguishing marks or logos, paid cash and left the shop without saying a word. He had driven to a quiet spot in the car park of a country park. He checked in all directions, but nobody else was around. Midweek, during the school term and a light drizzle falling from the austere Kentish sky (or should that be sky of Kent?) the location was ideal.

Marius opened the boot of his car and peeled back the thin

carpet that concealed the spare wheel. He looked around again. Nobody in sight. Then he took the tyre lever and prised the rubber back from the rim. He wedged the gap open with a piece of branch he had found in the car park and gently started to remove the packages. They were triple-wrapped but still he was careful. It took him almost ten minutes to remove the six packages. He forced himself to stop and look around after each one. Finally, he put the packages in the newly purchased holdall, forced the tyre back onto its rim and put it back in place. A spare tyre was a good concealment, but it wasn't fool-proof. Experienced Customs officers knew about it and if they were to remove it and bounce it on the ground it was very apparent very quickly from the weight and balance that something was amiss. A further problem arose if you had to explain why you had two spare wheels, particularly if one was not for the car you were driving. Or no spare wheel at all. Marius had solved the former problem for his contact, but much more importantly, he had solved the second problem for himself. He would not have to explain to some Customs officer or traffic cop why he had no spare wheel on his return trip to Tilburg.

Almost three hours late the white Peugeot pulled alongside him. The two occupants were laughing and joking. They didn't look about. They didn't seem to have any idea about security. Marius was glad to hand over the holdall and watch them depart. *Is it really worth it*, he thought, *to be so professional and cautious myself when at the moment of maximum risk my fate is in the hands of this pair of jokers?* He watched them leave and stood in silence, listening for the sound of roaring engines or squealing brakes. Instead, all he heard was the sound of the raindrops dripping from the tall trees into the shallow puddles that pockmarked the car park. Marius returned to his car, rolled himself a cigarette and waited. Ten minutes passed. The rain stopped. Marius sent a short text message and five minutes later he was heading for the Channel Tunnel, mentally composing the report that he would give Maas about his day's activities.

Gazza and Shane were heading for Lincoln. Instead of a text message they had made a phone call to Pyke. Gazza had let him know that they had collected the drugs and were now on their way home. He had told them so many times to be subtle, not to use such specific language, but it was no use. They just could not be persuaded to take things seriously. They weren't interested. Still, at least they had the merchandise.

*

Lake had been to look at Shane's home, or at least, the address where the white Peugeot was registered. Since Shane had become Tango Eleven his home would be Gold Eleven. Lake needed to know what the neighbourhood was like. Was it possible to put an observation van somewhere with a good view? Would it be too noticeable? Was there more than one exit from the premises? And most importantly of all, was the white Peugeot with the green wheels (X-Ray Eleven) there? The type of thing that he had done a hundred times before. When he got back to Scampton McBride was on the phone again. He made a vaguely interrogatory gesture with the stem of his pipe.

"No sign of X-Ray Eleven."

McBride ended his call. "They're almost certainly on their way back here in the Peugeot with gear on board."

"Two of them?"

"Yes. The Other Office are pretty confident about that. And we have to expect that Pyke is soon going to learn that we have seized fifty grand of his money at Ramsgate."

"Meaning?"

"I don't know. He may panic. He may not. He may tell those two jokers, Laurel and Hardy, in the Peugeot. He may not. Personally, in his position, I wouldn't. If he does tell them they might panic. Anything's possible. Here's what we'll do. The team is on its way back. We'll have them plot up on the A46 between Newark and Lincoln. Hopefully we'll pick them up on the way back. If we do, we'll see what happens to the gear and then we'll decide what we do in response."

*

Pyke didn't panic. He did what he always did when he needed to think. He went for a drive. McBride and Lake saw him leave the house and get into his car. But there was nothing they could do. The surveillance team was somewhere between Margate and Lincoln, and so they had to watch him go. And wonder.

Pyke phoned Maxi. He was almost home so they arranged to meet at the windmill. The windmill, or the mill, or something similar was such an obvious name for the pub that it was odd that the brewery had decided to call it 'the Pride of Lincoln' when it had been built ten years earlier in what one could generously describe as a faux-heritage style. Odder still was the fact that this name was written in five-foot-high letters on the tower of what was very obviously meant to look like an old mill.

Pyke arrived first. Or rather, he arrived before Maxi. He bought a pint of Guinness and headed for a table in the corner. A few minutes later Maxi entered. He didn't bother going to the bar at all but walked directly to Pyke's table, his face wearing a puzzled expression. Maxi didn't understand why he had been summoned. He had carried out his orders as instructed, as he always did. This meeting constituted a change from a well-practised routine and such deviations worried Maxi. Neither was he reassured by the expression on Pyke's face, which was somewhere on a spectrum between anxious and angry.

The two spoke, their heads close together. Neither noticed the young man with his back to them playing the fruit machine. But between the noise of the machine and the hushed tones being used by the two targets there was nothing that Lake could overhear. It didn't matter. He had seen what he needed to. He left and returned to his car, from where he called McBride.

Pyke and Maxi left twenty minutes later. Both returned to their respective cars. Maxi drove off immediately, but Pyke made a phone call first.

"Yeah?"

"Yeah, it's me. All okay?"

"Yeah, fine."

"No bother?"

"No bother at all."

"Did you see anyone I might not like?"

"No, nothing at all, no-one."

"Oh, okay, listen, I've got to go out tonight, so I won't be in when you get back. Can you look after my thing and come round in the morning? No. In fact, I'll call you in the morning."

"What's wrong, JP?"

"Nothing. It's all fine. I'll call you in the morning, alright?"

Pyke ended the call.

Gazza was puzzled. This wasn't all that unusual. A lot of things puzzled Gazza: long words, elementary arithmetic, basic English geography. But on this occasion, he wasn't just puzzled, he was worried.

"I think something's gone wrong."

"How do you mean?" asked Shane, who also spent a lot of his life slightly perplexed.

"JP doesn't want the gear right away. Wants us to hold on to it overnight."

The two sat in silence as they ruminated upon the possible implications of Pyke's unexpected instruction. They passed Alconbury Services, then Peterborough, then Stamford.

"Let's dump it. I mean, hide it. Let's stash it somewhere and come back for it tomorrow when we've had a chance to think things through and talk to JP."

"Where?"

"I dunno. We're in the country, we could put it in a barn or a haystack or something."

Shane indicated left and turned off the A1. Five miles down a winding country lane and not a haystack or a suitable barn anywhere in sight.

"Here, in here, this'll do."

The Peugeot pulled into the small car park. Dusk was falling. Both got out, Gazza carrying the holdall. They tried the door of the small building furthest from the road, but it was locked. There was another possibility nearby. Shane looked at Gazza; Gazza shrugged. He knelt down and started to create a cache. Together they disguised it as best as they could. It was only for a few hours, after all, and it was better than being caught red-handed with a holdall full of pills. They returned to the car park looking left and right all the while. One last look round to be sure that the coast was clear and then they got back into the Peugeot and headed for the A1 again.

Well, thought Michael as he stood in the shadow of the scorers' hut, *that was interesting.*

SIX

Michael decided to wait five minutes and finish his spliff whilst he mulled over what he had seen. It couldn't hurt to take a look. He walked back to the car park. It was empty. He went to the road and looked left and right. Leighton Parva was as quiet as it always was. The Peugeot had left at a speed and at a volume such that he was confident that he would have ample notice if it were to return. Then he made his way past the pavilion and the scorers' hut to where the pile of grass clippings edged the boundary at long on, or at fine leg if you were bowling from the pavilion end. He poked the pile with his toe and instantly met a faint resistance. He looked all around again and sunk to his haunches. Within thirty seconds he had retrieved the sports holdall. It was heavy. He looked around again.

There was a small gate leading from the club directly to the vicarage's back garden. A relic of some cricket-loving clergyman, perhaps. Michael decided it was the better route than walking across the field, through the car park and down the lane. He hefted the bag. It really was quite heavy. And he made for home. He had to struggle through a rhododendron bush that had escaped his grandmother's pruning shears and made for the back door. His grandfather would probably be in the front room doing his bit for the Scottish distilling industry. Except he wasn't. The old man was sitting at a table on the patio.

"Quiz night tonight," he said. Michael had forgotten. Thursday night was quiz night at the Old Volunteer.

"Leave that in the kitchen and we'll deal with it later. I shall have to go or they will send out a search party. Your oma and I used to go every week. Used to drive her mad."

"Why?"

"Your oma was very competitive. She hated the fact that we always came second. Hated the fact that it was by design too." He chuckled.

"You deliberately came second?"

"Oh yes. It was quite an art. Much harder than coming first. More of a challenge. But perhaps, just for a treat we'll win tonight. Let them think that you're the brains of the family."

And so, Michael and his grandfather had made the short journey to the Old Volunteer a little after eight. The Old Volunteer was the type of pub that you see on Sunday-evening television. It was the sort of place where a vicar's murder might be investigated by a detective with an amusing character trait, a fondness for model railways, perhaps, or vintage motorcycles. The walls were decorated with horse brasses and prints of hunting scenes. There were photographs of old football teams and cricket teams. Leighton Parva 1st XI 1911. The same names as on the war memorial mostly.

The fruit machine was discreetly tucked away in a corner and a blackboard announced that the daily special was 'Ploughman's Lunch'. Michael suspected that the daily special was often 'Ploughman's Lunch'.

The old man made directly for a small round table in the corner. Such was its size and location that it could only feasibly be occupied by two people, which was why he had chosen it, of course. Michael went to the bar. He perused the pumps – no

Abbot. The publican had taken two bottles of Pils from the cold shelf and was pouring these into a pint glass. He added two slices of lemon. "The major's usual," he explained. "And what would you like?"

Michael carried his pint of Ruddles County and his grandfather's drink over to the table. "Still prefer German beer?"

"It's a rough approximation. Not quite Berliner Kindl, but close enough. Now, do you think it would be more fun to win narrowly or to absolutely blow them all away?"

"It sounds like you'd enjoy winning narrowly more."

"Yes. Good lad, yes."

The quiz was similar to a hundred others that were probably taking place the length and breadth of the land. Small groups of pensioners argued in tense whispers about the exact location of Lake Titicaca, the year of the Battle of Bosworth and the film career of Cliff Richard. The old man was studying the other teams, of which there were five, but particularly a group of five men whose team captain, and there was not the slightest doubt as to which of them was the captain, was a rather florid-faced man.

"That's Colonel Roberts," said the old man.

"Parish council?"

"Yes, he's the competition. I'd like to beat him by one point."

The quiz was in rounds and teams were supposed to submit their answers at the end of each round. The questions mostly weren't particularly testing, and Michael was pretty sure that either he or his grandfather knew the answers to all of them. But at the end of each round the old man would score out one or two correct answers before submitting them. At the end of each round the quizmaster would give a running total of the scores. His grandfather and he were either tied for the lead or a point ahead or behind at the end of each round. The 'parish council' team were giving them concerned glances.

The final round was sport. "Peter's pretty good at sport. I think we'll have full marks on this round, please."

"Okay, Grandpa."

The old man had been correct. 'Team Florid Face', as Michael had renamed it, scored full marks too, and so the quiz went to a tie breaker.

From George the publican's point of view this was the ideal outcome. Firstly, it allowed him to indulge in his weaknesses for the dramatic. Secondly, by prolonging the event a few more minutes some customers might be persuaded to buy another round. After allowing ten minutes for exactly this purpose he called for hush, and when he thought he had secured as much attention as he was likely to, he asked, "And now, everything riding on this, ladies and gentlemen: who or what were Sherman, Lee, Stuart and Valentine?"

The captain of Team Florid Face immediately scribbled down his answer. He did not seek or entertain suggestions from his teammates. Neither did he show them his answer; he just handed it immediately to the quizmaster, a smug grin on his face. Michael understood now why his grandfather wanted to win but was privately amazed at how he had had the willpower deliberately to allow himself to be beaten by such an individual every week. What sort of a man enjoyed a victory that his opponent thought was his?

The old man pulled his sheet of paper and wrote deliberately in a clear hand, then gave it to Michael. Michael nodded, folded it carefully and handed it to the quizmaster.

"And now, to determine the winner..." George was really hamming it up. "The tie break question was: who or what were Sherman, Lee, Stuart and Valentine?"

"US Civil War generals!" called out the captain of Team Florid. He beamed at all those present. If he hadn't been pushing seventy, he might have performed cartwheels.

"No, I'm sorry, Peter. It was a good guess but only three of those were Civil War generals."

The captain of Team Florid had just become the general of Team Apoplectic.

"The correct answer is that Sherman, Lee, Stuart and Valentine are all examples of Second World War tanks. And we have a winner: Michael and Bernard."

There was a more than expectedly enthusiastic ripple of applause. It seemed that Team Florid did not enjoy much support. The old man nodded modestly. As he glanced down, he appeared to notice something. His eyes met Michael's. He glanced down again. His glass was empty.

*

Michael and his grandfather were back in the old vicarage. "So how come a brigadier knows so much about tanks?"

"Well, I ended up as a brigadier, but I was in the army for nearly forty years."

"How did you come to join?"

"I was he invited. We all were, summer of 1939. I was in the Officer Training Corps at university, you see?"

"You were at university?"

"Certainly, I was. You didn't think you were the only educated bugger in the family, did you?"

"No, sorry, I just never thought…"

"Well, I didn't finish. War got in the way. And afterwards, well, there didn't seem much point."

"So, you joined up? Volunteered, I mean."

"I did. I mean I would have been called up anyway. But I decided not to wait."

"So, you joined as a private?"

"No. I tried to, but they sent me to a Cadet Training Unit straight away. Then a wartime commission and then posted."

"What regiment?"

"I was a tanker. Fifth Royal Tank Regiment, 22nd Armoured Brigade, 7th Armoured Division."

"The Desert Rats?"

"Yes."

"Why didn't I know my grandfather was a desert rat?"

"It's not important. It was a long time ago. Anyway, I managed to get myself wounded in Tunisia and they made me the battalion intelligence officer, then the brigade intelligence officer. By the time the war ended I had almost forgotten what a tank looked like. In the summer of 1945, it was sheer chaos. I found myself in Berlin, there was a lot of intelligence work, and I met your oma and I just sort of stayed."

"For thirty years?"

"Yes, longer actually; it was the first place I had ever settled. My only home really, although Berlin is nothing like it was then anymore."

"Were you a spy then?"

"Spy is a very vulgar term. The British don't spy. We have intelligence officers, agents and assets."

"So, you were a spy."

The old man shrugged. He declined to debate the distinction.

"Did you enjoy it?"

"Oh yes! I absolutely loved it. It was all a great game, do you see? Us versus them, lies, subterfuge, blackmail, coercion, betrayal. It was terrific fun. Like Boy Scouts but with better beer and sausages."

"Do you miss it?"

"A little bit, yes. Life has been rather dull since I retired. The pub quiz is now the highlight of the week. Imagine that?"

"And you can't even tell that pompous old fool that you outrank him?"

The old man laughed. "Oh, it's much worse than that, much, much worse. I couldn't tell him, and you mustn't either... I'm a knight."

"A knight?"

"Yes, I'm a Knight Commander of the Most Excellent Order of the British Empire. I've got a medal somewhere."

"What did you get it for?"

"Skulduggery and mischief, dear boy, skulduggery and mischief."

"You mean like when you let your opponent think he's won when really you have?"

The old man eyed him. He appeared to be about to say something. But then he decided against it. "Next week we'll lose by one point. See if you can handle it."

He presented it like a challenge, which was absurd. As if Michael cared who won the weekly quiz in a little pub in the middle of nowhere.

"But for now, why don't you fetch that bag you found in the grass clippings, and we'll take a look at it, shall we?"

His grandfather had a knack, perhaps he had learned it in the military, of asking questions in a way that made it abundantly clear that they were orders. Michael wasn't sure what to do, so in the end he took the simple course and obeyed. The Taylor brothers had probably done something similar.

*

Gazza and Shane had been having second thoughts about hiding the bag at Leighton Parva Cricket Club. Gazza wasn't one hundred per cent sure of the name of the village and Gazza was having misgivings about the exact location. What happened to grass clippings? Were they taken away, perhaps by the council? If so, when? And how often? And whilst it seemed like a remote location at dusk, would it still be quiet and unoccupied whenever they returned? Each was mentally composing the account that they would give Pyke if it were needed and in each man's version the directing mind behind leaving twenty-five thousand ecstasy tablets in a field in Rutland was the other.

In the event neither had an opportunity to put their side of the story without the other being present. They were somewhere near Grantham when Pyke called.

"That thing you have. Don't leave it in the car overnight. Take it home with you."

"No need. We've stashed it."

"You've what?"

"We've stashed it. Somewhere safe."

"Where? No! Don't tell me. Come to my place."

"I thought you were going out."

"Change of plan."

"Okay. Be there in about half an hour."

Shane turned to Gazza. "I told you he was lying, didn't I?"

"No."

"Yeah, I did. I told you something was wrong."

Gazza pondered this. It certainly seemed like something was amiss. The plan had changed twice in an hour and that never happened. Pyke was getting nervous. Well, he sounded nervous. And when he got nervous, he got very bossy. Gazza didn't like that at all. He hated being told what to do. What was the point of being a criminal if you had to follow rules?

*

Michael placed the bag on the kitchen table. His grandfather handed him a pair of Marigolds. "They'll have to do," he said.

Michael put on the yellow rubber gloves, feeling faintly ridiculous, and unzipped the bag. He pulled out a clear plastic package that appeared to be full of small white tablets. His grandfather nodded at a set of kitchen scales. Michael very gingerly placed the package on the scales.

"It's not a bomb!"

"Two kilograms. Just over."

"That's the wrapping. How many packages?"

Michael returned to the bag. "Six."

"Twelve kilos, say half a gram per tablet, twenty-four thousand tablets. Might be twenty-five – weigh another one."

Michael couldn't help thinking that his grandfather was not responding the way that most seventy-six-year-olds might. He weighed a second package. It was just over two kilos.

"Weigh them all."

The third was two and a half kilos, the fourth was two, and so were the fifth and the sixth. Twenty-five thousand tablets. How had the old man known?

"How very interesting," said the old man. "What are you going to do with your lucky find?"

"I don't know. I don't even know what they are."

"Well, I doubt very much that they're aspirin. Did those two jokers look like retail chemists to you?"

How much had the old man seen? And how?

"I imagine that they are probably MDMA," said the old man.

"Eh?"

"Methylenedioxymethamphetamine, ecstasy."

No wonder the old man was so good at pub quizzes. He knew simply everything.

"The way I see it you have a number of options." The old man counted them off on his fingers. "One: you could put them back amongst the grass clippings. Two: you could phone the police – very public-spirited, of course, but a bit boring. Three: you could try to sell them. I wouldn't recommend that. You don't even know what they are or what they are supposed to be, and I hope, I hope, you don't have the contacts."

Michael waited; for some reason he was sure that his grandfather had a fourth option. He had.

"But I think that the most interesting and remunerative option would be simply to ransom them."

Michael was shocked. His grandfather was seventy-six! A pillar of the establishment. A knight of the realm, no less. He had at least two tweed hats that Michael had seen. He lived in an old vicarage, for God's sake! Yet here he was calmly suggesting – Michael quickly did the arithmetic – ransoming a quarter of a million quid's worth of what were almost certainly illegal drugs. And what was more, he was suggesting this with a twinkle in his eye.

"Your find. Your choice. But I don't think I'd be doing my duty as a grandfather if I didn't open your eyes to the potential for a bit of skulduggery and mischief. More interesting than anything else you might do round here and only slightly more illegal than lurking behind the scorers' hut and smoking hash."

SEVEN

Gold Eleven, Shane Hartney's home at 9 Furness Street, was in one of the narrow streets of Victorian terraces near the Lincoln City football stadium, Sincil Bank. It was an absolute nightmare for surveillance. Putting in an observation van was out of the question. Even if a suitable parking space could be found it would stand out like a sore thumb. It was simply impossible to find any position from which any car or pedestrian could keep watch on the front door of number nine. The surveillance team, who had been to Kent and back the following day and had not finished until McBride had stood them down at midnight, were tired and grumpy.

Andi Woodhead and Steve Bradford were parked in the Mondeo, which was starting to resemble a skip and smelled pretty similar too. Steve was wrestling with the cellophane on a fresh pack of Rothmans. He cracked the window open an inch, but it had started to rain and it was slanting in at the exact angle to go straight into his ear. Nick Harper was squinting at the junction of Furness Street and Kirkby Street. Beside him, in the driver's seat, Gill Murray was attempting *The Guardian*'s cryptic crossword, without much success. In the back seat, Chris Bolton, Monster, was working his way through a bacon and fried egg sandwich. At the other end of Furness Street, where it met Thesiger Street, Gerry Day and Carl Sanders were watching that junction whilst engaging in their favourite surveillance pastime of speculation and theorising.

"So yesterday, right," began Carl, "that was the money going out, right?"

"S'pose."

"But was it payment for goods delivered that day? Or was it payment for goods already imported and sold on?"

Gerry shrugged. "Or was it payment, or part payment, for goods yet to be delivered?" he offered.

There was a period of silence.

"How much cash can you get in a rucksack, do you think?"

"Depends on the notes, doesn't it? And the rucksack."

"I think it was for drugs delivered that day. Why else would the Tartan Terror keep us hanging around the A46 until midnight?"

"That's the wrong question."

"Is it?"

"Yeah, the right question is, why did he stand us down?"

Carl thought about this for a few minutes.

"That's right. He must have thought that something significant, like an actual importation, was happening. So why did he stand us down? What happened?"

"Presumably he heard something from the Other Office."

"I wish he'd tell us a bit more. I mean, here we are either racing about or sitting about and most of the time I don't know why."

"Perhaps he thinks you don't need to know."

Carl thought about this for a few minutes too, the resentment slowly building within him.

"And another thing, what are we supposed to be doing now? If there wasn't an importation yesterday, what are we doing? And if there was, well, we've lost the chain of evidence. And the gear is probably long gone anyway. None of it makes sense."

McBride had not had the time fully to debrief them on the events of the previous day. He had merely given them instructions to plot up on Gold Eleven, Shane Hartney's home address, and follow X-Ray Eleven, the white Peugeot with the green wheels, whenever it moved and wherever it went. Now, and Carl wasn't going to like this one bit, he was changing those instructions.

"*Andi, Andi, Control.*"

Andi Woodhead leant forward and pressed her finger against the small button on the dashboard between the fog lights and the heated rear window.

"*Andi.*"

"*Send one car, with one male and one female occupant, to the car park of Damon's restaurant, Doddington Road, near the A46.*"

"*Received.*"

"*Everyone else, notify me when X-Ray Eleven is mobile, but do not, do not, follow, receive?*"

"*Mark, Mark, Andi.*"

"*Mark receiving.*"

"*Looks like you and Julia get to have breakfast.*"

"*On our way.*"

Mark Hardy started the Primera engine, glancing quickly at Julia Hayes beside him. She shrugged. He put the car in gear and headed for Doddington Road.

Gerry and Carl returned to their speculation. Gill returned to her crossword and Monster produced a second bacon and egg sandwich from his jacket pocket. Steve further mentally postponed the date on which he would quit for good and fumbled for his lighter.

*

Back at Scampton Joe was watching television. Specifically, the long running non-drama that he had titled *Aged Mercedes Parked*

Outside Grotty House. McBride wasn't exactly pacing up and down in anxious thought like an expectant father in a hospital corridor, but that was the vibe. In fact, he wasn't pacing at all. His pipe was doing all the work required to put that image in Lake's mind. Lake's thoughts then drifted to how terrible McBride must be a poker with that belching 'tell' in the corner of his mouth all the time.

At first, he had slightly resented being kept back at Scampton whilst the others went out to play. Most investigators regarded surveillance as a treat. A chance to escape the office and most of the provisions of the Road Traffic Act. But actually, he reasoned, he was in a position to learn more about target work than anyone else in the team. In theory. Except he wasn't learning anything save that when McBride's phone rang, he mostly listened. Then there would be a brief period of intensive puffing and he would issue his orders. Lake had no more idea what lay behind them than the team grumbling and griping in cars all around Sincil Bank. He decided that he would gently introduce the topic and hope that McBride shared a little information, or wisdom, or something. He was just mentally composing how he would raise this delicate subject when something caught his eye.

*

Mark and Julia were already inside Damon's when the targets arrived. Criminals, even quite good ones, normally assumed that they might be followed. If they were worried about being the target of surveillance, they would look behind themselves. If it weren't for the advance intelligence provided by the Other Office that would be entirely reasonable. But by the time that the Peugeot pulled into the car park Mark and Julia were already sitting at a table sharing a stack of pancakes.

Shane and Gazza arrived first. Julia, who was facing the door, saw them immediately and pushed her foot down on Mark's. He raised his eyebrows one millionth of an inch. She nodded her head a little less than that. Then she looked at her wristwatch and wrote the time on the paper napkin by her right hand.

Shane and Gazza looked left and right before they were met by the restaurant's hostess. They asked for a table for four, explaining that their 'business associates' would be along later. Mark smirked. He couldn't help it. The hostess showed Shane and Gazza to a table about twenty feet from the two surveillance officers. Perhaps she wasn't really listening. Or perhaps she thought that a pair of young men in shell suits and wearing baseball caps were exactly the type to have 'business associates'. Or perhaps she didn't care. Her hosting duties performed, she disappeared, and it was a different young woman who arrived to take the order a few minutes later just as Pyke and Maxi walked through the restaurant's doors. They did not require the services of the hostess and made their way immediately to Shane and Gazza's table in time to order a pair of frankly preposterous breakfasts. There seemed little danger that they would be leaving in a hurry, and so Mark and Julia ordered top-ups to their coffees.

At the same moment that breakfast for four (four particularly hungry rugby teams by the look of it) arrived Andi's Mondeo pulled into Damon's car park and made a slow tour, Andi muttering all the time about people who couldn't make their mind up and tell their teams what the hell was going on. She observed Maxi's Renault 21 (X-Ray Four), then the white Peugeot (X-Ray Eleven). Andi parked at the far end of the car park, where she and Steve had a clear view of the restaurant's exit and the Renault. They didn't have a clear view of the Peugeot, but the deployment of Monster to linger near the public telephones by the petrol station covered that angle. The other cars took up positions a quarter of a mile distant in each direction.

The four targets collectively decided that nourishment should come before business and for the next fifteen minutes there was little to observe except an ambitious attempt at the world bacon-eating record. This completed, they waited until the plates were cleared and then started to speak, in low tones, heads close together. After a few minutes Shane left the table and headed for the doors. Steve saw him enter the car park and Monster saw him walk to the Peugeot and open the door. Three keys turned in three ignitions. Kevin Cleary got out of the back of a car and sauntered back to his Yamaha. Monster saw Shane reach in and withdraw something rectangular, shut the door and return to the restaurant. Three keys turned again in three ignitions. Steve lit another cigarette.

"*Mark, Mark, Andi, are you receiving?*"

Bzz bzz bzz.

"*Three clicks received, understand yes, yes. Have you eyeball on targets?*"

Bzz bzz bzz.

"*Three clicks received, understand yes, yes. Is Tango Five present?*"

Oh, I get it, thought Nick. *Three clicks for yes, three letters in the word yes.*

"*Four, Five, Eight, Eleven.*"

It was very faint. Obviously, Mark was whispering.

"*Do you require assistance?*"

Bzz bzz.

Two clicks, that must mean no, thought Nick.

"*Two clicks received, understand no, no.*"

Andi reached for the mobile phone. She called McBride and updated him.

*

McBride had put the phone on its speaker setting. When he had thanked Andi and hung up, he turned to Lake. "Well?" his whole body seemed to say.

Lake was learning to interpret McBride and his little idiosyncrasies. This was McBride's idea of instruction. Present the pupil with a situation, not even a question, just a situation, and see what he thought the answer was.

"So…" began Lake, "Shane Hartney and Gazza Barham, the two idiots in the Peugeot, probably collected a consignment of drugs yesterday, probably in South East England. But we don't know exactly where, and we don't know when."

McBride nodded and reached for a pipe from his rack.

"At some point and for some reason the two of them decided that instead of returning to Lincoln and handing over the goods to Pyke, that they would stash them somewhere."

McBride was slowly filling his pipe. *It's like being in the study of some Oxford don*, thought Lake.

"So, why did they do that? They weren't told to by Pyke as far as we know. So, something must have alarmed them. Now it wasn't us, because we were nowhere near them. Maybe they are just very jumpy, but that doesn't seem to fit with what we know about them and how they have behaved so far, so it was something else."

The first puffs of smoke were rising from McBride's pipe.

"Did Pyke tell them about the Dutchman being pulled at Ramsgate?"

McBride shook his head.

"Then I can't think what it was that spooked them. Anyway, they have stashed the gear somewhere between Kent and here. Maybe they have a safe spot for cases like this or maybe they improvised."

Lake focussed hard on McBride. What did he think of his reasoning? Did he actually know the answers to these questions himself?

McBride removed his pipe. "They improvised."

Lake couldn't work out how McBride knew this. If he knew this.

"So, if they improvised then it is likely that wherever they stashed it is not very secure. Therefore, they need to retrieve it as soon as possible. And they need to be extra sure that they aren't followed."

"Or…?"

"Or perhaps Pyke will go and fetch it. Which he can't do because he doesn't know where they've stashed it…" Lake was speaking faster as he became more confident in and excited by his reasoning. "And he won't want them to tell him on the phone and so he would need an in-person meeting."

McBride held up his hand to pause Lake before he got over-excited.

"So, the meeting is so…"

"Shane Hartney, Tango Eleven, and Gazza Barham, Tango Eight, can tell Pyke where they have stashed the gear and someone at the meeting is going to go and fetch it, probably soon."

"I agree," said McBride. "It works as a theory based upon what we know. In practical terms, right now, we need to decide who we follow from that meeting."

He picked up his phone and dialled. "Andi, it's Frank. Listen, we think the gang have stashed some gear somewhere, probably south of here. Someone from that meeting may be going to get it, but we don't know who. What can you tell me about the situation?"

"Very little. Tangos Eight and Eleven arrived in X-Ray Eleven. Five minutes later Tangos Five and Four arrived in X-Ray Four. They are parked apart. They had breakfast. They are talking. At one point Tango Eleven went to X-Ray Eleven and appeared to fetch a book or something."

There was a pause.

"Could it have been a road atlas?"

"Let me check… Yes, it's a road atlas."

"Okay, go with Pyke, in whatever car he uses."

"Okay, got it."

Andi reached for the transmit button. *"All cars from Andi, we are going with Tango Five when he leaves, Tango Five."* She turned to Steve beside her and shrugged.

Bzz bzz bzz bzz bzz bzz bzz.

"*Rapid clicks received, standby! Standby!*"

Gazza and Shane left the restaurant first. Shane was carrying a road atlas, but nobody noticed. It probably wouldn't have made any difference. It was too late to change targets at this stage. Andi watched them get into the Peugeot and head for the A46. She couldn't see whether they went north or south. A few seconds later Pyke and Maxi emerged. They walked briskly towards Maxi's Renault since it was starting to rain lightly. Andi stayed where she was and calmly described the scene. From his position by the petrol station Monster saw the Renault enter the roundabout and head north towards Gerry and Carl. The surveillance team followed. As the convoy approached the Ermine estate McBride and Lake began to pick up the commentary on the radio at Scampton.

"Shit! He's heading for home," said Lake. "We've guessed wrong!"

"Maybe," said McBride. "Or maybe Maxi is taking him home and Pyke will fetch it in his own car."

"Could be," agreed Lake. He went next door where on the monitor he saw Maxi's Renault pull up outside Pyke's home, Gold Five. Pyke got out, empty-handed, and walked up the front path. The Renault pulled away. Lake was standing in the doorway describing all he saw to McBride.

McBride reached for the transmit button in his desk microphone. "*From Control, stay on Tango Five, currently in Gold Five.*"

*

Meanwhile, ten miles south, Gazza and Shane were heading for Rutland.

EIGHT

"So, Mikey, have you decided?"

His grandson nodded. His mouth was full of toast.

"Good, it's not the real thing, of course, just a little tickle. But it will be fun just the same. Right, you are going to need some cash."

The old man walked down the passage past the barometer, the hunting prints and the various archetypal accoutrements of an old vicarage to the study. Michael's father's study at their home in Sussex had been tiny. The desk had taken up almost half the room and the rest was taken up with cheap Ikea bookshelves, poorly assembled and laden down not with law textbooks but with old copies of golf magazines, various minor trophies, paperbacks of minimal literary merit and photographs of his father and various cronies standing on first tees and eighteenth greens. There was no photograph of Michael, his sister Emma or their mother. His grandfather's study was completely different.

It was a largish room that might have merited the name 'library'. Floor-to-ceiling bookshelves lined three walls. In the centre was a back-to-back partner desk. His grandparents had obviously shared the room. The lamp on one half of the desk was from Tiffany, a delicate thing with coloured glass depicting a dragonfly. There was some lavender notepaper, a fountain pen and a pair of feminine-looking reading glasses. He wondered if his grandfather had been in this room since his wife died.

Now that he looked more closely, he saw that the books on the shelves at that end of the room were mostly in German. The opposite side was more English, and more male. There was a lot of military history and, Michael couldn't decide if this was ironic or not, some Len Deighton and John le Carré novels. The desk lamp at the male end was brass with a green glass shade. The more Michael studied the room the more he was aware of the subtle distinction between 'his' side and 'hers'. A single room divided into different zones.

The old man went to the top shelf and removed three or four books, all on the subject of Operation Husky. He retrieved an ancient tin tea caddy and placed it on the desk. It was absolutely full of bank notes. Pounds, Deutsch marks, French and Swiss francs, US dollars and others he did not recognise. The notes were bound in rolls secured with elastic bands. He selected one of the smaller rolls and tossed it to Michael.

"That's a thousand. You shouldn't need it all. Now, here's what you do…"

The old man spoke for fifteen minutes. It was a model of clarity and detail. Like a military briefing. Well, it would be. It was also quite involved and quite complicated. Above all it was very specific; no deviation or improvisation would be tolerated. It wasn't hard to imagine a man twenty years younger giving similar instructions in an office hard by the Berlin Wall.

Michael took his grandfather's Rover 800 and drove into Peterborough. He had been forced to memorise his instructions and tested twice before he was allowed go.

"Write down as little as you possibly can and *never* when you are in the field," the old man had said. Michael couldn't quite believe he was doing this, but it made his grandfather so happy, so transparently, absurdly happy that he was glad to go along. The old man seemed to have shed about twenty years and had been bustling around the kitchen at twice his usual speed. His eyes were actually twinkling. What harm could there be in making a grieving, lonely old man so happy? Well, quite a lot of harm if things went wrong, but Michael couldn't quite credit the possibility that they might.

Michael's first stop was at a large sports retail store where he purchased a holdall, similar in size to the one currently sitting in the kitchen of the old vicarage. He paid in cash. Then he went to the Co-op, where he purchased a Nokia pay-as-you-go mobile phone, also with cash. He was invited to complete a form, giving his details 'for warranty purposes', just as his grandfather had told him he would. How had he known? He completed it using the name and address that he had memorised.

Then he went to Woolworths, where he purchased a small pack of coloured stickers, a pack of ten of the cheapest ballpoint pens available, a small pad of writing paper, also the cheapest, and therefore the most common, in the land. At Boots the chemist, he purchased a box of latex gloves. Finally, he visited the Orange store and bought two more untraceable phones, Motorolas this time. On this occasion he gave the name of a company, which he assumed to be fictitious, and an address that he knew was.

He couldn't quite decide if this was thrilling cloak-and-dagger stuff and he was Rutland's answer to 'the Jackal' or whether he was just making a fool of himself indulging a slightly dotty old man.

When he drove back to Leighton Parva he noticed that his grandfather was sitting on the bench beside the war memorial, which seemed an odd thing to do until Michael realised that from that spot he would have had a view of the road in all three directions, the entrance to the cricket club, the pub and the village's sole telephone kiosk. Fifteen minutes later the old man was back in the kitchen.

Michael was wearing latex gloves. He had put all the mobile phones on to charge and was now moving the six plastic packages from the bag that he had found the previous evening to the one he had purchased in Peterborough. His grandfather nodded approvingly. Then, donning a pair of Latex gloves himself, he took a sheet from the middle of the pad of writing paper, and with one of the ballpoint pens he wrote the number of the Nokia phone. He put this in a shoebox and put the shoebox in the now-empty bag. He marked the Nokia with a blue sticker and the Motorolas with yellow and red stickers.

The old man walked upstairs to the little room at the back of the house with a view over much of the cricket club. It had once been the maid's room, probably. Now it contained two large trunks, a military kitbag and several largish cardboard boxes, and a stool, by the window. Michael walked through the back garden, through the cricket-loving clergyman's little gate and made a full circuit of the boundary. His grandfather watched approvingly. By the time Michael had completed his circuit and was re-entering the garden his grandfather was sitting in a chair on the patio with the original bag, containing the shoebox, at his feet. He nodded once and then returned to the house and upstairs to the room at the back. Michael picked up the bag and walked briskly back to the gate and diagonally across the cricket pitch, diverting only slightly to avoid the square, to the pile of grass cuttings. There he placed the bag into the little gully created the day before and, using his hands, raked the grass back over it until it was concealed entirely. He looked left and right, brushed the grass from his hands, and walked back to the house.

*

Shane Hartney was not what you would call an articulate man. He wasn't really one for speeches and he hadn't read a book since he had been expelled from school (running a pornographic magazine library from the lost property store – not his first offence). His vocabulary, in the broadest sense, was not extensive.

But in his specialist area, he was more than a match for any man. He ran through the full gamut of Anglo-Saxon profanity and back again. Then, like a freestyle jazz musician, he began to challenge the form of the medium. He turned nouns into verbs, present participles mostly, and adjectives. He turned verbs into adjectives and gerunds. It was quite a performance. If a professor of linguistics had been observing there was probably sufficient material for an entire paper. But no professor was watching, only an old man and his grandson standing by an upstairs window with binoculars.

Michael was using a pair of ordinary binoculars, the type available from the high street. His grandfather was using an older, heavier, less commercial pair that bore a Kriegsmarine serial number. He merited the superior equipment because, alongside who knew what other skills, he possessed the ability to read lips. He chuckled slightly as he saw Gary 'Gazza' Barham on his knees scrabbling at the pile of clippings, casting handfuls behind him like a terrier trying to dig out a rabbit hole.

"I don't think that this is a pair of criminal masterminds. And as for their choice of vehicle, they might as well be flying the skull and crossbones."

Michael panned his binoculars left to where the Peugeot was parked outside the pavilion. Everything about it said 'Scalliemobile'. It was a rolling invitation to be pulled over by any police officer who wanted an easy collar. Michael panned back again. The pair seemed finally to have accepted the evidence of their own eyes. The taller of the two pulled out a mobile phone.

"Jay Pee," murmured the old man, "we've got a problem. No, the bag's here. Something, something. But it's empty. There's a note. It's just a number. No, I told you. The bag's here! It's just a telephone number. No, nothing else. Okay, we're on our way back to Lincoln now – that's interesting! Lincoln!" The last three words were a commentary rather than a verbatim account.

"Probably take them an hour or so for them to get back to Lincoln."

"So, we should be getting a call in about ninety minutes. Fancy a cup of tea?"

NINE

Pyke turned the shoebox over and over in his hands. This was turning into a very bad week. £50,000 in cash had been confiscated and now somebody had ripped off twenty-five thousand tabs of ecstasy. His working assumption was that the two were related.

Turning to the first issue. He could see two possibilities. The first was that the Dutch cash courier had been the victim of a random or routine stop. These things happened. If it had occurred in isolation, he might have been willing to write it off as bad luck. But it hadn't happened in isolation, which led to the second possibility. That somebody had betrayed him. He examined the shoebox again. It was an ordinary shoebox. There was a small sticker, half the size of a postcard, that indicated that the box had once contained a pair of ladies' shoes, size four. A style called milady. A colour called café au lait. If this represented some type of clue Pyke couldn't decipher it.

The second scenario also had more than one possibility. He had been ripped off. But by whom? Prime suspects were Gazza and Shane. If it was them then he would probably know soon enough. They couldn't possibly move on that much merchandise without him learning about it. If they had any sense, they would know that. But they didn't have all that much sense. And if it was them, how had they tipped off Customs at Ramsgate about the cash? They knew about the cash, of course. Shane had been at the café when Pyke had given it to Maxi. But they didn't know who Maxi was going to give it to and they certainly didn't know the name or the number plate of the Dutch courier.

Unless. Unless they had followed Maxi. Maybe the story they had told him about being delayed in traffic was a lie. Well, obviously it was a lie. They had overslept. But supposing they hadn't. Perhaps they had followed Maxi and seen the handover or been in the neighbourhood and seen the Dutch car and put two and two together. That didn't work. Maxi would have seen and recognised Shane's Peugeot. Unless they were in someone else's car. Or it was a different crew altogether. Maybe Gazza or Shane had told someone else to follow Maxi. It didn't have to be both of them.

Shane was slightly less stupid than Gazza. But who was more likely to try to rip him off? The smart one (these things were relative) or the stupid one? And why the shoebox and the piece of paper with the mobile telephone number on it?

Could it be a trap? Could the police have found the gear and be trying to lure him to it? Well, he wasn't going to go near it. But he couldn't just walk away from that much product. He had customers waiting, customers who would soon find another supplier if he earned a reputation for being unreliable.

What would Maas have advised? That was easy. Maas would have told him just to walk away. In Pyke's particular financial circumstances this was not an option. So, given that, what would Maas have advised? Well, a few key principles for a start. Whenever there is an event, a pause, a resumption, a change of gear, start again at the beginning. He needed a new, untraceable phone. There was an independent shop in North Hykeham on the south side of the city that asked few questions. Pyke put the piece of paper in his pocket, picked up his car keys and headed for the door.

Outside the surveillance team was still waiting.

Pyke knew that sooner or later he would have to call the telephone number in the shoebox. He resented that he had to buy a new phone for a hundred pounds, but it was such an obvious thing to do he knew that he would be kicking himself forever if he spared himself the expense and something went wrong. It also gave him an opportunity to see if he was under surveillance, either official surveillance by the police or unofficial surveillance by... who knew who? He set off from home as fast as he could, tearing through the streets made narrower by cars parked on both sides. He doubled back twice and stopped suddenly three times. He saw a couple of cars that he didn't like the look of. One had two young men in it. Another had a man and a woman, but after a further five minutes of frantically darting this way and that he didn't see them again. He then moved to phase two of his anti-surveillance routine, haring around the A46 Lincoln ring road at close to a hundred miles per hour.

The surveillance team held back as far as they dared and left a lot of work to Kevin Cleary on the motorcycle, whose extra height meant that he could see further ahead. Surveillance was usually hard work, but this was on a different level. But Pyke's behaviour had sent a very clear message. He was trying to lose a tail and therefore highly likely to be about to do something significant. The team hung on to him for dear life.

Pyke eventually turned off and headed for the phone shop. It was true that the proprietor was willing to sell phones for cash with no questions asked but in truth so was almost everywhere else. In fact, the shop was poorly chosen. There was a bus stop, ideal for lurking surveillance officers, directly opposite. A little further down the street was a cycle shop with some of its wares set out on the pavement. From there Monster took three photographs of Pyke emerging with a Nokia carrier bag.

Pyke had intended to drive home as quickly and as erratically as he had come, but within thirty seconds of drawing away from the phone shop, he saw a marked police car in his rear-view mirror. He drove back around the A46 and into the Ermine estate like a driving test candidate, always two miles per hour below the speed limit.

When Pyke returned home, he immediately put his new phone on to charge. New phones took a little while to charge and he needed to think. Within five minutes he was out of the house again and driving out of the Ermine estate, this time at a more sensible speed. He headed north and drove out towards Market Rasen. The surveillance team did the same.

Pyke parked in the small square in the centre, from where it was less than thirty seconds' walk to the Aston Arms. Within a minute he was sitting in a corner nursing a pint of Guinness and watching the door. He glanced at his watch: thirteen minutes past one. A minute later two young men walked in and went directly to the bar. They appeared to pay him no attention. But Pyke had made a poor choice of pub. The Aston Arms was an old-fashioned sort of place. It was decorated in a traditional style: dark wood, burgundy velour stools, a carpet that was the shade of a ripening bruise and walls covered with mirrors advertising the wares of breweries that had long since been swallowed up by the huge corporations that now dominated the British beer industry. Monster and Carl could choose to look in any direction and see Pyke.

Pyke could see them too and was watching keenly to see if they ordered fruit juices or some non-alcoholic beverage that would mark them out as coppers on duty. He had it in his head somewhere that police officers weren't supposed to drink on duty. But the pair of young men were drinking Guinness too. There was no such thing as alcohol-free Guinness and nothing else that looked quite like it. He decided on balance that these two were not his enemies. In any case, one of them looked too short to be a copper.

Pyke tried to consider his options, but in reality, there were only two. He could call the number in the shoebox or he could not. If he didn't, he would lose his merchandise. And he had all his working capital tied up in those pills. He doubted that Maas would let him have a whole consignment on sale or return. It was either call the number or start again. And he couldn't do that. His customers would go elsewhere. He had to make the call. He had no choice. He finished his pint and headed for the door. As he reached it, he glanced over his shoulder at the two men at the bar, but they seemed to be paying him no attention. Within half an hour he was home.

The new phone was almost charged. Pyke lit a cigarette and called the number.

"Yes?"

"Who is this?"

"What do you want?"

"You have something that belongs to me."

"Yes."

"I want it back."

"Put a thousand pounds where you left it. You will have it back twenty-four hours later."

"Listen! I don't think you realise who you're dealing—"

The line went dead.

*

Pyke glared at the phone in his hand. His first reaction was anger. Then he tried to think calmly. The man on the phone had been young. But he wasn't from Lincoln. At least, he didn't have a local accent. He didn't have any accent really. He sounded a bit like a newsreader, sort of, neutral, or slightly posh, or was that just southern? What he did not sound like was anyone who might be an acquaintance of Gazza or Shane. Their social circles didn't even include people who read newspapers.

Pyke drew on his cigarette and tried to think what Maas, or Don Corleone, would have done. On the one hand a thousand pounds was a small price to get back merchandise that he could probably sell on for a hundred times that. But he had no guarantee that he would ever see that merchandise again. Would his thousand be met with a demand for a second thousand? Or was it a trap set by the police? The sum was very small, which meant that it might be the work of that pair of geniuses, Shane and Gazza. Small-time was very much their style. It hadn't been either of them on the phone, of course. It wouldn't be.

He thought about what Shane and Gazza might do with a thousand pounds. They hadn't the sense to put it under the mattress. He would hear about it within twenty-four hours. And if he kept a note of the serial numbers…

*

Lake was watching the monitor. "He's home!"

McBride came and stood behind him. "So he's just made a thirty-mile round trip to have a pint?"

"Looks like it… Wait, here he comes again. What's that?"

"It looks like a shoebox."

"Do we go with him?"

McBride lit his pipe. "No, no, he's behaving like he's looking for a tail. There's nothing from the Other Office to suggest that he's doing anything We'll let him go. Tell the team to stand down and come back here. I've got something else for you to do.

"It's called 'Oasis' or something like that," said McBride. "Anyway, it's the database for cross-Channel ferries. Look for our Dutch friend with the fifty grand. See how many trips he's made, how often, what routes. What vehicles he's used. And then look for Dutch vehicles on the same day. Anything that might give us a connection or might give us a pattern."

Lake nodded.

*

McBride had gathered Lake, Nick Harper and the team's three senior officers – Andi Woodhead, Julia Hayes and Kevin Cleary – for a briefing.

"It's all gone quiet. There's a bag full of pills somewhere and we don't know where. Those two clowns have stashed it. We don't know where. We don't know if they've collected it, or whether someone else has, or whether it's lost forever. If the gang has it, they have to move it. They need customers and they need cash."

"So do we just stay on X-Ray Eleven until that gives us the answer?" asked Andi.

"It's an option. But I'd rather not risk exposing ourselves. You saw what Pyke was like today, racing around like a maniac, making a completely unnecessary journey to a pub in Market Rasen. We might be behind them for days, learn nothing and be seen ourselves. We could be here for months. We don't have to dismantle the organisation on the first day."

"And supposing we do find them with a bagful of gear in the boot?" asked Julia. "We can't tie them to an importation. We're Customs officers. We prosecute drug-smuggling not possession with intent to supply."

"So, what are we going to do?"

"It's a target operation. We wait for the intelligence and respond accordingly."

TEN

Maxi was the reliable one. So, Maxi would be sent down to Rutland to deposit the cash. Pyke was as confident as he could be that Maxi would not be part of any plan to rip him off, but it didn't hurt to check. After all, Maxi was still the likeliest source of the security leak that led to the cash seizure at Ramsgate. He drove to Maxi's house, just half a mile away on the St Giles estate, and gave him his instructions. He told him that the cash had to be deposited at four o'clock exactly.

What he did not tell Maxi was that he planned to park on the A46 a little south of Lincoln between two thirty and three thirty and watch for Maxi's Renault (which he hoped to see) and a white Peugeot with green wheels (which he hoped he wouldn't).

Maxi drove past Pyke's position a minute or two before three o'clock. The shoebox was on the passenger seat beside him. He did not see Pyke's Mercedes. At a quarter to four he turned off the A1 and a few minutes later he was driving slowly through Leighton Parva's main street. He did not notice the old man sitting on the bench by the war memorial and did not see him make a short call on his Motorola. Did not see him rise and walk to the drive of the old vicarage and did not see the maroon Rover pull out and drive towards the A1.

Maxi looked at his watch. It was five minutes to four. He pulled into the cricket club car park and manoeuvred such that his Renault was facing the exit. At one minute to four he picked up the cardboard box and walked across the cricket pitch to the pile of grass clippings that Pyke had described to him. He did not bother to avoid the square. In the upstairs window Michael, watching his progress through binoculars, tutted.

Maxi reached the pile and looked about. He saw nobody. He put the shoebox on the ground and with his hands shovelled some grass over it. He stood back to inspect his work, returned to the clippings and shovelled a little more. He stood back again, this time satisfied. He returned to his car, again walking directly across the square, and got into his car. Michael saw him pick up his phone. A minute later the Renault was out of sight. Michael picked up a mobile phone of his own and called his grandfather.

Within a minute of ending his call Michael received a call himself. On the third phone.

"I've paid. I want my property."

"Twenty-four hours."

Michael ended the call. This was genuinely thrilling. For the first time in weeks, he felt his pulse rising. It was absurd but he felt alive. The man on the phone had sounded angry, and menacing... and something else. Michael pondered... desperate, that was it, desperate and anxious, and maybe, just a little bit frightened.

Maxi drove through Leighton Parva, then through Leighton Magna and two more villages before re-joining the A1. He paid more than his usual attention to his rear-view mirror and varied his speed between forty-five and eighty miles per hour. He saw no-one and nothing unusual. By the time he had reached Grantham he had grown bored of this and settled into his usual driving style for the rest of his journey back to Lincoln. He did not notice the burgundy Rover joining the A1 behind him at Foston.

*

McBride had told the team to go home early. He was expecting a busy day tomorrow. Lake had been mowing the lawn when Bella got home from work. Married life, having an actual house with an actual lawn, it was all still a bit of an adventure. He was enjoying 'playing house', buying furniture, linen, crockery. He was absurdly proud of his lawnmower, which in truth was far larger and more powerful than he needed. But since the start of Operation Bagration he had been spending less and less time at home. Bella was working hard too, a teacher at a nearby school, but she seemed to find more time for domestic chores. Every time Lake came home, or more accurately every time he noticed, there was some new addition to the household inventory. So, he was pleased to be making some contribution at last. He also enjoyed playing with the mower. But he didn't really know what he was doing, which was why at the exact moment Bella came home he managed to get half a tin of engine oil all over himself. He was trying to rub it off, and actually merely distributing it over an ever-wider area of himself, when he noticed Bella standing at the back door wearing an expression of mild exasperation and affection that he found so adorable.

"Hello, handsome! Are you oiling yourself up for me?"

Lake smiled sheepishly. "I thought there might be something stuck in the… err… carburettor. I was trying to clear it."

"Shower! Now! I'll be up in a minute."

*

Andi had not made it home in time to catch Marcus before he went to collect their children from school. But she couldn't have missed him by much. If she hurried, she might just make it to the school gates in time to be there when the Polly and Jamie came out.

Andi hadn't time to change. She was in surveillance garb. The emphasis was very definitely not on glamour. Practicality

86

and anonymity were the key ingredients. Plenty of pockets for notebooks, handcuffs, pens, spare radio batteries and the rest of the crap that James Bond never seemed to need to carry. Dull colours, jackets that could be quickly removed, reversed even. Andi was thirty-six but prided herself that with the right clothes and the right posture she could pass for anything from late twenties to fifty. At least it was a sense of pride when she was at work. Away from work, well, perhaps not so much.

She hurried towards the school. She met no parents coming towards her, heard no happy squeals or yells from children set free from the academic day. She was going to be on time. Just. She rounded the corner and saw that the pavement outside the school was full of parents. Well, more realistically, mothers. There was one father, a studious-looking man who could have used a haircut. He generally wore a corduroy jacket and a frown. He was in his usual spot on the fringe of the gossip, a pencil clasped between his teeth and a few pages of paper in his hand. Somebody had told her once that he was a professor at one of the universities. He certainly looked the part.

There was one other father, of course: Marcus. He was right at the centre of things, taller by almost a head than most of the mothers, beaming his snow-white smile, enjoying the attention. Around him were half a dozen young and not-so-young women who aspired to be 'yummy mummies', hanging on his every word, cooing and fawning. She should have felt pride. Marcus was still a very handsome man. Even though he was approaching forty he had kept himself in shape and his shaven head, a necessary concession to male-pattern baldness, seemed to suit him. She ought to have felt pride, but instead, conscious of her own dowdiness, almost frumpiness, she felt jealous. And she didn't like the way that woman was pawing at his arm.

*

Lake spent the following morning interrogating the Channel-crossing database. Every now and then he would make a note. With each note he became just a little more puzzled. After an hour it dawned on him. He was embarrassed and angry with himself that it hadn't made sense earlier. It certainly wouldn't have taken McBride that long.

McBride spent the morning poring over an exercise book that he kept locked in his desk drawer. Just before one o'clock the Other Office phone rang.

"Meeting at the Lindum Café!" said McBride. "Four cars and the bike. Everyone, go! Now!"

"Scramble! Scramble! Scramble!" said Monster. But this time he meant it. Nine Customs officers hurried from their seats; newspapers and sandwiches went flying. McBride's pipe sent out a cloud of satisfaction.

"X-Ray Five is still at Gold Five!" shouted Lake from the room with the monitor. But nobody was listening.

*

It's safe to say that Egon Ronay probably never visited the Lindum Café. If he had he may have charitably described it as being typical of the genre. If he had felt like being a little more objective, he might have described the genre as 'greasy spoon'. He probably would have had little positive to say about the hygiene standards, the chipped Formica-topped tables or the consistency of the plastic bottles of ketchup and brown sauce. But he could not fail to have been impressed at the temperature at which tea was served (a point midway between molten lava and the surface of the sun) or the cholesterol per penny ratio of the most popular dishes. Monster was sitting at a corner table with a plate of egg and chips when Gazza and Shane walked in. His choice of table had not been accidental. His right ear, containing his radio earpiece, was hidden from the rest of the customers.

"*Tango Five is sweeping the plot.*" He recognised Kevin's voice. "*He's been past me twice.*"

"*Tangos Eight and Eleven into the café.*" That sounded like Carl.

"*X-Ray Five is parked. Tango Five towards the café.*"

Monster reached for his tea.

"*Tango Five into the café. Eyeball to you, Monster.*"

Pyke waited until the proprietor had returned to the counter with his order for three teas.

"Shane, Gazza, I want you to go and fetch that bag you left down south."

"But it ain't there no more."

"It is now. It's back!"

"But how? We looked properly. I swear we did."

"It's back. And I want you to fetch it. Be there at four. When you've got it, I want you to take it to the Golden Gloves in Sheffield. Got it?"

"Anything to collect?"

"No. I'll sort that out. I'm seeing Lee tomorrow."

Three mugs of tea arrived.

Monster looked at his watch. It was one thirty. Best practice would be to remain where he was until the three targets had left. To leave before them would mean walking directly past their table. But he needed to tell the team to follow Shane and Gazza in X-Ray Eleven, not Pyke in his Mercedes. He rose and walked swiftly past the three conspirators and out of the door. He turned left away from the café, his left hand in his trouser pocket.

"*Andi, Andi, Monster.*"

"*Andi.*"

"*We go with X-Ray Eleven. X-Ray Eleven. Receive?*"

"*That's received. From Andi. All units. We are going with X-Ray Eleven, X-Ray Eleven.*"

*

McBride was thinking. This much was obvious from the small re-creation of the Flying Scotsman at full speed that he was performing. The decision to go with Gazza and Shane was undoubtedly the correct one. It seemed likely that they would shortly be in possession of a large quantity of controlled drugs. But Julia had been right. There was no evidence to tie the pair to an importation. The obvious solution would be to tip off the police and have them arrest the pair and make the seizure.

It was McBride's grand strategy to work at Pyke's organisation from the outside in. He would attempt to pick off his underlings and lieutenants first. This would increase the pressure on Pyke. People under pressure made mistakes. By cutting off his associates Pyke could perhaps be lured out and forced to perform tasks himself. Tasks that could be observed and recorded in officers' notebooks. And finally, finally, perhaps he would be foolish enough to expose himself to arrest. If this could be achieved without Pyke having any clue that Customs were after him then so much the better.

But there were disadvantages to the idea too. The first was that the police might cock it up. They might not take it seriously; they may not react at all or send too small a team to deal with it. The second is that the police would be aware that there was a mysterious source of intelligence (the tip would be anonymous) about a Lincoln gang. Police canteens being what they were it wouldn't be long before there were a hundred people enjoying this gossip. And they might include Pyke's cousin.

Finally, the credit for the seizure would go to the police. McBride himself couldn't care less about this, and he knew that the Other Office wouldn't, but he had a feeling that Howard Spencer would. In the end McBride had very little choice. He couldn't allow an unknown but substantial quantity of drugs to end up on the street.

*

A little after three o'clock Shane and Gazza set off for Rutland. They did not see the Mondeo parked a little down the road from the block of flats. They did not see the Nissan Primera that followed them down Nettleham Road or the Renault Laguna that slipped in behind them as they joined the A46. Neither did they see the maroon Rover that joined the A46 South near the Bentley Hotel. They were slightly late, as usual, but Shane was confident that his car and his driving skills were sufficient to shave a few minutes off the expected journey time. The Peugeot rattled and roared as he performed an ambitious overtaking manoeuvre on the single-carriageway stretch of the A46. He did not notice the cars behind him performing similar overtakes on the maroon Rover.

Pyke was parked in the car park of a McDonald's on the A1 at Colsterworth when he heard the tinny chirrup of a mobile telephone. He was puzzled at first, but then he remembered the second mobile in his jacket pocket.

"Yes?"

"Your boys have got a tail."

He didn't recognise the voice. "What?"

"Those two idiots in the Peugeot. They have a tail."

"Who is this?"

But the line was dead.

Pyke drummed his fingers on the steering wheel. He had only used this phone to communicate with whoever had ripped off his merchandise. Nobody else knew the number. But this person, whoever it was, was not whoever he had been negotiating with. He sounded far older for a start. But whoever it was, he knew that Shane and Gazza were on their way. Pyke didn't like that at all.

Were his two associates being followed? If so, by whom? The police, presumably. And if not, was this a trap? And if it was, who was setting it, and why? Maas would have told him to just abort the whole thing. Tell the boys to go back to Lincoln and write off the drugs as lost. Throw away the phone and cease all contact with whoever had just called. But Maas was big time. He could afford to walk away from tens of thousands of pounds. Pyke couldn't. He had customers who valued his reliability.

If he let Shane and Gazza continue, they might be being followed by the police and could be arrested in an hour. If they were, would they keep their mouths shut? If he called them off, he could send Maxi. But if it was a setup and Maxi was caught 'hands-on' with twenty-five thousand tabs Donna would never forgive him. The final option was to go to Rutland himself. Plus side: he would have his merchandise. He could supply his customers. He was back in business. Minus side: he could be walking into a trap. It was twenty to four. Whatever he chose to do he needed to decide quickly.

*

Michael sipped his tea and gently flexed the fingers of his left hand. They were still sore. But in another couple of weeks he might risk a guest appearance for the Leighton Parva Sunday side. His grandfather had suggested that he get himself in position a little earlier than he had originally planned and so he was standing at the rear window with a pad and pencil by one hand and the pair of U-boat binoculars by the other. He had placed the bag of pills back amongst the grass clippings at five that morning.

Because he was at the back of the house, he didn't see the bottle-green Mercedes drive past the old vicarage and past the entrance of the cricket club. Neither did he see Pyke walk past and step into the village's only telephone kiosk, where he made a call, consulting his own mobile phone for the number.

"Where are you?"

"Almost at Grantham services."

"Okay, wait there until I call you. Wait there. Got it?"

"Got it."

Pyke walked back to where he had parked his car. In his head he could imagine what Maas would have said: "Just walk away. Walk away. There is always another deal."

Pyke drove slowly into the cricket club car park. He waited. And waited. In the upstairs window Michael wrote down the number plate. Pyke waited. There were no shouts. No sounds of screaming engines or running feet. Just the gentle rustle of the wind in the trees. He got out, walked briskly across the field until he reached the pile of grass clippings. He looked about. Nothing. Pyke turned and knelt. He groped amongst the clippings. Immediately he felt the bag. Not his bag. Another bag. Similar in size. Similar in heft. It was too late to walk away now. He picked up the bag, walked back to his car and threw it in the boot. Quickly he unzipped it. It was full of clear wrapped parcels of white tablets. He closed the bag. Closed the boot. This would be when it would happen. If he had been set up. If this was a trap. It would be now. He felt his heart pounding, felt the bile rising in his throat.

Nothing happened. His pulse rate began to recede. He glanced about and for the first time started to appreciate how beautiful his surroundings were. A cricket club, a timbered pavilion with a little terrace, green, green grass, a parasol of ash and elms on the southern edge providing dappled shade that at teatime would almost reach the square. Birds chirruping merrily somewhere. When he made it big, when he was a success, he would live somewhere like this. Pyke got into the Mercedes and turned the key. He pulled out of the car park and turned left and back towards the A1.

*

Pyke was not surprised to find that he was sweating; it was, after all, a warm day. But he was surprised at how euphoric he felt. He had gambled. He had won. He had disregarded the silent voice of Stanley Maas and he had been correct to do so. Now all he had to do was drive up to Sheffield and see how much product he could persuade Lee to take off his hands. He paused at a petrol station on the A1 near Newark, phoned Gazza and told him to go home. Gazza was puzzled but did as he was bid. Behind him four cars full of Customs officers were just as puzzled. When Pyke reached Worksop, he phoned Lee.

*

The Golden Gloves Gym's walls were not decorated with pictures of various alumni who had gone on to win Golden Gloves, or any other titles of note. In its thirty-year history it had produced only two professional boxers, and one of those had a career that lasted only one fight. The gym had been founded by Lee's father, Ernie, once a promising welterweight, whose career had peaked and indeed ended in an ABA title fight in 1950. Ernie believed that the youth of Sheffield had been distracted and softened by the liberal attitudes of the 1960s and deplored the ending of National Service. He had founded the Highfield's Boys' Club in the year that Lee had been born and ran it until his death in 1993 on the day that Sheffield Wednesday beat United in the FA Cup semi-final. It may have steered one or two errant youngsters onto the straight and narrow path, but it largely went unnoticed. Until Lee took over.

Lee's first act as proprietor was to change the name of the gym. His second was to change its whole purpose. His management of the club was based not on a worthy social ideal but on a fiscally sound, albeit utterly illegal, business plan. A few adolescents would occasionally spar in the single ring. If you were lucky, you might see a gangly youth skipping or a big lad on the heavy bag. These days the main reason for visiting the Golden Gloves was purely pharmaceutical.

To begin with it had been anabolic steroids and various performance-enhancing products aimed at customers whose career prospects relied upon the size of their biceps. Later the bill of fare broadened to include more recreational products. By 1997 the Golden Gloves was, to all intents and purposes, a front.

Pyke walked directly through the gym itself to the cramped

room filled with a small desk and two large safes that Lee called his office. The tang of embrocation and sweat did not revive any happy memories in him. He hated training and more than that he hated the chiding, the shouting and the abuse that formed a large part of his coaching. His own brief career in the ring had not been built upon an appreciation of the finer points of the noble art. He just liked hurting people.

Fifteen minutes later Pyke left with an empty bag and Lee's safes were full. Pyke was well satisfied with the deal he had made. One third for cash (payable tomorrow) and two thirds on sale or return. He decided that this constituted enough for a day's work and decided to head for home. As he pulled out of the small piece of wasteland that served as the gym's car park he passed Lake's car, parked in the road opposite.

*

Pyke was feeling pretty good about himself. He was willing to admit to himself that he had been worried. And he was willing to admit that perhaps he had been too worried. He had broken one of his own rules. He had personally gone to fetch the merchandise from the cricket club. He had promised himself that he wouldn't do that. Partly because it was bloody dangerous, of course, but mostly because it did not fit in with his self-image.

Pyke considered himself a player and a professional. He wasn't a petty grifter. He headed an organisation. He was a boss, in his own mind at least. And bosses didn't take the risk of being caught 'hands-on'. But it had been a calculated gamble. He hadn't been pushed into a hasty and foolish decision; he had weighed the risks carefully. He had made his decision and he had been proved right. Proved brave, more importantly, proved wise, or shrewd, or something. He felt more confident now that when the next crisis came, and hopefully it never would, he could rely on his own judgement. That felt good.

But it was only possible to enjoy a limited amount of self-satisfaction at leading a gang if your gang was, well, limited. Maxi was fine. Reliable. But he was limited in as much as he had promised that he would never be 'hands-on' either. And he wasn't exactly over-brimming with initiative. Gazza and Shane, well, they occupied a place on the spectrum somewhere between useless and a bloody liability.

There was no point in seeking to learn what had gone wrong with the Ramsgate money by questioning Maxi. He didn't know and he wouldn't have noticed anything that might have provided a clue. Pyke's position, when he spoke to Maas, was that there had been no problem at the English end. He had taken extra precautions. The way that Pyke was going to tell it, and he hadn't decided that he was actually going to say anything, the unscheduled stash at the cricket club was a carefully prepared contingency plan. It was either bad luck or Maas's bag man had done something that caused him to be searched by Customs on his way home. Pyke thought that this was probably true, but in any case, it had to be his opening position when he spoke to Maas because he wasn't going to give him a further fifty grand.

Settling this issue with Maas was his first priority. His second was finding someone a bit more reliable than Shane and Gazza to move his merchandise. Maas's people would probably do it for a price, but if Pyke introduced Maas to Lee at the Golden Gloves and to his other customers then Maas wouldn't need Pyke anymore. No, the better option was to find better associates. Then, if they were good enough, they could collect the merchandise on the continent and bring it in themselves. Merchandise was a lot cheaper if delivered in Calais rather than Canterbury.

Maas would probably have said, had said in fact, many times in the past, that it was better to have a limited crew that you knew and trusted than more professional operators whose loyalty might be more uncertain. Possibly that was true in Holland. But here, if Pyke was going to grow his operation, he needed better staff.

And probably he needed more of them. So, he decided that he would, very discreetly, put the word out amongst the boxers and the bouncers that there might be opportunities for reliable people. He could try them out and then select the best and most reliable. Shane and Gazza could be quietly side-lined.

But before any of that he had to speak to Maas. And for that he needed to get a new mobile phone. An annoying additional expense. Actually, no, he didn't. He could just re-purpose the phone that he had bought, especially for the bastard who had ripped him off for a thousand pounds in Rutland. He hadn't used it for anything else. It was clean and it was a new number to Stanley. *Small economies like this are what keeps an enterprise profitable*, he told himself as he punched in Stanley's number and texted him.

*

The old man arrived home at about six. He put on the kettle and asked Michael for a full debrief.

"There's not a great deal to tell, really. At one minute to four a green Mercedes arrived—"

"Index?"

"Eh?"

"Number plate."

"Oh, Alpha, Four One Four, Delta Delta Oscar."

The old man nodded. Michael had done his homework. "And then?"

"Remained parked for two or three minutes. I couldn't see the driver, so I don't know if he made or received a call. Then the driver got out."

"Description?"

"White male. About thirty. Short light brown hair, very short. Clean shaven. Medium height. Slightly overweight. Jeans, black Harrington jacket. He walked directly to the pile of grass clippings, paused for a second, looked around, then knelt down and retrieved the bag. Put it on his shoulder and walked directly back to the car. He opened the boot. And I think, I think, he opened the bag for a quick look. Wasn't more than a second or two. Closed the boot. Got back in the car, turned round and left. He headed east towards the A1. There was no-one else in the car. I saw when he turned round."

"And then?"

"I went to the front window, like you said. There didn't seem to be anyone following him."

"Two minutes?"

"Yes, I waited two minutes, like you said, three actually, no other traffic."

The old man nodded. "And he was definitely-clean shaven?"

"Yes."

"And his hair was brown, not black?"

"Light brown, yes."

"Good, well, that was fun. I doubt that we'll be seeing him again. Unless it's in the paper. His fellows in the white Peugeot had a tail. At least three cars."

"Police?"

"I suspect not. I rather think that they might have been Customs and Excise."

"Why do you think that?"

"A couple of reasons, three actually. One: it's hard to tell when someone is in a car, but I think that one of them was too short to be a copper. Two: the cars. They had had the middle letter Y in the number plate. That usually indicates that the vehicle was first registered in Central London. Lincolnshire police probably have locally registered cars. Whereas Customs and Excise is a civil service department. It has civil service procurement policies, centrally sourced vehicles, do you see? Central London."

"You said three reasons."

"Oh yes, well, they were pretty good. County drugs squads usually aren't specialists in mobile surveillance."

"And Customs are better, are they?"

"Bloody ought to be!" growled the old man.

ELEVEN

Lake walked in carrying a spiral-bound notebook. He looked slightly puzzled and slightly excited.

"What've you got for me, Joseph?"

"Okay, I've been through the cross-Channel database for the last six months. Last Tuesday, the blue Audi, GG-67-05, came in on the morning Dunkirk to Ramsgate ferry, passenger's name is Bakker. That's been through ten times in the last six months. Always the same route and time but different days of the week. Always in the UK for four hours."

"That's good, why the expression?"

"Because last Tuesday Bakker, or a Bakker, was on the Channel Tunnel too. Arrived eleven thirty or so, left about 1800. Registration was MJ-42-30. I don't know that model or colour."

"Dover will."

"Yeah. This Bakker is a regular visitor too. Always the same day as the blue Audi. Usually in the country for just a couple of hours. But he makes other trips too. Sometimes just for a couple of hours. Sometimes for longer. On a couple of occasions his initial is given as M, sometimes E, usually no initial at all. And sometimes Bakker, or E Bakker, comes in the blue Audi. There are one or two other Bakkers too, but I don't think they are relevant."

McBride nodded. Then he fished a five-pound note out of his pocket. "Go and buy some bog roll, and get me a scotch egg or something. I need to make a phone call."

*

After a second successive day in which very little had happened the team were hoping that they might be allowed to go home at five o'clock. The initial novelty of working at Scampton had started to wear off. For those who had to travel in each day from Nottingham or beyond it was starting to become a chore. There was even the suspicion of a groan when Lake stuck his head around the door of the room known as 'dispersal' and called, "Briefing, ten minutes."

Any weariness had disappeared within thirty seconds.

"It's on! Tomorrow. Pyke is meeting the Dutchman. Don't know where, or when, or even why. But it might be a cash handover. That is a sideshow, though. Tangos Eight and Eleven, Gazza Barham and Shane Hartney, are receiving a consignment. Down south somewhere. So, cars fuelled, batteries charged. Bring an overnight bag, cuffs, spare notebooks if you need them. Everyone here seven tomorrow morning. I'll have an up-to-date briefing sheet by then."

*

McBride was puffing happily on his second pipe of the morning. He was confident that this time he would get the result he wanted. Gazza and Shane had set off, half an hour late, but at least they were on the road. The surveillance team was behind them, keeping a more than usually discreet distance since McBride knew, or hoped he knew, where they were headed. Pyke would be on the move soon. McBride didn't have a second surveillance team. He had to trust that Lake could handle anything needed on his own.

The journey south mostly proceeded smoothly. Andi gave McBride regular updates by phone as the team passed Newark, Grantham and Peterborough before turning east on the A14. A little after noon McBride received a phone call from the Customs staff at Harwich. Lake was checking the database for the Rotterdam to Hull ferry. Having confirmed what he expected to see he took one of the two remaining cars at Scampton, a Volkswagen Golf, and drove up to the small town of Market Rasen, where he found a quiet spot from which he could observe traffic coming from Lincoln on the A46. Everything was in place. McBride had literally everything that could be controlled, planned for, anticipated or expected covered.

Except for Howard Spencer. Spencer had enjoyed the early stages of Operation Bagration. He didn't need to waste his time on the day-to-day management of his team. No need to listen to their hopes and fears, their expectations or their grumbles. It freed up so much time that could be used positioning himself politically, emphasising, exaggerating or, if necessary, inventing his little triumphs and making sure that news of these reached the right ears. Not directly, of course; Spencer was far too smooth an operator for anything so crass. Just an off-hand comment here, a casual remark there. His idler moments he gave over to fantasising on similar remarks that he would make in the future. When he was back in London. When he was far away from the grubby world of investigations.

"Oh, if you had my experience of life at the sharp end you might realise how very naïve you sound."

"Well, I think until you have got your knuckles dirty on the street as I have you don't fully understand all the implications of these policy choices."

He was looking forward to sailing smoothly through a Whitehall cocktail party whilst in his wake hushed voices said things like, "That's Howard Spencer. Hard as nails, they say." Or, "Oh, Spencer. Don't underestimate him. He's been where the fists were flying, you know."

In fact, it was while enjoying one of these innocent little daydreams that he had received a telephone call from his manager, Alan Hawkins, the assistant chief investigation officer, enquiring as to the status of Operation Bagration. He dealt with it smoothly, of course. A confident assertion that everything was running like clockwork, with just a hint that this was in no part due to his steady hand of the tiller. When he had hung up it occurred to him that actually he hadn't the first idea what was going on at Scampton. Such updates as he solicited from McBride were mostly delivered in monosyllabic grunts seasoned with various slang or technical terms, Spencer wasn't sure which. *Perhaps*, he wondered, *I ought to take a trip up to Scampton and treat the team to a pep talk and share some of my wisdom with McBride.*

Spencer was halfway to Scampton before he remembered that his Ministry of Defence pass had not arrived. It didn't matter. He was could simply phone ahead and have one of the team meet him and escort him onto the base. Better yet, he could arrive unannounced, talk his way onto the base and conduct a spot inspection. The more he thought about it the more that idea appealed to him. He also thought that it might represent an opportunity to remind McBride who the leader of this team really was. He would invite McBride to talk him through his strategy, his tactics and the thinking behind them. Then he would pick a decision, dismantle it and demonstrate to McBride that he had been wrong and therefore, by implication, why he should be checking more of his decisions with Spencer. The fact that Spencer had only the vaguest idea of what his team were doing and almost no idea why did not in the least dissuade him from the notion that his strategy would be superior to whatever the team was currently doing.

Stefan had read that day's *Daily Express* and was now working his way through *Auto Trader* when Spencer's Jaguar pulled into the main gate at Scampton and paused in front of the barrier adjacent to his tiny guard hut. Stefan had got used to seeing the Customs fleet of vehicles arriving each morning and coming and going throughout the day. This car did not look like any of the others. He picked up the peaked cap that his employers had provided in a misguided attempt to confer some authority upon him and walked slowly towards the driver's side of Spencer's Jag. The window slid down smoothly, accompanied by the almost inaudible sound of a small electric motor. Spencer smiled broadly. Stefan decided that he didn't like Spencer. Stefan mostly didn't like anybody that he met in the course of his professional life.

"Please?"

"Oh, hello! I'm afraid I've not got my pass with me at present but if you wouldn't mind letting me through…"

"No pass?"

"Well, no, not actually on me. It's probably just inside actually. Very recently issued, you see?"

"Wait, please, one moment."

Stefan returned to his little hut. He was sure that he had a list of permitted vehicles somewhere. He eventually found it underneath some empty cans of Pepsi Cola. It was quite badly stained. He took the sheet and added it to the top of a clipboard that was hanging from a nail on the inside of the door. Everything looked more official if a clipboard was involved. He returned to Spencer's open window.

"Wait, please, one moment."

Stefan slowly walked around the car. He noted the rear number plate and then, when he had reached the front, he noted that too. They were the same. Finally, his circumnavigation complete, he found himself back at Spencer's window.

"Your car, not in list."

"No, well, nevertheless I am the SIO of the team working inside."

"You are Air Force?"

"No."

"Please leave. This is Air Force military base. Very restricted.

You must leave, please."

"No, you misunderstand. I'm from Customs. I'm the SIO."

"No Customs here, Air Force military, you must leave, please."

"No, there is, Customs, I mean, look, let me call them. Someone will come out and vouch for me."

Spencer picked up his mobile phone and Stefan retreated to his little guard hut. Spencer phoned McBride first, but his line was engaged. Then he phoned Lake. But his line was engaged too. Finally, he phoned Andi Woodhead.

"Hello?"

"Ah, yes, Andi, listen, I'm out at the front gate and I need someone to come and buzz me in…"

"Call Frank. We're all in Cambridgeshire somewhere." The line went dead. Spencer pursed his lips.

This was not the way that he expected to be addressed by his subordinates. He tried McBride again. Lake wasn't there to see it, so we will never know whether he would have been able to interpret the smoke signals as McBride came round the corner of the administration block, mobile phone clamped to one side of his head, pipe between gritted teeth. He completely ignored Spencer and walked to Stefan's guard hut. "It's alright. He's with me."

McBride turned, again without acknowledging Spencer, and walked back to the building. The barrier rose and Spencer followed, his Jaguar barely purring at three miles per hour. Spencer pulled up beside the van, the last vehicle in the fleet. McBride was standing in the doorway, phone still clamped to his ear. As Spencer approached, he held it open. "Okay! Thanks!" He ended the call and followed Spencer inside.

Spencer had never visited Scampton before and so he was standing just inside the passageway, unsure which way to turn. This was not the entrance that he had planned for himself, but he hadn't planned on ninety per cent of his team being absent either. He hated the idea that he would have to ask where they were and what they were doing. Even worse was the fact that he didn't even have an opportunity to do that. McBride was already on another call as he strode past him down the passage, and had ended that and started another before he reached the little suite at the far end that housed McBride's office. Or 'Wee Frankie's Hoose o' Fun', as the handwritten sign above the door now labelled it.

When McBride had finally finished Spencer said, "If we're short of signs I'm sure I could order up a few 'No Smoking' ones from headquarters."

He was rather pleased with what he thought was a clever way of addressing the fact that McBride had not extinguished his pipe. He was looking forward to the reaction and the opportunity to reassert himself, but unfortunately, at that moment McBride's phone rang again.

When McBride ended his call Spencer seized his opportunity. He had intended to deliver his question coolly, but he was slightly rattled by the fact that McBride might receive another call at any moment and he blurted it out like an over-anxious child. Even to Spencer it sounded a little like an adolescent whine.

"Where is everybody?"

"What did you say to Stefan?"

"Who?"

"Stefan, the security guard, what did you say to him?"

"Well, nothing really, he seemed to think I was in the Royal Air Force."

"What did you say to him? Did you mention Customs?"

"No, well, possibly, I don't remember actually."

"That was *not* helpful."

Spencer was affronted. "I think you need to remember to whom you are talking, Frank."

The world's universities are full of professors of linguistics who will assure you that it is simply impossible to deliver five full sentences in the English language in a growl. They are all wrong. But to be fair, they had probably never met Frank McBride. "You wanted a target operation. You have one and you have one because

I have a certain reputation in London and certain connections at the Other Office. We agreed that I would run the operation and that I would do it my way. If you want to re-visit that agreement, we can certainly do so and I shall advise the Other Office of our new arrangement. Of course, it will be for the Other Office to decide if we will continue to benefit from our current facilities."

Spencer was silent. He appeared to be considering the merits and demerits of a hundred possible responses.

"Now you've picked an unfortunate time. We have a cash handover in Lincolnshire right now and very likely a drugs handover in East Anglia in a couple of hours. We will probably be making a few arrests today. Your MOD pass is on that table, remember to take it with you when you go."

McBride's phone rang again. He picked it up. "Oh, and Howard! Never, ever bring that car here again!" He turned his attention back to the phone. "Yes, yes, got it. Okay, come back here, yeah, chicken, and some crisps. I don't care! And buy some bog roll!"

Spencer picked up the pass. By the time he had reached the spot where his Jag was parked, he was mentally debating four different ways of bringing Frank McBride down to size.

TWELVE

Pyke had expected his conversation with Maas to have either involved a heated dispute about money or an assurance that the business partnership would continue exactly as before. He wasn't expecting to hear that for the next transaction Maas himself would be arriving to collect the money and that he wanted to meet Pyke and not Maxi or any other anonymous bag man. Neither had he expected – although now he thought about it, it made sense – that the delivery of the merchandise would take place in a different location to usual.

Shane and Gazza were on their way to Essex rather than Kent to make their rendezvous with Maas's associates. He had wanted to warn them to be more than usually vigilant about looking for the police. However, on reflection it seemed like a mistake to put that idea in their heads. He hadn't totally forgiven them for dumping thousands of pounds' worth of stock in a cricket club. Although he resented paying a thousand pounds to whoever had ripped him off, it might easily have been worse. It could have been found by some public-spirited citizen who had handed the lot over to the police. Worse yet, the police might have used it as bait in a trap. He didn't want the pair of them to panic again and risk losing his merchandise.

He wondered now about the phone call that he had had advising him that Gazza and Shane had been followed the day that they were to have collected the pills. There was no sinister motive at play here. It didn't seem to have been contrived to lure him out into the open. If it had he would even now be in Lincoln Prison awaiting trial. It made no sense. Unless they actually really had been being followed and the rip-off merchant from Rutland was some sort of bizarre guardian angel. Perhaps they had been followed. Pyke didn't know exactly what Shane and Gazza got up to when they weren't working for him. Who knows what unwanted attention they drew to themselves? Another reason to ease them out and find more reliable associates. Pyke glanced at his watch and reached for his car keys.

*

Lake was pleased with the spot that he had found. It was a natural place for a parked car to be. He had a good view of the road from Lincoln but could not easily be seen himself. Finally, it was a simple left turn to join the main road behind Pyke when he came past, as he now did. Lake counted to ten before starting his engine and pulling out onto the main road. He could still see Pyke's Mercedes, X-Ray Five, about 150 yards ahead. He followed at a distance into the centre of Market Rasen, where Pyke pulled into the main square. Lake cruised past and pulled over on the left. He hopped out of the car and walked briskly back to the main square, looking for the green Mercedes. But it was the BMW he saw first. A navy-blue, Dutch-registered, BMW 7 Series, a white male sitting in the driver's seat. Almost as soon as Lake saw this the green Mercedes pulled alongside the BMW. They were close enough for the two drivers to speak easily through the drivers' windows, but Lake couldn't see if they did. Almost immediately the Mercedes pulled off again and Lake saw the first puff of smoke from the BMW's exhaust. The Mercedes turned left onto the high street again, heading east. Lake didn't bother to see if the BMW was following. He hurried back to his own car. As he reached it, he saw the BMW pass him. This was the tricky part. Lake could either bank what he had already witnessed or he could twist and try to follow the two cars.

What Customs used to call 'one-up' surveillance was not recommended. There was a high risk that whoever was being followed would notice. This risk was amplified when there were two targets and amplified further when they were probably up to no good. They would be especially nervous, especially watchful. Nevertheless, Lake decided that he would risk following them for a very short distance. He set off down the Louth Road.

Not for the first time Lake reflected upon the fact that surveillance in rural Lincolnshire was not like surveillance in London. Within a hundred yards he, the Mercedes and the BMW were the only cars on the road. He was clearly visible in the BMW's rear-view mirror. He had decided that he would abandon the tail at the first opportunity. That didn't mean just stopping. That would be absurdly suspicious. It meant taking the first opportunity to turn off. He saw a sign for the Market Rasen Rugby Club just ahead. That would be ideal. Except that Pyke turned into the rugby club car park, followed by the BMW. Lake carried on towards Louth. After a mile he pulled into a golf club car park and phoned McBride to report.

*

Pyke was sitting in the passenger seat of Maas's BMW. He was impressed. Leather upholstery, four-litre engine – this was the type of car that he would have next.

"Johann, we need to talk about what happened last time."

"Yes."

"It is very important that I protect my people. It is very important that my organisation is secure. You understand?"

"Yes, of course."

"Losing a little money is not good, you understand? The police will be watching me. I cannot afford to have suspicions. If my people are noticed, then I will be noticed. You understand?"

Pyke indicated that he did.

"At the moment I am taking all the risk…"

"Which is reflected in the price." Pyke didn't want this conversation to all be going one way. He wasn't about to allow Maas to talk to him like a headteacher.

"Correct. And I can afford to lose money. But I cannot afford to lose security. If you cannot guarantee the safety of my people, then we will not be able to do business the way that we have. I am happy, of course, at any time, to supply you in Tilburg at a more competitive price. Do you understand, Johann?"

Pyke nodded. He got out of the car and went to the boot of his Mercedes. He took out a sports holdall and returned to the passenger seat of the BMW. "Twenty-five thousand, English," he said.

Maas nodded. He did not look in the bag. He picked up his mobile phone, selected a number from the contacts list and dialled. "*Hallo, Marius, het is goed. Ga je gang.*" He tossed the bag onto the back seat. He passed a small piece of paper with a telephone number on it to Pyke and shook his hand, indicating that the meeting was over.

*

Marius had arrived at Harwich in the early afternoon on the ferry from the Hook of Holland. He was a little nervous as his Volvo crawled through the shed at Customs. There were half a dozen officers in uniform. They stood in a variety of casual poses, their faces a blend of feigned indifference, but Marius felt their eyes sweeping over his vehicle and settling on his face. He was fighting panic, an urge to stamp his foot down on the accelerator and race through the shed, leaving them spinning in his wake. He forced himself to act naturally, don't make eye contact, try not to look too nervous, or bored or anything, just a few more metres to go. At the exit from the shed, a little beyond the uniformed officers, was a middle-aged man, not in uniform, with his arms folded across his chest. He seemed to be staring at Marius, but as the Volvo approached, he turned away and went through a small door. Marcus was through and heading for the A120 towards Colchester.

He had decided that this would be his last trip. Being a drugs mule was not a profession that one could pursue indefinitely. It would only be a matter of time before a Customs officer got lucky, or some careless link in the chain exposed him. Or until it suited somebody, somewhere, to betray him. His brother Edwin and he had promised themselves and each other that they would work for Stanley Maas only for as long as it took to earn the money required to open a little bar in Tilburg. They had made this mutual pact before they had fully understood the cost of acquiring a lease, re-fitting and refurbishing, buying glasses, and glasswashers and the hundred other things that are necessary to get a bar off the ground. So, the original target of €100,000 had become €150,000. They were now a few thousand short of that target, but Edwin's experience at Ramsgate the previous week had rattled them. They agreed that the time to quit was now.

Of course, privately deciding to get out of the game was not exactly the same thing as telling Stanley Maas. The Ramsgate episode seemed like a good opportunity to raise the subject. Edwin and he had spent a lot of time debating exactly how they were going to tell Maas. It wasn't that he was exactly frightened of Maas. Although any sensible person would know that Maas was not a good man to disappoint. He respected Maas and was grateful to him for the opportunities he had provided and the lessons that he had learned. It had to be handled carefully.

Maas had been surprisingly understanding. He had even offered to invest some cash in their bar himself and become a silent partner. It had been quite a challenge politely to decline that offer, but it had to be done for two reasons: firstly, Edwin and Marius were determined that their business would be entirely legitimate. They did not want Maas to use it as a front or a money-laundering operation. Secondly, if Maas started as a silent partner, he was sure, sooner or later, to become the dominant partner, and shortly after that they would lose control altogether. Of course, the brothers couldn't say any of this to Maas. It was all very delicate. But they had, somehow, managed to do it. With Maas having been so understanding it was almost impossible to refuse him one last favour. Maas explained that he had a commitment that he had to honour. Edwin could stay at home, he explained. He just needed Marius. So, this would be the last time.

Edwin and Marius had seen plenty of films where the protagonist allows himself to be persuaded to do 'one last job' and it almost never ended well. But Marius tried not to think about that. This was real life, not Hollywood, and he was only doing what he had done over a dozen times before.

Maas was a professional, Marius told himself. He was cautious and he was disciplined and he insisted that anybody who worked with him was too. And he cared about the people who worked for him. Marius knew that if he heard nothing for six hours he was to dump the pills he was carrying and return home. No questions asked. And he would still receive half his money. Maas didn't want people taking unnecessary risks. In fact, he received the call only thirty minutes after he had got off the ferry: "It's all good. You can go ahead."

Marius pulled off the A120 just before Colchester and started to look for a suitable place to rendezvous. Amateurs who thought that they were professionals arranged all these things in advance. But arrangements made in advance can be leaked in advance. If you didn't know where you were going to make the handover, neither could anybody else. He cruised through the small Essex villages until he found a suitable spot, paused briefly and, having satisfied himself that it suited his purpose, drove on. He stopped a few miles away in a slightly larger village and waited.

*

Shane and Gazza were also approaching Colchester, but from the opposite direction. Unlike Marius, the two had not spent their journey weighing up the risks of what they were doing. And neither did they have any long-term objective. Making a collection for Pyke meant five hundred pounds each and they were debating how to spend it. Manchester United had been drawn in the same Champions League group as Feyenoord and Gazza wanted to make the trip to the away match. There followed a brief argument about whether Feyenoord was a place or just a team. They were not professional, and they thought it slightly comic that Pyke had tried to engender some discipline in them.

Gazza's phone buzzed, a text from Pyke. It consisted only of the number on the piece of paper Maas had given him. Gazza immediately made a phone call.

"Hallo."

"Hallo. We've come to collect."

"Go to a place called Wivenhoe. Then call me."

"Okay."

Shane consulted his road atlas. Wivenhoe was less than ten miles away, a medium-sized village a couple of miles south of Colchester. This represented a new procedure from the Dutch. They had previously preferred to meet in towns. A quarter of an hour later Shane pulled over outside a post office. Gazza phoned the same number again.

"Hallo."

"We're here."

"Alresford Village Hall, Ford Lane, Alresford. Five minutes."

"Okay."

Gazza turned to Shane. "The cloggies are being extra careful this time. We've got to go to Alresford Village Hall. Place is even smaller than this."

Shane shrugged. "Which way?"

"Right here, I think. It's only a couple of miles."

Marius had parked in the car park of a pub called 'The Pointer' on the Wivenhoe to Alresford road. He saw the white Peugeot pass his position and waited, looking for any cars that might be following. After waiting a minute he saw none. He put his Volvo in gear, pulled out and slowly drove through the village, regularly looking in his rear-view mirror. He saw a green Renault Laguna behind him, driven by a man with a young woman in the passenger seat. That might mean trouble. He pulled over but the Renault cruised past him. He glanced at his watch. More than five minutes had passed since his call. It was time to decide.

He had chosen the location well. Apart from the Renault he had seen nothing unusual. In five minutes he could make his handover and be on the road home, for the last time. Or he could abort, receive half his fee and have to do it again. (He was certain Maas would not allow an aborted trip to be his last.) He drove slowly to the village hall. The car park was empty except for the white Peugeot with the green wheels. The streets were empty. There were no suspicious parked cars.

He had decided to go ahead, but then he saw the green Renault again, coming towards him this time. He decided to drive past the village hall. It had a large car park and he had chosen it because it was so exposed. Anything he did could be observed but any observer would have to be visible himself. There were no bushes in which to hide, no café to sit outside, no bus shelter at which to loiter. He drove past slowly again. The Peugeot was there and there was no-one else in sight except a dog walker on the edge of the playing fields. At least Marius assumed he was a dog walker. He saw no dog, but the man was carrying a lead.

Time to decide. He pulled into the car park and drew up alongside the Peugeot. Without saying a word he got out and went to the boot. Shane and Gazza did the same. Marius looked round. All clear. He opened the boot. Shane did the same. Gazza lifted the spare tyre from the back of the Volvo and put it in the Peugeot. Marius shut the Volvo's boot. Returned to the driver's seat and was out of the car park and away in less than thirty seconds.

*

Shane and Gazza didn't hurry away. Gazza phoned Pyke and told him that the handover was complete. His hand went to the ignition key, but he paused. Be cool. A simple handover. Accomplished in seconds. In the middle of nowhere. No witnesses. Gazza lit a cigarette.

"What an old woman! You know, I sometimes think that John is losing his nerve."

"How do you mean?"

"Well, all this nonsense about being cautious, being professional and all that. I think he's losing his bottle."

"Yeah, and I don't like the way he talks to us. It's like he's our dad."

Gazza had never known his father. "Yeah, or a teacher."

Shane wasn't very familiar with teachers. "Yeah," he agreed.

Monster, put the lead that didn't have a dog back in his pocket was walking back to his car, trying all the while to keep the Peugeot in view. In his other pocket was the transmit button.

"*Handover complete. Handover complete. A spare tyre. A spare tyre.*"

"*Okay. That's received.*"

"*Dutchman is manoeuvring. Manoeuvring.*"

"*From Andi, Carl and Mark, go with the Dutchman. Wait for my call.*"

"*From Monster, Tango Eight is making a call on his mobile.*"

"*Okay, hold back. Let him finish.*"

Monster had reached Andi's car. He tossed the lead onto the back seat and pulled out his handcuffs. This was it. This is why he did the job. The feeling, the unique indescribable feeling of the few seconds before a knock. Like a fighter waiting for the bell to sound round one. No, like a sprinter on the blocks. No, not quite that either. The heart pounding, the sound of blood pumping in his ears, the dry mouth, this, *this*, was why he was an investigator.

Come on! thought Monster. *Come on, let's do it. Call it! Call it now!*

"*All units from Andi, knock knock knock!*"

The car park was gravel. Andi had noticed it. No need to go crazy. No need to send it spraying, no need for skids or wheel spins. There was only one exit, unless they wanted to set off across the playing fields. She put the Mondeo in gear and cruised slowly into the car park. Gill, in the Vectra, was just behind her. She parked the car nose to nose with Shane's Peugeot. Gill pulled alongside. Monster ran to the passenger door.

Such was Gazza's speed of thought, or lack of it, that he didn't realise what was happening until he saw the handcuffs. Shane needed a moment or two even after that.

*

It was done. Marius realised that he had been sweating. But it was done. His career as a drug smuggler was over. His career as the joint proprietor of a bar near the Konig Willem II Stadion in Tilburg was about to begin. His last task was to call Maas. "*Allemaal klaar. Ik ga nu terug.*"

He pulled out of the car park and headed east. Suddenly the gnawing fear was gone but replaced instantly by something else. The adrenaline left his system and he started to feel tired. No, not tired, exhausted. Utterly spent. He realised that he was shaking. Then he began to feel nauseous. He pulled over to the side of the road and wound down the window. A green Renault Laguna passed him! Was it the same one he had seen earlier? So what if it was. Just a local. He was clear. It was over. His breathing calmed as he started to think about his bar. Edwin wanted a dart board. He thought a pinball table would be better. He allowed himself a wry smile. This was his biggest problem now. Arguing about lampshades, choosing a model of till. It had all been worth it. He was grateful to Maas for the opportunity but now his brother and he would slowly drift away from him. When he was fully calm, and the nausea had subsided, he realised he was hungry.

He glanced at the clock on the Volvo's dashboard. He had over two hours before his return ferry to Holland and decided that he would celebrate with some fish and chips from a shop that he had seen in Elmstead Market. Five minutes later he saw the Laguna again. But this time he didn't give it a second thought.

Marius was lucky. He was able to find a parking space only twenty yards past the chip shop. He turned off the ignition, treated himself to another little sigh of relief and got out of the car. The chip shop didn't open until five thirty and that was still a minute or two away. Marius waited outside, taking in what he hoped was his last view of England. At least for a while. He had nothing in particular against the country or its people but for him England had meant risk, peril and, if he was honest with himself, a little bit of fear.

A green Laguna cruised past. This was getting beyond a coincidence. Was something wrong? The panic started to rise in him. Something was wrong! Get back in the car. Drive like hell. Anywhere. But there were two young men walking towards him. They would reach his car before he did. They looked slightly tense and excited. Something was wrong! He turned the other way. A middle-aged man and a young woman. People don't walk that quickly or purposefully towards closed chip shops. Oh no. Oh no, no, no! He turned again. He knew he was panicking. He knew he looked like he was panicking, but he couldn't help it. He could swivel. He could spin, but he couldn't leave the spot. The two men were level with his car. They started to break into a run. Something was wrong! He turned again.

"Mr Bakker? Mr Bakker, my name is Sanders, British Customs. You are under arrest."

THIRTEEN

Pyke glanced at the clock on the mantlepiece for the third time in five minutes. He wasn't worried. He wasn't even angry, not quite. Gazza and Shane were late checking in again. They had probably got lost, or stopped for a meal, or run out of petrol. Just as likely as any of those was that they were safely back at home and had just forgotten to call him to let him know. He had to find somebody better. A little more reliable. Maas's people were always on time. Always followed orders. There had to be similar people in Lincoln he could use. He just didn't know who they were.

Students, he thought. Surely some of them were intelligent enough, poor enough, desperate enough. But discipline wasn't a word you normally associated with students. Soldiers then? But he didn't know any of those. Fighters. Fighters had discipline. At least the best ones did. And those who took their training seriously didn't have a lot of time to hold down regular, well-paid jobs. Maybe fighters were the answer.

The doorbell sounded. Those morons had better not have brought the gear here. He sprang from the couch and strode angrily to the front door. Ready to deliver a massive bollocking to the pair of hopeless... It wasn't them. It was Diane, and she was crying. He opened the door wider and she rushed past him. She was heading for the front room but changed her mind and turned and faced him in the hall. "You bastard! You stupid, stupid bastard!" And then she broke down sobbing.

Donna came down the stairs wearing her 'Friday night' dress, her head half covered by a towel turban. "What is it? Di babe! What is it?"

"Ask him!" She pointed at Pyke, a gesture full of anger and hate and fear. "Ask him!"

Donna looked at Pyke. A look of horror was slowly making its way across his features. He turned and hurried out the front door. He reached the street and looked right and left. Nothing. He rushed back in, shut the door and put the chain on.

Donna and Diane were now in the front room. Diane was sobbing into Donna's shoulder. Pyke knew what had happened, or he thought he did. But he needed to know some details. Above all he needed to know how much time he had. The expression on Donna's face told him that now was not the time to seek information from Diane. Instead, he went upstairs and flushed all of his and Donna's personal-use cannabis down the toilet. He gathered up all his old mobile telephones, removed the SIM cards and flushed those too. He turned his current phone off and wrapped it in cellophane, and then put it in a freezer bag. He went into the back garden and paused. He could only hear the usual sounds of the Ermine estate on an early Friday evening. He walked to the back corner of the garden and knelt down. He removed the loose plank and, reaching through, placed his phone deep within the pile of lawn clippings that his neighbour had piled up against their mutual back fence. Even if they found it, it wasn't on his property. Their search warrant wouldn't cover it. He went back inside and scrubbed his hands in the kitchen sink until he was sure there were no signs of grass stains.

He gathered together his four old phones, now minus their SIM cards, and went back outside. He looked left and right.

Nothing. He half jogged, half trotted down the street. The last building was a small block of flats. There were four bins in the communal area at the back. Pyke thrust a phone deep into the rubbish in each and checked that they were invisible to a casual inspection. He walked slowly back to his house looking in all directions. Nothing. He re-entered the house and hovered at the doorway of the front room.

Diane was a little calmer. "You've got to get him out. You've got to."

"Slow down, slow down. What's happened? What's happened to Gazza?"

"He's been arrested."

"When? Where?"

"Today, this afternoon."

"Did you speak to him?"

"He said he's going to prison. Ten years. He said he's going to prison. You have to get him out. You get him out, JP, or I swear I'll tell them everything. I'll tell them everything!"

"Don't talk like that! No need to talk like that. John will get them out, won't you, John?"

Pyke nodded. "Tell me everything. You need to tell me everything. First, where is he?"

"In prison. He's been arrested."

"They don't take you to prison when you've been arrested. They take you to a police station. Did he say where he was?"

"No."

"I'm going to make some phone calls. I'll be back in an hour." Pyke headed for the door. "Don't let her leave."

Pyke drove to Nettleham, a village a couple of miles away. He parked beside a public telephone box and rooted around in the Mercedes' ashtray looking for loose change. First he called Gazza. But his phone was switched off. Then Shane's, same result. Then he called Leanne, Shane's girlfriend.

"Hi, it's me, have you heard from Shane?"

"No, is that JP? I thought he was with you, or Gazza."

"Okay, thanks." He hung up and thought hard. He stepped out of the kiosk and looked up and down the street. There was no sign of anyone. He stepped back in and called Maas.

"Hi, it's Johann. Listen, my friends have run into some trouble."

"What sort of trouble?"

"Legal trouble, I think."

"What about my friend?"

"I don't know."

"Okay, are you at a public phone?"

"Yes."

"Call me again tomorrow." Maas hung up.

Pyke cruised slowly down his road looking for unfamiliar faces, unfamiliar cars, anything unusual. He didn't see anything, but he wasn't really sure what he was supposed to be looking for. He hadn't memorised the models and colours of all his neighbours' cars. Perhaps he ought to start doing that. He completed a loop and parked outside his house.

As soon as he crossed the threshold he was hailed by Donna. "In here."

He entered the front room, where he saw that Diane had been joined by Leanne, Shane's girlfriend. Both appeared to have been crying. Pyke braced himself for another avalanche of recriminations, entreaties and threats, but there was none. He looked at Donna, trying to frame a dozen questions with a single expression.

"I'll put the kettle on," she said. Pyke followed her to the kitchen.

"It's worse than we thought. Shane and Gazza have been arrested and they are at Colchester Police Station. They had your parcel with them. They were caught completely red-handed."

"Shit!"

"Leanne said that Shane sounded really frightened. How much did they have?"

"Enough."

"Are the police going to come here?"

"Depends. If they keep their mouths shut, no. If they do turn up, we'll know why."

"What are you going to do?"

"There's nothing I can do. Tell the girls to go home and get rid of anything incriminating."

"You tell them."

*

It was too late. The search teams had already arrived at Shane's house near Sincil Bank and Gazza's flat on the St Giles estate. Since they had the keys taken from them at their arrest, they had no need to wait for Diane or Leanne to return home to gain access and indeed, by the time they returned the search was almost complete.

Leanne's Fiat pulled up outside the block on the St Giles estate, where Diane shared a flat with Gazza directly behind a maroon Vauxhall Vectra. Diane needed a moment or two to compose herself and as she rooted around in her handbag for a tissue a young man left the block of flats carrying a black bin bag. He walked to the Vectra and opened the boot.

"Do you think?" began Leanne.

But Diane was already out of the car and racing for the block's entrance. Halfway up the stairs she met a young woman also carrying a bag. But this one was transparent and appeared to contain a number of smaller transparent bags. Diane barged past her and, reaching the first-floor landing, saw that her front door was open.

Leanne had attempted to follow her and now met the woman with the bag at the bottom of the stairs.

"What's going on?" she asked.

"Do you live here?"

"No. My friend does, what's going on?"

"Was that your friend I just passed?"

"Yes, tell me what's going on. I have a right to know."

It was an immutable law when dealing with the public that any person who claimed to have a knowledge and understanding of their rights almost certainly didn't. What they usually had – no, what they always had was a deep sense of grievance combined with a certainty that they were entitled to immediate justice and restitution based on their own terms.

"Let's go upstairs. I'll try to explain."

The officer who met Diane in the doorway of her flat was trying to say something similar, but Diane was far too angry, far too frightened and far too loud for him to make himself understood.

"You've got no right! Where's your warrant? Where's Gazza?"

Damn, thought Pete Wood, *another five minutes and we would have been finished and out of here. Now I have to deal with this.* Pete was from Nottingham B, the commercial fraud team. He preferred the type of investigation that could be done from his desk. Hysterical women in council flats were not his idea of an enjoyable day's work. He guided Diane to the sofa in the flat's living room and pulled out his notebook.

"Okay, okay, let's see if I can answer your questions. Firstly, who are you?"

"I live here. I want to see your warrant. You are not allowed in without a warrant. If you've broken in I'll have you in court."

Pete sighed inwardly. This sort of thing didn't get any easier.

Debbie was having a similar but slightly more productive conversation with Leanne in the kitchen. Productive, that is, until Leanne disclosed her address and Debbie told her that the little house she shared with Shane was also being searched.

"I want to phone my lawyer."

"By all means. I'm not stopping you."

Unfortunately, Leanne did not have a lawyer and didn't even know a lawyer. But she did know Pyke, so she phoned him instead. He wasn't answering so she phoned Donna. "Donna, it's Leanne,

I'm at Diane and Gazza's. There are people here searching it. I don't think they have a warrant. They're not police. I want to speak to John. I need a lawyer, what do I do?"

Donna passed her phone to Pyke.

"John, I'm at Gazza and Diane's. They're searching it. Talk to them. Tell them they can't."

Pyke hung up. 'Talk to them'? Was she mad? This was bad. Gazza and Shane nicked. Their homes being searched. Who knew what incriminating material there might be there? And Leanne and Diane. What might they say? Using Donna's phone, he called Leanne back.

"Don't say anything. Not a single word. And tell Diane not to. I will sort this out. I guarantee it but you have to say nothing. Do you understand? Tell them nothing."

"You'd better sort this out, John Pyke. You'd just better! I'm warning you!"

"I will sort out everything. Trust me. Just say nothing… and don't use my name."

*

"This is an interview with Shane Patrick Hartney. My name is Kevin David Cleary, officer of Customs and Excise, also present is Christopher John Bolton, officer of Customs and Excise, and…"

"Samantha Castle, Mr Hartney's legal advisor."

"Today is Friday 8th August, 1997, and the time by my watch is nine forty-five PM. We are in an interview room at Colchester Police Station. Mr Hartney, you do not have to say anything, but it may harm your defence if you do not mention when questioned something that you later rely on in court. Anything you do say may be used in evidence. Do you understand?"

"No comment."

"Are you Shane Patrick Hartney of 9 Furness Street, Lincoln?"

"No comment."

"Earlier today you were arrested in Alresford, Essex. At that time you were searched and in your pocket was a wallet. I am now showing you that wallet marked 'Bolton A'. Is this your wallet?"

"No comment."

"Contained within this wallet was a driving licence in the name of Shane Patrick Hartney of 9 Furness Street, Lincoln. I am showing you this driving licence now. Is this your driving licence?"

"No comment."

"Why were you in Alresford earlier today?"

"No comment."

"Do you drive a white Peugeot with the number plate G416 HEW?"

"No comment."

"Do you know a man named Gary Phillip Barham?"

"No comment."

"Do you know a man named Marius Bakker?"

"No comment."

"Did you at any time today meet a man other than Barham in Essex?"

"No comment." Shane smirked.

"Mr Bolton, have you any questions for Mr Hartney at this time?"

"Just one. Shane, what did you think was in the spare tyre?"

"No comment."

"Very well. We shall take a short break for now. We may have further questions for you later. Ms Castle, is there anything that you would like to say, for the record?"

"No, thank you."

"Okay, the time is nine fifty-one and the time elapsed counter on the recording machine is showing six minutes. I am suspending the interview now."

Shane smirked again.

*

Samantha Castle had spent three years studying law at university, a further year doing her legal practice course and had almost finished her two-year training contract. In less than three months it would all have been worth it. She would be a solicitor of the Supreme Court. But it was ten o'clock on a Friday night and she was in Colchester Police Station debating the finer points of legal jurisprudence with Shane.

"So, what do you reckon? They've got nothing on me, have they? I'll beat this rap, you reckon? Eh?"

"We don't know the full extent of the evidence against you at this stage or what further evidence might be gathered later. I can't possibly give you a definitive answer at this stage."

"But they got nothing. That interview, six minutes! Six minutes, they've got nothing."

"Mr Hartney, from what they tell me there are many thousands of tablets, presumably illegal drugs, in a Volvo spare tyre in the boot of your Peugeot. They tell me that they observed Mr Bakker put it there with your assistance. They have asked you to account for your presence here and you declined to answer, meaning that if, when, you give an explanation for your movements today you are likely to be disbelieved. Your instructions to me are that you are completely innocent and know nothing about any drugs. However, I would not be doing my job if I didn't advise you that the evidence against you is really quite strong. I consider it likely that you will be charged with an offence. I consider it likely that you will be refused bail. And I consider it, well, quite possible that you will be convicted. Although it is too early to say at this stage."

Shane looked puzzled. "You mean, you mean I might go down?"

"Yes. That is exactly what I mean."

"How long?"

"Hard to say."

"Will I be out by Christmas?"

Ten o'clock on a Friday night and here she was talking to this idiot. Samantha had learned to contain, or at least to disguise, the exasperation that most of her clients provoked, but she didn't have a one hundred per cent record.

"Mr Hartney. You won't be out for the millennium!"

"What?"

"Mr Hartney. If those tablets are MDMA, ecstasy, that is a Class A controlled drug. The maximum sentence is life imprisonment."

Shane was sick. Samantha only just avoided getting it on her shoes.

*

There is a reason why the makeover programmes on Channel 4 never speak of 'Police Canteen Chic'. And it's not because they don't all conform to a recognisable style. Colchester's looked like all the others that Kevin and Monster had had the privilege to patronise over the years. It was closed for business, of course. The shutters were pulled down and there wasn't a copper in sight. At nearly 10PM on a Friday night the canteen's potential customers would be preparing themselves for a couple of hours of dealing with Colchester's party people on the pavements outside the city centre's pubs and bars. But it wasn't empty when they walked into the canteen on the top floor. The rest of the Customs team were sitting around two tables that somebody had pushed together. Nick Harper was making a list.

"We're down south. I don't even know if they have curry sauce. They probably won't have peas or gravy."

"Well, just get me a saveloy and chips."

Harper looked up.

"Yeah, that'll do. Saveloy and chips for me too," said Kevin.

"Me too. But two saveloys. What?" Monster's face wore an expression of aggrieved innocence.

Harper scribbled something on a piece of paper and made for the door.

"So? What's the score?"

"No comment."

"Yeah, Barham was the same. We'll put them to bed and have another go in the morning. Their homes are being searched now."

"What about the Dutchman?"

"Mysteriously lost the ability to speak English. We'll have a translator in the morning."

"Has anyone found us a hotel?"

"Working on it."

"Has anyone updated McBride?"

"Yeah, I'll call him again in the morning."

*

Woody the cowboy was having a fight with a Tyrannosaurus Rex. Michelle was trying to dry Maisie's tutu with a hairdryer. Saturday mornings were ballet class and the highlight of the week. McBride was sitting on the edge of the sofa beaming down on Frankie Junior when the phone rang.

"Okay, tell me. And make it concise."

He listened for a full five minutes, not interrupting once.

"Mr Spencer will have to make the decision. If he asks you can tell him that my decision, sorry, my recommendation, is that we charge all three, object to bail and object to bail again at the Magistrates' Court on Monday morning. Got that?"

Andi hung up. Kevin looked at her.

"Well?"

"What do you think? Charge them all. But Spencer has to approve it. Funny thing, though. I thought I heard kids in the background. Small kids."

"McBride hasn't got kids. He's far too old."

"How old is he? Does anyone know?"

"About a hundred and ten," said Monster.

"No seriously."

"I have no idea, is it important?"

"No. Not really, I suppose not. Joe, do you know…"

"Well, despite appearances I believe he is between the ages of fifty-two and fifty-seven."

"How do you reckon?"

"He told me once his dad was killed in the war before he was born. So that makes his date of birth somewhere around 1940–45. So, fifty-two to fifty-seven."

"Ah!" said Nick.

"Of course, he might have meant the Zulu war, in which case Monster is right."

*

Colchester Magistrates' Court would not be the first choice to represent the majesty and solemnity of British justice. It could have done with a lick of paint for a start. Monday mornings were particularly chaotic. As well as the routine cases scheduled weeks in advance the daily list included all the poor souls who had spent some part of the weekend, in some cases up to three nights, in one of North Essex's police cells. The public area was very busy. Solicitors bustled to and fro clutching briefs that could mostly be written on postcards and in some cases actually were. There were defendants trying to find their lawyers and lawyers trying to hold urgent conferences with their clients in noisy corners or in the coffee bar upstairs. Samantha had drawn the short straw at her firm and would be representing Gazza and Shane. Her slightly more senior colleague had pulled rank and insisted that she would benefit from the experience of confronting Customs and Excise in court.

"They very likely won't even have a lawyer," he had said. "They tend to be represented by an officer. Good on the facts usually, but with little or no understanding of the law. If you can persuade the bench to ask them a few detailed questions about the Bail Act, they ought to fall apart, and you can get our two heroes out."

Samantha was not entirely convinced. However inexpert a criminal advocate a Customs officer might be, if they were able to utter the words 'street value of a quarter of a million pounds' and 'maximum sentence, life imprisonment' there was a good chance that her clients would be refused bail, remanded in custody and she would have to bear the opprobrium back in the office of having been beaten by an amateur and probably have to make several trips to Colchester Prison to receive instructions from her clients for the next few months.

She recognised Andi Woodhead, dressed as she had been yesterday, definitely not court garb, wrestling with the cellophane on a packet of cigarettes. Andi had given up. Officially. But on special occasions… and at times of high stress… and this counted as one of those. Professional lawyers hated losing bail hearings to amateurs, but Customs officers lived in fear of losing a bail hearing and having a suspect abscond.

"Hello again. I'm afraid smoking is not allowed here." She pointed at a sign directly above Andi's head. She shrugged. "Want a chat?" She was already heading for the exit. Samantha followed. As they reached the doors, they were joined by a young man wearing a suit that would have looked slightly out of date on his grandfather. Samantha knew what that meant. Inwardly, she sighed.

"Oh. Hullo! Are you for Hartney and Barham?"

Samantha nodded. She treated Andi to an apologetic look.

"I'll be outside," she said, lighting her fag as she walked through the doors.

"Justin Grantleigh." The baby barrister extended his hand, then hurriedly withdrew it. Barristers are not supposed to shake hands. "I'm for Bakker."

"Samantha Mitchell."

"My instructions are to seek unconditional bail. Yours similar?"

"I'm afraid I can't discuss my instructions with you." This was just what she needed, some posh boy five minutes out of law school who was going to make an arse of himself and possibly damage her application for bail into the bargain.

"Oh, no, of course not." He looked embarrassed for about a tenth of a second and then the misplaced confidence came flooding back. "I was just chatting to the crown prosecutor, but she said she knows nothing about our case."

"She wouldn't. It's a Customs case. One of the investigating officers will be representing the crown. That was just her actually."

"Really? Can they do that? Well, makes things pretty simple, I should think."

"The facts are… not helpful."

"Ah, yes, I was going to ask you about that. My brief is rather sketchy, I'm afraid. Something about a few pills. My chap in the wrong place at the wrong time, I expect. Being Dutch in a built-up area or something. Immigration giving in to their habit of arresting any foreign national in sight."

"Customs, not immigration. And it would be a mistake to underestimate them."

*

Shane and Gazza had not enjoyed their time as guests at Colchester Police Station. They had both been interviewed again on Saturday morning and for a third time on Saturday afternoon. Dozens and dozens of questions, some of them quite detailed. They hadn't answered a single one, but it didn't seem to make any difference. The questions just kept on coming. Where did they live? How did they earn a living? Why were they in Essex? It was unrelenting. The officers were completely unfazed by their lack of co-operation. They seemed confident almost to the point of indifference, as though they were going through the motions because the end result was inevitable.

Samantha Mitchell hadn't been much of a comfort either. She had seemed to be determined not to see any silver lining anywhere.

She was supposed to be on their side but mostly she just seemed unfriendly and exasperated.

They had been far more impressed by Justin Grantleigh when they had seen him walk into court. He was a proper toff who used long words and carried himself with effortless confidence. Shane wished that he had been representing him. Until the hearing started.

It was really unfair. That Customs officer, the woman dressed as if she had spent the early part of the morning mopping floors, just stood up and started telling her story about how they had been seen meeting the Dutchman and putting his spare tyre in their boot. Then she started talking about the number of pills and their value. Even Shane could judge the effect this was having on the magistrates. By the time she sat down Shane could see why his solicitor had been so pessimistic.

Then it was Grantleigh's turn. And even Shane could tell it wasn't going well. The magistrates kept correcting him. He got everybody's names wrong. He got the times and the dates wrong, and then, for some reason, he started talking about Holland.

"That ponce is going to get us all hung!" whispered Shane.

"Hanged," muttered Marius, who had been a good student of English at school.

When the decision came it was no surprise.

"Mr Bakker, Mr Hartney and Mr Barham. I have listened carefully to the representations made on your behalf by your legal representatives. However, in view of the serious nature of the offences with which you have been charged, the weight of the evidence against you and the likelihood of a substantial custodial sentence should you be convicted, bail is refused. You will be remanded in custody for seven days and appear again here on Monday 18th August. Take them down, please."

FOURTEEN

It was actually a perfectly good delivery. It wasn't rapid, of course, this was Melton Mowbray and District Division Two, but it was straight. If you were being generous, you might say it had a small amount of away swing. If you were being harsh, you might say it was a foot or two over-pitched. Michael took a big stride to meet it and drove. The ball raced away, half an inch above the turf. It perfectly bisected the fielders at mid-off and cover, and reached the boundary rope, where it lifted slightly before landing in the pile of freshly mown grass clippings that Michael knew better than most. He smiled. He glanced at the scoreboard. He was now on fifty-one. Time to retire. He nodded at the opposition captain, tucked his bat beneath his left arm and walked towards the pavilion whilst removing his gloves.

There was a polite smattering of applause from his teammates and from the opposition scorer. As he reached the pavilion steps his grandfather put down the local newspaper that he had been reading and clapped four times. Michael smiled again and entered the pavilion, where he removed his pads.

A few seconds later he came to join his grandfather, who was sitting on a chair perhaps twenty yards from where everyone else had gathered. He was in his usual tweed jacket and cavalry twill, a slightly battered Panama hat the sole concession to the August sun.

"Did you enjoy that?" enquired the old man.

"Yes, yes, I did actually."

His grandfather nodded, and went on nodding as he seemed to hold a small internal debate. Having resolved it, he picked up his paper again and turned to pages four and five. Without a word he passed it over.

"Lincoln men arrested in £250,000 drugs haul," said the headline. The article was accompanied by two photographs of young men.

"Is this who I think it is?"

"Read."

Michael read through the article quickly, and then again, more slowly. "Customs and Excise, you were right."

"I was right about them being hopeless amateurs and bloody liabilities too."

"You didn't say that to me."

"Didn't I? I said it to him."

"Who?"

"The man in the green Mercedes. I told him. I told him they had a tail, and he should come and collect his property himself. And he did. Sensible fellow."

"You enjoyed it, didn't you? All the old cloak-and-dagger stuff, you enjoyed it."

"Well, an old man stuck out here in the country has to find ways to amuse himself." He chuckled and then blew his nose on a yellow handkerchief.

"Are you going to call him again? Mercedes Man?"

"What for?"

"Because you like it. And that's what retired people do, isn't it? Take on a bit of part-time consultancy work, just to keep their hand in."

"Is it? Is that what we're supposed to do? I've been getting it wrong for years then. And what about you? Your paw is mended. You can't tell me that village cricket is satisfying."

"I don't know. The teas are quite good."

"I mean, are you going to go home? Back to your parents, I mean."

Michael's face clouded over. "Do you mean I'm no longer welcome?"

"Of course you're welcome. In fact... In fact, I was wondering if you might like to join me in my new... what did you call it? Consultancy business. As a junior partner, of course."

Michael looked surprised. Was this another example of the old man's slightly peculiar sense of humour? There was a muted roar from the fielders. "I think that's the end of the innings. Would you like me to steal you a sausage roll?"

Michael trotted off to the pavilion.

*

Pyke had retrieved his old phone from his neighbour's grass clippings and was transferring the contact details to his new one when it rang. He was frozen for a moment, not knowing what to do.

"Hello."

"I told you that pair were useless."

"Who is this?"

"You know very well who it is. I told you that pair in the white Peugeot were useless. My question for you now is whether you are sufficiently serious to engage a professional."

"Listen. I don't know who you are but—"

"You have my number. This time tomorrow."

Pyke glared at the phone in his hand. He had problems enough without some smart arse goading him. Not just that, but someone who had ripped him off for a thousand pounds. He finished inputting the numbers, not including Gazza or Shane. He couldn't call them, and he didn't need anything linking him to them.

He was slightly surprised that he hadn't received a visit from the police, or from Customs, who apparently were the people that had nicked his couriers. Nicked the Dutchman too. Maas had not been pleased. He now had two problems. He needed to replace Gazza and Shane, and he needed to persuade Maas that it was safe for them to continue to do business. That wasn't going to be easy.

Word had spread that Gazza and Shane had been nicked and anyone with the ability to put two and two together had quickly realised whose gear they had been transporting. Pyke needed to get back in the game as quickly as possible before his customers had time to find alternate suppliers. But finding somebody to step into Gazza and Shane's shoes when everyone knew what had happened to them was going to be difficult. And what made it even worse was that Maas had insisted that any future business required Pyke, or one of his organisation, to collect the drugs on the continent. No more handovers in Essex or Kent. This made the job of courier even more unappealing since it would be necessary actually to import the drugs and pass through Customs controls at the port.

Using Maxi was out of the question. Donna had made that very clear. Another option would be to do it himself, but there were two very good reasons to avoid this. The first was the obvious risk, multiplied by the fact that he didn't know what Gazza or Shane had told Customs. He could very easily be a marked man. To try to import his stuff personally might be suicidal. The second reason was a combination of personal pride and business credibility. Pyke saw himself as head of an enterprise, not a mere mule. And it was important to him that Maas saw him in the same light.

Finally, there was the issue of trust. Pyke's business model, he genuinely thought of himself in these terms, was to be a middleman. If he were to allow his supplier, Maas, to know his customers then the two could cut him out altogether. He would be adding no value to the transaction chain. The thing that concerned him most was that the likeliest replacements for Gazza and Shane were either his customers or people more closely linked to his customers than they were to Pyke himself. They owed him no loyalty.

Pyke decided that he needed to think. He picked up his car keys.

"*Standby! Standby! Tango Five from Gold Five. Heading for X-Ray Five.*"

"*Received. All units, standby, standby.*"

"*He's into X-Ray Five, facing south.*"

"*Received.*"

"*He's mobile, mobile heading south.*"

"*Thanks, Control, we've got him.*"

Pyke headed out of Lincoln, careless of where he was going. He took the Gainsborough Road, heedless of the convoy of cars behind him. When he reached the village of Saxilby he remembered that he was hungry and, noticing a fish and chip shop, he pulled over.

"*It's a stop, stop, stop outside the chippy!*"

"*I've got him, my footman is out.*"

Carl Sanders strolled over the post office on the opposite side of the road and loitered by the door.

"*He's on his own, going into the chippy. Nobody else around. Everyone, hold back.*"

Pyke ordered a portion of chips. His order was taken by a middle-aged man whose proprietorial air and impressive girth indicated that he was the business's owner and quite possibly its best customer too. He raised his eyebrows slightly. Pyke added a battered sausage to his order.

When he emerged from the shop Pyke looked left and right. He noticed a young man at the post office window. Could he be a copper? Or a Customs man? Pyke told himself he was being silly. Why would anybody be following him to see him buy sausage and chips? He returned to his car and began to eat, whilst weighing his various options.

He didn't like it, but he kept coming back to the offer (had it been an offer?) from the mysterious rip-off merchant from Rutland. In some ways he was ideal. He could collect the merchandise from Maas's people in Holland, hand it over to Pyke, or better yet, someone who would work for Pyke and Pyke could move it on to his customers.

But he knew literally nothing about this person. He didn't have a local accent. Sounded a bit posh, actually; he sounded quite old. Pyke finished his chips. He felt a little better. The more he thought about it the more he liked the idea that this man was cautious. And he had been right about Gazza and Shane. And he had been true to his word. He could have just taken the thousand pounds and disappeared. But he hadn't.

Pyke started the car.

"*Standby, standby. Smoke from exhaust.*"

He pulled out and performed a U-turn.

"*He's pulling a snake, a snake.*"

Pyke drove home still thinking. On one hand this seemed like a heaven-sent solution. But on the other he could lose an entire consignment. He kept coming back to the fact that the man had kept his word last time. Finally, he decided that he would, what was the word, engage this man. But only, only if he could meet him and learn who he was.

*

Michael had made a pot of tea. His grandfather always insisted on a pot. In fact, he had only recently reconciled himself to the concept of tea bags. He was not ready, not even nearly ready, for tea stewed in a mug. It had to be a pot. Because it was a special occasion there were biscuits too. On a plate, naturally; eating biscuits directly from the packet was not something that could be countenanced in the kitchen of the old vicarage.

Next to the plate of biscuits lay the mobile telephone with the blue sticker, newly charged. *The whole scene has a sense of drama about it*, thought Michael. If the director knew his business the phone should ring just as the grandfather clock in the hall chimed three. It chimed. It rang. Must be Hitchcock.

"Hello."

"It's me."

"Oh, hello, thank you for ringing."

"First things first. I want to know who you are."

"You can call me Peter."

"Okay, Peter, I might be willing to have a meeting to discuss your proposal."

"No. No meeting. You and I shall never meet. Are you in Lincoln?"

"It doesn't matter where I am."

"There's a pub in Cherry Willingham called the Wishing Well. There is a public telephone just outside. I shall call you at three thirty-five. Goodbye."

The old man picked up his car keys, then turned to Michael. "Shall we?"

Michael assented, although he had no idea to what he was agreeing. He followed the old man out of the door and got into the Rover. Together they drove towards Peterborough before turning off into the small village of Marholm. The old man parked beside a public telephone and consulted his watch, an Omega Geneve. It was three thirty.

"Now, let's see if we can't do business with this man. Come on."

The pair walked to the telephone box and, slightly awkwardly, both entered. The old man fished a telephone card from his pocket. He consulted his watch again, inserted the card and dialled.

"Hello."

"Good. You are there and on time."

"What do you want?"

"The question is rather what do you want, or what do you want me to do for you? Let me begin by setting out my understanding of the situation and you can let me know if there are any inaccuracies."

"Alright." Pyke had no idea what or who he was dealing with, but he decided that there could be no harm in allowing things to play out.

"Good. Now you are an importer and distributor of illegal controlled drugs. You head an organisation. I am not sure of its size, but I imagine that it is rather small. Slightly smaller now that Messrs Hartney and Barham have been arrested. Am I correct so far?"

"No comment."

"Good. And your business model, if I may call it that, is that you receive your merchandise from a supplier on the continent who delivers to your representatives in the UK. Am I right?"

"No comment."

"But you and I both know that your representatives were unprofessional and unreliable. And now your supplier knows this too. And anybody that you may wish to engage to replace Hartney and Barham are now very aware of the risks that come with working for you. Am I right?"

"Go on."

"So, now we come to the areas where I have no direct knowledge and am forced to speculate. I am assuming that the price for your merchandise is higher if delivered to the UK than if collected abroad. And it may be, in any case, that your supplier is no longer willing to deliver to you in the UK after what happened to Mr Bakker. Yes?"

"Go on."

"So, this is my proposal to you. I am a specialist consultant. I offer a range of services from pure consultancy to import facilitation. For a fee I would be willing to advise you on making your organisation more efficient and secure. Or you could subcontract to me whatever elements of your operation you choose. In short, I will import your drugs for you."

Michael couldn't believe what he was hearing. Had the old man gone mad?

The old man's frankness had alarmed Pyke too. He didn't know how to react, what to think, what to say. He panicked. "I am not an importer of drugs. I know nothing about it. And if I did, I wouldn't discuss it on the telephone. And I don't do business with people I haven't met and don't even know."

"Very well. You need time to consider. I understand. When you are ready to do business this is what you do: place an advertisement in the *Grantham Journal* advertising left-handed gold clubs for sale. Give whatever telephone number you are using at the time but transpose the last two numbers. Do you understand?"

"Swap round the last two numbers?"

"Exactly. Goodbye."

The old man hung up. He did not appear disappointed. He put the phone card back in his wallet, made a note of the telephone number of the phone box and the pair walked back to the Rover.

"Do you think we shall ever hear from him?" asked Michael. He was still reeling from what he had witnessed.

"I really couldn't say. He has to continue supplying his customers or they will go elsewhere. He will find it hard to find volunteers to replace Hartney and Barham, harder still if they have to import the drugs personally. Either he will find someone else, who will be caught, or he will do it himself, in which case he will be caught. Or he will be in contact. We shall have to wait and see."

*

Pyke stepped from the phone box and looked long and hard in every direction. He saw no lurking pedestrians, nobody sitting in parked cars. The Wishing Well was at the end of an L-shaped parade of shops. Some of them had flats above. There could be somebody behind any one of those windows, watching, taking photographs. Pyke shrugged. He was getting paranoid. He needed to get a grip. Try to understand what had happened. Try to work out what he was going to do next. He was unnerved by the fact that the man on the telephone seemed to have diagnosed his problem perfectly. Who was he? How did he know so much? Was he being set up? If so, by whom?

He drove home, carefully checking his rear-view mirror all the way.

*

At Scampton Andi and Joe were in McBride's office. Andi had just returned from Cherry Willingham.

"Are you sure?"

"Yes."

"One hundred per cent?"

"One hundred per cent. He didn't make a call. He received one."

"And he didn't call anyone on his mobile first?"

"From the moment he left the car to the moment he was in the telephone kiosk his phone was not in his hand."

McBride reached for his pipe. "Okay, thanks." Andi headed for the room with the kettle. Joe remained.

"Thoughts?"

Joe considered for a moment. "Either he's getting more cautious or those he's dealing with are."

McBride nodded. "Those are the two likeliest explanations. But there's a third. Maybe he is dealing with a new person who is more careful, more professional."

"That'd be annoying."

McBride treated him to a look that was part exasperation, part annoyance and just a hint of scorn.

"What are you talking about? It's what we want. We are not here to catch the amateurs. The better they are the more I like it."

McBride leant back in his chair. His pipe started to emit contented little puffs.

Grandmaster who has found a worthy opponent, thought Lake.

*

Andi knew that McBride would be talking things through with Lake, or using him as a sounding board at least. In different circumstance she might have resented this. She was, after all, the senior officer in the team and if there was to be a caucus of wise and experienced officers she ought to have been part of it. But she had other things on her mind. Marcus had been, well, just a little bit odd recently. It wasn't the fawning attention of the mums at the school gate. She had got used to that years ago. Sometimes she found it amusing, sometimes it gave her a little sense of satisfaction that other women found her husband so attractive. No, this was something different. Marcus had been different. He wasn't quite a full-time house husband. He did quite a lot of scouting. But that was in the football season, of course, not the summer. Now, when she asked him about his day, he was slightly evasive. And he wasn't very good at it.

And he had bought a briefcase, one of those 'executive' ones with a combination lock. He had never had a briefcase before. His scouting notes were mostly scribbled in a small notebook, or on the back of supermarket receipts, parking tickets and takeaway menus. And he kept it locked. Andi could have opened it in five minutes. Combination briefcases weren't hard if you had a decent torch and perhaps a magnifying glass. But she hadn't. That would have been a breach of trust, or a lack of faith, or something. She felt slightly guilty just thinking about it. So, she hadn't. Yet.

She decided to give him a call while waiting for the kettle to boil. But the home phone was engaged. That had been happening more and more often recently too.

*

Ideally things would have been a little quieter than usual for the team at Scampton. There was no Gazza and Shane to follow around and most people expected Pyke to be less active. In fact, just the opposite was true. He seemed to be on the road almost every day. He visited the Golden Gloves Gym in Sheffield twice and boxing gyms in Doncaster, Scunthorpe and Grimsby. The team spent so much time following him that they had to swap their cars with those of Nottingham B. Those who had spent a month cultivating beards had to shave them off. Monster had gone one stage further and had a crew cut.

Whenever they were not on surveillance the team were putting together the case against Gazza, Shane and Marius Bakker. There were witness statements to be written, court orders to be sought and a thousand other little tasks that were mostly tedious but always critical to a successful prosecution. The team had expanded further into the administration block accommodation. There was now an office with half a dozen old RAF desks where the team worked. The dispersal-room television was getting a lot less use and everyone was getting a little tired and a little fractious.

McBride shared his thinking only with Lake and not always with him. Andi Woodhead and the other senior officers were starting to resent being sent out on tasks with little or no context. The discontent was very close to boiling over. Somehow, from within his little office, McBride seemed to sense this and called a meeting, not in the briefing room but in the more informal atmosphere of the dispersal room.

"Our friend has been busy. He's calling in debts because he needs readies. But it's more than that. He is trying to set up a distribution network. Some of these gym owners are new contacts. He's setting up customers for future importations. But he has a problem. We've nicked his couriers."

"So, will he make the run himself? Will he go 'hands-on'?"

"He doesn't seem to be stupid enough or desperate enough for that yet. But I have a question for you all. Does anyone here know if Pyke is left-handed or right-handed?"

There was silence.

"He used to box right-handed. I've seen pictures."

"Not conclusive."

More silence.

"I think he's right-handed. He uses his phone right-handed."

There were a few nods.

"Okay, has anyone seen anything, anything at all to suggest that Pyke might be a golfer?"

More silence, blank and puzzled looks were exchanged.

"He's placed an advert in the Grantham local paper. Left-handed golf clubs for sale. I don't think he's selling left-handed golf clubs and if he were, why would he advertise them in Grantham?"

FIFTEEN

When Michael came down for breakfast his grandfather was not in the kitchen. He briefly considered the possibility that he had overslept or chosen to lie in before dismissing the idea as absurd. The night before they had competed again in the Old Volunteer pub quiz. His grandfather had insisted that on that occasion they should lose narrowly. Michael had agreed but actually he had found it harder than he expected. Team Florid Face were taking the whole thing far too seriously and had spent a large portion of the evening casting suspicious or downright hostile glances in his direction. Michael had overheard one of their number questioning George, the landlord, as to the legitimacy of Michael taking part since he was only a temporary resident of the village. It required a certain power of will intentionally to score only four out of ten on the final round. Even though it was absurd, Michael still felt a little bitter and resentful. His grandfather had taken almost no interest in the final round. He didn't even glance at the answer paper. Nevertheless, Michael had deliberately omitted answers to six questions and handed it in to the landlord/question master with a rueful smile. As if he didn't know who had won the 1953 FA Cup Final!

Team Florid Face accepted their victory with as little grace as a school bully winning an arm-wrestling contest. Worse still, his grandfather had insisted that they remain for another drink, thus condemning them to a further forty minutes of ill-disguised gloating.

Michael was considering whether to have a second cup of coffee when his grandfather entered through the back door. He was dressed in his usual uniform of Rutland retired major but wearing an expression of ill-disguised glee.

"Want to buy some golf clubs?" He threw a copy of the *Grantham Journal* onto the kitchen table.

"You're kidding!"

"No. Our little friend from Lincoln wants to do business. We shall give him a call later. But we have some errands to run first." He sat at the kitchen table. "But first, some coffee, and proper stuff, not that instant rubbish that you drink. And then I need to get changed."

*

PWJ Motors was the type of establishment that gave used car dealers a bad name. It occupied a small lot of ground on the outskirts of Grantham where perhaps two dozen vehicles of doubtful provenance and road worthiness sat with windscreens wearing such effusive enticements as 'Good Runner' or 'Three months MOT'. P or W or J or perhaps all of them occupied a cluttered and filthy Portakabin that served as office, sales room and the Grantham Museum of Greasy Chip Papers and Fag Butts. Michael and his grandfather took a slow walk around the lot, clockwise and then anti-clockwise.

"What are we looking for?"

"The most inconspicuous vehicle we can find. That Sierra will do. The silver one in the corner."

The Sierra was indeed inconspicuous as evidenced by the fact that Michael had walked past it twice in the previous ten minutes and had absolutely no recollection of it. 1.3 million Sierras had been sold in the UK. And quite a lot of them were silver. Even PWJ had found it difficult to identify any special characteristic of the vehicle. The only message on its windscreen was the price, £3,995.

The old man indicted by a gesture that Michael had no role to play in the sales negotiations. He went alone into the Portakabin. Five minutes later he emerged holding two sets of keys and a copy of the car's logbook, including the section that PWJ was supposed to send to the DVLA with details of the new registered keeper.

The old man tossed a set of car keys to Michael. "Lincoln," he said.

Michael drove, steadily at first as he got used to the unfamiliar car, and then more confidently as he approached Lincoln. His grandfather directed him through the city's southern suburbs and then asked him to pull over in a side street opposite the entrance to the Canwick Road Cemetery. Together the two walked between the rows of gravestones until the old man found what he wanted. In one corner there was a set of three graves. Each was marked by the standard headstone of the Commonwealth War Graves Commission. From the inscription it was clear that the three young men, who had all lost their lives on the same day in March 1944, were part of a RAF bomber crew. Two of them had been Michael's age, one a year younger.

Seemingly satisfied, the old man led Michael back to the Sierra and together they drove to the city centre where at two different shops they each bought a pay-as-you-go mobile telephone. On each occasion they paid cash and registered the phone in a false name. They then visited a branch of Halfords, where they made a small purchase whose purpose dawned upon Michael only as they were leaving the shop. Finally, in a newsagent near the cathedral, they bought a tourist map of Lincoln. As they walked back towards Steep Hill his grandfather explained to Michael what he wanted him to do. Michael nodded. He understood his instructions very clearly, even if the purpose was somewhat opaque.

"Hello, this is Peter."

"You got the message then."

"I will meet you in the Magna Carta in fifteen minutes."

"I thought you didn't want to meet—"

But the old man had hung up.

There are only a few copies of the Magna Carta left, and one of those is kept at Lincoln Castle opposite the more famous cathedral. Between the two old buildings are a few more modern ones, one of which was a pub called the Magna Carta. Pyke glanced at his watch and picked up his car keys.

As the front door of Pyke's house opened Lake called, "There he goes." But only McBride was listening; the rest of the team were scrambling, this time without any sense of irony, for the cars parked behind the administration building. The first car reached Westgate Car Park a few seconds before Pyke's Mercedes pulled in.

"*X-Ray Five into Westgate Car Park, Westgate Car Park, all cars hold back.*"

"*Tango Five from X-Ray Five heading generally towards the castle.*"

"*From Carl, I'm going into the pub now, need one for back-up.*"

"*From Monster, I'm coming in too, keep separate.*"

"*From Andi, I'll take eyeball on the entrance.*"

Outside the Lincoln Visitor Information Office Michael sat on a bench peering over the top of his tourist map. He saw first one young man hurry into the pub and thirty seconds later a second. A few seconds after that a woman sat down on the bench next to him.

A minute or so later he saw Pyke, the man he had seen collect the parcel from the cricket club, walk briskly towards the pub. The woman on the bench next to him started to mumble into her shoulder. Pyke entered the pub but within seconds he was out again with a mobile phone pressed to his ear. He walked diagonally across the little square to a public telephone box. As he opened the door the phone started to ring.

"Hello."

"It's Peter."

"Right."

"How can I help you?"

"What are you offering?"

"I will collect your merchandise for you from your contact in Europe and deliver it to you in Lincoln. The price is two thousand pounds per kilogram of product."

"Two grand, you're joking!"

"Considering the discount that you will get for cash and carry it is a better deal than you will get elsewhere. Payment will be due within seven days of delivery. If you require me to make payment to your suppliers in Europe that will be an extra five thousand pounds, payable out of the sum transported. Delivery will be according to my timetable. When you are ready you will provide me with the contact details of your supplier. I will arrange everything after that. If my terms are agreeable, you can contact me by placing a postcard in the window of the newsagents in Long Bennington advertising poodle puppies for sale and giving your current telephone number with the last two digits transposed, understand?"

"Long Bennington, Poodles, right."

On the bench the woman was still mumbling into her shoulder. As Pyke left the telephone box and headed north up Bailgate she mumbled some more. Michael continued earnestly to study his map, or at least that is how he wanted it to appear.

"*North on Bailgate, back towards X-Ray Five.*"

Michael saw the two young men exit the Magna Carta together and hurry across to the junction with Bailgate before settling into a normal stride as they rounded the corner. The woman rose and walked to the telephone kiosk, where she appeared to make the briefest of calls. She turned with her back to the device and looked directly at Michael. Michael hurriedly looked down at his map. It was at that point he noticed that it was upside down. The woman emerged from the kiosk and gave Michael a long look before also setting off up Bailgate, back towards the Westgate car park.

Michael's phone rang. "Time to go home."

*

The team had gathered in the dispersal room. The general mood was one of frustration. Lake was beginning to doubt his ability to interpret McBride's mood by means of smoke signals. He appeared to be… well, certainly not frustrated. He appeared to be… excited? Thrilled? Elated?

When everybody had written up their notes McBride hosted a debrief.

"Let's take it from the top. Pyke is summoned to a meeting at the Magna Carta."

"He appeared to leave the house hurriedly. He looked at his watch as he walked to his car." This was from Lake, who had been viewing the monitor.

"He was still in a hurry as he left the car in Westgate car park."

"I saw him come into the pub. He was looking all around him."

"Looking for a tail or looking for someone he was meeting?"

"I was watching him, not reading his mind. Anyway, he was in the pub about ten seconds when his phone rings. He turns around and walks straight out."

"That's right. He was there for a matter of seconds. Then he comes out, he's looking around, then he sees the phone box and heads straight for it."

"Was he hurrying?"

"I'd say not."

"Was anyone in the telephone box when he arrived at the pub?"

McBride was met with shrugs.

"There was someone on the bench outside. He had a tourist map. It was upside down."

"Description."

"White male, twenty to twenty-five, dark curly hair, dark jacket."

"Get the CCTV tapes."

Andi nodded. She decided not to mention that she had been transmitting whilst sitting next to this young man. She continued, "So he's in the phone box for two or three minutes..."

"Did he make a call or receive one?"

"Don't know. Receiving, I would guess."

"Did you mark the call?"

"Yes, straight after, called my own mobile."

"And then he's back to Westgate Car Park and straight home."

"Arrived back at Gold Five at fifteen forty-three."

"So, what do you think, Frank?" This last one was from Andi.

"I think we've finally got a target worthy of the name."

"What, Pyke?"

"No, not Pyke, whoever he spoke to. I'm going to call him 'Lefty'." McBride puffed on his pipe. Lake had been right. He was thrilled.

*

"Tango Five on the move imminently. Scramble! Scramble! Scramble!"

Another wave of warriors launched an attack on Rorke's Drift, but nobody was watching. They were all heading for the cars.

"*From Control, Tango Five from Gold Five towards X-Ray Five.*"

"*He's mobile, mobile, heading south. Towards you, Monster.*"

"*Yeah, I've got him.*"

Pyke didn't notice the surveillance team behind him. He drove steadily down the A46 to Newark and then onto the A1 at Newark. After ten miles he turned off into the small village of

Long Bennington. He drew to a halt outside a shop that served as village grocers, newsagent, tobacconist, confectioner and about a dozen other things.

The cars darted into side streets and Nick Harper leapt out to investigate on foot.

He looked left and right. How were you supposed to do surveillance in tiny places like this? There was literally no cover. No telephone box, no bus stop. Nowhere to stand without looking like a surveillance officer or a weirdo.

Nick took a deep breath. "*From Nick, I'm going in. Earpiece out.*" He removed the earpiece from his right ear. He could no longer hear the rest of the team's transmissions but he dared not be in such close proximity to Pyke with a visible earpiece.

"It's five pounds for a month, dear."

"Okay, thanks." Pyke turned, almost bumped into Nick and left the shop.

"Can I help you, dear? I'll just be a moment. I have to put this in the window while I remember." The shopkeeper shuffled out from behind the counter clutching a postcard. Nick didn't make any excuses. But he did leave.

*

When the team gathered again in Scampton Nick shared with them what he had seen and learned. "He put a postcard in the window. Poodles for sale. Five hundred pounds. And a mobile telephone number."

"Those will be left-handed poodles, I expect," said McBride. His pipe said 'grim satisfaction'.

"Joseph! A word, if you please." McBride turned towards his office.

Lake allowed two people to call him Joseph. His mother and Frank McBride. And there was a similarly short list of people to whose summons he would respond with the same promptness with which he hurried off to Wee Frankie's hoose o' fun.

"Yes, Francis, what is it?"

McBride raised one grey shaggy eyebrow. But he didn't say anything. Instead, he gestured to the chair opposite him with the stem of his pipe.

"Shut the door."

Lake braced himself.

"I'm taking a week's leave next week. I have just got off the phone with Mr Spencer. We have compromised upon a protocol for my absence. You will be 'in the chair'. You will receive the intelligence from the Other Office. But the final say in operational decisions will be his."

Lake raised a less shaggy eyebrow.

"As I say, it's a compromise. Mr Spencer will be here at Scampton all next week. There is… an art in interpreting intelligence and an art in what you share and how. You understand?"

Lake nodded.

"The decisions that Mr Spencer will make will be informed by what you tell him about the intelligence that we have received. I hope I'm making myself clear. Now, let me give you my appreciation of the situation and we can discuss the possible implications of any intelligence that we might receive and what courses of action an intelligent and experienced investigator might take in response."

Lake was at once excited and nervous. He was expected to tell Spencer whatever information that he judged would steer him towards the decision that McBride himself would have taken. On the one hand it showed that McBride was placing a lot of faith in his judgement and wisdom. On the other, this was far beyond anything that he had ever attempted before. Lake was slightly puzzled as to why McBride was having this conversation with him and not with Andi Woodhead or one of the other senior officers. It was a compliment, of sorts, or a test, or both.

"Pyke's just booked a ticket for a cross-Channel ferry. He's going next Wednesday."

"Do we know why?"

"Looks like he's going to visit Maas and to give him some money."

"Money he owes or payment in advance."

"It's not clear. Probably the latter."

"So, what do we do?"

McBride started to fill his pipe. Lake lit a cigarette.

"So, as usual we have a number of options, and, as usual, we have to choose based on incomplete and imperfect information. Possibility one: it's just a cash run. Possibility two: Pyke will be coming back with gear on board. Possibility three: this is payment for an imminent importation."

"So…" Lake was thinking aloud, "if it's just a cash run, we could either pull him on the way out and seize the cash, or… do nothing?"

"Correct."

"If Pyke is importing it himself, we can have him pulled at the port or follow him until he hands the gear over."

"Also correct. But Pyke is the principal target of Operation Bagration. We catch him hands on at the port, that's it. Mission accomplished. If we follow him trying to identify his customer or customers there's a chance that we could lose him. We may have to sit on him for days. He may have multiple customers. We would have to knock the job when he hands over to the first; we can't just let that gear go into the market. So, if it's option two, realistically we pull him at the port. But I don't think Pyke will be carrying."

"Why not?"

"Because of our friend the left-handed golfer and poodle fancier. He's good. Very, very careful. We have no idea who he is or where he is. Why would Pyke hook up with a professional like that and then make a suicide run himself?"

"You think that Lefty will do the actual importation?"

"It seems likely. Of course, we could pull Pyke anyway, belt and braces, but it would mean that he'd know we were targeting him."

"If Lefty the golfer is making the importation, he will have to hand over the gear to Pyke at some point. We could just sit on Pyke, wait for the handover and then move in."

McBride had finished filling his pipe. He extended a hand. Lake passed him a box of matches.

"Have we got a source of intelligence on the left-handed golfer?"

"No. And I don't think we're going to either. I get a feeling, it's just a feeling, you understand. He seems to be old school."

"Old school?"

"A regular John le Carré type. Coded messages, dead letter drops, trefs, you know?"

"What's a tref?"

"Two-second meetings, brush by handovers, that sort of thing. Get yourself a couple of spy novels, le Carré, Deighton. You may find them instructive reading."

"So, we let Pyke go to Holland, or wherever, and then we follow him from the moment he comes back until he either receives or hands over a package."

"And if Spencer wants to do something different."

"The intelligence that you will relay to him will make it very clear that that is the correct course of action."

SIXTEEN

It was Monday morning. Lake's first day 'in the chair'. The phone rang. Not Lake's phone, not McBride's. *The* phone. Lake answered.

"Lake."

"It's Tommy Stone, from the Other Office. You're in the chair this week, right?"

"Right?"

"Okay, here's what we think we know about today."

Lake opened the desk drawer and withdrew 'Frank's Book'. It was an ordinary A4-sized hardback exercise book, but to Lake's knowledge this was the first time that anybody except McBride had ever handled it, let alone opened it. He selected a fresh page and wrote the date.

"I'm listening."

When the call was finished Lake sat and considered what he had heard, what it might mean and, most importantly of all, what he was to tell Spencer. When he had finished making his notes in Frank's book, he locked it back in the desk drawer and went to see his SIO.

"I've just been speaking to the Other Office," he began. "Indications are that Pyke is travelling to Tilburg on Wednesday."

"Indications?"

Lake considered for a moment.

"Strong indications. The Other Office are pretty confident." He decided to push ahead before Spencer could interrupt again. "He will probably be travelling with Tango Four, Stephen Pettigrew, known as Maxi. They are likely to be staying overnight. We can check for the crossing and booking. It looks like he will be carrying cash out."

"What will he be bringing back?"

"The Other Office thinks nothing."

"Thinks?"

McBride had warned him about precisely this. He said nothing.

"So, he may have drugs?"

"All the indications are not."

"Indications! I'm not sure that I can allow potentially hundreds of thousands of class A drugs into this country on the basis of 'indications'!"

McBride had warned him about this too.

"As soon as we have the booking, we can send a team to the port. Keep our options open. We can have them pulled, follow them away, anything. We probably have forty-eight more hours to learn more. We don't have to decide now."

"Learn more! Learn more 'indications', you mean!"

Spencer was getting quite agitated and rather shrill. If this was what he was like discussing matters forty-eight hours in advance, what was he going to be like 'in the heat of battle'?

"I'll get to work on finding the booking, shall I?" Lake was looking for an excuse to leave before Spencer had a stupid idea.

"That should be underway already! Why isn't it being done now?"

Lake sighed and then tried to disguise it. "I thought you would want to be brought up to date on the latest intel straight away. I'll get on it now." He hurried away. McBride's instincts had been right. Howard Spencer MA (Oxon) was a bloody liability.

Howard Spencer would be the first to admit – in fact, it might even have been a source of pride – that he was not especially close to his team. He had arrived at Nottingham only a few months earlier as part of the office's expansion and had not sought to establish close relationships with any of the people working for him. But now he was re-thinking his strategy, with two aims in mind, one professional, one personal.

Professionally he was anxious that firstly Operation Bagration should be a success and secondly that he should garner the maximum possible level of credit. Although he wouldn't have minded if those priorities were reversed. Personally, he wanted to cut Frank McBride down to size. Partly because he didn't like him but also because, from what he had learned from his frequent trips to London, there might be additional kudos due to whoever was able to tame Big Bad Frankie. But for this he required allies. He immediately dismissed Nick Harper. Harper might be a source of limited information, but he doubted that McBride would share too much of his thinking with him. Besides, he seemed to be utterly enthralled by McBride. Lake was a better prospect. He thought perhaps that as a graduate he might be inclined to side with the Oxford man rather than the gruff Glaswegian. But disappointingly he seemed to be more concerned with operational matters than office politics. Spencer did have one further option, though.

A year ago, Andi Woodhead had been the senior investigator at Nottingham. Not technically. Technically, Neville Sands, the SIO of Nottingham B, the VAT team, was senior, but for all practical purposes Andi was top dog. It occurred to Spencer that Andi might be a little resentful of McBride and his star status, might feel that she was dropping down the pecking order, and Spencer might use this to his advantage.

Spencer had decided that he needed his own office at Scampton. He had selected one at the opposite end of the building from McBride's. Partially for that reason and partially because it was substantially larger. He probably wouldn't have admitted it to himself, but it was true, and the firm belief of the whole team that there was a third reason. The name plate on the door to Spencer's office read 'Wing Commander Alistair Munroe, DSO, DFC & Bar'.

Since Spencer had installed himself at Scampton use of the dispersal room had reduced to almost nothing. The officers busied themselves in the newly established 'office room', the games of cricket in the corridors – played using improvised bats, balls and wickets salvaged from a cupboard somebody had found – had ceased altogether. The whole atmosphere was more subdued.

Spencer had taken advantage of a not-quite-accidental meeting with Andi at the tea point to invite her for a little tête-à-tête in Wing Commander Munroe's office.

"You're probably wondering why it is that Joe Lake is 'in the chair' instead of you." There was something about the way that Spencer used investigation parlance that always sounded incongruous. It never sounded quite right, always somewhat out of place. It was like hearing an archbishop swearing. He just couldn't carry it off.

Andi treated Spencer to her best blank expression.

"Frank and I had quite a disagreement about it actually. But in the end, I let him have his way, just this once. But I shall be keeping a very close eye on things. I don't want to step on any toes, obviously…" Inspiration struck him. "And that is part of the reason why I set up office a little out of the way, but I shall be keeping a watching brief."

Another blank expression.

"But I shall need you to alert me if I need to intervene. If, in your opinion, which I value highly by the way, there is something I ought to know, Lake struggling, for example, or Frank overstepping… well… you know."

Andi nodded. She did so to indicate that she understood, not that she had agreed with or to anything. She would need to consider things very carefully before she chose a side in any impending civil war.

"Yes, well, that's all really. Do let me know, and of course, I may need you to step up at some point. If it's necessary, you understand?"

Andi nodded again and, taking advantage of the silence, rose and left. She didn't turn left back towards the end of the building where everyone else was gathered, though. She turned right out through the door and, fishing in her handbag for her cigarettes, began a long, slow circuit of the small cluster of buildings immediately behind the administration block. Andi preferred to think slowly. Some people made the mistake of thinking her unintelligent, which she certainly was not. She just liked to weigh things carefully before she committed herself. Three laps and two cigarettes later she returned to the building.

*

Mondays meant a pub lunch, but this week Michael and his grandfather eschewed the Old Volunteer and instead ate at the Wheatsheaf in Long Bennington. Michael was beginning to enjoy driving the Sierra and was starting to think of it as 'his car'. The old man was in an especially good mood having seen the advertisement for poodle puppies.

After lunch they drove to Lincoln. They stopped near a telephone box in North Hykeham and made a note of the number, then bought a Lincoln Street atlas.

"Allow me to explain to you how mobile surveillance, as practised by Customs and Excise works."

Michael pulled over. "I'll need my full attention for this."

"Yes, you will. Let's start with conventional mobile surveillance. We can deal with technical mobile surveillance later if I think we have to. A surveillance team will usually consist of between three and five cars. Popular makes and models, and in common and nondescript colours. Each car will usually have a driver and a passenger. There will usually be a motorcyclist too. The best way to spot those is that they will be doing their best to look nondescript too. The helmet will be a dull, dark colour; the leathers will have no decals or logos. The motorcycle will be a sports tourer, not an out-and-out racer, and not one of those 'sit up and beg' BMWs either. They just scream 'police'. There will only be one car behind the target at any given time. The others will either be further back or on parallel routes. The bike is for emergencies. The final giveaway is that the cars often won't indicate and never will when they are in the target's rear-view mirror."

Michael nodded.

"The cars and their passengers will communicate by encrypted radios, so scanners are a waste of time. The purpose of mobile surveillance is chiefly not to see where a target goes but to see and hear what he does. Therefore, the cars are primarily to get the footmen, as they call them, to where they need to be. Radios these days are pretty small and covert, so don't bother looking for them, but they will have an earpiece. It looks like a deaf aid. When a target stops you can almost guarantee that there will be at least one passenger out of a car within seconds, probably getting up close to the target. A second will usually be somewhere around so that they can report when the target is heading back towards his car. The first one won't be able to transmit, you see, in case the target, that's us, hears."

Michael indicated that he was still following. He couldn't decide what to think about hearing himself described as 'a target'.

"If a target makes a phone call from a public telephone an officer will make the next call from that phone. They call it 'marking'. It is so they can later identify the number that the target called by looking at the call listings kept by BT. Now, we are going to see if our friend is being followed today. Before that we have one last little job to do."

Michael pulled out and continued towards the city centre before stopping near the Canwick Road cemetery. His grandfather left the car and walked alone amongst the graves for five minutes. When he returned, he said, "I'll drive from here."

The old man drove the short distance into the village of Canwick, where he pulled up alongside a telephone kiosk. He took two ten-pence pieces from his pocket and gave them to Michael.

"Call our friend. Tell him your name is Peter and that you want to meet him in fifteen minutes at the bowling alley on Westborough Road. Then hang up."

"And if he gives me any problems?"

"Then hang up."

Michael called the number from the poodle advertisement, with the last two numbers transposed.

"Hello."

"This is Peter."

"No, it's not."

"This is Peter. I will meet you at the Bowling Alley on Wellingborough Road in fifteen minutes."

He hung up.

Pyke looked at his watch. It would take at least ten minutes to drive to Westborough Road. He could do his thinking on the way. He picked up his keys and called to Donna, "I've got to go out for a bit."

Pyke hated being at the beck and call of the mysterious Peter. He liked it even less now that it was obvious that Peter was more than one person. But he needed to supply his customers, and soon, and so, for the time being, he recognised that he had to allow himself to be used like a puppet on a string. But he determined that as soon as he could he was going to discover who Peter and the Peter organisation was.

*

"Pyke's on the move," said Nick Harper, who had been watching the monitor. Next door the phone was ringing.

Lake shouted, "Scramble!"

Eleven sets of footsteps thundered down the corridor, past the office being used by Howard Spencer, and towards the cars and motorcycles. A minute later Spencer was standing in front of Lake demanding an explanation.

"Pyke is going for a meeting with Lefty the courier," said Lake, with a lot more confidence than he felt.

"Who is Lefty the courier?"

"That's what we're trying to find out."

*

"Now," said the old man, "we shall find out how good Customs are. A good team will send two cars beyond the halt, ideally on either side of the road. That means one in the golf club car park and one down by the sewage works. The third car will probably plot up in Hall Drive, the fourth in South Park. The second car will drop off a footman at the bowling alley. From here I should see them all."

Five minutes later Pyke drove past in his green Mercedes. He was followed by a silver Vectra and a maroon Mondeo. He drove into the bowling alley car park and parked directly in front of the CCTV security camera. He got out and looked around. Nothing. He walked into the reception area of the bowling alley, passing a young man who was leaving. The public telephone in reception was ringing. He picked it up.

"Listen, I'm getting a little tired of this."

"In the cemetery. Next door, not the crematorium, the cemetery. The grave of Flight Sergeant Packman. It's towards the back, on the right."

"Fuck off!"

"Flight Sergeant Packman."

The line went dead.

"*Tango Five is out of the alley, towards X-Ray Five. He's at the car. Into the car. Back to the road. He's gone right, right, right.*"

"Yeah, Andi has eyeball on the junction Wellingborough Road and Canwick Road."

"From Andi. He's not made the junction. My footman is out."

"From Monster, X-Ray Five parked and empty, Wellingborough Road."

"Where's Tango Five?"

"Wait… I think he's in the graveyard. I can't go in there. There is no-one else here. He'll spot me for sure!"

Still muttering curses under his breath, Pyke walked through the cemetery. It was warm and he was starting to sweat. Was he supposed to look at every grave in the place? And what for? After ten minutes he found it. Flight Sergeant T M Packman, died 16th March 1944. RAF crest. What was he supposed to do now? He stood looking at the headstone. It looked exactly the same as the two either side. The only difference was that Packman's grave had one of those small wooden crosses with a poppy at its centre. Pyke didn't normally associate poppies with August. Packman had died in March. He bent down and picked it up. On the back was written, "Public telephone box, outside Froggie's News, 231 Lincoln Road, North Hykeham, 6PM."

It was a quarter to six. Pyke hurried back to his car, still carrying the little wooden cross. He tossed it onto the back seat and headed for North Hykeham. Behind him four cars and a motorcycle did the same. He reached Froggie's News at five to six, entered the telephone box and pretended to make a call. At six o'clock he hung up. The phone started to ring immediately.

"Peter?"

"Yes." It was the older man's voice this time. "How can I be of service?"

"Well, you can stop running me all over the county for a start."

"But that is all part of the service. That's what you are paying for. Security. Now, what can I do for you?"

"I need you to fetch something for me from Holland."

"Approximate weight?"

"About five."

"That will be ten thousand pounds. When do you need it collecting?"

"About a week?"

"Very well. I shall need the name of my contact. A number. And an assurance that he or she is willing to conduct themselves in a professional fashion. As you know I have high standards and I do not compromise them for anyone. When will you have that information?"

"Thursday."

"Very well. I shall contact you next Friday."

SEVENTEEN

Pyke had made all his arrangements with Maas from a public telephone. The same one each time. Directly opposite the Lincoln Imp, his local pub.

He didn't think that he was imagining it. Maas was being extremely cautious, suspicious even. But at least he was still willing to do business. He set off from home at nine in the morning, two days' clothes and twenty-five thousand pounds in cash in an overnight bag. He picked up Maxi on the way. Since he couldn't use him for anything except cash he might as well make the most of what he could do. His plan was that Maxi would take charge of all payments to Maas. Ideally, he would have liked to have given him responsibility for collecting money from UK customers too, but Maxi always seemed to come away empty-handed or with half the cash and a promise. It wasn't his fault. He just didn't have the necessary, what was the word, presence, to collect debts from drug dealers. He was so obviously one of nature's nice guys. And, frankly, a bit weak. None of this mattered if he was making payments. People were always happy to receive cash from anyone, even someone like Maxi.

"Got your passport?"

"Yep, and I brought some Pesetas along as well, you know, just in case. We had some left over from Benidorm last year."

Perhaps he needed to re-think his plan about making Maxi his 'money man'.

*

Nick Harper and Monster had driven down to Dover the previous evening. Or rather, having previously experienced the culinary delights and nightlife of the town, they travelled instead to Canterbury, armed with the details of a good hotel and a shortlist of recommended Indian restaurants. Nick decided that this was a good opportunity to tap into Monster's considerable experience to add to his knowledge and understanding of investigations work. Monster was happy to oblige him his technical explanations liberally sprinkled with examples from his own career. Examples in which the role of hero always seemed to be played by Monster himself.

At ten past nine Lake had called to tell them that Pyke had left home and at half past Mark Hardy had called to let them know that the green Mercedes was heading south with Pyke and Maxi on board. Monster, who had already consumed an enormous plate of bacon and eggs, glanced at his watch and decided that he had time for another cup of tea and a few slices of toast. They were in Dover in plenty of time to take up a position to see Pyke and Maxi check in and to ensure that they were not intercepted by Customs or Immigration on the way out.

It was three hours from Calais to Tilburg and with the hour's time difference, which Pyke had forgotten to build into his calculation, it was almost half past seven when they arrived. Maas was at the football. Willem II, Tilburg's team, were playing NEC Nijmegen at home in the first match of the season. They arranged to meet at the Superkruiken Bar in the city centre, the following morning at nine.

The Superkruiken was less of a bar and more of a shrine to Tilburg's Willem II FC. The walls were covered in photographs of past players and teams. There were shirts, scarves, pennants everywhere. Any bar looks a little odd at nine in the morning. The lighting, the smell, the ambiance is not what a bar should be. The Superkruiken was no different. It seemed like a living thing stripped of its soul. When Pyke and Maxi arrived a young man was pushing a broom to and fro, and a zombie, who later in the day would perhaps become a young woman, was loading glasses into the dishwasher.

"*De bar is gesloten*," said the young man, barely bothering to look up.

"We're here to meet Stanley," said Pyke.

The young man shrugged.

"Would you like a beer?" the zombie asked. "Please sit in that corner. I haven't done it yet." She nodded to the far end of the bar.

Pyke and Maxi walked further into the gloom and Maxi hefted the rucksack on his shoulder. After a minute or two the zombie brought over two glasses of beer and placed them on the small round table. She picked up the three empty glasses and ashtray and walked away, this time swaying her hips slightly.

Maas arrived at about half past nine. He saw Pyke and Maxi sitting in a corner when he arrived and gestured for them to follow him. He opened a door at the end of the bar and led them up a narrow and surprisingly steep set of stairs into a small room, at the centre of which was an octagonal card table covered in green baize. Maas waved the two Englishmen to a seat. He picked up a phone attached to the wall and uttered a couple of words in Dutch.

"I am sorry to have to tell you that I am very disappointed." He paused to allow his words to sink in. Pyke started to feel uncomfortable.

"We lost. Two one. This is not a happy day for me and I hope that you will be bringing me good news."

Pyke was about to speak when the door opened and the young woman, who was now no more than fifty per cent zombie, entered, carrying three large glasses of beer on a tray. She placed them in the centre of the table and left while three sets of eyes ogled her retreating form.

Maas picked up his glass and took a deep draught. "Now… to business."

Pyke explained that he wished to continue to purchase tablets from Maas but that he proposed to pay for and collect the goods in continental Europe. Maas nodded. Pyke explained that under his new system Maxi would be travelling to Tilburg to make payments and that another associate would contact Maas to make arrangements for collecting the merchandise. He decided not to reveal that he had never met his new 'associate' and had no idea who he was. Instead, he emphasised that his new associate was a professional and that his engagement, he actually used this word, ensured additional security for everybody involved. Maas nodded again and took another swig of his beer.

"Very well."

"Since I am now bearing the transportation costs and a greater share of the risk, we shall have to agree a new price."

Maas nodded again. "What do you have in mind?"

"I was thinking of half the previous price."

"Three quarters!"

"Shall we say two thirds?"

"Agreed. Have you brought money?"

"I have twenty-five thousand English. That's 12,500 tablets, yes?"

"It is agreed. When shall I meet your new associate? What is his name?"

"His name is Peter and you will probably never meet him."

"Then how will I—"

"Leave that to Peter – all I need are the contact details of your courier."

Maas reached into his back pocket. He withdrew a small number of business cards. He briefly sifted through them before selecting a bright yellow one. He handed it over. Tricolore Cabs. The card listed a local number and beneath that three names and mobile telephone numbers.

"Call the number on the card for Ruud. Ask for Sebastiaan. He will require twenty-four hours' notice."

Maas indicated that the meeting was at an end.

*

Michael was spreading his toast with butter. It was obvious from the expression on his grandfather's face that he did not approve.

"You're going to have to do a little shopping for me today. In Leicester. I've made you a list. I've to go up to London. I suppose you would say down to London. There are a couple of people that I need to see."

Michael nodded. He had had a very difficult conversation with his father the night before and had been forced to confront the issue of his future career. He had mentioned it to his grandfather, but he had seemed unconcerned.

"It may take you a little while. We shall need two identical... what do they call those little suitcases, overnight bags, with wheels?"

"Wheelie bags."

"Yes, two of those, almost but not quite identical, but purchased at separate shops. And get yourself a largish rucksack too. The type that back-packers use. And you will need two hundred pounds' worth of French francs and about twenty-five pounds' worth of Belgian francs, and one of those little 'GB' stickers. You're quite sure you are willing to do this?"

Michael wasn't sure. But he nodded anyway.

"Good. Now I shall need you to give me a lift to Peterborough Station and collect me again at half past six. I can't drive myself. I'm expecting rather a good lunch."

Howard Spencer and Joe Lake were alone in Scampton. And about as far apart as it was possible for two people to be within the old administration building. At half past nine Lake emerged from *the office*, where he sat to receive calls on *the phone*. He needed to update Spencer but didn't feel that he could do so without the fortification provided by a cup of coffee. In the drawer in the desk where 'Frank's book' was kept he had found a packet of bourbons. He munched one now as he waited for the kettle to boil, making a mental note to have replaced the now much-diminished packet before McBride returned on Monday. Pyke and Maxi, Tangos Five and Four, were on their way back from Tilburg. Lake estimated that it was three hours at least to Calais. Half an hour or an hour to get aboard, a ninety-minute crossing, deduct an hour for the time difference. It was half past nine now, Lake calculated that the earliest that X-Ray Five could be coming ashore was in four hours' time. The surveillance team had set off at eight. They should be at Dover in plenty of time. The kettle boiled. Lake made a cup of coffee for himself. He didn't need to make one for Spencer. He had installed a percolator in his office.

"Tangos Five and Four appear to have left Tilburg. It's five hours or so before they will reach Dover."

"Assuming that's the route they take."

"Yes, assuming that. They have a return ticket."

"Assumptions are dangerous things in investigation."

Joe Lake knew that assumptions were dangerous. Joe Lake had been an investigator for ten times as long as Spencer. Given that the team was on its way to Dover it was a bit late to start hypothesising that the targets might take a different ferry, use the tunnel or hijack a bloody hovercraft.

"And what do the soothsayers at the Other Office foretell about what the targets might have on board?"

"All the indications are: nothing."

"Indications and assumptions. A dangerous combination, don't you think?"

"What do you suggest we do?" Lake was struggling to keep the exasperation from his voice.

"Well, for now we shall have to trust to the Argus-like properties of our colleagues at the Other Office, I suppose."

"And when they arrive at Dover, if they do?"

"That is a decision that I shall make nearer the time when hopefully we have something a little firmer than assumptions and indications to inform us."

What a dick! Lake nodded and began the long walk back down the corridor.

Within half an hour it was obvious that X-Ray Five was heading for Belgium and Northern France rather than Rotterdam or the Hook of Holland. Lake decided not to share this information with Spencer. It wouldn't make any difference and he didn't trust himself to remain calm if he had to endure another conversation like the last one.

Stephen 'Maxi' Pettigrew didn't have many qualities and even fewer qualifications, but he could read a map. Pyke's Mercedes reached Calais a little after one o'clock. From the cafeteria on the upper floor of the terminal building Monster saw them. He called Andi Woodhead in Dover, then Lake in Scampton and then headed for the next departing ferry as a foot passenger.

Lake walked back down the corridor. Spencer had added a 'No Smoking' sign on his door, which was shut. Lake carried on past, out into the car park and lit a cigarette. He inwardly debated whether to call McBride. After considering the merits and demerits of this course of action he settled on a compromise. He sent a text:

T5 & T4 @ Calais, expected inbound, prob empty

Then he went and knocked on Spencer's door.

"They've arrived at Calais. Next ferry leaves in half an hour. Crossing is ninety minutes. The surveillance team is plotted up."

"The Other Office?"

"No change."

Spencer needed to decide or, better yet, delegate the decision to Lake. He didn't.

"We still have two hours to decide."

"What we choose to do now effectively makes the decision for us. If we decide to pull them at the port our search teams are all in Dover, over two hundred miles from Lincoln. If we are going to pull them at the port, we need those officers on the road back here now. We stand to lose time in which evidence could disappear."

Spencer didn't appear to hear. He sat there, paralysed.

"Do you think we should call Frank?"

It was a mistake. Suggesting that McBride was better placed to make a decision was guaranteed to rile Spencer and to make him decide whatever he thought the opposite of what McBride would have done. Spencer seemed to emerge from his trance.

"No. We pull them at Dover. Bring everyone back."

"Not everyone. We will need a couple of people to supervise things. And two interview teams."

Spencer looked startled. "Yes, obviously, leave two teams there. Bring everyone else back."

"You're sure?"

"I think I have made my instructions perfectly clear. Leave four there. Bring everyone else back."

"Okay."

Before Lake had even left the office Spencer was mentally rehearsing how he would tell this story. "I sensed that the operation was starting to drift and so I decided to put myself in a position where I could see everything for myself. It was lucky I did because McBride didn't have a handle on things at all. Indications and assumptions were all he could give me. So, I took charge, ordered that the job be knocked and... well, events have borne out what a very wise decision that was." Yes, that was it. He had imposed himself upon the situation and rescued the operation.

Lake returned to the car park. He didn't want Spencer to overhear this conversation. "Hello, Andi. Yeah, it's me. Spencer wants them pulled at Dover… Yes, I know… I know that too… What can I say? He's the bloody SIO… No, I haven't spoken to him… Yeah… Yeah… Leave two interview teams down there. Everyone else back to Lincoln in case we have to do house searches… No. No, I don't. I think it was just a money run. Yes, they think so too… Of course, I told him… Yeah, well, I'm not exactly thrilled myself."

He texted McBride:

HS ordered pull at Dover

He didn't know whether Frank was checking his messages or how often. He lit a cigarette. His phone buzzed – incoming message:

Photocopy every piece of paper they have, diaries, wallets, EVERYTHING – FMcB

*

The officer stepped into the slow-moving queue of traffic and waved the green Mercedes into the examination bay. Pyke's first reaction was a tide of relief that Maxi and he had nothing to hide. They were completely clean and pure as the driven snow. The second thought that occurred to him as Maxi and he were led to separate interview rooms was that because they had nothing to hide, they hadn't agreed any common story to account for why they had driven to Tilburg and returned just over twenty-four hours later. The third thing that occurred to him was that Maxi's strengths definitely did not include a talent for improvisation. Who knew what he might say? This could all get very complicated and very unpleasant.

Even without the benefit of the short conversation that he had had with Andi Woodhead half an hour earlier, the local Dover Customs staff would have quickly arrived at the decision that they were going to take the Mercedes apart.

Pyke had claimed that he had travelled to Tilburg to watch the football match that had taken place in the city the previous evening. As an explanation it wasn't great, but it was the best that he could think of in the circumstances. Unfortunately, his account gave rise to further and more detailed questions. The score? Two one to Nijmegen, he knew that. What colours did the teams wear? Well, based upon what he saw in the Superkruiken Bar he was pretty sure than Tilburg wore red, white and blue. Except that Tilburg's team wasn't called Tilburg. It was Willem II FC. And he couldn't describe Nijmegen's kit. Or name a single player. He didn't know the name of the stadium. He hadn't got a programme or even a ticket stub as a souvenir. Pyke sensed – no, let's be fair, he knew this wasn't going well, and his anxiety was not improved by wondering what Maxi might be saying in the room next door.

In fact, Maxi wasn't saying anything at all. For all his faults Maxi was able to remember and follow instructions. He just wasn't necessarily able to understand them. It had been impressed upon him that if he was ever arrested, he should reply to any and all questions with, "No comment."

But Maxi hadn't been arrested. He wasn't even being interviewed under caution. It didn't matter. Maxi didn't understand the difference. After ten minutes the officer had become bored and frustrated and left to speak to Andi in the tearoom.

Andi was embarrassed. She was a senior officer in the National Investigation Service and her targets were letting her down. The NIS was supposed to be working on the best criminals, the international dealers in death who made millions from the illegal trade in narcotics. Instead, she was having to listen while some uniform from Dover laughingly recounted what this pair of fools were saying.

Monster entered at this point. "I have photocopied everything they had, including every page of the road atlas that had a scribble, squiggle or stain on it. How are they getting on searching the car?"

Andi looked at the uniformed officer. He promised to enquire, and after he had left, Monster and Andi decided to share a few thoughts about the quality of their targets and of Howard Spencer's decision-making.

EIGHTEEN

It was almost five o'clock by the time that Pyke and Maxi were on the road home. The experience had unnerved Pyke and he was angry with himself for having failed to agree a convincing account of why he had been in Holland. When Maxi proudly told him that he had answered every question, including the one about whether he'd like a cup of tea, with 'No comment' Pyke felt even worse. But they had been clean, and no harm had been done.

The bigger issue, mused Pyke, *is why were we stopped?* He could think of three possibilities. The first was that it had been purely random. That was possible, but they had been there for almost two hours, long enough to search the car extremely thoroughly. He tried to imagine what Maas would have said. After a few minutes' thought he realised that he didn't have to imagine. Maas had lectured him on this subject when they had been in Bijlmerbajes.

"Johann, this place is full of people who are guilty of thinking wishful. They see something that they do not like. They get a bad feeling. They mistrust. And they ignore it. Do not ignore it. It is not coincidence. It is not bad luck. If something bad happens there is a reason for it."

Okay, so not random. The second possibility was that there was something about Maxi and him that marked them out for closer examination. Well, it was August. Almost every other person on the ferry had been part of a family from returning from holiday. There must have been at least a dozen caravans on the ferry, and the same number of motorhomes. And he had lost count of the number of cars with roof racks, filled to the brim with beach balls and sleeping bags and buckets and spades. Two young men in a Mercedes did stand out. A further thought occurred to him. Maxi and he had travelled out the previous day. There was probably a record of that. In fact, he tried to recall the questions he had been asked; did the Customs officers know that before he told them? He thought perhaps they had.

So that was a possible explanation. But was it also what Stanley would have called thinking wishful? Pyke considered the facts. The Dutch money courier had been stopped at Ramsgate and relieved of £50,000. Shane and Gazza had been arrested in the middle of nowhere, somewhere in Essex. And the Dutchman too. That was three unhappy coincidences. Four if you counted today. *I have to face facts*, thought Pyke. *I'm being targeted.*

Maas had lectured him on this subject too. "If you are being targeted, you stop. You stop at once. It doesn't matter how much you lose. It doesn't matter how little more you have to do. You stop. The police have budgets. The politicians set them targets. If you give them nothing, nothing for three or four months, they will go away. They have to. So, you stop. You stop straight away."

That was easy for Maas to say, of course; he had a well-established business. He probably had lots of legitimate sources of income. Pyke thought that he probably owned that bar, or part of it. And perhaps others like it. And other businesses. Cash businesses, like launderettes, taxi companies. Maas could afford to stop for three or four months. He had twenty-five thousand pounds of Pyke's money for a start.

Pyke didn't have any of those advantages. He had commitments. He had promised Diane and Leanne some money. Who knew what they might do or say if he didn't provide for them while Shane and Gazza were inside? But he had Peter. Let Peter take the risks. The cash he would earn from moving on the merchandise he had ordered from Maas would be enough to take care of Diane and Leanne, and then he could decide what to do.

*

Back at Scampton Spencer had left. Not before throwing a minor tantrum and cursing the Other Office, McBride, the uniformed officers at Dover, everyone, in fact, except Pyke. Lake had listened to it all with the blankest expression he could muster, inwardly hoping that this meant that the SIO wouldn't be showing his face at Scampton again any time soon.

Lake was feeling profoundly depressed. Not because the search of Pyke, Maxi and the Mercedes hadn't found anything. He had expected that. But because he had failed to dissuade Spencer from the foolish and totally unnecessary decision to order the search at all. He was completely sure that somehow McBride would have prevented Spencer doing so much damage. Even now, Lake was sure, Pyke would be driving home and inching, probably slowly, towards the inevitable conclusion that he was being targeted. And if he had any sense, and Lake was in no position to make such a judgement, he would be packing up or at least laying low for a while. If that was the case then the Other Office would grow bored, decide they had better uses of their time and facilities, and Nottingham's first and only target operation would be shelved. Who knew when they might get another? Lake blamed himself.

He was alone now in Scampton, and no-one would be arriving that day. Those who Spencer had ordered to race back to the Midlands to perform house searches could all go home. Andi Woodhead and those still in Dover would do likewise. In Lake's imagination they would all be cursing him all the way back to the Midlands.

It was time. If not now, when? He opened the desk's second drawer. The one below that which held 'Frank's book'. He pulled up the small box and put it on the desk in front of him. Why not? Nothing he did could make him a bigger figure of scorn than he was now. Four days 'in the chair' and the job was in ruins. He opened the box.

It was a complete starter kit. As well as the pipe itself there were filters and cleaners and a funny little tool similar to the one that he had seen McBride use. Not for the first time he examined the pipe from every angle. He tentatively tried it in the centre of his mouth, then in the corner à la McBride. He practised waving it about airily. He used the stem to point at imaginary interlocutors. He sucked then blew air through it. He did everything bar fill it with tobacco. And it was not the first time that he had run through this little routine. On every previous occasion he had ended by putting everything back in the box. A thirty-year-old! With a pipe! You might have got away with that sort of thing fifty years ago, but today, today it was to invite ridicule.

He reached into the box. "What brand?" he had been asked in the tobacconist. He didn't know. Literally anything except McLintock's would do. He didn't even want to imagine what people would say if they learned that he was smoking a pipe and that he had filled it with McBride's preferred tobacco. So, he had St Bruno. He broke the seal and took a pinch and placed it in the bowl. He tamped it down. Then he took another pinch and a third. That was too much; he took half a pinch out. He tamped it down the way that he had seen McBride do. Oddly, he was starting to feel a little better.

There was nothing more to do now except to light the damn thing. The absurd, pretentious, ridiculous thing. Lake placed it almost reverently on the desk. He rose and walked the length of the corridor. He checked that Spencer's Jaguar was gone. He reversed the journey, re-inserted himself behind McBride's desk and looked at the pipe without touching it. The phone rang.

"Joseph, it's Frank."

"Listen, Frank—"

"No need to say anything. I know all about it. There's nothing you could have done. The man's a fool and that's all there is to it. Don't worry. Pyke has paid twenty-five grand up front. The importation will be in a few days, a week at most. He simply can't afford to walk away. When you look at the photocopies tomorrow, look very carefully and think about what you have and what it might mean. Now go home and have a glass of Scotch – just one, mind. We live to fight another day and that begins tomorrow."

Lake put down the phone and picked up the pipe. He reached for the matches.

NINETEEN

The Sierra had a flat tyre so Michael and his grandfather had to use the Rover. It was almost a thirty-mile detour to go via Retford, but the old man had a lifetime's experience and it had taught him never to cut corners. He called Pyke from the telephone box nearest the railway station.

"It's Peter. Do you still wish me to run that errand for you?"

"Yes."

"Magna Carta, 2PM."

He hung up and walked back to his car. It took fully three quarters of an hour to drive to Lincoln and in that time Michael's grandfather had plenty of time to explain precisely what he wanted him to do.

*

In Scampton Lake looked at his watch, cursed and picked up the phone. The Other Office told him that time was tight, but it could probably be done. He walked into the dispersal room, where a tired and dejected team were watching *The Bridge on the River Kwai*.

"Tango Five will be on the move shortly, we think," he began. "Let's try to flood the city centre, focussing on the castle and cathedral area."

Monster was the only one who appeared to have heard him. "Now?" he asked.

"Yes, now! Now!"

The team, exhausted and demoralised, grumbled from their chairs at a great deal less than 'scramble speed' and sulked towards the door. Lake couldn't blame them. In their position he probably would have been the same. He hated playing the sergeant major and could all too easily imagine what the team would be saying about him. He walked back to McBride's office, musing bitterly that the loneliness of command was real. And it was crap.

When he reached McBride's desk he reached for the pipe. McBride had been right. Somehow it helped.

*

"*From Monster. X-Ray Five into the Westgate Car Park. Tango Five on board.*"

Pyke strode briskly towards the Magna Carta. He was slightly late. Donna had been moaning to him about Diane and Leanne. As he approached the pub his phone rang. "I know, the telephone box, right?"

"No. Go to the cathedral. Keep this line open."

Pyke turned left past St Mary Magdalene's church and through the Exchange Gate into Minster Yard.

"*From Gill, he's away from the pub. Away from the pub towards the cathedral.*"

Pyke still had his mobile phone clamped to his ear. "On your left as you go in, side chapel, second last row on the left, hymn book, between pages 100 and 101. Got it?" Michael hung up.

"*He's into the cathedral, into cathedral.*"

Pyke put his phone in his pocket and entered the cathedral. He turned left, walked briskly into a side chapel where, without sitting or kneeling, he started to riffle through hymn books. In the second he found a slip of paper. He glanced at it, put it in his pocket and walked back towards the main entrance.

Five yards away Gill Murray muttered something she would not ordinarily say in church. She looked around. Was there anyone here who might be Pyke's secret correspondent? How could she tell? That group of Japanese tourists? The old man in the tweed jacket? The couple lighting a candle? The young man browsing some booklets on the subject of Christian missions? It was impossible to tell. Whatever Pyke had collected may have been there ten minutes or twenty-four hours.

Pyke left. Gill pressed the transmit button concealed in the strap of her handbag several times.

"*Rapid clicks received, standby! Standby! From Carl Tango Five from the church towards the castle.*"

Pyke walked back up Bailgate towards his car.

"*He's heading for X-Ray Five. Everyone, get back to your cars. We're going with him. We're going with him!*"

Pyke drove west, then south around the back of the castle. In the narrow streets Kevin Cleary was having to do most of the work on the motorcycle. He continued heading south down Spring Hill and then Hungate then east through the city centre towards Broadgate then south again over the river and Sincil Dike.

"*He might be heading for the cemetery.*"

He turned left at the cemetery.

"*Heading for the bowling alley.*"

He went past the bowling alley.

"*He's gone right, right, right. We're overshooting.*"

"*He's into the golf club, the golf club.*"

Pyke parked at the far end of the car park and waited. It was ten to three. At five to three he walked into the clubhouse, past the secretary's office, the pro shop and the bar, and up to the public telephone that started to ring at exactly three o'clock.

"*Is anyone wearing anything you can wear in a golf club?*"

"*From Gerry, I'll go.*"

But Gerry made the mistake of checking the bar first. By the time he had established that Pyke wasn't there he was already on his way back to his car. Twenty minutes later he was back at home.

*

"Do you know," said the old man, "'Now, Maitland! Now's your time!' He never said it."

"Who didn't?"

"Wellington. Never said it. They probably made it up for the film. Artistic licence or some such."

Michael's grandfather was about a hundred pages into a million-page book on the battle of Waterloo. "Well, I thought I may as well get my money's worth."

"I'm sure it's all very interesting, but can we go over it just one more time? I want to be one hundred per cent sure." His grandfather put down the mighty tome.

*

The bus left Leicester at half past ten. The old man handed his new burgundy wheelie bag to the driver, who put it in the luggage compartment. He boarded the bus, took a seat about halfway back by a window and opened a far smaller book. Michael, standing outside, waited for the old man to look out of the window so that he could give him a parting wave, but he never looked up. Michael eventually gave up and walked back to his Sierra. The bus had a few stops en route to the coast. He would likely be in Calais before his grandfather.

The drive to Folkestone had taken longer than he expected. He had planned to have something to eat at the Channel Tunnel terminal but strangely he had no appetite. By the time he reached Dunkirk at about four o'clock it had returned. He stopped for a sandwich and a glass of iced tea. When he had finished it was half past four. He had two hours to drive before he made his phone call.

At half past seven the Battlesite Expeditions bus pulled up outside the Ibis hotel in Waterloo. Forty weary passengers, mostly slightly past their prime, disembarked. As they stretched and yawned the driver opened the luggage compartment and started to line up the bags and suitcases. The tour guide, he had previously introduced himself as 'Geoff', assured his charges that they need not worry about their baggage as the hotel staff would take it up to their rooms. They were invited for a welcome drink in the bar at eight o'clock where the guides would explain the itinerary for the following day. Most of the tourists saw this as an opportunity for a thirty-minute lie-down, but Bernard had other ideas.

"Rifleman?" said Bernard.

"Royal Green Jackets, twenty-two years. You?" replied Geoff. Neither of them needed to reference the small badge that Geoff wore in his lapel.

"Tanker. Fancy a pint, or whatever passes for a pint around here?"

The two old soldiers headed for the bar, where Geoff, unwittingly, provided Bernard with all the information he needed.

*

Sebastiaan had been slightly surprised to have received such explicit and detailed instructions from his English contact and positively astonished to have received them in near-flawless Dutch. His father had told him that he would be dealing with a professional and that he was to learn as much as he could about him. It looked as though this would not be possible. At half past nine he pulled off the E19 into a set of motorway services just north-east of Antwerp and after completing two full circuits of the car park drew into a spot behind a motorhome, where he was confident that he was out of the vision of any CCTV cameras. He made his phone call.

His second set of instructions were equally explicit. He stepped from the driver's seat and took his time looking in all directions. He locked the car and, walking to the rear, placed the keys inside the still-warm exhaust pipe. Then he walked towards the building. As he crossed the threshold, he received another call. He continued past the shop and the café bar to the entrance to the toilets. The public telephone on the wall was ringing. Some people might have been exasperated at the precautions that the Englishman was insisting upon, but Sebastiaan was not a run-of-the-mill mule. He was Maas's son and he had been brought up to conduct himself as a professional, to learn his trade. One day, he would inherit the family business. He answered the phone, looking about him in case he might see the Englishman using a mobile telephone. He didn't.

"Have you done as I said?" The voice had switched back to English.

"Yes."

"Very good. Now I would like you to tell me a story?"

"What story?"

"Any story, it doesn't matter, and in any language. I just need to hear you speaking for about five minutes."

"Because if you can hear me speaking you know that I am here in the services, and I cannot see who is at my car."

"I just like stories. Start talking."

Michael walked through the dark car park, his phone clamped to his ear, whilst Sebastiaan told him about the boar with the golden bristles. He retrieved the keys, opened the boot and removed a holdall. He locked the car and replaced the keys. He walked to the Sierra, also in a CCTV blind spot. He had parked next to a black Range Rover whose size and angle meant that his own English number plate was all but invisible, threw the holdall in the boot and got into the driver's seat. He started the engine and let it run for a minute or two, revving very slightly occasionally.

"*Bedankt. Dat was een mooi verhaal.*"

He hung up, turned off the engine and waited. Thirty seconds later he saw Sebastiaan run across the car park, get into his car and roar off onto the eastbound carriageway.

Very good. Bright boy. If you really put your foot down, you might catch up with an English-registered car heading for France. Michael waited ten minutes then started his Sierra and headed for Brussels. He by-passed the city using the ring road and headed south towards Waterloo. Just about the point where the notional boundary between Flanders and Wallonia crosses the N5 there was a small kidney-shaped lake. At its narrowest point it was fifty yards wide. The mobile phone sailed in a perfect parabola and landed in the centre.

It was ten o'clock when the Sierra pulled into the car park of the Waterloo Ibis hotel. Michael went to the boot and retrieved the holdall and the second burgundy wheelie bag. In five minutes, he was in his grandfather's room. Five minutes later he was on his way carrying only the empty holdall. By eleven thirty he was at his hotel in Brussels. The following afternoon he was back in Dover with a boot full of cheap wine and beer bought at one of the many hypermarkets in the Calais area that specialised in serving the English travellers making short trips to the continent to stock up on alcohol and tobacco.

Michael briefly considered making a small diversion to visit his parents in Sussex but decided that he couldn't face questions as to his plans for the future and definitely didn't want to explain what he had been doing for the past few weeks or why he was driving a ten-year-old Sierra full of Belgian beer. Instead, he headed north. When he reached Stamford, he stopped to pick up a takeaway curry. By nine o'clock on Saturday night he was sitting at his grandfather's kitchen table, sipping a glass of Frambozenbier and attacking a chicken jalfrezi.

Two hundred and fifty miles to the south-east Bernard was in his hotel room. He had spent the day standing on various hills and nodding knowledgably as Geoff had spoken of Hougoumont Farm and La Grande Batterie. Then he had eaten his evening meal at a table with five of his fellow battle enthusiasts. Four of them were perfectly normal people with a more than normal interest in military history. And then there was Gary.

Gary was in his early fifties and regarded himself as an expert on… well, just about everything really. He began by taking issue with many of the facts that Geoff had imparted that day and then went on to outline his critique of many leading historians of the battle. Mistaking the lack of response from his dining companions for rapt attention he then went on to outline some of his pet theories on the subjects of other battles in other wars, in some cases on other continents. He finished by offering a detailed criticism of the performance of the 7th Armoured Division in the battle for Caen in June 1944. Bernard said nothing but idly wondered whether he could spare a few tablets to add to Gary's luggage. In the end he decided that that was a luxury that he could not afford. He remained silent, made his excuses as early as he decently could and retired to his room.

Bernard donned a pair of rubber gloves. Using antiseptic wipes, he cleaned the wheelie bag that Michael had delivered inside and out. He placed the four polythene parcels containing 12,500 tablets inside and set the combination lock to Gary's date of birth, just for fun. Geoff had had a list of the tour party and their passport details. Bernard was pleased to learn that he could still read upside down. He wrapped the gloves and the wipes in a copy of *De Standaard*. He would drop the parcel in the litter bin in the hotel's lobby the following morning.

The second day was very much like the first except that as the day, and Gary's provocative questions and pedantic interruptions, grew more tiresome the group dispersed and rather than listening to Geoff's commentary (and Gary's counter-commentary) wandered the battlefield. Bernard made sure that he was at a different table for dinner that night.

If an investigator had questioned those who had attended the tour of the Waterloo battlefield in August 1997 some, but not all, would have remembered an elderly man of military bearing who had said little and largely kept himself to himself. A few might have remembered that he introduced himself as 'John'. Most, even Geoff, would have struggled to say anything about the man who had merely said that he was from 'the Midlands'.

On Monday morning the tourists gathered at about nine thirty outside the hotel, where each deposited their luggage beside the coach and took their places. Bernard was the second to deposit his luggage, the wheelie bag that bore his name and address on a little label and contained his clothes and toiletries. Instead of boarding the bus he returned to the hotel. At nine thirty-five he placed a second similar bag, with very dissimilar contents, at the end of the row of suitcases and holdalls. This bag bore no identifying features. Bernard settled himself in a seat as far as possible from Gary and feigned sleep.

The coach left Waterloo at ten and reached Coquelles at a quarter to one. By half past it was on board the train for the Channel Tunnel. Shortly after noon (UK time) Bernard and his fellow tourists were back in the UK and heading up the M20. The first drop-off point was at Ashford. Four passengers exited the coach and retrieved their luggage. The second was at Luton, the third, Northampton. By the time the coach had reached Leicester half the tourists had disembarked. Bernard and five companions climbed down and shuffled to the side, where the driver opened the luggage compartment once more. A couple from Blaby retrieved a pair of slate-grey bags. Bernard picked up a burgundy wheelie bag bearing no markings and walked across the street and around a corner, to where, out of sight of the other passengers, a young man was standing beside a silver Ford Sierra.

Bernard put the wheelie bin in the boot and climbed into the passenger seat. From the glove box he took a Halfords bag and from that bag he took a small rear-view mirror. He fixed it to the windscreen a little below and to the left of the main mirror.

"Okay, let's go home."

Michael drove. His grandfather kept his eyes firmly on the second rear-view mirror. When they reached Oakham, he told Michael to pull into a supermarket car park.

"Now, a quick test. If we were being followed what would happen now?"

Michael thought for a moment. "The car following us would probably overshoot and take up a position ahead of us with a view of the road home."

"Yes."

"The second car would follow us into the car park and park where they could see us."

"Yes."

"Third and fourth cars would hold back. The third would position itself such that it could become the lead car…"

"The eyeball car."

"The eyeball car, if we resumed towards home."

"And…"

Michael looked blank.

"Do you see any cars of popular make and model in common colours in this car park?"

"Well, yes, obviously, lots. But none with a pair of people sitting in them."

"Neither can I. Now, I want you to go to the telephone box over there and make a call."

"And you will see if a surveillance officer comes and makes one straight after?"

"Exactly. Then you go to fetch a supermarket trolley and together you and I shall do some shopping."

TWENTY

Back at Scampton Frank McBride had returned from leave. The whole team were gathered in the dispersal room going over the events that they had witnessed in the cathedral the previous week.

"So… Let me be clear that I have this right," said McBride. "Tango Five, Pyke, is summoned to central Lincoln, specifically to the Magna Carta. Where we know he has been summoned before."

There was a general mood of assent.

"And on that occasion, he received a call directing him to the telephone box just outside…"

More assent.

"But on this occasion, he doesn't get to the Magna Carta. As he reaches the bottom of Bailgate he receives a call that causes him to turn not right towards the Magna Carta but left towards the cathedral. Now, on the previous occasion he received the call telling him to use the box as he entered the pub, right?"

"That's right. I heard it ringing as he crossed the threshold."

"So, boys and girls, what do we think? Was he being watched?"

"Not necessarily."

"I agree. But it's possible. Now, when he goes to the cathedral, he goes immediately to the side chapel, where he starts going through hymn books, am I right?"

"Yes, straight away. He looks at three and I think he took a slip of paper from the third one."

"Okay. So can you see the bottom of Bailgate from the cathedral?"

"No, and you could hardly stand in the cathedral and make a call without attracting attention."

"I agree. So therefore, whoever called him was not in the cathedral. But, but, and this is just a theory... How long do you suppose that note was in the hymn book for?"

There were shrugs. Lake offered, "Not too long. Risky. Might be found, might be moved, might be in someone's hands whilst they raised their voice in praise of the Lord."

"If it were me," said McBride, "I would put that note there at the last possible moment, which means that Pyke's correspondent was in the cathedral a few minutes before Pyke arrived. And Pyke's interlocutor..."

"What?"

"The person he spoke to, was not in the cathedral at that time."

"So, there was a pair of them. They were right there, under our noses, and we didn't see them."

"We haven't seen them yet. Monster, get back to the office and get a bigger telly. And get some Dictaphones. As many as you can. Gill, get down to the city council and get the tapes for the city-centre security cameras. And buy some bloody bog roll!"

*

McBride emerged from his little office with what, for him, seemed like indecent haste. He was still clutching the phone he only used to talk to the Other Office.

"Scramble! Scramble! Scramble! Get yourselves to Wragby as soon as you can! You too, Joseph!"

They ran for the cars. Lake leaped into a Golf being driven by Monster. "Where the hell's Wragby?"

"Ten miles east of here. God, I've spent too long staring at that bloody map."

Stefan glanced over the top of his newspaper as four cars tore out of Scampton. He shrugged and reached down to his thermos flask. He usually enjoyed a coffee and a cigarette at about this time. They turned right towards the ring road. A few seconds later the motorcycle did the same but Cleary rode with a more elegant and assured manner. His place was at the back, and he knew that he had the acceleration to make up ground if he needed.

"From Control. X-Ray Five is mobile, mobile, acknowledge." For some reason McBride's accent was far stronger on the radio. Or perhaps it was because he was actually agitated.

The convoy left the ring road and headed east on the A158. Monster glanced in his rear-view mirror. "I think he's behind us."

Lake looked in the passenger-door mirror. He pressed his thumb down on the transmit button. *"X-Ray Five is in the middle of the convoy."*

Ideally you never want the target to be behind you. He has too long to look at you, remember your number plate or, more likely, your car. More time to remember that he has seen your car somewhere before. Ahead Andi turned off on the side turning towards Nettleham.

"Julia has eyeball. I'm behind him. Everyone else, get off the road."

Monster swung his Golf off the road and almost met Andi, who had performed a rapid U-turn, coming the other way. Gill Murray and Nick Harper worked out that they too were ahead of the target and sped up to increase the distance between them and Pyke before turning off onto the road to Sudbrooke.

Pyke drove through Langworth. Only then did it occur to him to check for a tail. By then it was too late. The surveillance team had sorted itself out and everyone was in their approved positions strung out behind him. Everyone relaxed and settled in to see where the day might take them. Pyke slowed as he approached the outskirts of Wragby, if a village that size can really be said to have outskirts. He turned right in the centre and immediately pulled over outside the chip shop. He glanced at his watch.

"*He's stopped outside the chip shop.*"

"*He's just sitting in the car.*"

Lake looked at his watch too. Two minutes to ten. What was Pyke doing? He might just be looking for a tail. Driving around aimlessly and suddenly stopping every now and then and checking his mirrors, looking for cars darting into side streets. Scanning the pavements for young men walking hurriedly, one hand in a trouser pocket. Mumbling into their shoulders. Then Lake saw the telephone kiosk. He realised its significance just as Pyke got out of the car.

"I bet he's receiving a call in that TK at ten o'clock."

"TK?"

"Telephone kiosk, canary, phone box!"

"Oh, right, could be," agreed Monster, who was regretting that the chip shop was not yet open.

"Yeah, he's going to the phone box now." Lake was surveying the scene in the nearside-door mirror.

"So not looking for a tail then?" Monster wondered.

Lake was experienced and his intuition, which is really just subliminal experience, was improving but he didn't make the next logical leap.

"Is he on the phone?"

"No, he hasn't touched it yet, hang on, he's out again."

"*From Andi, he's back towards the wheels. He's got something in his hand. Looks like a bottle.*"

"*Fanta bottle, Fanta bottle.*"

"*Towards X-Ray Five! Into X-Ray Five with a bottle.*"

Pyke couldn't decide whether Peter's precautions were a silly, annoying game or further proof of his wisdom in employing someone who was so absurdly security-conscious. A message in a bottle! Really? He had to use his car key to retrieve it. It was a pretty short note, but it was detailed and highly specific. He shrugged, re-inserted the keys and started the engine, and headed south towards Bardney.

The surveillance team followed cautiously. The country lanes of rural Lincolnshire did not suit themselves to mobile surveillance. They did not want Pyke to be able to look back and see four cars and a motorcycle lined up behind him. He didn't need to. He now had people for that.

"It's a stop, stop, stop outside the post office."

"There's a canary on the offside."

If anything, Bardney was even smaller than Wragby. When Pyke stopped opposite the telephone kiosk in the village centre the team hurriedly tried to find hiding spots in side streets. It was too late. Michael had seen them all as they entered the village. He had noted the colours and models of the cars, one or two number plates, and one or two faces.

Pyke waited five minutes, as he had been instructed, and then pulled off again, now heading east.

"I think he's just leading us round the houses," said Monster.

"What bloody houses?" said Lake, surveying the bleak and featureless Lincolnshire scenery.

"You know what I mean. He's looking for a tail."

"Or he's got someone else out looking for him. Damn. That's what this was about. Here we are all lining up behind him showing our faces and our number plates to anyone who chooses to stand on a street corner." Lake picked up the phone to call McBride.

As he did so Pyke entered the village of Branston and parked directly outside the telephone kiosk in the centre of the village. The radio crackled in the background as Lake outlined the situation and explained his fear that the team was being deliberately exposed.

"You've got to stay with him. We think the gear is being delivered today and it's being delivered to Pyke." Lake could imagine McBride pacing the empty corridors of Scampton, smoke belching from his pipe.

Pyke checked his watch, left his car and entered the telephone kiosk, one of the old-fashioned red ones that were effectively soundproof. The phone started ringing immediately. He looked around suspiciously. Was someone watching him or was it a coincidence? He saw a Volkswagen Golf parked down the street. Had he seen that before? He thought perhaps he had. But black Golfs were ten a penny. He answered the phone. "Yeah?"

"He's definitely on the phone this time!"

The man calling himself Peter spoke slowly and clearly. Then he asked Pyke to repeat his instructions back to him. Pyke resented this. He resented being treated like a backwards schoolboy. He even resented the patient, patronising tone that the old man had taken. But business was business. We would see who was so clever and security-conscious when Pyke finally discovered 'Peter's' true identity, or rather identities. It was just a pity that he hadn't the first idea how he was going to do that. Yet.

Pyke returned to his car and headed for home. He looked in his rear-view mirror more than usual, but he didn't see a black Golf. He did see a maroon Mondeo, though. Had he seen that before? Maybe, but there were millions of those on the road too.

Pyke arrived home and walked briskly down the drive. He badly needed a cup of coffee. The surveillance teams took up their standard positions for a departure from Gold Five. Lake called McBride to bring him up to date, but he had already learned from listening to the cars' radios, which were now in range of the antenna at Scampton.

Due to a shocking lack of foresight on behalf of the world's sports administrators there is no biathlon for pipe-smoking and swearing. Perhaps they just assumed that Frank McBride would be so unbeatable that it would not provide an arresting spectacle. He now added pacing and muttering to his athletic compendium.

The bowl of McBride's pipe was so hot he could barely hold it. He put it down and started filling his spare. His emergency pipe. He phoned the Other Office and recounted the events of the past two hours. Then he listened for thirty seconds. His emergency pipe still unlit, he reached for the transmit button.

"From Control. Stay with Tango Five. Stay with Tango Five. I will give the lift-off from here." He took a seat opposite the monitor and lit the pipe. Deep down, or actually, not all that deep down, he loved this. The thrill of the chase. The requirement to make instant decisions on imperfect or incomplete information. He just loved it. And he was going to miss it.

Fifteen minutes passed. Then Pyke emerged from his house.

"Standby, standby! Tango Five from Gold Five, into X-Ray Five. Wait. He's mobile, mobile, heading south on the Gold Road."

"Monster has eyeball."

Here we go again.

Out of the Ermine estate and onto the ring road. On to the A46, heading south, towards Newark and the A1. Where was he going? What was he up to now? He left the A1 at Newark and headed for a small retail estate. The team followed. Almost immediately he indicated right, turned at a set of traffic lights and pulled into the car park of McDonald's. The surveillance team moved immediately to the correct positions. The eyeball car cruised harmlessly past and out of sight of Pyke's rear-view mirror. The second car, the back-up, entered the car park and parked as far from Pyke's Mercedes as possible and out of his eyeline. Lake leapt out of Monster's car, tested that his radio was transmitting and headed for the restaurant itself. Other cars found positions from which they could cover a departure in either direction. The motorcycle held far back, ready to respond should things go wrong.

Lake was in the restaurant before Pyke and took up a position from where he could observe everything discreetly. He glanced around, looking for anyone that might be there to meet Pyke.

Nobody stood out as an obvious candidate. It was the usual blend of young families and groups of teenagers.

"*Takeaway, no meeting, no meeting.*" His voice was barely a whisper.

Pyke walked straight past him carrying a brown paper bag. By now Gill was in the car park doing her best to look like a harassed young mother.

"*Back towards X-Ray Five.*"

Andi had taken advantage of Pyke's time in the restaurant to re-position her car so she had a clear view of Pyke's Mercedes.

"*It's okay. Andi has eyeball. Everyone, return to your cars and hold well back.*"

Andi could see each individual French fry leave the bag and enter Pyke's mouth. She wasn't gifted with hawk-like vision, but she had a very compact telescope. The situation was under control. She looked left and right. No unusual vehicles in the car park. Nobody sitting in a parked car except her and her passenger, Carl, and Pyke having his lunch. Andi's breathing was calm. Her pulse was under control.

At Scampton McBride was trying to follow the action on the radio, but Newark was at the very limit of its range. He chewed at the stem of his pipe and then at his fingernails. This was the hard part, the part where you had made your call and then live with your decision, powerless to affect the course of events.

Then Pyke's car door opened.

"*Standby! Standby! Tango Five, out of the car. Wait.*"

Pyke walked a few steps across the car park and tossed the brown bag into the litter bin. Then, without looking left or right, he walked back, hopped into his car and turned the ignition.

"*He's back in the car. Standby, standby! X-Ray Five is mobile, back towards the main road.*"

That was the last transmission that McBride heard. The range was just too great. Nobody in the surveillance team heard his urgent instruction.

It seemed to Monster that this had been like an intermission in a play, a brief pause in the drama while everybody had a chance to regain their composure and reflect upon what they had seen so far. Now they were ready for act two. For some reason his mind turned to choc ices.

Pyke turned back onto the main road and headed for Newark town centre. The team, playing their role in this saga, slipped in behind him. Pyke indicated left and turned into Northgate.

"*He's heading for the station!*"

Pyke bought a ticket for Grantham. Immediately behind him in the queue Nick Harper overheard him and bought two himself. He passed them to Gill Murray and Carl Sanders, just as he had been trained, and then left the station. He looked left and right for Julia's car.

"*From Andi: Gill, Carl, make sure he boards. Then go with him.*"

Andi paused for a few seconds. "*Julia and Nick, head for Grantham now. Julia, go halfway to Grantham, await instructions.*"

Julia's car, the silver Vectra, would be at Grantham in twenty minutes, well before the train. Steve, alone in the silver Peugeot, could be there in ten minutes once Pyke was confirmed on the train. The other two cars, Andi's and Monster's, and the bike, would have to hold back here in case Pyke doubled back. If he did, then the car sent to Grantham would be out of the game completely. Steve might, just might, be able to catch up.

A train rolled into the station, but it was northbound, towards Doncaster, away from Grantham. Andi was trying to decide whether, when Pyke boarded the southbound train, she should send all the cars south or leave one in Newark to watch the Mercedes. She was inclining towards leaving one car in Newark when everything changed.

"*Tango Five crossing to the other platform.*"

Oh no! What was this? Some French Connection nonsense?

"*He's boarding the northbound train.*"

"*Go with him! Go with him! What's the first stop?*"

"*Doncaster.*"

"*All cars to Doncaster, as fast as you can!*"

Monster grinned. Lake checked his seatbelt and said a little prayer. He remembered what Monster had been like on their surveillance course. On the A1 Julia and Steve searched frantically for an opportunity to turn round. Andi could see the train pulling out of the station.

"*Is he on board? Is he on board?*"

"*Yes, yes.*"

Andi cursed and put her car in gear.

*

It is thirty-eight miles from Newark Northgate to Doncaster Station. The train makes the journey in just under half an hour. But the train doesn't have to worry about the traffic leaving Newark, or the two and a half miles from the A1 junction to the centre of Doncaster. To beat the train a car would need to average approximately one hundred miles per hour on the A1. Monster arrived with three minutes to spare, seconds ahead of Kevin Cleary on the Yamaha. Andi was a minute and a half behind him. She hadn't driven that fast since her police driving course eleven years earlier. And she hadn't enjoyed it at all. The other two cars were still fighting their way through Doncaster traffic. Monster, needless to say, was still grinning when he saw Pyke emerge from the station with Gill a few paces behind him.

"*Monster has eyeball,*" said Monster, and he couldn't keep the smugness out of his voice. Beside him Lake was trying to prise his fingers away from the door handle he had been clutching in terror for the past half hour.

"*Didn't meet anyone on the train. No meeting on train.*" Gill was whispering.

Lake had been in McDonald's with Pyke. Nick had been behind him at the queue for tickets at Newark Station, and Gill and Carl had boarded the train with him. That was four footmen burned and Pyke hadn't actually done anything yet. Not counting the morning they had spent following him around deserted country lanes east of Lincoln. Pyke was behaving like someone who had suddenly learned how to be surveillance-conscious.

In fact, Pyke was nothing of the kind. He was just doing exactly as Peter had instructed him and he was finding it all very boring and unnecessary. He was wondering how much all of this was for his protection and how much was for Peter's benefit. After all, Peter was the one carrying the ingredients of a double-figure prison sentence at the moment.

*

Actually, that hadn't been true for the past fifteen minutes. Michael sipped his coffee. He was by no means a coffee snob, but this was awful. He glanced at his watch. Twenty minutes had passed since the green Mercedes had departed. Pyke, if he obeyed his instructions, would be on a train by now. He rose and walked out of the restaurant and across the car park. He reached into the litter bin and pulled out the brown paper bag that lay on top. Glancing inside he saw the steel shining. He left the car park and walked across the road to his Sierra. When he was sitting in the driver's seat he opened the bag again. He retrieved the set of Mercedes keys and picked up his phone. The Motorola with the red sticker. The one he used only for calls to his grandfather. Ten minutes later he handed him the keys.

"I think we'll have a copy made, just in case."

The young man at the key-cutting shop had been told, more than once, that before making copies of car keys that he should ask for evidence that the customer actually owned the car concerned. But the old man in the tweed hat didn't have any and began to become quite distressed and so he relented. *After all, it's hardly likely that he's a master criminal,* he told himself.

Michael walked across Newark Station car park, a wide-brimmed hat shading his features and a rucksack on his back. He took his time, looking for any of the cars that he had seen in Bardney earlier that morning, but they were all tearing up the A1. He reached the Mercedes, opened the boot and emptied the rucksack into it. He closed the boot, went to the passenger door and opened it. He spent less than a minute looking at the contents of the glove compartment, enough to provide him with the information that he wanted. He opened the rear nearside window about three quarters of an inch and stepped out of the car. He locked it and posted the keys through the gap at the top of the window. They fell to the footwell behind the passenger seat. Glancing left and right he hefted the now-empty rucksack and left the way that he had come.

*

Pyke strode away from Doncaster Station and headed for the high street. There he adopted a more leisurely pace, pausing occasionally to examine a shop window. The surveillance team were hanging as far back as they dared. They had three footmen on the street with the cars doing their best to keep up on parallel course. If Pyke received a package they would move in and make the arrests. Three might not be enough for that, they had to keep as close as they dared.

After about fifteen minutes Pyke entered a pub. Lake followed him. Pyke ordered a Guinness and took a seat in the corner where he had a good view of the door. Lake remained at the bar. "*Hold back!*" he whispered.

Andi decided that it was time she brought McBride up to date. She spoke for almost five minutes uninterrupted, describing the events of the past couple of hours. "And now he's in a pub, apparently waiting for someone," she concluded.

"Where's X-Ray Five?"

"Newark Station car park."

"Have you got anyone sitting on it?"

"No. Shit!"

There was a long pause; when McBride next spoke there was a weary resignation in his voice, tinged with something else – what was it? It couldn't be... it couldn't be admiration, could it?

"I think we've been done. Properly done. He's sold us a beautiful dummy, feinted south, so you sent half the team south. Then he went north, and we've sent the other half after him, leaving the Mercedes unattended. It's probably too late to get a car to Newark right now."

"Shit! Shit, shit, shit! This bastard is better than we thought!"

"No. No he's not. But someone is."

It was too late, of course. Pyke finished his pint, glanced at his watch and wandered back to the station. This time nobody accompanied him on the train. They were all racing for Newark. But by now the Doncaster traffic was too heavy. Even the motorcycle couldn't make it through. Pyke got into his Mercedes and drove off. There was no-one there to follow him.

McBride filled his pipe and swore. Not necessarily in that order. Pyke headed for the Golden Gloves Gym in Sheffield. He made three other stops before he arrived home shortly before midnight. It was then that he remembered about the spare keys and found them on the floor behind the passenger seat. As he walked up the drive to his front door, he hummed a happy tune. No parcel, no bag, no package of any kind. McBride swore again. And again. And again.

TWENTY-ONE

The team arrived in ones and twos the following morning. They were tired, but that wasn't important. They felt defeated – not the Grande Armee's retreat from Moscow defeated, more like playing another school much better at rugby defeated. Bruised and humiliated. Over a hundred miles of mobile surveillance takes its toll. Multiple sudden stops, foot surveillance in and out of shops and pubs, boarding trains, chasing trains, and for what? Ten people had spent fifteen hours on duty and observed almost nothing of evidential value.

As the team drank tea and coffee, passed a newspaper to and fro, and asked Monster where he had bought his bacon, sausage, black pudding and egg sandwich. McBride remained in his little office. He must have been waiting for everyone to arrive because a minute or so after Kevin Cleary came in, removing his helmet and leathers, McBride made his own appearance. He stuck his head around the door. "Briefing. Half past ten."

Gill looked at Lake, her eyebrows raised. Lake returned her look blankly. McBride hadn't told him anything. But there was something about the morning's smoke signals – the little puff, puff-puff, puff-puff – that bizarrely seemed to indicate contentment.

Maybe there was some new intelligence from the Other Office. Or maybe Lake couldn't read McBride's pipe as well as he thought he could. It was still only ten past ten. He decided that he would have a little chat with McBride.

"So, I see that you have taken up the pipe," began McBride, "or is it just when you're in the chair. Or just when no-one's around?"

Lake turned and left. Less than a minute later he was back with his pipe and his tobacco, "In view of yesterday's fiasco, would you mind telling me what you are so happy about this morning?"

"You're not damping that down enough. You want a firmer consistency for an even burn."

"Well?"

"I am happy, young Joseph, because we have a worthy adversary."

"You've said that before."

"Yes, I have, and I was right, but it's even better than I thought. Whilst you lot were careering all over Lincolnshire to no useful purpose yesterday, I was examining the CCTV footage from the area outside Lincoln Cathedral. And I have identified our Professor Moriarty."

"What's his name?"

"I don't know his name. But I know who he is. And he is our Tango Thirty. Print that picture and put it on the wall. No. Wait. Gather the team first."

*

The team gathered in the briefing room and Lake moved the TV and video recorder to a place at the front of the room on a very old filing cabinet. He took his seat in the front row.

McBride marched in at ten twenty-five. Everyone was present so he began.

"Some of you might know that many years ago I was a drugs liaison officer overseas in Bangkok."

Everybody knew. Everybody knew that alright. That was when Frankie McBride had punched some Foreign Office toff in the face and tried to drown him in the punch bowl (the exact details of the accounts varied).

"Now in those days, and probably still today for all I know, DLOs used to receive some counterintelligence training from the spooks. You can imagine the sort of thing. How to tell if you are being followed. How to tell if you're being followed without looking as if you are trying to tell if you are followed. How to lose a tail. How to lose a tail and make it look like you weren't trying to. That sort of thing. Well, when I did it – I don't know ten, twelve years ago – it was mostly done by surveillance specialists from MI5. Lamplighters if you are a le Carré fan. But the whole thing was designed, co-ordinated and run by a soldier. Forty years in military intelligence or something. Ended up head of station in Berlin before the wall came down. And he was good. What he didn't know about counter-surveillance wasn't worth knowing."

McBride nodded at Lake. He got up and pushed the play button on the video recorder. The screen was filled with black and white footage from the area between Lincoln Castle and the cathedral. It was from four different cameras in four different locations and the point of view changed every half second or so.

"*Pause!* Now, we never knew this man's name. Everyone always called him 'the brigadier'. But ladies and gentlemen, boys and girls. *That's him!*" McBride stabbed a finger at the screen, where there was a grainy image of an elderly man walking into the cathedral.

*

"Andi, can you give me a lift to Newark Station? I need to go to London and speak to a few old friends. Joseph. You are in the chair."

*

210

It was a quiet day at Scampton. Some of the team put the finishing touches to their witness statements for the trial of Shane, Gazza and Marius Bakker. Others set about charging radio batteries, checking the camera kits and other little tasks. Nick Harper, because he was the junior man and likely to be asked anyway, spent the day checking over the cars, checking oil and tyre levels, light bulbs and filling the wash/wipe reservoirs. Lake had spoken to the Other Office and been told that little was expected that day. He decided to find a quiet corner and smoke a pipe. He wasn't quite ready to do so in front of his teammates yet, although he suspected that some had guessed.

He had had plenty of time to explore the administration block whilst he had been alone at Scampton. He had found a set of office-door name plates wrapped in a copy of the *Daily Telegraph* from 1965. All the names had post-nominal letters indicating various awards for bravery. Scampton wasn't exactly full of ghosts, and Lake definitely didn't believe in ghosts, but when it was very empty, and very quiet, well, it was hard not to reflect upon the fact that this place had been the last safe and familiar place on earth known by men even younger than himself.

At the end of one corridor was a door that looked as though it was for a cupboard but actually led into an anteroom, and from there was a door opening into a slightly larger room, one of the few whose windows could actually be opened. This, Lake thought, was the ideal spot to give his pipe another run out. He shut the door to the anteroom behind him and was taking it from his pocket when he pushed the second door open.

Both were surprised and both were embarrassed. It was hard to say which the more so. Lake considered it briefly, but it was too late to hide the pipe. Monster had seen it. Monster couldn't have hidden the source of his shame even if he had wanted to. The evidence lay all around the chair he was sitting on and even in his lap.

Lake was the first to regain his composure. "I won't tell if you don't."

"It's too late. Everyone knows. Pipe tobacco stinks. But I'd be grateful if you... you know."

Lake nodded. He picked up the book nearest to him. "What's tort?"

"A civil wrong. Something you sue people for. Negligence, defamation that sort of thing."

"Oh! And you..."

"Just started, Nottingham Law School."

"But why?"

"I can't do this forever. A man with responsibilities can't be chasing around in cars all day and spend his evenings in the back of vans or police canteens."

Lake didn't want to hear this. He didn't want to hear out loud the nagging little voice that had been in the back of his head. And he certainly didn't want to hear somebody else articulate it. Because one day Bella, would very gently, very tactfully, say something similar and he would know that she was right.

"Hang on! What responsibilities? You haven't got any responsibilities!"

And Monster blushed. He actually blushed.

TWENTY-TWO

Michael couldn't understand those people who were so enthusiastic about the dawn chorus. To his mind it was just an unwelcome and unnecessarily shrill cacophony. If he had been willing to be honest with himself, he might have admitted that his partly the result of the dull throbbing in his head. He had spent the latter part of the previous evening in the Old Volunteer drinking Rutland County and growling at the fruit machine. Then there had been two, or was it three, large scotches with his grandfather in his study. He couldn't remember what they had talked about.

The earlier part of the evening had been spent on the telephone to his father. He had talked, or more accurately listened, about his future. In the end he had given in and promised to enrol upon a law course, starting in just over a month.

The most annoying part was that his father's arguments had been difficult to refute. He could hardly explain that he was very busy gaining valuable experience as an apprentice drug trafficker. How had that happened anyway? It was obviously absurd, but the simple truth was that he had been led astray by a seventy-six-year-old man. He was now an international trafficker in misery and death, and he had become so because his twinkly eyed, tweed-clad grandfather was mischievous and bored.

He could hear him downstairs, pottering about in the kitchen and humming something by Beethoven, or Bach, or, well, someone German anyway. Michael flinched as he raised his head from the pillow and, reaching for a dressing gown that was probably someone's unwelcome Christmas present in about 1955, he grumbled downstairs.

"Tea?" The old man was indecently breezy. Michael managed a slight inclination of his tortured skull and slumped into a chair at the table.

"Did I ever tell you about my old pal Dickie Shardlow?"

Michael began to shake his head but quickly realised that this was too ambitious a manoeuvre.

"Wonderful chap, Dickie! Bit dim but wonderful just the same. Retired now and on just about every committee in the county. I think he likes the free biscuits. Anyway, I gave him a bell. Are you listening?"

Michael indicated that he was by means of a vaguely affirmative groan.

"Anyway, up to you, of course, but if you like, you can turn out for the Leicestershire seconds against Lancashire next week. If you fancy it. You know?"

Michael perked up. "Really?"

"Oh, yes. I told Dickie about your fifty at Lords. Didn't think I knew about that, did you? And he was all for it. Owes me a favour or two anyway, from the old days."

This might have meant anything. Had his grandfather lent Dickie a fiver for a taxi home or exfiltrated him from behind the Iron Curtain one moonless night? No point in asking. His grandfather would just have chuckled.

*

There are great cathedrals of cricket: Lords, obviously, the Wanderers, the Melbourne Cricket Ground. And there are beautiful chapels. Grounds nestling amongst bucolic pasture in English villages or atop cliffs leading down to where the azure Caribbean laps against sandy coves. And there is Grace Road, home of Leicestershire County Cricket Club. Grace Road was neither a cathedral nor a chapel. It was more like a register office that used to be a telephone exchange. It is not particularly beautiful. Nor it is glamorously situated. But it is a first-class county ground and Michael would be playing there. If it ever stopped raining.

A psychiatrist would probably have a thing or two to say about it, but when Michael was playing cricket nothing else on earth mattered. He was able or rather unable not to immerse himself utterly in the game. Nothing else mattered to him, and he was able to set aside his cares and troubles, both acute and chronic, and just play. The issue of his future, of his slightly bizarre present, the apprentice to a geriatric Fagin, mattered not at all. The sweet scent of new-mown grass, the crack of leather on willow, polite ripples of applause, fetching a sprig of cress from a sandwich from between his teeth. The prospect of three whole days of nothing but bat and ball was bliss. When he arrived at Grace Road, he couldn't have been happier.

It was hell from start to finish. It rained all the first morning. Michael sat on the players' balcony of the pavilion, gloomily watching the drizzle start, cease and restart. It never properly stopped, and it never properly rained. It was in a perpetual no man's land between play abandoned for the day and umpires' inspection in forty minutes.

The weather wasn't the only source of Michael's gloom. It quickly became very clear that he was very much the outsider. The rest of the team all knew each other; in some cases they had done for years. The dressing room was full of in-jokes and inexplicable nicknames. He hadn't been awarded a nickname himself yet, at least not so far as he was aware. He had an uncomfortable feeling that when he was it was likely to be uncomplimentary. He suspected that the rest of the team rather resented his presence. He understood. He really did. He had no connection whatsoever with the county. He had been parachuted in by Dickie, a committee member of whom the players had almost certainly never heard. He didn't know whether his teammates knew that he had been captain of cricket at Cambridge. He certainly wasn't going to tell them. It wouldn't help.

At three fifteen the umpires had announced that the pitch was not yet playable, and that tea would be taken early prior to another inspection at four fifteen. At three sixteen the rain ceased and the sun broke through. The skipper suggested that it might be a good time to have a little practice in the nets. It did not go well.

Michael first faced the club's overseas player, Bonzer, an Australian bowler far faster than any that he had previously faced. Michael heard the ball as it fizzed past. It was even close enough to his nose that he could imagine he smelt it. But he certainly didn't see it. Or the next one. The third one he felt as it crashed into his ribs under his left armpit. His teammates gathered in a little arc to enjoy the spectacle.

"Stop tickling him, Bonzer! Bowl properly!"

Bonzer tickled Michael black and blue for ten minutes before the skipper decided to replace physical pain with emotional humiliation.

"Hey, Cherub! Have a little bowl at this 'un. He doesn't seem to like the quick stuff."

Cherub's nickname was not hard to decipher. He was short of stature but had yet to shed his puppy fat. His hair was a nest of golden curls and his eyes were baby blue. No-one would have been the least bit surprised if Cupid's bow and arrow had been found in his kitbag. And he was far, far too good for Michael. He groped and prodded at the ball but never seemed to touch it. And the little arc grew like crones at the guillotine steps.

Things didn't improve when it stopped raining. Leicestershire lost the toss and so fielded first. Michael fielded at Fine Leg, traditionally the position occupied by the least gifted fielder. That was fair enough; after all, he was new, nobody had seen him play, nobody knew how good he was. Based on the very limited evidence of his performance in the nets it was no surprise. But he hadn't expected to be at Fine Leg from both ends. Every five minutes he had to leave his position in the north-east corner of the ground and trot 150 yards to its mirror in the south-west corner, and back again, and back again. By the close of play Michael had run about two miles and touched the ball once.

The second day began the same way. Michael spent two hours trotting from north-east to south-west and back again. The Lancashire captain declared at lunch. Michael had given up trying to fit in with the rest of his team and had spent most of the afternoon session sitting in a quiet corner of the pavilion reading a law textbook. He knew that this would lower his standing still further with his teammates if he was discovered but he didn't care. If this was professional cricket it held no appeal. He had taken stock of his situation and found it unsatisfactory. He was unemployed, or apprenticed to a septuagenarian rogue, depending on your point of view, living in the middle of nowhere and about to embark, grudgingly, on a career that held absolutely no appeal to him. On the table in front of him was a textbook on contract law that would have served as ballast on a battleship and was about as interesting.

About half an hour before close of play Michael heard a loud curse from the middle. Bonzer was striding back towards the pavilion, his bat under one arm and a stream of antipodean obscenities on his lips. Michael picked up his bat and skipped down the steps. As he did so he glanced at the clock and the scoreboard. Leicestershire were 240 for five and the skipper was still at the crease on ninety-one. Michael was pretty sure that he knew what message his captain would have for him.

"I'm going to declare when we get past 250 or when I get my century first. Just try not to make a fool of yourself."

As pep talks went it was not exactly a classic but at least Michael knew what was expected of him. He let two away swingers from a talented but inconsistent teenager drift past his off stump to see out the over and took up station at the non-striker's end to await his captain's hundred and his declaration.

The skipper was clearly in a hurry. He swung wildly at the first three deliveries without making contact. He slashed at the fourth too, caught an inside edge that missed his off stump by a whisker, bisected the wicketkeeper's legs and raced to the boundary. Ninety-five. He slashed at the fifth too. This time an outside edge flew high over a fielder's head, bounced twice and clattered into the pavilion steps. Ninety-nine. Michael was resigned to the fact that the next delivery was likely to signal the century and the end of the innings. All he would have to show for his two day's cricket was half a day in the field and two deliveries, both of which he ignored.

The bowler could tell what was in the skipper's mind too. He sent down a bouncer that any sensible batsmen would have left well alone. But batsmen on ninety-nine are not sensible. The skipper whirled his bat above his head as though he was either trying to screw himself into the ground or achieve heavier than air flight through an improvised willow helicopter blade. He got nowhere near the ball. And neither did the wicketkeeper. It sailed over his head and ran down to the boundary. Leicestershire had passed 250. They had their batting point, but Michael knew that there was not the remotest chance of a declaration whilst the captain was on ninety-nine. His role would be to push a quick single, allow the skipper to complete his century and then get off.

The bowler sent down a good delivery, but Michael met it firmly. The ball struck the middle of the bat and rolled back to the bowler. The bowler, whose body language was broadcasting a message of utter contempt for Michael, attempted to casually flick the rolling ball up into his hand with the toe of his boot. Unfortunately, he had dedicated too much of his attention on projecting an attitude of utter scorn and he mis-kicked. The ball clipped of his heel and rolled back onto the stumps behind him. Michael's skipper, desperate to get to the striking end so that he could complete his century, had edged down the wicket. He scrambled to get back, but, in turning, slipped on a damp patch of grass and measured his length on the pitch. And his length, including the length of the bat stretched out in front of him like a man grasping for a life belt, was ever so slightly shorter than the distance to the crease.

Out. Out on ninety-nine. And technically run out by Michael. It wasn't his fault. He hadn't done anything wrong. He had made no error of judgement or execution. It was not his fault. It was a freak occurrence. No fair or rational observer could possibly attach any blame to Michael.

"You utter tosser! You useless, fucking educated wanker!"

The skipper, it seemed, was neither a fair nor rational observer. He declared the innings close with a snarl that contained no vowels but more than made up for it in terms of vehemence. The pair trudged back to the pavilion. The skipper was met with polite applause and cries of, "Bad luck, skip!"

Michael was met with a wall of scorn and loathing. The rest of the team were obviously neither fair nor rational either.

*

That evening, after he had returned to the old vicarage, Michael decided to share his feelings with his grandfather.

"Grandpa?"

"Yes, Mikey."

"Are you… are you planning to do any more smuggling?"

"I thought I might try it just once more, why?"

"I'm not sure that I really want to smuggle any more drugs. I mean, I enjoy it, the game, the fun of it. I just don't like the idea of pedalling narcotics."

"I know how you feel. It is a bit distasteful. Fun, though. What do you say we just do it once more? Just for my sake."

The old man detected a little hesitancy. "Did I ever tell you about old Frank Lambert?"

"No, I don't think so."

"Marvellous chap, Frank, worked with him in Berlin, first rate. Well, anyway, Frank went into the consultancy business. I'm not sure of the details. Sorting out people's messes mostly, I think. Anyway, the interesting thing about Frank, I remember him telling me this, more than once, I think…"

Michael was starting to wonder where this story was going. But it was going somewhere. He had no doubt of that. His grandfather liked to play the role of the rambling old man, but Michael was no longer fooled. All this had a point. One just had to be patient.

"Frank absolutely loathed all his clients. Without exception. 'Bernie,' he said to me one day, 'every last man jack of them are stupid, venal and ungrateful. I despise them all.' And he did. Absolutely did. Anyway, he must have been able to tolerate it because he put up with them for years. Lives mostly in St Lucia these days. But Frank was like that. A very high tolerance level. I used to have a high tolerance level myself, but these days I find myself having less time for the venal and stupid. So, one last time, eh? What do you say? Just to make an old man happy?"

"I suppose it will provide a nice diversion from Partridge and Crittenden. I'm on page 46 of a five-hundred-page book and I already want to tear my eyes out."

"Oh, I shouldn't worry about that if I were you. Something is bound to turn up." The old man visibly brightened. "Now, can you tell me the single most dangerous thing that you can do when playing the great game?"

Michael knew the answer to this; the old man's lessons were slowly seeping in.

"Doing the same thing you did last time?"

"Exactly. And so, we are going to Peterborough to do some shopping and to put your beloved Sierra in a crusher. No paperwork required. If anyone has seen it there is nothing to connect it with you. One more thing. We are going to need what Lenin used to call a useful idiot."

"A what?"

"A useful idiot. White male between twenty and twenty-five. You must know dozens. After all, you spent three years in Cambridge. Place must be chock-a-block with idiots. Certainly used to be."

*

The third day dawned bright and dry. The two umpires, who might easily have featured in a film called *Laurel and Hardy Go to Lords* mooched out to the middle and, after a short discussion, declared the pitch fit for play. It isn't possible to resolve a three-day match in one day, and so a result was impossible. But this was a second eleven match. There were twenty-one players, anxious to put in a notable performance to impress the selectors and help to stake their claim for a place in the first eleven. Twenty-one plus Michael, who no longer cared. Possibly the skipper noticed or perhaps he just forgot, but in the event, Leicestershire were 145 for six when Michael was eventually called upon to bat, just after tea.

"See if you can get us to 250 for a bonus point," called the skipper as he made his way down the steps. Michael didn't care about a bonus point. Or the result. Or even his own score. He just wanted to stay in the middle where he didn't have to endure the company of the rest of his team or read any more about legal cases involving snails and ginger beer. Accordingly, he resolved to play defensively until it was time to pack up and go home.

First ball! First bloody ball! And not even a good one. It was fast enough but it started wide and swung wider still. Michael decided, he didn't know why, that he would treat the spectators, of which there were about four, to an extravagant leave. He thrust his left leg forward and raised his bat above his head as if poised to slay a dragon. The ball passed by six inches from his pad.

"Owzat?" It was less of an appeal than an embarrassed cough. But it was enough to arouse the corpulent, myopic, inattentive clown from his daydream. He had been idly picking his nose and gazing somewhere towards Narborough when his reveries were interrupted. He pursed his lips and frowned as though weighing the many factors impacting upon his decision, and then he raised the index finger of his left hand. First bloody ball!

Michael marched off towards the pavilion. The injustice. The incompetence. The humiliation. His only consolation was that it couldn't possibly get any worse. And then it started to rain again. And then he saw Giles.

The Honourable Giles Templeton was twenty-five per cent of the crowd. Michael hadn't noticed him earlier. He had no idea how long he had been sitting in the second row of an otherwise empty stand. Michael's walk back to pavilion was completed in total silence. He skipped up the steps and walked briskly to the changing rooms to remove his pads... and to curse.

*

"Amongst the worst decisions I've ever seen," offered Giles, "including some I've made myself." Giles was actually a very good umpire, but an even better friend. He was negotiating his way through the eastern Leicester suburbs at the wheel of a Land Rover, one of many that were used on his father's estate. One of his father's estates.

"Really doesn't matter. I was just pleased to be able to go home really. Anyway, what brings you down here?"

"Well, I had to pop down to see my big sister and since I was almost passing your door on the way home, I thought I'd drop in. Your grandfather said that you would be here, so…"

"Could you stay for a day or two? I could use the company."

"Oh, I expect so. The mangelwurzels are ripening nicely and we have more or less taught the grouse to hover directly in front of the guns. So, everything is pretty much under control and will doubtless tick along nicely without my steady hand on the tiller. I expect I can afford to spend a few days in your bucolic idyll."

The pair of old friends chatted amiably for the remainder of the journey back to Rutland. Others often wondered why they were so close. On the face of it they had little in common. Giles was a genuine aristocrat who lived in a castle that some king or other had gifted to one of his ancestors. He had studied land management as preparation for taking over the management of two hundred thousand acres one day. But the pair had met on their first day at university and had been virtually inseparable ever since. Michael the brilliant linguist, Giles the plodding yet conscientious student. Michael the gifted cricketer, Giles the diligent scorer. But now Giles was settling into what would be his life for the next sixty years and Michael was dreading the future and forestalling it by indulging the eccentric and illegal whims of his grandfather.

"Giles, has anyone ever described you as a 'useful idiot'?"

"I don't think anyone has ever called me a useful anything actually. Why do you ask?"

"Oh, no reason really. I just wondered whether you might like a little adventure before you settle down to a lifetime of allowing New York bankers to trample about in your trout streams and judging bonnie baby competitions at the village fete."

"Are you leading me astray again, Mr Butcher?"

"Absolutely! What do you say?"

"Well, I've always rather enjoyed being led astray."

"You're going to love my grandfather then."

TWENTY-THREE

"Howard? Could you spare a few moments?"

Spencer was in the process of rising from his seat; he sat down again. The fortnightly branch meeting was one of two lowlights of his month. Firstly, he had to drive all the way to Birmingham and then sit there listening to a range of tedious subjects being discussed by his peers, the other Nottingham SIO and the six from Birmingham. There were arguments about petrol budgets, boring anecdotes about people he didn't know and a lot of tedious detail about operations he had never heard of. It was all so... provincial. No strategy, no blue-sky thinking, just a collection of under-educated has-beens bickering about cars and cameras and who knew what else? Not one of them had ever picked up a management handbook in their lives.

Sometimes Howard felt like he was talking another language entirely. And so were they! They seemed to be doing it deliberately – the technical jargon, the slang, the references to nicknames, some of which seemed to belong to individuals and some, more bizarrely, to roles or functions. The most galling thing of all was that they all seemed to think less of him because he was educated and forward-thinking. And all of it presided over by Alan Hawkins, the assistant chief investigation officer. Spencer resented him most of all. Hawkins was his manager. He had to show him some deference, but it irked him.

"No, not here, my office."

Hawkins wove through the piles of paper and the various other obstacles that littered his office floor and installed himself behind his desk. He glanced at the wall clock. Not quite noon so the bottom drawer containing the bottle of Wray and Nephew remained closed. Instead, he pulled an over-brimming ashtray towards him and emptied its contents into a wastepaper basket, where they continued to give off a tiny wisp of smoke. Had there actually been any wastepaper in the basket it surely would have been an inferno in minutes. He lit a cigarette and gestured vaguely in the direction of the room's only other chair. Spencer navigated his way to it as best he could, doing his utmost not to allow the sleeve of his jacket, or anything else, rub against any surface. He imagined that he could feel the grime from the carpet soaking up through the soles of his Gucci loafers.

"I'm concerned, Howard."

Spencer felt a small bolt of panic rising in himself.

"I'm concerned that we are not making the best use of your talents."

That was better. Finally!

"I mean, running an investigation team is obviously great fun and I hate to tear you away, especially since you have a target operation running. But I may have something that would be right up your street."

Spencer did his best to remain impassive. On the face of it this sounded good. But he had learned the hard way that some of these investigation types, rough-edged and ignorant though many of them were, often possessed a level of low cunning. It was best not to commit himself or even demonstrate any enthusiasm until he had the opportunity to consider things from all angles. Well, from one angle actually: the benefits and prospects to and of Howard Gideon Spencer.

"You've probably heard the rumours that the department is considering setting up a National Intelligence Service to sit alongside the National Investigation Service."

Spencer nodded. He had heard nothing.

"Well, the chief is setting up a working party, half a dozen or so of the great and the wise, chaired by some Whitehall mandarin to explore the idea. The chief asked me to nominate someone with operational experience but who could bring some real strategic analysis to the issues. Naturally, I thought immediately of you."

Spencer nodded slowly.

"It would be in London, of course, six weeks. Couple of months maximum. I'd quite understand if you think you can't leave Operation, er, Bagration at this delicate time. But I thought I'd offer you the chance anyway. Just let me know by the end of the week." He stubbed out his cigarette.

Spencer was thrilled. And not quite as good at hiding it as he thought he was.

"Well, it's a kind thought, Alan. I mean, good of you to think of me. And, of course, I'd like to help if I can…"

His mind was working furiously.

"As you say, Bagration is at a delicate stage… Give me a day or two and I shall let you know."

*

Spencer, once he had slalomed his way out of Hawkins' office between the teetering towers of files, camera cases and takeaway cartons, almost skipped down the corridor. Finally, an opportunity to do something interesting, something more deserving of his talents and something that might represent an escape route out of investigation. From the Customs National Intelligence Service to *the* Intelligence Service, MI6, couldn't be that much of a leap, surely. And as for Bagration… Well, if it went well, he was still the case SIO and if, as Spencer privately thought more likely, it fizzled out or went badly, well, he had the perfect alibi.

*

Hawkins lit another cigarette. He was not a stupid man. He didn't have a prejudice against the educated. His own wife was a headteacher and two of his children were at university. And he didn't immediately dismiss people just because they came from a privileged background. In short, he did not suffer from inverse snobbery. He was not prejudiced. He just thought that Howard Spencer was a conceited, ambitious and unscrupulous waste of space. He reached for his phone.

"Hello, it's me, Jumbo... Yeah, I gave him the spiel... Well, he said he'd think about it for a day or two, but basically he swallowed it, hook, line and sinker... Well, consider it a favour repaid... How's it going, by the way? Okay, well, let me know if you need anything... Yes, of course, now tell me. How is my favourite goddaughter? And the little 'uns? That's great. See you soon, Frank."

*

Leanne and Diane sat at either end of the sofa wearing identical expressions like a pair of badly disgruntled bookends. Diane had clearly been crying. She seemed to have spent most of the last week crying.

"There's two grand for each of you there," said Pyke, indicating a pair of envelopes on the coffee table. "Same every month while Shane and Gazza are away. Shouldn't be long. They're sure to get off."

"And what if they don't, John Pyke? What if they don't?" Leanne had apparently appointed herself the pair's spokeswoman.

Pyke sighed. They almost certainly wouldn't get off. The pair had been caught about as red-handed as it was possible to be. But it wouldn't be helpful to explain that at this point. Neither was there any point in explaining that Shane and Gazza's predicament was chiefly of their own making. Again and again, he had tried to impress upon them the value of conducting themselves like professionals. But they wouldn't listen. They wouldn't take elementary precautions. They had been sitting in a car full of drugs at the handover location smoking a fag when they should have been putting as much distance between themselves and the scene of the crime as possible. Their fate was surely sealed. The best that Pyke could hope for was that they, and Diane and Leanne, kept their mouths shut. Which is why he was here handing over four grand of his hard-earned to a pair of ungrateful and potentially treacherous women. It was a temporary solution and a temporary expense. Once they had been convicted, he would cut them all loose. He was better off without them.

"So long as everyone holds their nerve, it's all going to be fine." He could tell that neither of them believed him. But two grand apiece had bought him a little time.

*

Leanne and Diane aside, Pyke was actually pretty happy with how things were going. He had a network of customers at various gyms and he was confident that each of those gyms would want more and more product as various fighters/bouncers became alive to the opportunities of making money. He was buying product more cheaply than before, even allowing for Peter's transportation fee. The risk was minimal. Admittedly Peter insisted on a lot of silly running around and jumping on and off trains, but the fact remained that he only had the merchandise in his possession for a few hours. If he found someone to play that part for him the risk would be, as near as possible, zero. With additional volume came additional discount and additional profit.

He felt that he had a new and improved business model. It annoyed him that he didn't know who Peter was, but on the other hand that meant that there was nothing linked to him if anything went wrong and Peter got caught at Dover, or Heathrow or wherever he was coming in. The only nuisance was Leanne and Diane, but actually, how much harm could they do him? No. Everything was good. He spent the next week visiting his various customers collecting payment and taking orders for his next shipment. The miles were starting to take their toll on his ageing Mercedes, but another month or two, another shipment or two and he could upgrade that as well.

*

Monster and Andi were growing a little tired of Operation Bagration. Andi's husband had started to complain about the long hours. Her children were missing her. Monster's rugby team had grown tired of him missing training or, on one occasion, an actual match. Almost three months of tearing around the East Midlands, sitting in parked cars, eating lunches bought in chip shops (actually, they rather liked that part) and what did they have to show for it? Shane Hartney and Gazza Barham behind bars. It was hardly Pablo Escobar or Al Capone, was it?

The pair had spent so long together that they had almost run out of things to talk about. Almost. But that was okay. Both had other things on their minds.

Monster was at a crossroads. He had spent the past six or seven years living the work hard, play hard life of the bachelor investigator. And he was going to miss it. But to his surprise, and what must have been everyone else's utter shock, he was in love. And not just in love: he was on the brink of changing everything about his life. Because Susannah had twins, Becky and Rose. And so, Monster had enrolled on a law course. He hadn't actually started yet, but he had decided to get in a bit of early reading. It was going to be hard. It would take a few years, but he was going to be a solicitor, wear a suit, be home to tuck the girls into bed, not sitting in a parked car eating dinner purchased from a petrol station.

Andi had a lot on her mind too. Marcus was still behaving very oddly. Scrutiny of the telephone bill had revealed that he was spending a lot of time on the internet. The briefcase was still locked. She had started making a note of the combination reading. It was changing regularly. Which meant it was being opened regularly and that Marcus was conscientiously re-locking it each time. She had continued to resist cracking the combination and checking the contents, but she had done something else. Something that she knew was probably worse.

Marcus had told her that he was going away for a golfing weekend with the boys. So, she set a little test. No. Not a test, let's be honest. She set a trap. Marcus kept his golf clubs in the garage alongside the lawnmower, the barbecue and a hundred other items used much less frequently. Andi simply took all the golf balls out of the bag. Whatever Marcus was up to he would surely take his clubs with him. But if he was genuinely playing golf, he would need to buy balls, and when she checked the bag on Monday morning there they would be. If the clubs had spent the weekend untouched in the boot of the car, then the little compartment would still have no golf balls. It was now Wednesday, and she hadn't yet summoned the courage to look.

*

The pair had been following Pyke for three days straight and were now sitting across the road from the Golden Gloves in Sheffield. It was the second time Pyke had been there this week.

"Perhaps he's coming out of retirement," said Monster. He scrunched up a Mars Bar wrapper and tossed it over his shoulder onto the Mondeo's back seat.

"I don't know much about boxing," said Andi. "Is there a fat slob weight division?"

"I think it's more likely that all these gyms are his customers, or his distribution points at least."

"In which case he's either made another run that we don't know about or he's collecting payment."

"And so, he'll be making another run soon."

"Or someone will. Maybe that old man that Frank is so fixated with."

"I can't see it. I just can't see it. I mean, he may have been James Bond when Frankie was a lad, but smuggling ecstasy? Really? The whole thing is probably a coincidence. I mean, what do we have, really? One rather grainy piece of CCTV footage of an old codger at a Cathedral... Hold on, here he comes."

"*From Andi, Tango Five from the gym towards X-Ray Five. Standby, standby!*"

*

Lake knew that eventually somebody would discover him smoking his pipe and he knew that the ribbing would be prolonged and merciless. He knew also that he was earning a reputation as Frank McBride's boy. He decided that he had to either abandon the pipe or ask Frank if he could be relieved of the number-two role on Operation Bagration. All logic and reason told him to ditch the pipe, but he had grown very fond of it. He found it comforting and, this was probably his imagination, it helped him think. He still hadn't decided exactly what he was going to say when he walked into Frank's office in Scampton on a Tuesday morning. It didn't matter. Frank had an entirely different topic of conversation in mind.

"I know some of them think I'm daft. Maybe you do too. But I've been doing this a long time and I don't like coincidences."

Lake sipped his coffee and waited for Frank to explain.

"The bloody brigadier is Lefty, the poodle-fancying golfer. The more I think about it the more I'm sure. It's just got his fingerprints all over it. Not just the discipline, there are lots like that – well, a few, anyway. It's all that, plus… plus, it's just so old-fashioned. I mean, left-handed golf clubs for sale! Notes in hymn books! You can imagine Burgess and MacLean doing that sort of thing."

"Supposing you're right…" began Lake.

Frank looked at him. Lake re-phrased.

"Let's assume you're right" – that was better – "and the brigadier is involved. The first thing we have to do is identify him. You don't know his name, but others will. They might have retired or something, but someone knows who he is. You said he was military intelligence. Is he getting a pension? A member of some Pall Mall club, something like that?"

"I've tried all that. No trace of him at all. I've asked everyone that I can think of. They've all said they can't help. I've just got one more line of enquiry out there and frankly it's a long shot. We'll have to do it the hard way. I want you to get details of every time Pyke has made or received a call from a public telephone and trace the number of the person he spoke to. They will almost certainly be public phone boxes or untraceable mobiles, but perhaps we can trace him to an area. Or at least triangulate him."

"Do you think that will work?"

"Frankly, no. If it's him he'll be making calls and buying phones at unique locations every time. I'm trying ten things that I don't think will work. Because one of them might. I'm in the market for any other bright ideas by the way. And I'm asking you because you're clever. And because I can't very well throw it open to the whole team because half of them already think I'm chasing a ghost and if I admit I can't find him the other half will too."

Lake leaned back in his chair. How do you find a ghost? A ghost who doesn't want to be found. One who is probably a professional in not being found. This was difficult, and therefore fun. He let his mind wander. It fell upon an idea and then he dismissed it, then another. No, that wouldn't work. He sat in silence for about fifteen minutes. He thought that he had been immobile, but he couldn't have been. His lit pipe was in his hand. How had that happened?

*

Lake had found a large cork board in one of the abandoned offices and had hung it on the wall of the briefing room. McBride had pinned a map of the East Midlands to it. Red pins marked the locations of the public telephone boxes used by Pyke. Green pins marked the locations of the public phones used by whoever he had been talking to.

McBride and Lake stood back and looked at it.

"This tells us nothing. He could be anywhere."

"Right, you won't like this. Get the CCTV footage for that day the brigadier was at the cathedral. Concentrate on the nearby car parks. Run every number plate of every car through the Police National Computer. Get the registered keeper and address."

"That won't tell us his name."

"No. But when we have his name it might give us his address. Get everyone to do an hour. They won't like it, but there's little else to do at the moment. They're not paid to watch *The Blues Brothers* all day. Anyway, you can't spend longer than that staring at a screen without going mad. I want the results in twenty-four hours. I want this man found."

*

McBride was half singing, half humming to himself. Something about starvelings and slumber. His pipe was sending off a message Lake hadn't seen before.

"I've got the details of every car that was in a central Lincoln car park that day."

McBride extended his hand. He didn't say a word. Lake handed him several sheets of paper. McBride started to leaf through them. After a few moments he smiled. "Let's go and have a look at that map again, shall we?" He rose from his desk, and this time Lake could interpret the smoke signals – satisfaction!

McBride ran his finger down the map. He scratched his head. "Road atlas!"

Lake fetched one from the office. "Where are we looking for?"

"Leighton Parva, Rutland."

Lake consulted the index and then turned to the correct page. He looked again at the map on the wall. "There!"

"But how did you...?" McBride had already started to walk back to his office. "Shut the door!" he ordered as Lake followed him in.

"I'll tell you, young Joseph, but if you ever, I mean ever, breathe a word to another living soul I shall tear you into a thousand pieces and scatter you to the crows, understand?"

Lake nodded.

"Years ago, I was awarded an OBE."

Lake nodded. This was not exactly a secret.

"The thing is, if you are admitted to an order of chivalry... are you smirking? If you are admitted to an older of chivalry you are entitled to a coat of arms drawn up by the College of Heralds. You had better not be smirking!"

Lake opened his mouth but the expression on McBride's face caused him to close it again.

"Look, I know it's ridiculous. And frankly, I can't even remember what it looks like." For the first time McBride had told Lake a downright lie.

"Is it red, yellow and purple by any chance?"

McBride treated Lake to an expression that started with surprise, eased through into anger and then morphed into admiration. He decided not to respond.

"Well, to cut a long story short, I got on very well with one of the printers there, a guy called Sid, and I gave him a call. You see, there's all the gongs you see in the New Year's Honours and all that. Those listed in *The Times* and so forth. But there's a second list, much shorter list, of secret honours."

"The sort given to senior figures in military intelligence when they retire?"

"Exactly, so, it was a long shot, but I called Sid…"

"And you found your Mr X?"

"Sir X, actually, knighted in 1990."

"And he lives in Leighton Parva?"

"Yes, he does. Now get someone down there to take a look at the place. Should be easy to find. It's the old vicarage."

TWENTY-FOUR

Howard Spencer wasn't usually attracted to strong or confident women. This was partly due to his innate misogyny, but to be fair he didn't much like strong and confident men either. But he definitely preferred his women fawning and ideally somewhat in his awe. The woman who gave her name only as 'Phillipa' was definitely not fawning and didn't seem to be in awe of him or anyone else on the nine-person committee. She was, he judged, perhaps five years younger than him but carried herself with a confidence and authority that suggested a rank that she could not possibly have held at her age. Perhaps it was a confidence born of her position. She had been introduced as 'someone from the intelligence service'.

She certainly didn't dress like a junior civil servant. Spencer didn't exactly think of himself as a connoisseur of couture, but he recognised a Chanel suit when he saw one, and a Cartier wristwatch. Phillipa said little at the meetings and took no notes. Yet she didn't seem bored or uninterested. She just sat there like a well-tailored and well-coiffed sphinx. And she was attractive, really attractive, even in formal office wear and with her hair in a business-like ponytail. Spencer resolved to get to know her a little better and sought to intercept her at the afternoon tea break. She swerved past him effortlessly. "Sorry, busting for a fag." She skipped down the stairs and through the double doors at the back of Custom House and joined the other nicotine fiends on the steps facing across the Thames to HMS *Belfast*.

The following day Spencer was prepared. He had purchased a pack of six slim panetellas at a tobacconist near the Monument and he was ready. But Phillipa had been busy on her mobile phone at the morning break. He finally cornered her after lunch.

"How are you enjoying the talkfest so far?" Spencer tried to convey the sense that he found the committee that he had been thrilled to join a little dull for him.

"I've known worse."

"Well, yes, me too. But committees aren't really my thing. I lead an operational team as my day job."

"Yes, I think you said, yesterday, and possibly once or twice today."

"Yes, I really ought to be back in Lincoln, minding the shop, but a good leader has to be able to delegate and I've got one or two good chaps up there."

"Lincoln?"

"Yes, well, there and abouts, you know? It's a target operation. With assistance from the Other Office, if you've heard of them."

"I'd hardly be much use on a committee considering the future of intelligence in Customs and Excise if I didn't know who the Other Office were."

"Well, no, of course not."

"Perhaps you could tell me about it later. If you have time for a quick drink after work."

Bingo! Mission accomplished. A quick drink with the lovely Phillipa and who knew what next? Spencer beamed.

"Why not? After all, if you can't keep a secret, who can?"

*

The pubs around Lower Thames Street would all be full of Customs officers, but Spencer knew a little wine bar near Fenchurch Street where he could share tales designed to impress. His usual tactic would be to hold a little information back, to allow his audience (Spencer usually had audiences, not interlocutors) to infer that there were more, juicier details that he could not disclose. But actually, with respect to Operation Bagration he knew so little that he could convincingly outline the full extent of his knowledge and understanding and achieve the same effect. This he did. He told Philippa about John Pyke and his gang, about Stanley Maas and his. He told her the size of his team and the number of vehicles it had. And he told her about Scampton.

"Operation Bagration! How very droll," she had said at one point.

Spencer frowned momentarily. He had always meant to find out what that word meant, but it hadn't seemed important. At the end of their first drink Spencer realised that he had run out of things with which to impress Phillipa. It didn't matter because she had meant it when she had said a quick drink (singular) and by half past six she was on her way.

*

Pyke was doing his accounts. Not literally, of course. There was no double entry bookkeeping involved, just a few scribbles on the back of the envelope he had received by post that morning. He had received most of what he was likely to receive from his contacts at the various gyms. Altogether it amounted to almost fifty-five thousand pounds. He had paid off Leanne and Diane, at least for the moment, at a cost of four thousand pounds, and he owed 'Peter' ten thousand pounds. He had paid twenty-five thousand for the merchandise, so that made fifteen thousand pounds' profit in a couple of weeks. Not bad. And his experience at Dover had convinced him that his new approach of buying cheaply in Tilburg and allowing 'Peter' to take the risks was a winning formula. The only risk at his end was collecting the merchandise from 'Peter' and distributing it to half a dozen of his customers. Once he had found someone else to take on that role, he had the perfect set-up. However, to repeat the methodology meant that he would have to pay 'Peter' the ten grand that he had agreed.

Pyke picked up the letter that had been in the envelope:

Dear John,
If you are still interested in selling those golf clubs, please re-advertise them on the same basis as before.
Best regards
Peter

Pyke pondered. The message itself was clear. Place an advertisement in the *Grantham Journal* advertising left-handed golf clubs and giving his current mobile telephone number with the last two digits transposed. What puzzled him was how had Peter known his name and address.

*

Donna was giving Pyke a hard time again. Leanne and Diane had been complaining. He couldn't believe it. He had given them two grand, each, less than a week ago and they were already bellyaching. And Donna didn't want Maxi to deliver the money to Tilburg either. How had she even known about that? Stupid question. Maxi must have told her. He should have known better, but Pyke hadn't explicitly told him not to. How could he? "Don't tell your sister, my girlfriend, because we can't trust her." That wasn't going to go down well, was it? And now Donna was changing gears. Now she was complaining about how much he had given Leanne and Diane. When was she going to get something nice? She was on the brink of accusing him of having an affair with one, or the other, or both when mercifully his phone rang.

"Hello."

"It's Peter."

"What do you want?"

"Ten thousand pounds, of course. Magna Carta, 2PM tomorrow. Alright?"

"Alright."

The line went dead. Pyke considered whether he should take Peter – it was the younger version this time – up on his offer to use him as the cash courier. But he – well, not him, the other Peter – had wanted five thousand pounds. Maxi would do it for five hundred. Five thousand pounds represented a large chunk of his profit. That was too much. Perhaps he could do it himself. But he hadn't enjoyed the two hours he had spent being questioned at Dover last time. On the other hand, what might Maxi do or say if he was questioned a second time?

*

Pyke had picked up four cans of lager at the Co-op on the way home. He was looking forward to a quiet evening in his favourite armchair watching football. He felt like he deserved it. He had had a hard day. He had been at the Golden Gloves Gym in Sheffield negotiating his next sale of product and had visited other gyms in Gainsborough, Grimsby and Hull. Some of these visits had been utterly futile. Time wasters who either wanted to drive the price down, or wanted tiny quantities, or wanted enormous quantities but only on a sale-or-return basis. He was exhausted, and a little worried. He had seen a blue Mondeo twice. He couldn't be sure it was the same one, but on the second occasion it had pulled up right behind him and he had had a good look at the occupants in his rear-view mirror. The passenger was a chunky lad and Pyke thought that he might have seen him somewhere before, loitering near a burger van, perhaps? He couldn't be sure. But he was feeling uneasy.

Pyke went to the kitchen to put his beers in the fridge. Donna would normally have been there about that time preparing the evening meal. Instead, he found her in the living room sitting on the sofa with an expression that said his evening might not unfold as he had anticipated.

"What have you done now, John Pyke?"

She seemed to have been crying.

"Nothing. What? What's the matter?"

"Maxi has been arrested!"

"What? How? What for?"

"What do you mean, what for? You know what for. You've got him mixed up in something again. First Gazza and Shane, now Maxi. You promised me! You promised me Maxi would be safe!"

She was furious, and frightened. Pyke was nonplussed.

"But he hasn't been doing anything. Not for me, anyway. When was he arrested? Where? Who by?"

"Don't you interrogate me, John Pyke. Don't you dare! It's bad enough that Maxi is being interrogated. You promised me!"

"Babe! I don't know what this is about. I promise you. Where is he?"

"Lincoln Police Station, I think."

Pyke slumped into his armchair. Donna was beginning to think that perhaps he was telling her the truth. Perhaps he had no idea what had happened or why. Pyke pulled out his phone. But who to call? Maas had told him that whenever any member of an organisation had been arrested it was safest to assume the worst and react accordingly. But what was the worst? Maxi hadn't done anything since he and Pyke had travelled to Tilburg. Even if he cracked, and Pyke thought that unlikely in view of his performance at Dover, what could he tell them? He didn't know where Pyke stored his merchandise and even if somehow he did there was nothing there. The only thing that Pyke had that might incriminate him was fifty-four thousand pounds in cash and that was hidden below the false floor of his wardrobe. Maxi didn't know it was there. But if the police, or Customs, came to search his house would they find it? They might. They easily might. He needed to move it somewhere safe, and quickly.

Just then the front doorbell rang. Too late! Should he flee? Could he make it out the back door, through the garden and over the fence? Could he trust Donna to keep quiet if he ran away while her beloved little brother was in custody? He froze.

"Donna! JP! It's me."

Before he could say anything, Donna had leapt from the sofa and was running to the front door.

*

Pyke was studying the copy of the bail notice that Maxi had given him. Both were sipping from cans of beer while Donna was in the kitchen.

"Slow down, Maxi, and begin at the beginning."

As the story unfolded Pyke began to feel less and less worried. Maxi had been arrested by the police on suspicion of handling stolen goods. His flat had been searched and a few car radios had been found. What a fool! He had been bailed for now, but there was a good chance he would be charged when he returned to the police station in four weeks' time. But Maxi had never been convicted before. He would probably get a fine or community service.

"I didn't tell them anything, JP. Nothing! I didn't say a word. Not even to the posh woman."

"What posh woman?"

"I don't know, a posh woman. You know? Well spoken. Elegant."

"Who was she? What did she ask you?"

"She just asked me if I knew a long list of people."

"What people?"

"I don't know? I didn't know any of them, I swear, JP. Just a load of foreign names."

"What names? Can you remember any of them?"

"No, Jan someone, something Van der something. I didn't know any of them and I didn't say anything."

"This posh woman, was she police?"

"I don't know. She wasn't in uniform. Like I said, she was elegant."

Pyke didn't like the sound of this at all. Anyway, Maxi was now a marked man. He couldn't send him to Tilburg again to pay Maas. He would have to think of something else. Or go himself.

*

Michael and Giles had pretty much exhausted all Leighton Parva's entertainment possibilities by lunchtime. The had toured the village from east to west and back again, pausing at the pub, which did not open until noon, the cricket club and the war memorial. They had even made it as far as the hill, from where they could see the (ironically) slightly smaller village of Leighton Magna and the imposing edifice of Leighton Hall.

"Built by some nabob on his return from Calcutta in about 1800, I believe." Michael, for some reason, felt the need to act as a tour guide. "Used to be a borstal or something. It's empty now, I believe."

Giles nodded politely. "You mentioned, I think, that the pub opened at noon?"

Michael brightened. "Yes indeed, finest watering hole in, err, well, it's a pub anyway. But we had better check in on Grandpa first."

When they returned to the house the old man had prepared a detailed briefing paper related to various tasks. As usual he insisted that they committed it all to memory and made no notes of any kind.

"You boys are quite sure about everything you need to do?"

Michael nodded. Giles nodded. Together they rose and Giles picked up the Land Rover keys from the kitchen table. Michael picked up the rucksack containing the cash.

They decided to begin by looking for the cars. It didn't seem like a very difficult task. Two cars. Common make and model, similar age, and identical in colour. The only condition was that they couldn't be a silver Sierra. It took them most of the day visiting used car dealers in the Grimsby and Scunthorpe area. Eventually Giles pointed to a blue Austin Montego. "Didn't we see a car just like that in Barton upon Humber?"

"If we did it will probably still be there tomorrow. Let's come back then and get the pair of them."

"Maybe buy this one now and come back tomorrow for the other?"

Michael agreed and walked over to the little Portakabin where deals were done. Half an hour later he was back, four thousand pounds lighter and clutching two sets of keys. He had been slightly surprised when his grandfather had instructed him as to the name and address to give the dealer, but presumably the old man knew what he was doing. On the way home, as he had been instructed, he bought a copy of the *Grantham Journal*.

The following day Giles and Michael travelled up to Barton upon Humber, where they paid slightly more for a slightly worse example of a 1988 Montego, also in Atlantic Blue. This accomplished, they set off for the second part of their mission. Both had expected this to be the more difficult part of their task but, mostly through good fortune, they found what they were looking for almost straight away. Again they paid in cash, again they gave the name and address that Michael's grandfather had mandated. There was one final trip to a DIY store to buy a padlock and some tools, and then they were almost finished.

*

Two days later, while Giles had gone into Stamford to buy some more clothes, his stay in Rutland lasting somewhat longer than he had expected, the old man summoned Michael for another briefing at the kitchen table.

"I'm sure that it's not very fashionable to say so, but it's the truth just the same. One of the skills that you will need in life is the ability to bully, cajole or dupe people into doing things for you."

"Are we talking about useful idiots again, Grandpa?"

"We are – specifically, young Giles. Now, do you think you could persuade him to perform a few simple tasks?"

"Probably, what sort of tasks? Would there be any risk?"

"A small amount of risk, but very manageable, I think."

"And how much should I tell him?"

"The minimum necessary."

"Giles is my friend. He trusts me."

"That should make it easier then."

Michael felt a pang of guilt. Giles, dear, loyal, faithful Giles.

"Now, I have another little task for you. We have to assume that Customs have changed their cars. So, we need descriptions of the new fleet. We shall take our friend Mr Pyke for a little tour. Give him plenty of stops. Now, pass me that map of Lincoln and I shall show you where a good team will plot up for each of them."

"Are they a good team?"

"Pretty good. That makes it easier actually. You're going to need one of those things, you know, the tiny little tape recorders."

"A Dictaphone."

"Is it? Yes, one of those. Means you can keep your eyes on the road. You remember what to look for?"

"Common makes and models, unremarkable colours, four years old or less."

"And with a 'Y' or a 'U' in the number plate. And a motorcycle, sports tourer, probably, plain helmet, plain leathers. Do you remember what any of the officers look like?"

"One or two."

"Alright then. I shall give him a call tomorrow. Now, I'll show you where I will make him stop. And you can tell me where Customs will go and where you will be to see them."

Michael knew it was childish, like some sort of adult game, but he felt his pulse quicken slightly. He forgot his misgivings about Giles.

TWENTY-FIVE

At Scampton Monster had found a stack of old logbooks from the war and was reading excerpts to the rest of the team. To begin with he was looking for comical turns of phrase and reading them in a sort of Biggles meets Prince Philip type of voice. After a while the text became more poignant and he dropped the accent; a little while later he was forced to give up completely. The words of young men who had faced indescribable horror and presumably one night had not returned brought home how very insignificant by comparison the team's efforts to put John Pyke behind bars. Monster gathered the logbooks and returned them, almost reverently, to the cupboard at the end of the corridor.

In his little office McBride was addressing his usual audience of one. A copy of the *Grantham Journal* was on the desk in front of him, open at the classified advertisements.

"I don't like it." McBride took the unlit pipe from his mouth.

"I don't like it." He replaced the pipe in his mouth and then appeared to notice for the first time that it was empty. He reached for his tobacco pouch.

Lake knew the rules of this game by now. He wasn't actually required to say anything, at least not at this stage. He was there solely to prompt McBride's chain of thought.

"It's careless. Doing the same thing twice. And giving us his new mobile number as well. Assuming that it's the last two numbers switched around like last time."

"Either he's lost contact with the brigadier, and this is his only way of contacting him…"

"Or?"

"Or something else." McBride lit his pipe. "Anyway, I've let the Other Office know the new number."

At this moment Andi and Nick came in.

"We've been to Rutland."

"And?"

"It's a nightmare! Completely unobservable. Tiny place. Maybe a hundred houses, a pub and a cricket club. Nowhere you could possibly put a van without standing out and I'd guess everyone knows all their neighbours. Place like that, the only chance you'd have is to be born there and then spend twenty-five years settling in."

"Telegraph poles?"

"Well, yeah, obviously."

"Does it have water? Electricity? Gas?"

"Probably not gas."

"But an electricity van would be okay, for a few hours?"

"I suppose so, but we don't have one. London does, but we can hardly park a South East Electricity van outside his house."

"British Telecom?"

"Do we have one?"

"I can get one."

"Okay, but not yet. We can probably only use it once."

*

The following day Lake was in McBride's little office when the Other Office phone rang. McBride pushed it across the desk towards him. Lake raised his eyebrows a little. McBride shrugged. Why not?

"Joe Lake."

"It's Tommy from the Other Office, are you Frank's boy?"

Lake took a deep breath. There was nothing to be gained from antagonising the Other Office.

"What have you got for us?"

"Pyke's been told to go to the Magna Carta at 2PM. I assume that means something to you."

"It does. Thank you." Lake searched for some cutting remark, some way of articulating his deep resentment at being referred to as 'Frank's boy', but nothing occurred to him in time.

"Well?" said McBride. "What's the plan?"

"We absolutely flood the place. The castle, the cathedral, the Magna Carta and everywhere in between. We'll need some cameras, the covert video bag, everything."

McBride nodded.

"The call is scheduled for two, so everyone in position by half past one."

McBride nodded again and returned to the task of cleaning his pipe. It was clear he was going to offer nothing further. Lake rose and walked to the 'dispersal room', where Carl and Kevin were trying to fix a dart board to the wall and arguing about what height it should be.

"Briefing! Fifteen minutes!"

*

Pyke checked his rear-view mirror again and again as he drove down Riseholme Road. On Broadway he stopped suddenly and checked in all directions for other cars suddenly stopping or darting into side streets. He didn't see anything. The surveillance team were already ahead of him. Ten men and women lurking on street corners, loitering at bus stops and lounging in doorways from where they could see every inch of the route between Westgate Car Park and the Magna Carta. If Pyke had been a little more professional, he would have not used the same car park that he always used. But he wasn't. So, he did. He parked in Westgate, as he always did. For some reason the car park seemed to have more than its usual share of desirable vehicles today. Pyke mentally listed them, imagining he was in a showroom. He liked to indulge himself occasionally with dreams of a more successful and prosperous future. That Mercedes looked nice, but he wasn't sure about the colour. The silver BMW was nice, and the red Audi and the black Range Rover, but, in his fantasy, he settled on the white Saab convertible. To Pyke, it said 'class'.

As he walked down Bailgate his phone chirruped.

"*Tango Five is receiving a call.*"

"Where to?" Pyke didn't enjoy being bounced around the city by Peter every time, but he had grown used to it and had very little choice now that Maxi was off the team.

"The telephone kiosk opposite the Magna Carta." It was old Peter this time.

"*From Control: he's heading for the known TK.*"

Pyke stepped into the telephone box. After thirty seconds the phone began to ring.

"Yes."

"Do you have the money?"

"It's at… it's nearby."

"Okay, here's what you do. You put it in a carrier bag inside an orange rucksack. You can buy one in the camping shop on Bailgate. You deliver to a lock-up garage in Newark. It's padlocked. The code for the padlock is written on page 100 in a book like the last book. Do you remember?"

"Yeah, I remember."

"In the same place, exactly the same place. Then you go to Canwick Park Golf Club. Do you know it?"

"Yeah."

"There's a noticeboard for the ladies' section. There's a notice for the club championship. Behind it on the noticeboard, pinned underneath is the address of the lock-up. You deliver there between five and five thirty. Got it?"

"Why can't you just tell me?"

"Between five and five thirty. But buy the rucksack first, Bailgate. Oh, and John, if you need me. An advert in the *Newark Advertiser*, poodle puppies for sale, your number, last two digits reversed."

Pyke, who had been moaning to himself about the lack of professionalism of his local crew, was now inwardly grumbling about his new hyper-security conscious, what was he, partner? He set off up Bailgate, wondering why it was necessary that the money should be delivered in an orange rucksack and why he had to travel all over the city to learn where to deliver it. Why couldn't Peter just have told him? He was in a public telephone box. It was hardly likely to be tapped. But Peter had made it clear that his (their?) various precautions were non-negotiable. And he needed Peter more than ever. Unless he just stopped. Or paused for a while. He had twenty thousand. Thirty if he bilked Peter. He could live comfortably for a while. But Leanne and Diane would want regular handouts. And if he stopped supplying his customers somebody else would soon step in to fill the void. He had no choice but to do as he was directed. And since he had no choice, he didn't trouble himself too much with the question why.

"*Tango Five is going north on Bailgate, north on Bailgate.*"

Five Customs officers made the same journey. Two were close enough to see Pyke and three more were relying on radio commentary.

"*Tango Five, at junction with Eastgate.*"

"*From Andi. Message from Control: he might be going to a camping shop. If he does get the camera in there.*"

"*Monster, yes, yes, wait... Tango Five into Lincoln Camping and Leisure.*"

"Get the camera in there."

Carl hefted the rucksack from his left shoulder. He pressed the 'record' and 'play' buttons and checked to see the blinking green light that told him the camera was functioning, then removed the earpiece from his right ear and entered the shop.

"From Andi, message from Control, someone get to the cathedral. And call Control."

"From Gill, on my way."

The surveillance team took up positions outside the shop, on Pyke's likely route and from a position where the entrance to Westgate car park and Pyke's Mercedes itself, X-Ray Five, could be seen.

None of them noticed the young man outside the travel agents. Or the second one by the chemists. And one of those two didn't notice the young woman with the ponytail holding a tourist guide to Lincoln. The other did. It would have been very odd if he hadn't.

Pyke must have walked past Lincoln Camping and Leisure a thousand times. But he had never given it a second's thought. Now he was inside the range of equipment was baffling. After a few moments he saw a selection of rucksacks near the till. He walked past the young man with a rucksack over one shoulder and selected an orange bag that, according to the label, had a capacity of thirty litres and approached the till. Twenty quid! For a bag. These outdoor enthusiast types must have money to burn. He was going to take it out of Peter's payment!

Pyke left the shop and turned right, back towards the castle, the Magna Carta and the cathedral. One officer mumbled into his shoulder. A minute and a hundred yards further on another did the same.

"He's heading for the cathedral."

*

252

Gill Murray was a senior officer who had spent all eleven years of her investigation career in Nottingham. Target operations were new to her, but she was rather enjoying herself, even if a lot of the time she had no idea what was going on. She walked briskly into the cathedral's side chapel and began to thumb through the hymn books. In her ear she could hear the surveillance team describing Pyke's movements. In the fourth book she found a four-digit number written in the margin in blue biro. She memorised it, glanced at her watch and retreated to a position at the back of the chapel, where she sat down and tried to look pious. She didn't notice the old man in the tweed jacket.

*

Pyke made no pretence at piety. He walked directly to the rear pew and began rifling through the hymn books. After a few seconds Gill saw his lips moving as he walked briskly past Gill towards the exit.

Gill counted to twenty and then rose and followed him. As she rose subconsciously she swept her auburn hair back behind her right ear, exposing the earpiece. The old man in tweed inwardly tutted and shook his head sadly.

*

Joe Lake pulled into the car park of Canwick Park Golf Club and parked next to a black Range Rover, wondering how he would explain his presence if challenged. In fact, nobody challenged the slightly scruffy young man as he walked past the bar to the noticeboards outside the changing rooms. It took him only a moment to remove the bottom two drawing pins that held the details of the forthcoming tournament and read the details written on the small piece of paper tacked underneath. Now, could he find a spot from which to observe someone else doing the same?

The door swung open and Pyke started to make his way down the corridor. Lake swiftly turned and went into the gents' changing room. He passed through the locker room into the toilet and shower area, and locked himself in a cubicle. Only then did he realise that he was still holding the two drawing pins that had been securing the notice. He waited ten full minutes before he emerged. By that time there was no sign of Pyke and no sign of his Mercedes in the car park. Lake returned to the noticeboard. The note with the details of the lock-up garage in Newark was gone. He replaced the two drawing pins and returned to his own car, from which he called McBride.

"Get yourself down there pronto and check the place out. Then give me a call."

*

The town planners of Newark had not overtaxed their imaginations. Cherry Holt led to Sycamore Close and Lilac Close, and just beyond them, Birch Close. Birch Close was a short cul-de-sac, perhaps sixty yards long. On both sides were a small number of semi-detached houses, mid-sixties, local authority housing if Lake had to guess. He parked on the main road and decided to inspect the 'plot' on foot. At the end were two five-storey blocks of flats. To the left of those was a playing field and to the right the road led around the back of the blocks to a parking area with two rows of lock-up garages, back to back. There were twenty in all. Some still bore the original double doors of thirty years earlier. A few had the more modern 'up and over' doors, and a couple, including number seven, had a roller door that was secured by means of a padlock attached to a hoop or staple set into the ground. The padlock, which had a combination lock, looked substantial... and new.

Lake looked about. The rear windows of the blocks of flats all overlooked number seven. And all of the garages could be seen from the playing fields, where two young men kicked a football about in a desultory fashion. Even at a distance Lake could see that one was a natural athlete, the other less so. On the other side was a fence to the back gardens of another street of houses. The view from those would probably be too far and at too shallow an angle. The best view of all was from the parking spaces directly opposite garages numbers one to ten. A car or van parked there would have an interrupted view of garage number seven at a distance of no more than forty feet. There was only one space free. Lake decided to save it with his own car and then retreat to a safe distance and call McBride.

*

It was already five thirty-five when Pyke found the garages behind Birch Close Flats. He had been seized by some irrational fear that because he had missed the time window prescribed by Peter, there might be adverse consequences, although he couldn't have said what these might be. Anyway, he was flustered, and anxious, and in a bit of a hurry. He parked outside the first two garages, took the orange rucksack from the boot and walked down the row. Behind the one-way glass in the Astravan Monster's camera clicked as he fired off almost a whole thirty-six exposure reel of film. Pyke knelt at the base of the door and turned the wheels of the combination padlock until it read 9876 and unlocked. He felt apprehensive, but he couldn't have said why. Taking a deep breath, he rolled up the garage door to reveal... nothing. Well, not exactly nothing. It was an empty lock-up garage. What had he been expecting? A door to a parallel universe? A dozen police officers? Peter?

He placed the rucksack on the floor, just inside the door, and stepped back. Only then did he glance around. It was just starting to get gloomy. He saw nothing that alarmed him. He shut the door, affixed the padlock and span the chambers to re-lock it. When he got into the Mercedes and drove off, he realised he was sweating.

By half past eight it was completely dark. Monster stretched and reached for his radio. *"Mark, Mark, Monster. Visibility is now zero. Time to pull me out."*

*

McBride had called in a couple of favours to get Cyclops at such short notice. It was an Escort van, plain white with twin windowless rear doors that almost, but not quite, met at the top. The gap was where the 16mm lens was sited. If you looked really closely you could see. But few people did. The infra-red video camera was attached to a standard video recorder. If you ran it at one eighth speed, that is at six frames per second instead of the usual fifty, a three-hour tape would last twenty-four hours.

"We'll change the tape every morning before it gets light and view the tape here," said McBride. "We've only got the van for a week so let's hope that the brigadier comes to fetch his money before then."

"If it's him. If he hasn't got it already."

"Oh, it's him! I'm sure it's him. I just can't work out what he's playing at."

TWENTY-SIX

Howard Spencer prided himself on his ability to find a well-crafted phrase and he was enjoying himself. Normally writing annual performance reports was a bit of a chore. Spencer didn't like to spend too much of his time considering what those below him in the pecking order were doing, much less how well or poorly they were doing it. But this was different. He was composing a masterpiece. A pen portrait of Frank McBride that blended a wistful acknowledgement of glories past set against a forensic dismantling of current performance. 'So sad that it has come to this', was the tone he was trying to find. An unwillingness to embrace new techniques. A failure to work productively alongside colleagues. A casual attitude towards the ever more stringent legal guidelines and policy requirements. A dinosaur unfit to cope with the modern world and unable to play a useful part in it. All wrapped up in a gossamer-thin veneer of affection and respect.

When he had finished Spencer was well pleased. Poor old Frank. One of the old school. Feted for past glories but just not up to it anymore. And it took someone with the perspicacity, and the courage, of Howard Spencer finally to say so. Although, in truth, we all knew it really, didn't we? So long, Frank! Well done, Howard!

The written report was only half the job, though. Spencer also had to have a face-to-face annual performance review. Spencer, who had been so proud of the written report he had crafted, was slightly less confident in his ability to deliver the stern messages that had appeared on the page in person. McBride could be an intimidating presence. There was something about the way that he listened that filled you with doubt. Spencer's plan had been to begin the interview by asking McBride how he thought had had performed and then disagree. He thought that it would be easier to downplay or undermine McBride's achievements than to cite examples of where he had fallen short. The fact was that Spencer had little idea what McBride did or how well he did it. To admit that, however, was to admit of a failing of his own and he certainly wasn't going to fall into that trap.

"So, Frank, what sort of a year do you think you've had?"

McBride removed the unlit pipe from his mouth and peered into the empty bowl. He appeared not dissatisfied with what he saw and replaced it in the other corner of his mouth.

"I understand that you are seconded to this intelligence working party for at least six weeks. Official instructions say that for any absence of over two weeks a temporary SIO should be appointed as cover. I think the team would very much like to learn who you will be nominating as your temporary replacement. And I know that some of us would be interested in learning why you have not put arrangements in place already, considering the delicate stage of Operation Bagration."

Spencer couldn't believe that his meeting had gone off the rails as quickly as this. He had intended it to be a sixty-minute dressing-down of McBride complete with a list of shortcomings and chastisements. Now he was scrambling to think of excuses not to promote the wretched man. He toyed with the idea of blurting out that he would temporarily promote Andi Woodhead, but he couldn't be sure that Andi would accept and he wasn't entirely sure whether his decision needed to be approved by Alan Hawkins, the

ACIO. Did he want to explain to Hawkins why he had overlooked McBride, who was the obvious choice? He had a horrible feeling that Hawkins and McBride may have been old friends, although neither had ever said as much.

In the end Spencer had chosen the path of least resistance. He had promoted McBride. And because that created a vacancy for a senior officer, he promoted Joe Lake too. In some ways this was an even more bitter pill. He had had high hopes of Lake, an educated man. He thought that he may have had the good sense and the political antennae to recognise where his best interests lay. Instead, he had thrown in his lot with this old dinosaur! Spencer had even heard a rumour that he had started smoking a pipe.

*

A hundred miles to the south another report was being written. The subject this time was Howard Spencer himself and instead of being a hand-crafted masterpiece it was a frank and brutal machine-produced document. It listed vanity, inattentiveness and conceit together with a poor grasp of theoretical concepts and the practical implications of policy choices. Normally these would have been a serious but not necessarily fatal blow. However, the final paragraph was like a bullet to the head. It was titled 'Security Awareness and Discretion' and it set out in detail the information that Spencer had shared with Phillipa in the Fenchurch Street wine bar together with the policies, guidelines and relevant sections of the Official Secrets Act and other less well-known pieces of legislation that it breached.

Howard Spencer would never work for the Intelligence Service. He would be lucky if his next posting was to the Ministry of Paperclips.

Phillipa did not sit back and admire her prose. She did not indulge herself in imagining how the document would be received or the consequences for the vain and conceited man who had robbed her of forty-five minutes of her life and forced her to drink a very mediocre Pouilly-Fumé. She pressed 'send' and moved directly to her next task.

*

McBride was sitting on the sofa while Maisie was explaining, in great detail and with great enthusiasm, the concept of Beanie Babies. Frankie Junior was making a spaceship, or possibly a dinosaur, out of Lego when Michelle came downstairs.

"How do I look?"

"You look beautiful, of course!"

"No, really, Dad, seriously, am I presentable?"

"You look lovely. Don't be so anxious."

"I know. It's silly. I'm like a giddy teenager."

McBride felt a momentary stab of guilt. He had missed Michelle's teenage years. He had no memory of her changing her clothes five times in the ten minutes before a date, or of unsuitable boyfriends. He had never found a used pregnancy test kit in the bathroom bin, or a pack of condoms in a coat pocket. He simply hadn't been there. He had only met Tony once before the wedding.

"What's so special about tonight? You've been seeing him for nearly a year."

"Exactly a year. A year today."

"And you like him, this Simon? You really like him?"

Michelle blushed.

"When can I expect an interview with this young man where he humbly seeks your hand?"

"Dad! The kids!"

McBride chuckled. The doorbell rang. Michelle checked her lipstick in the wall mirror and hurried towards the door.

"And this one, Granddad," Maisie presented a Beanie Baby for inspection, "I call this one Vladimir," she said with the solemnity that only six-year-olds can muster.

"Good girl, good girl."

McBride had promised Michelle that the children would be in bed by eight. He actually achieved this by half past nine, beating his previous record by fifteen minutes. When Michelle got home, he had been dozing in the armchair for over an hour.

"And so?"

"What?"

"And so?"

"You're not at work now, Dad, your interview techniques won't work on me, you know."

"That's alright. You're a grown woman. You don't have to tell your old dad everything."

"You are a nosey old git. Do you know that? A nosey old git! But a very sweet one, and so I'll tell you, even if somehow you seem to know already. Yes, Simon has asked me to move in with him."

"And the kids?"

"Yes, obviously and the kids."

"So, you won't need me – well, not as much."

Michelle leaned over and kissed him tenderly on the cheek.

"Oh, Dad!"

*

Maxi's arrest had given Pyke a bit of a fright. He had over fifty thousand pounds in cash in the bottom of his wardrobe. He couldn't afford to lose it and he couldn't trust anyone to look after it. After mulling it over he decided that the safest place for it was probably in Stanley Maas's safe. If he paid Maas fifty thousand then the money could sit there and he could obtain product, imported by Peter, at such time and in such quantities as he wanted. Also, the fewer trips that he made to Holland with cash the better. He was resigned to the fact that he would have to do this himself.

Maxi wouldn't, Gazza and Shane couldn't, and there was nobody else that he could trust with that sort of money.

This time he needed a better excuse for visiting Holland. PSV Eindhoven were playing Dynamo Kyiv on 17th September. That would have to do. He could buy a ticket from a tout and attend the game. He would have a ticket stub and perhaps a matchday programme to show Customs if he was stopped on the way back. Eindhoven didn't hold particularly fond memories for him. He hadn't been back since he had been arrested there a couple of years earlier, but it was less than an hour's drive from Tilburg. The timing and the location were ideal. His last consideration was how to conceal fifty thousand pounds mostly in five- and ten-pound notes. The obvious place was the spare wheel, but that hadn't worked out well for Gazza and Shane, so he settled on concealing the money within the headrests and the upholstery of the rear seats. He called Maas from the telephone box outside the Lincoln Imp and arranged to meet him on the evening of 16th September at the Superkruiken Bar.

Maas was in a much better mood than when they had last met. FC Willem II had won three of their last four games and the Superkruiken (now it made sense) were riding high in the Dutch league. His already broad smile widened further when Pyke handed over £50,000 and explained that his courier, 'Peter', would be in touch shortly to arrange the collection of a further twelve thousand tablets. Maas reached into a desk drawer and pulled out a business card. As before it was for Tricolore Cabs. "It is Ruud, again, but you ask for Sebastiaan and the number is different. Twenty-four hours' notice, as before, yes?"

Pyke agreed and pocketed the card.

"Now!" Maas finished his beer in a single gulp. "I have just acquired a new club that I think you will like very much. Very sexy girls, and since we are business partners, for you, there is no charge – we go now, yes?"

Pyke had enjoyed his evening at the Fancy Pants club and had enjoyed the match too. Kiev had won three one. He returned to Tilburg directly after the game, arriving around midnight, and was slightly disappointed to see that without Maas he had no VIP status at the Fancy Pants. But he enjoyed himself just the same. He set off for home late in the morning and reached Coquelles in time for the 2PM crossing.

He was stopped by Customs. This time he had a well-prepared story to tell. And it was ninety-nine per cent true. He had visited Tilburg to see an old friend. Attended the match. Spent a second night in Tilburg and then come home. No, he hadn't brought anything back, except this match programme, see? Oh, and a ticket stub, see? And a hotel receipt. He thought it all went pretty well.

In the inspection bay Monster was taking photographs of the headrests.

Pyke was back in Lincoln by a little after seven. A useful and enjoyable couple of days. And he hadn't needed Maxi, or Gazza and Shane, or anyone. His poodle advertisement would be in tomorrow's paper. All he had to do was wait for his next consignment to arrive and swiftly move it on to his customers. He was a one-man gang. Two or three days' work each month. Minimal risk and twenty or thirty thousand pounds' profit. More when he cut Gazza and Shane loose. Things were looking pretty good.

*

In the movies the gangster's children all grow up to be doctors and lawyers and politicians. The Godfather aspires to respectability for his offspring. Stanley Maas was not like that. He wanted Sebastiaan to be a gangster, to learn the family trade and one day take over the family business. Sebastiaan was happy enough with this plan.

At one time had had hoped that he would become a professional footballer, and for a while that seemed possible. Part of him wished that he could point to some major injury caused by a vicious tackle from a less talented peer from which he had never totally recovered. But it hadn't been like that. He simply wasn't quite good enough. Almost, but not quite. He had spent a year in Willem II's youth team, mostly as a substitute, and even before the coach took him aside one morning in May he knew. He was never going to play for the Superkruiken. He intended instead, one day, to own the club.

It was a good life. Even in a small town like Tilburg. He enjoyed the pleasures of being a rich man's son. He worked too. Or at least what was called work in the Maas family. And, from time to time, he would attend his father's office above the Superkruiken Bar for a personal seminar on business studies, as practised by the Maas family. It was on one of these occasions that his father and he were discussing Pyke.

"Johann is a nice boy," said his father, "but he is not premiership, not first division. He is a useful outlet for a few thousand tablets each month. He is a reliable payer, but he is not a reliable partner."

Sebastiaan nodded. There would be more to come.

"Our business is like all business. Revenue, costs, overheads, stock on hand, supply chain, routes to market, but with one other critical element."

"It's mostly illegal."

"Exactly, which carries an entirely different set of risks. Our suppliers, mostly, are not honest people. Our customers also. We do not have recourse to law to settle commercial disputes. But most critically of all, if we choose our partners unwisely, well, I am not anxious to see the inside of Bijlmerbajes again. And so, we must be selective, and cautious."

"And so, Johann, from England?"

"He is a risk. If I thought that he could open up more markets my attitude might be different. Or if I thought that he could achieve the standards of professionalism that we require. But he is sloppy. Uses the same phone too often. Employs very poor staff. He is a customer we do not need."

"But you took his money for another consignment."

"I did. I did. And for one reason only. I am intrigued by his associate, 'Pieter'. Tell me again about the handover last time."

And so Sebastiaan recounted the tail of the motorway services, the telephone call and the tale of the boar with the golden bristles.

"Pieter, I like. The next time I want to know who he is. Take as many people as you need. Don't frighten him off, but I want to know more about him. I think it is likely that we shall hear from him soon. Johann is not the type of man who can afford to bear the cashflow of having fifty thousand English in my safe for long."

TWENTY-SEVEN

The brigadier had risen early as usual and when Michael came downstairs; he was sitting at the kitchen table reading a simply enormous book by AJP Taylor.

"You said something about not doing the same thing twice?" The young man's tone was disapproving.

"Calculated risk, Mikey. Of course. If you've got a better idea. I'm willing to listen."

"You could just do nothing. Just stop."

"But then the mission would be incomplete. Loose ends. We would have achieved nothing."

"I thought this was just a bit of fun to indulge your desire for a little mischief."

"Oh no. Well, yes, it's mostly that, but not entirely. Anyway. We may be past that stage. Would you do me a little favour? Would you take this to the pillar box outside the pub and post this for me?" He indicated a small manilla envelope on the kitchen table. Michael noted that it was addressed to 'The Occupier', The Old Vicarage, Church Street, Leighton Parva. The old man doubtless had his reasons.

When he returned to the house less than five minutes later, he was agitated.

"Grandpa!"

"There's a van parked outside."

"Hmm?"

"A British Telecom van. The middle letter is a U!"

"Well, it would be, wouldn't it? I'm sure that BT buys all its vans centrally and probably registers them all centrally too. It is a national organisation, after all."

"Well, yes, but…"

"Hmm?"

"There's a copy of the *Evening Standard* on the dashboard."

"Hmm?"

"The *London Evening Standard*. How many Rutland BT engineers read the *London Evening Standard*?"

"Very good, yes, very good. You're definitely coming on, Mikey."

"But what do we do?"

"Do? We don't do anything, of course. Well, not until tomorrow. Then I want you to buy a copy of the *Newark Advertiser*."

*

Michael had been dozing. His grandfather must have been pleased with him because, as a treat, he had allowed him to win the pub quiz. They had built up a large lead in the early rounds and allowed the parish council team slowly to rein in that lead before scoring full marks in the last round to win by a couple of points. Michael was starting to enjoy the game within a game of winning or losing at will and in a manner of his own design. The old man was starting to influence him, and he couldn't quite decide if he was happy about that or not. And then it dawned on him. It didn't hit him like a lightning bolt. It dawned. A gradual gentle meniscus of light started to form at the edge of his brain, first red, then pink, then peach until slowly a crystal-clear bright light of understanding showed everything in perfect clarity.

"You old bastard! You fiendish, evil, manipulative swine!"

He almost skipped downstairs. He peeped through the window beside the front door. The British Telecom van was gone. He picked up the key to his grandfather's Rover (the Montegos were safely stored elsewhere).

"I'm going to buy the paper. Anything else you want?"

The best place to buy a copy of the *Newark Advertiser* is Newark. And the best thing to do having bought a copy is to have a full fry-up breakfast at the Jolly Boatman café on Albert Street. Michael was feeling pretty good. In a pointless act of self-discipline Michael resolved not to pick up the paper until he had finished his breakfast. The absurdity of this exercise struck him midway through, but he persevered until he had finished the 'bacon and eggs' portion and then, regarding this as a compromise that preserved honour whilst recognising common sense, he picked up the paper as he settled down to finish his tea and the two rounds of toast.

God but life in a small town was dull. Really, if this was an example of the most newsworthy and interesting things that had occurred in East Nottinghamshire in the past seven days why did they bother? The sports pages were similarly poor fare. There were pictures of broadly smiling septuagenarians clutching a crown green bowls trophy and speculation as to the likely impact on a new signing on Newark Town's chances in the Rymans League. Pages and pages of estate agents' advertisements, and finally, the classified ads. Near the bottom was the advertisement for poodles. Same number as before. Careless. Michael finished his tea and glanced out the window. There was a public telephone a few yards down the street. That would do.

*

Marcus had forgotten his briefcase. Or perhaps he hadn't needed it. Anyway, it was sitting beside the kitchen table. He was dropping the kids off at school and then going for a meeting at the Nottingham Forest training ground. The briefcase was just sitting there. The previous evening Andi had gone into the garage to fetch a screwdriver. The golf bag had just been sitting there too. Without thinking she had checked the ball compartment. It had been empty. And now the briefcase was just sitting there.

It was locked, but that wasn't a physical obstacle. It might have been a spiritual obstacle, a betrayal of trust, but... the golf balls. This wasn't merely snooping. This was following a reasonable basis of suspicion to a likely source of evidence. Part of her hated herself for thinking in professional investigator terms. Part of her wanted to just forget it and go to work. But she knew that she wouldn't be able to forget it. She hadn't forgotten the golf balls. She had barely slept. The pulled the briefcase towards her. Using a penlight she squinted at the gaps between the rotors, looking for the slight scored line on the barrel mechanism. In two minutes, it was unlocked.

Andi made a cup of tea. It went cold. Still, she hadn't opened the briefcase. She put the kettle on again. And then she opened it.

She was still reading three quarters of an hour later when Marcus came in through the back door.

"Babe! Did I leave my briefcase in here?"

*

Michael missed his Sierra. The Montego was a far inferior vehicle. He was rather looking forward to the day when he would consign it to the crusher. In the meantime, he was sitting in the queue to join the Channel Tunnel shuttle. The first time he had done this he hadn't been at all nervous. It had been exciting, and he hadn't fully appreciated the risks. He was a little better informed now, and perhaps slightly wiser. Also, he was haunted by all those 'one last job' films he had seen. But all this made him edgier and also more alert. It was like when a batsman's score reaches the nineties. The fear of failure outweighs the thrill of potential success. Michael knew that feeling and knew that he had to find a way of achieving a sensible balance between boldness and caution. He couldn't just scratch about until he missed a straight ball. He couldn't allow his wariness to morph into paranoia.

From Coquelles he took the A16 coast road and crossed the border into Belgium between Dunkirk and De Panne. He bypassed Ostend and Bruges and then halted at a motorway services near Maldegem a couple of miles from the Dutch border. Slowly he walked around the service area and twice around the car park. He noted the positions of the overhead lights and surveyed which parts could be seen from the entrance and the exit to the car park. Finally, he went to the fuel station and studied the angles there. Satisfied that he had seen and learned all that he needed, he went to the café and ordered a coffee. The café had a poor view of the car park. Ideal. He returned to the car and retrieved a mobile telephone from the glove box. He had fixed a sticker to the back marked with the number '2'. He switched it on and made a call.

TWENTY-EIGHT

Michael could have chosen anywhere in South Holland or North Belgium. But, possibly inspired by his desire to find a balance, he compromised and chose both. There was no real operational or security reason to choose Baarle Nassau. Since the creation of the single market and the Schengen agreement national borders on continental Europe didn't really mean anything. He just thought that it was an interesting place and wanted to see it.

Baarle Nassau is a small town in the Netherlands, except that it isn't. Within the Dutch town are twenty-two enclaves that are actually Belgium. And within those are eight that are actually Dutch. There are a couple of border posts that exist mostly so that tourists can have photographs taken standing beside them but for the most part one can wander from Belgium to the Netherlands and back again just by crossing the street. One of the enclaves is less than half the size of a football pitch. At one point the border runs through somebody's front door. The buildings in Belgium have their numbers written in black on a yellow background, the Dutch in white on a blue background. One place was as good as another so far as Michael was concerned and it seemed like fun.

He wandered around the town for an hour, childishly thrilling as he passed from one country to another. After an hour he had found the perfect spot. A café on the corner of Sint Annaplein and Burgemeester de Grauwstraat. From a nearby public telephone he called Ruud/Sebastiaan.

Michael's Dutch wasn't good enough to pass as a Dutchman but it was pretty close.

"Hello, Sebastiaan, it's Pieter."

"Hello, Pieter. Have you come to collect your parcel?"

"Yes. I am in Baarle Nassau. Can I meet you in the Green Butterfly café on Sint Annaplein at seven?"

"Sure, when you say meet—"

But Michael had already hung up.

*

At six o'clock Michael called Sebastiaan again.

"Are you using the same car as last time?"

"Yes."

"I want you to park in Klokkenstraat. Leave my parcel in the boot. Sit at a table on the terrace outside. Order a bottle of beer and a coffee. At seven fifteen get up to go to the rest room. Leave your car keys on the table. Understand?"

"I understand."

Michael hung up. Sebastiaan immediately called Tobias and Vincent. Tobias went immediately to Klokkenstraat to see the lay of the land. Vincent cruised the area looking for an English-registered car. He found it at about a quarter to seven in the car park at the top of Molenstraat, five minutes' walk from Klokkenstraat. It was a blue Austin Montego.

At a minute to seven Ruud sat down at a table outside the Green Butterfly. He ordered a coffee and a beer, and casually surveyed his surroundings. Pieter had chosen well. He might be any of the dozens of pedestrians milling around the town's central square. It was also starting to get dark. Sebastiaan was impressed, but not overly so. He had just received a text from Vincent informing him that the Montego had been found and was being watched. At seven fifteen he rose from his seat and, placing his keys on the little silver coloured box that dispensed paper napkins, he entered the café proper and went to the toilets. He didn't try to look around himself, or to linger where he might catch a glimpse of 'Pieter'. He didn't try to be 'smart' at all. He had people for that.

A minute later Michael walked past the table where he had seen Sebastiaan sitting. It took less than a second to pocket the keys. Two minutes later he was at the boot of Sebastiaan's car. A further minute later he was in Belgium walking down Klokkenstraat clutching a red sports bag. The keys were in the exhaust pipe. Michael wasn't trying to be smart either, but he couldn't help but notice Tobias loitering in the gloom near the entrance to the firework shop. He turned right into Kapelstraat and left into Molenstraat. By the time he reached his car it was starting to get dark. He threw the sports bag on the back seat. And set off south. He was back in the Netherlands for a hundred yards, then Belgium again, then the Netherlands again, for seventy yards this time. Within five minutes he had joined the N260 leading out of town towards Turnhout. Five minutes later the road became the N119. He was in Belgium proper. An hour later he was past Antwerp and heading for Bruges and the Channel ports. It was now dark, but Tobias and Victor had no difficulty keeping track of the Montego in their respective cars. They were still in contact when Michael pulled into a motorway services.

Michael had spotted the Opel Vectra and the Volkswagen almost as soon as he had left Baarle Nassau. For a while he thought that a Volvo might be following him too, but it had overtaken him and proved to be occupied by a young family. Just the two to worry about then. He drove into the services car park and completed a slow, very slow, loop before accelerating away and re-joining the motorway. The Dutch would be sure to think that he was looking for a tail. Fifteen minutes later he pulled off at the services he had visited earlier that day. Again, he performed a very slow lap of the car park. At the furthest and darkest point, and sure that neither the Vectra nor the VW could see him, he stopped. Giles pulled out in front of him in the other Montego, completed the second half of the lap at slow speed and then accelerated rapidly to re-join the motorway. Tobias and Vincent followed Giles. Michael parked, put the sports bag in the boot and went for what he considered to be a well-earned cup of coffee in the café upstairs.

The café was almost deserted. Aside from Michael there was an old couple leaving as he arrived and, in the far corner, a very attractive young woman in a business suit. There was something oddly familiar about her and yet Michael couldn't remember ever having met her before, and he was sure that he would have remembered. After five minutes the woman got up and left without giving Michael so much as a glance. Michael saw her again as she exited the services building below him and headed for the car park. A minute or two later he saw a dark Range Rover drive past the front of the building on the way to the exit. For some reason the Range Rover rang a faint bell, somewhere at the back of his mind, but try as he might, he couldn't bring the elusive memory forward.

*

Giles drove steadily. He reached Coquelles by eleven French time and was through the tunnel just after eleven English time. He headed for a hotel just off the M20 near Ashford. He parked in the easternmost part of the car park. He arrived just as the bar was closing so he had time for a drink. He ordered two. The first didn't take him very long. Only then did he casually look round the bar looking for Dutchmen. He didn't see any. They must be freezing their arses off in cars outside.

In fact, only Tobias was sitting in the hotel car park. Vincent had gone off to Ashford in search of supper. By the time he returned an hour later, slightly apologetic and clutching a lukewarm and mediocre kebab, Giles was tucked up in room 114 and fast asleep.

In the morning, Giles treated himself to a full English breakfast and a leisurely perusal of the others present in the hotel dining room. At ten o'clock, wearing a different coat, he turned left out of the main entrance towards the westernmost part of the car park where, at two minutes past ten, he hopped into a waiting black Range Rover.

"Late as usual!" said the driver.

At about noon the two Dutchmen who had been sitting in parked cars and shivering all night finally admitted to themselves that something had gone horribly wrong. At the same time Tobias started to wonder whether the blue Montego didn't have a different registration to the one that he had seen parked in Klokkenstraat.

*

The Menin Gate Memorial was unveiled in 1927 and since then at eight o'clock each evening the last post is sounded to commemorate those who lost their lives in and around Ypres. The memorial is to the nearly fifty-five thousand British and Commonwealth soldiers with no known grave. Their names are listed on the memorial itself. Two of the Taylor brothers' names are on the memorial: 9th Battalion, Leicestershire Regiment, 1917. A third brother lay in another cemetery a little west of the town. The fourth brother's name appeared on the Thiepval Memorial on the Somme battlefields fifty miles to the south. As was usual a small group was gathered to attend and observe the ceremony. Amongst them were forty-five who had made the trip with Battlefield Tours and a further thirty-six from the party organised by Great War Tours. Amongst the second group was an old man of military bearing who earlier in the day had spent some time alone at the memorial before visiting the war graves near Poperinge.

A little after the final notes of the last post died away the crowd began to disperse. The old man and his fellow travellers walked the short distance back to the Flanders Lodge Hotel. Unlike most of his fellow tourists the old man who had introduced himself simply as 'John' had travelled alone and had said little. The others mostly left him to his own devices.

Michael reached Ypres just as Giles was boarding the shuttle at Coquelles. He checked for CCTV cameras and, having satisfied himself that there were none, he opened the boot. He put the contents of the red sports bag into the turquoise wheelie bag and headed for the reception of the Flanders Lodge Hotel.

In his grandfather's room the old man seemed uncharacteristically anxious.

"Did you remember the receipts?"

"I did. One for coffee in Holland. Another for coffee in Belgium and one for fuel, also in Belgium. But why do you want them?"

His grandfather didn't answer' he just slipped them into the inside pocket of the wheelie bag.

"You said that the biggest mistake was to do the same thing twice in a row."

"I did. And it is."

"But isn't that exactly what we are doing?"

"Not exactly. Not exactly. For example, I don't want you going back to England. Go to Germany, anywhere will do. Only return when you hear from me. And then only if I use the words 'hunky dory', got it? And if anything goes wrong you call this number from a public telephone in Germany. In Germany, understand?"

He handed over a slip of paper with a German telephone number printed clearly upon it.

"No. I don't understand. This started out as risk-free fun and now you're behaving like you're going over the Berlin Wall again. Let's just dump the gear and go home."

"Are you losing your nerve, Mikey?"

"No. No, I'm not. I'll take the gear back myself if you want. I just don't want you getting into trouble."

"Listen, Mikey. I'm a war hero, a spook and a bloody Knight of the Realm. Nothing is going to happen to me that I can't handle. Now I want you to prove you can follow orders."

"Orders?"

"Yes, orders. Now what do you do?"

"Go to Germany. Wait for hunky dory. Call this number if anything goes wrong."

"Good lad. And don't worry."

"Okay, Grandpa."

"And one more thing. When you come back, see if you can't get me a couple of cases of Berliner Kindl, would you?"

*

Monster and Joe Lake had spent a frustrating morning at the offices of Newark and Sherwood District Council. It had been a relatively simple task to establish that the lock-up garage visited by Pyke was owned by the council, but the bureaucrat had steadfastly refused the name of the tenant who had recently rented it. He cited data protection considerations and client confidentiality, and finally, and this was the point where Lake had almost lost his temper, gave a brief lecture on the sacred bond of trust between the council and people who rented lock-up garages for eleven pounds a week. Lake sought to use his charm, then he begged, finally he threatened, but everything he tried seemed to make the bureaucrat more intransigent. Finally, Monster and he left, muttering darkly about court orders. Honestly! These people were impossible! When they reported back to McBride they were not expecting to be well received. Instead, McBride didn't seem the least bit concerned. In the past few days, he had been unusually quiet, almost introspective. It was not like him.

Andi was holding court in the dispersal room. Her story was being interrupted by gasps and giggles and eventually raucous laughter. Monster stuck his head around the door to learn what was causing all the merriment.

"And then, then I found his latest essay on the causes of the Spanish Civil War. He seemed to think it was mostly about Real Madrid and Barcelona!"

Monster looked puzzled. He met Andi's eye.

"My old man, the silly old sod! He's studying history at the Open University. He's been keeping it secret!" She could hardly speak from laughing, and relief, and the release from fear.

"He's been claiming he's away on boys' weekends and instead he's been in Milton Keynes attending lectures about the Corn Laws. He says he was ashamed of not being educated. Said he wanted to improve himself. The silly old sod."

Monster went red and withdrew.

*

McBride was at Michelle's again. He had managed to get his grandchildren to bed and was watching a documentary on the history channel. It was about his father. Or men just like his father, at least. He had never known the man. He hadn't returned from the war. McBride had been born a month later. McBride had been raised to believe that his father had died a hero fighting for a just and worthy cause. He still believed that.

When the programme paused for a commercial break, he flicked through the estate agent's details that Michelle had left on the coffee table. He was almost sure that she had intended for him to see them. Well, she hadn't put them in a safe and she knew what he was like, so that counted. Simon had been transferred to Corby. He and Michelle were looking for a home big enough for a family. The prices these days were shocking. McBride picked up the details of a nice-looking house that someone, Michelle presumably, had marked with an asterisk. He grunted when he saw the address. That would be ironic!

The advertisements during all these war documentaries were always the same. Invitations to buy gold, or commemorative plates, old newsreaders extolling the advantages of funeral plans or equity release. And coach companies offering tours of European battlefields. *Bloody hell!* thought McBride. *I wonder. I wonder!*

He reached for his phone. He had already dialled before he noticed the time.

"Joseph!"

"Hello, Frank. Do you need me to go somewhere?" He sounded tired.

"No, no, nothing like that. I need to ask you something. This cross-Channel database…"

"Oasis."

"Oasis. Does it show the names of all the passengers?"

"No, just lead passenger, sometimes with initials, sometimes without, and the car registration."

"Car registration or vehicle registration?"

"Vehicle."

"So, if a car had a passenger, we wouldn't have their name."

"That's correct."

"And if it was a bus, there could be fifty passengers whose names we don't know."

"Well, yes, but do you really think Pyke is travelling by bus?"

"No, of course not. But his courier might be. Do you know about the double-bag smuggle?"

"The one with one dirty bag and one clean one. You pick up the dirty one and if you're stopped you say, oops, silly me, that's my identical bag over there."

"That's the one. Any reason it couldn't work on, say, a coach party?"

"No reason at all."

"I want the names of anyone who travelled by coach to Europe in the last two months. And any booked to travel in the next two weeks."

"Who are we looking for?"

"The brigadier, of course. Pay particular attention to these tours that visit old battlefields."

*

Lake had made a special effort to get in to Scampton early. He had called an old friend based at Dover and obtained the last two months' passenger manifests. He waited until McBride had had his first cup of coffee (approaching him before that was like marching into a dragon's lair wearing a 'I hate lizards' T-shirt) and brought in his findings.

"Do you want the good news or the bad news?"

"Don't arse about."

"Well, I've found the brigadier. Made a trip with Battlesite Expeditions a few weeks back."

"Does that tie in with the time we left X-Ray Five unattended outside the station?"

"Yes, it does."

"That's good."

"But no trace on him on any car, bus or coach in the immediate future."

"Are there any trips to battlefields?"

"God, yeah, there are several every week."

"Keep checking then. Once a day. And one more thing. Get on to the tour company and ask them what the procedure is if someone forgets to take their suitcase off the bus."

Lake nodded and reached for his pipe. He turned and headed for the room next door.

*

McBride had arrived at Scampton wearing a tweed jacket over a check shirt. This represented a substantial departure from his usual sartorial style, which was a Marks and Spencer suit from the budget end of the range that had usually seen better days. In the introspective submarine-like atmosphere of Scampton this had provoked much comment and speculation. Lake was deputised to investigate.

When Lake entered the little office at the end of the corridor McBride was having one of his periodic pipe-cleaning sessions, indicating that he had a lot on his mind.

"Pyke has been promising his customers that he has a consignment arriving shortly."

"Meaning?"

"Well, meaning he might have a consignment coming, or he thinks he is, or he hopes he is. Or he is afraid that unless he tells his customers he has a consignment coming soon they will take their business elsewhere."

"And so, what do we do?"

"What we're doing now. Keep the camera van in on the lock-up. Follow Pyke wherever he goes. Observe everything he does. And I think we need to keep a closer eye on the old vicarage."

"Tricky! It's not exactly the place you can hang around."

"I want to know if the brigadier, who must be 'Peter', moves. Put an eggshell under the front wheel of his car or something. Drive by in the evening. See if the lights are on. Look for a note for the milkman."

"They probably bring a cow door to door out there."

"It's Rutland, not Lilliput. Put Monster on it. He lives nearest."

Lake turned to leave before remembering his mission.

"New jacket?"

McBride put down his pipe and tools. He looked Lake squarely in the face. "Aye," he said in a tone that suggested that further discussion on this topic was not welcome.

Lake bravely pressed on. "Suits you."

McBride sighed and appeared to have a little inward debate. After a few seconds his face wore his 'I have decided' expression.

"I think I told you once. My father died before I was born."

Lake was nonplussed. "Yes, you said, in the war."

"Aye, but I never said which war, did I?"

McBride sometimes made cryptic remarks for the sheer mischief of it. And sometimes he did it as a test. And sometimes he did it because he wanted to impart information without actually having to articulate it himself. Why did the man have to be so bloody oblique? What couldn't he just say what he meant?

Lake wasn't sure into which category the 'which war' remark might have fallen until he remembered the mug. He made a phone call to the office with an excuse about needing the information for some official purpose. It took the administration staff a few minutes to find it, but when they did it confirmed Lake's suspicions.

"Frank?"

"Yes?"

"Were you going to tell anybody or were you just planning to disappear one day and not come back?"

"You're supposed to be a team of investigators. I shouldn't have to tell you anything."

"But you are going to retire? On your sixtieth birthday? In a few weeks?"

"Aye."

"So, this is one last job?"

"Aye."

"And who is going to run Operation Bagration when you are off tending to your begonias or whatever?"

"The man I've been training, of course."

Lake grinned. "And your father?"

"International Brigade. Died defending Brunete. It's near Madrid."

TWENTY-NINE

Michael had spent an enjoyable term studying at the University of Bonn, and so, lacking any other ideas, that is where he headed. The city had not been Germany's capital for seven years and the process of decanting government functions, offices and staff was still ongoing. It was nevertheless returning to being the quiet university town it had once been. Michael booked into a small hotel near the city centre and decided to indulge himself in a little student nostalgia. And to wait.

The sensible thing would have been to avoid the old student haunts even though the chances of him being recognised were small. In fact, the sensible thing would have been to avoid Bonn altogether. If he had he would not have been spotted by the blonde girl with the brown eyes.

Her name was Luise and she was studying political science. She was from Cologne but had chosen to study in Bonn partly because Konrad Adenauer had been a hero of her father's. Michael explained that he had been a student in Bonn some years before and had returned, on impulse, to visit some of his old haunts. She complimented him on his German (which was excellent). He complimented her on her English (which was merely proficient).

When it was obvious that the bar would soon be closing Michael realised that he didn't want the evening to end there. He wasn't very good at reading the signs, but he thought that Luise felt the same way.

As they walked through the narrow streets of the old town back towards Luise's apartment, she told Michael all about her plans for the future. To her father's exasperation and disappointment, she was a committed member of the Green Party and a passionate advocate for the decriminalisation of cannabis. When she had reached the end of her five-minute monologue on this subject, she asked Michael for his views.

Michael wasn't exactly drunk. He had four or possibly five beers. Actually, it might have been six, but he sobered up suddenly. He had no illusions as to his attractiveness. He did not possess film-star good looks. Teenage years spent at an all-male boarding school had not imbued him with charm or confidence where the female of the species was concerned. And yet, here was a simply beautiful young woman whom he had met only hours earlier holding his hand and gazing into his eyes with a level of devotion that he could not possibly have inspired in so short a time.

Was this a… what were they called – a honey trap? How could it be? Nobody knew he was here. Unless they had followed him. Maybe they had. After he had dropped off the merchandise with his grandfather in Ypres, he hadn't been looking for a tail. But who? Who would have followed him? And why? To set up a honey trap? Luise? Was it possible? They had reached the door to her apartment building. He looked down at her angel-like face.

Michael kissed her. He kissed her lightly, on the cheek. He mumbled something about having to make an early start and made his way back to his hotel alone.

*

Donna was worried but not as worried as Pyke.

"What do you mean they've offered him a deal?"

"They say that if he provides them with useful information they will drop the handling stolen goods charges and he won't have to go to prison."

"He won't have to go to prison anyway. A few car radios? And he's clean. He's never even been nicked before. They're bluffing."

"But he's frightened, John, you know what he's like. He wouldn't last five minutes in prison."

"He's not going to prison. No chance! They're bluffing. He should tell them to get lost. Did he? Did he tell them to get lost?"

"He said he's thinking about it. I don't want him to go to prison. How much harm could he really do you anyway? You told me you never got him involved in… in whatever it is that you do."

"Don't you start. You know exactly what I do. And this is your house. It's not just me he could harm. I'll have to speak to him."

"And you can give him some money too. You gave all that money to Leanne and Diane and all they've done is spend it on themselves and go around town slagging you off."

"They what?"

"Slagging you off. Saying that Shane and Gazza are going to do ten years because of you, and you tried to buy them off."

Pyke felt the beginnings of a headache coming on. Leanne and Diane shooting their mouths off. Maxi considering becoming a grass. Customers pestering him for more product, and he didn't know where it was coming from. He was entirely at the mercy of 'Peter', whoever he was, or they were. Almost all his money was tied up in a consignment that might be intercepted or seized. A life of crime was a lot more difficult and a lot less fun that he had imagined. And was a net closing in on him?

*

Pyke was still worrying about all these things the following morning when Diane and Leanne arrived. He wasn't expecting great news, but what they had to say truly shocked him.

"Fifty grand?"

"Each."

"Fifty grand each. You're insane! Where the hell do you think I would get that sort of money?"

"That's your problem, John Pyke. It's fifty grand each or Gazza and Shane tell them everything they know." Leanne was being utterly impossible.

"You must be out of your minds. Firstly, I don't have a hundred grand. Secondly, what do you think would happen to Gazza and Shane if the whole nick knew they were grasses?"

"They won't go to nick. If they give you up, they'll be let off."

"Who told you that? You're crazy. They were caught red-handed. Nobody is going to let them off."

"Well, we'll just have to see, won't we?" She folded her arms.

"Look, next week I can let you have ten grand, but that's it. That's all I have, and I don't even have that yet."

"Each?"

"No, not each. Ten grand. That is all I have."

"Ten grand each, next Friday, or we tell them everything."

Pyke was pretty sure he could have them killed for less than that.

*

The brigadier packed the second turquoise wheelie bag with clothes he expected never to see again. He was at the coach ten minutes early, able to ensure that it was loaded first and therefore pushed to the very back of the luggage compartment. Fifteen minutes later he was back with the bag full of drugs, which was loaded almost last and therefore amongst the most accessible pieces of luggage. He took his seat towards the rear of the bus and opened his book. He had said almost nothing to his fellow tourists for three days and he didn't expect any of them to seek to engage him in conversation now.

Despite his confident words to Michael, he was starting to feel a little apprehensive. Doing almost exactly the same thing twice *was* risky. If Customs were able to establish that he had 'accidentally' left his bag on a bus twice, that coincidence might be a little too much for a jury to believe. However, there were several obstacles for them to overcome. The first was proving that 'he' was 'he'. He regretted having travelled under his own name on the trip to Waterloo, but there had not been time to make alternative arrangements. Now he was John Burriss. They could scroll through passenger manifests as much as they like, and they would not find him. John Burriss had died as an infant in 1921 and his passport would be consigned to the flames as soon as he reached home. There would still be a photograph on file, of course, but it was an old one. It resembled him closely enough to pass muster at immigration, but it was not a sufficiently close resemblance to represent proof beyond reasonable doubt.

The trouble with pretending to sleep on a coach is that coach seats are a lot more comfortable than they used to be. And if you are seventy-six years old it's all too easy for pretending to doze to become actually dozing. The brigadier didn't wake until the coach had reached Maidstone and the first few tourists were getting off. He had, he assumed, sailed through Customs whilst sound asleep. On the positive side that was one hurdle successfully cleared. On the other hand, he didn't know whether the coach had been stopped. Was it possible that Customs had examined the baggage compartment and found the drugs? And if they had, did they leave it there as bait in a trap? Was there a surveillance team even now tailing the coach and waiting for someone, for him, to pick up the 'dirty bag'?

He silently cursed himself. He was too old for this game, after all. It had been sheer hubris to imagine that he could come out of retirement and beat the system. Unless, of course, he had. It was possible, likely, highly likely, that the coach had sailed through the controls at Cheriton, and he had nothing to worry about.

The next stop was Cambridge. Only two tourists alighted here, but the coach halted for a few minutes to allow the passengers, many of whom were as old as the brigadier, to use the lavatories. The brigadier took advantage of the opportunity to stretch his legs and to look for a tail. So far as he could tell there were no surveillance vehicles in any of the obvious places. That didn't mean anything. They may have had an opportunity to fix a tracker to the coach, maybe even inside the dirty bag itself. The important thing was not to panic. The important thing was not to do anything unnatural. Don't give in to the temptation to look in the bag. Bring it home like a normal person would. Maybe leave it in the front hall for an hour or two. Then open it. "Imagine my shock, Officer, when I realised that not only had I picked up the wrong bag, but when I saw the contents!"

The coach reached Peterborough at ten minutes to five. The brigadier and three other passengers disembarked and walked to the nearside of the coach, where Steve the driver was opening the luggage compartment. The brigadier picked up the turquoise bag and walked away, resisting the urge to look about. The young man hurried towards him and relieved him of the bag.

"We're just parked over here. It's the black one. You sit in the front. I'll watch behind."

*

Back at the old vicarage the brigadier set out his plans for the final stages. Giles looked nervous.

"If you don't want to go through with it, Giles, I will understand entirely."

Giles glanced at the third person present and was treated to an expression of utter scorn. It was not the first time he had seen it.

"No. I said that I would do it. And I will do it." He returned the scornful look with one of defiance. He was sorely tempted to stick his tongue out.

Over tea and crumpets in the drawing room of the old vicarage in Leighton Parva three people made the final arrangements that, if produced in evidence, could have led to them all facing life sentences. When they had gone over every detail, twice, and were as certain as they could be that the plan was fool-proof, the brigadier handed Giles a mobile telephone.

"Remember, short and sweet."

Giles sat up straight and cleared his throat. "Hello, John, it's Peter."

Pyke was caught off guard. This was a third Peter. Young, definitely posh this time.

"Yes."

"Your parcel has arrived. I should be able to deliver it tomorrow. Shall we say the Magna Carta, at 4PM?"

*

Giles loaded the five polythene-wrapped parcels into the carrier bag. He was wearing rubber gloves, but Pyke hadn't been when he had placed the money in it a couple of weeks earlier. The carrier bag went into the orange rucksack and so too did the coffee receipts and the petrol receipt. The brigadier shook Giles' hand. The solemnity of the moment was rather undermined by the fact that Giles was still wearing the rubber gloves.

It took Giles forty minutes to reach Newark. He parked on the other side of the playing field and made his way across it. The chances of anyone seeing him at midnight were almost zero, but just in case the orange rucksack was covered in a black bin liner. Making sure that he was never in view of the camera van he made his way to garage number fourteen. He unlocked the door – it was an up-and-over door opened with a key, not a roller door affixed with a padlock – opened it and stepped inside. Only then did he turn on his torch. He removed the bin liner, folded it neatly and put it in his pocket. A task that was more difficult than he expected in rubber gloves. Finally, he went to the back of the garage, where it backed on to number seven and crawled through the hole that Michael and he had made earlier. He placed the orange rucksack in the exact centre of the floor and then crawled back into garage number fourteen. He turned off his torch. Opened the door and stepped outside. He paused and listened. Nothing. He closed the door, locked it and then set off across the playing fields the way he had come. By 1AM he was back in Leighton Parva.

*

Back at the old vicarage the brigadier had been persuaded. No, that wasn't right. The brigadier had accepted that he could not refuse the request that had been made of him. Logically the reasoning that lay behind it was impeccable. But he didn't like it. Was he getting soft in his old age? Or was he just not as professional and ruthless as he used to be? He thought of all the cruel tricks that he had been forced to play for decades. The promises broken, the promises made knowing that they would be broken. But this was different. He did it anyway.

"Hello, Mikey... Yes, it's your grandpa... Did you find any Berliner Kindl? Excellent. Thank you so much... I'm looking forward to seeing you... Yes, everything's hunky dory... That's what I said, hunky dory... See you soon."

*

Michelle waited as her father perused the estate agent's details. It was four pages long. When he had finished, he went back to the beginning and read them again.

"Well," she said, "what do you think?"

"A barn! You want me to live in a barn?"

"It's a barn conversion, Dad. They're very popular these days. And it's very nice. Look. All on one floor. Modern kitchen, living room and a little study for you to… you know?"

"Study? You think I'm going to study?"

"Well, I don't know, do the crossword, write your memoirs – you're always saying you've never had time for a hobby."

"If you say stamp-collecting…"

"Look, Dad, it's perfect. You know, for when you're a little older."

"A decrepit cripple, you mean?"

Michelle wasn't going to fall into that trap. She pressed on. "And we'll be right next door. And we can pop over. And you can see the kids anytime you like."

"And babysit them while you and Simon are out gallivanting, I suppose."

"The last time we were out gallivanting you were mortified at the prospect that we wouldn't need you anymore."

This was true. McBride was arguing for the sake of arguing. The fact was, he was feeling a bit odd about his impending retirement. Michelle was right, curse her! The arrangement was perfect. They would have a lovely old farmhouse with a big garden for the children. He would be forty yards away in the old barn.

"Well, is there at least a pub?"

"Yes, Dad. It's called the Old Volunteer. It's very nice."

"Don't you dare say pensioners' specials."

"You'd have room for a dog. You always wanted a dog."

In fact, the thought had already occurred to McBride. He had already chosen a name, Laika. But Michelle didn't need to know that just yet.

*

It was late, but McBride couldn't sleep. He was at home browsing through a copy of *The Complete Golden Retriever Handbook* when his mobile telephone rang.

"McBride."

"This is Jack Norton from the Other Office. I'm on the night shift."

"Hello, Jack."

"It's on, tomorrow. Unknown male. Posh. Mean anything?"

"Nope."

"Magna Carta at sixteen hundred."

"That's likely the telephone kiosk just outside. Do we have it?"

"You know we never tell operational teams that sort of detail."

"This is me you're talking to."

There was a long pause. This was Frank McBride, after all. "If you were still working here, would you have it?"

"Of course I bloody would!"

"Well then."

"Who's on the early shift?"

"Sid Baker."

"Okay, good, thanks, Jack."

McBride hung up. He glanced at his watch – almost midnight. He rang the paging service.

"BAGRATION. POSSIBLE KNOCK TOMORROW THURS. MEET RAFS 0800."

Howard Spencer was not included on the circulation list.

THIRTY

The team were tense, and excited, and nervous, and about a thousand other things. Lake was musing on the fact that whilst this was a big day RAF Scampton had had more important briefings for more important missions. Nevertheless, this felt special.

McBride was usually oblique about the intelligence received from the Other Office but on this occasion, he prioritised clarity of message over etiquette and discretion.

"We think Peter, Tango Thirty, or one of his associates in the smuggling organisation, will be making a delivery today. And circumstances being what they are it is highly likely that Pyke will have to go 'hands-on' himself. If he does, we knock it."

The assembled nodded.

"First point of contact is going to be the Magna Carta. Probably around four o'clock. That might mean the boozer itself, it might mean the telephone kiosk outside, it might mean the cathedral, or it might just be the starting point for a paperchase. We are going to need to be sharp and I have to be kept up to date on every development. Andi, you are in command on the ground. Joseph, you are my conduit for information. If you think that Pyke, or anyone else, has spotted us you tell me. Immediately.

The decision on calling the knock is mine, although I may delegate as circumstances dictate. Finally. If we are sure, I mean sure, really, really sure, that Pyke has his hands on the gear anyone can call the knock. Is that all clear?"

Some nodded. Some swallowed nervously. Monster actually licked his lips. But nobody said a word.

"Right. I want a van in on the lock-up. Take the camera van out, but I want a video in the obs van. Monster, that's you. One car as minder. That's you, Nick. Gerry, get down to the cathedral. Look in every hymn book and look under every notice you can find, and don't forget to look on the back. Look at the litter bins too. Mark, check out that golf club. Same deal. When you've done that, I want the pair of you in the cathedral area. Everyone else plot up on Gold Five from two o'clock. I'll call the lift-off from here. Questions?"

There were none.

"Right, cars fully fuelled, cuffs, sledgehammers, exhibit bags and labels, and get some pies and sandwiches. It might be a long day. If anything goes wrong, you know where Lincoln Hospital is. Now make sure everything is charged up and ready. I want you all in position by two but ready to go at a moment's notice from, well, now. Gerry, Mark, as soon as you're ready, go! Joseph, a quick word…"

The team got to their feet and began checking radios, batteries, phones and, in Monster's case, chocolate. Lake followed McBride into his little den.

"Shut the door. Listen, Joseph. If Andi is hesitating, if she seems to be dithering or losing her nerve and if you think we need to knock it then you call it. Call it as 'from Control'. I'll back you up."

Lake nodded. The responsibility hit him in the gut just as the excitement was coming the other way.

*

Pyke didn't intend to have possession of the merchandise for one second longer than necessary. He spent the morning on the phone to his customers making arrangements to deliver his product as soon as possible. At half past three he left the house.

"*All mobiles from Control. Tango Five is from Gold Five. Commander, acknowledge.*" McBride's voice was as calm and measured as if he was announcing an impending raffle over the tannoy of a village fete. It always took him like this. The more tense the situation, or the more urgent, the more he sounded like a slightly bored newsreader on regional television.

"*Andi, acknowledge.*"

"*Tango Five is now in X-Ray Five. He's manoeuvring, manoeuvring.*" He sounded like the station announcer on a heritage steam railway now. "*X-Ray Five is mobile, mobile, south, out of my sight.*"

"*Andi, acknowledge.*" Andi sounded like a five-year-old who had just learned there was ice cream on the vintage steam train.

Pyke drove the mile or so into the city centre and parked, as usual, in the Westgate car park. He didn't notice the Nissan Primera parked outside the Castle Hotel.

"*From Steve, X-Ray Five past our position into Westgate Car Park.*"

Pyke looked at his watch. He had plenty of time. It would only take three or four minutes to walk to the Magna Carta. He stepped out of his car and looking around lit a cigarette. Maas would have known what he was looking for; Pyke didn't. He saw nothing.

"*From Steve. X-Ray Five parked at Westgate. Tango Five is out of the car. Tango Five on foot heading east towards Bailgate.*"

*

Mark had reported that he could find no trace of any note, message or clue at the golf club. Gerry could find nothing at the cathedral. McBride told Mark to take up a position on the south-west outskirts of Lincoln. He didn't really know why. Was it guesswork? Instinct? Or something within the subconscious vault of twenty-five years' experience? He didn't know.

"*Tango Five headed down Bailgate, towards the Magna Carta.*"

"*Yeah, Joe has eyeball... past my position, past the White Hart, towards you, Gill.*"

"*I've got him. He's into the square... wait.*"

Pyke had dawdled and looked in shop windows for a tail. He had seen someone do that in a film once. He didn't reach the Magna Carta until four.

"*Tango Five receiving a call... no... belay that. Tango Five receiving a text. Receiving a text. He's done a snake, it's a snake, back towards you, Nick.*"

"*I've got him. Seems to be hurrying. North up Bailgate.*"

"*Joe has eyeball. North Bailgate. Everyone else, back to your cars.*"

It was the limit of range, but McBride could just receive the transmissions. The Other Office phone rang. He listened for thirty seconds.

"Are you one hundred per cent sure?" McBride reached for the radio. "*All cars from Control. He's heading for the lock-up in Newark. The lock-up in Newark.*"

Pyke reached his car. And looked about. He was clear. He hopped in, turned the ignition and engaged reverse.

"*From Control. Let him go, repeat, let him go. Everyone to Newark now!*"

The order had come a few seconds too late. Two cars and the motorcycle got out of the city ahead of Pyke. Joe and Carl's cars were forced to follow him. Thus, as the convoy made its way down the A46 there were two cars and a motorcycle ahead of Pyke and two cars behind him.

Meanwhile Monster was in the observation van in Newark with Nick nearby in the Renault Laguna.

Pyke was looking for a tail but since most of it was in front of him, he didn't see it. He drove steadily and after taking a wrong turn once quickly realised his error and was back on track, pulling into Birch Close at a little before five. He stopped outside garage number seven and paused.

"*From Monster. X-Ray Five on the plot. He's stopped outside the garage. Wait.*"

A few feet away were ten thousand tablets that he could sell for fifty thousand pounds. He could deliver them all today and have almost all that money by midnight. Nearly fifty thousand pounds was enough just to get in his car and go. He could get out of this life, this city. Everything. He could forget about Gazza and Shane and Leanne and Diane. He could just go.

If it had been twenty-four hours earlier, he may have done exactly that. Today it wasn't an option. Donna was pregnant. This time he was going to do a proper job of being a father. Provide for his family in a way his father had never done. Be a man. He couldn't just flee.

But being a father, a family man, carried other responsibilities as well. The main one:being staying out of prison. He looked at the text he had received less than an hour earlier.

SAME GARAGE. SAME COMBINATION.

This was not ideal. He was a few feet away from fifty thousand pounds, but he was also a few feet away from ten years or more in prison. He didn't like the look of that van. Had it been here last time? He couldn't remember. What would Maas do? Well, he wouldn't be here for a start. He would some other sucker to actually go and get his hands dirty. Pyke didn't have anyone else. He got out of the car and looked around.

"*Monster, what's going on?*" Andi was anxious.

"*Wait.*"

Perhaps he could come back after dark. But what good would that do? If the garage was being watched those watching would hardly go home for tea at five o'clock. Anyway, why would anyone be watching? Peter, or the Peter organisation at any rate, was good. All this obsessive security. Being bounced around the city. Phone boxes, messages on graves, in hymn books; they made Maas look like an amateur. They were hardly likely to have made a mistake.

"*From Monster, wait.*"

There were two cars at the entrance of Birch Close, plus the motorcycle. Carl and Joe had parked in a parallel street. Joe had made his way on foot to the playing fields.

"*From Monster, wait.*"

Lake called McBride. "Frank, it's Joe. He's at the garage. Parked outside. Hasn't gone in yet."

"*From Monster, Tango Five towards the garage. He's kneeling. Wait.*"

The two cars at the bottom of Birch Close started to creep forward. Gill and Steve had handcuffs in their hands.

"*...padlock... wait... doors open.*"

Andi was sweating. The radio transmitter was slippery in her hand. Lake crept as near as he dared.

"*From Monster, garage doors open, wait, garage appears to be empty, wait, Tango Five into garage, wait.*"

Eleven investigators held their breath.

"*He's got a bag, an orange rucksack.*"

Andi's words were part scream, part war cry.

"*Knock, knock, knock, knock, knock, knock!*"

THIRTY-ONE

Michael had crossed the border at Aachen and was by passing Liege when he decided that he ought to stop for lunch. He found a suitable motorway services and took advantage of the opportunity to remove any item that might be the least bit incriminating. It all went in the car park waste bin. His mobile phones went into the Gent-Brugge canal just outside Bruges. By the time he reached Coquelles he was as satisfied as he could be that he was clean. He spent the journey inventing and memorising an account of his, largely fictitious time in Europe. It was not because he expected to have to use it but because it represented one last part of his adventure before he had to take up the burden of a career in law.

*

Vince did not think of himself as a bitter man but, as in so much of his self-evaluation, he was badly wrong. He was standing in the green channel at Dover docks exactly as he had every working day for six years. And he was bitter about it. Vince considered himself a cut above the average Customs officer. He considered himself more highly qualified than most, which, viewed from a certain perspective, he was. He considered himself more intelligent than most, and perhaps he was, marginally. But Vince's annual performance reviews had not matched his self-estimation. No manager had ever suggested that he be promoted or even that one day in the future he ought to be. Vince considered this unjust and plain wrong, but that was not the chief cause of his bitterness. Not generally, and certainly not today.

Today Vince had arrived on shift to find a thin, a depressingly thin, manilla envelope in his pigeonhole. As he picked it up, he knew that it contained bad news. The 'good news envelopes' were large, bulkier and full of necessary information. The rejections were more austere. This was the third that Vince had received, and he promised himself that he would not be applying for selection as a specialist investigator when the annual exercise was announced again next year. Vince was convinced that he would be an excellent investigator. And he was similarly convinced that many of the investigators based in Dover or those who regularly arrived, unannounced, urgent and full of themselves, from London were less capable than he. So today, he admitted he was bitter. He just wasn't ready to the face the reality that today was not exceptional.

One of the local investigators had breezed in, confident, assured and patronising, and asked him to pull a blue Montego and question the passenger. No explanation. Arrogant sod. And worse still, he had been given a set of questions that he was to ask that made no sense. He was supposed to put all sort of propositions to this passenger, and he had no idea whether any of them were true. And the final indignity, some woman, presumably another investigator, was going to sit quietly in the corner while he went through this routine like a trained parrot. Her name, he had been told, was Philippa, and she barely looked at him, let alone said anything.

He glanced again at the manifest. He should be on this ferry, Michael Butcher, blue Montego, D826 XFF.

"If you wouldn't mind stepping this way, sir. Shouldn't take too long. No, leave the keys in the ignition."

It wasn't a cell. It would be stretching it a bit even to describe it as an interview room. There was no tape-recording machine, or any microphones, at least none that he could see. As far as Michael could tell it was just a room a few feet from the green channel. There was a desk and a couple of chairs. The officer invited him to be seated. He did as he was bid while deciding how he would play this. He decided, almost immediately, on playing it as a breezy idiot who was doing his best to be co-operative. *But try not to sound like Bertie Wooster*, he kept saying to himself. *And try not to sound like Giles. That was almost as bad.*

"Just a moment, er…"

"Michael. Michael Butcher."

"Just a moment, Mr Butcher, one of my colleagues will be joining us."

This didn't alarm Michael; he assumed that even these very informal interviews (he hadn't been cautioned) were usually a two-man affair. In fact, the officer's colleague was a woman. And unlike him she was not clad in blue serge with a double row of gold-coloured buttons. She was wearing a very smart business suit. Possibly expensive, but Michael didn't really know very much about such things.

It was the woman from the services in Belgium. Again, he felt a powerful sense of familiarity. Again, he couldn't remember ever meeting her. But he was sure she had been in the café the day he had given the Dutchmen the slip. Was she part of a surveillance team? Had he been followed to Ypres? Where was his grandfather? What had happened?

The woman examined a slightly dirty tubular steel chair in the corner of the room and decided that, lacking better alternatives, it would have to serve. She sat and studied Michael with what seemed to him to be a relatively low level of interest. The uniformed officer removed two sheets of paper from his breast pocket and began asking questions in a tone somewhere between bored check-in assistant and speak your weight machine.

Michael slipped into his useful idiot persona. Yes, he had been on the continent for a few days. He was visiting friends in Bonn. He had studied there and kept in touch with a few people. It was a short holiday before commencing his studies in law. He hadn't had a holiday earlier because he had injured his hand playing cricket. Did the officer play at all? Pity. Not too late to take it up. His uncle was still playing every week and he was fifty-four. The car had been a gift from his uncle. It was typical that he hadn't got around to registering him as the new keeper. No, he had driven directly to and from Bonn. Had he made any other trips to Europe earlier in the year? Well, yes. He had attended a stag weekend in Amsterdam with some friends. He preferred not to name them because it had been a pretty wild affair and some of the party had been well known. Or, at least, the sons of people who were well known. Yes, university friends. Yes, Cambridge. Look, I'd really rather not say.

Occasionally Michael would risk a glance at the woman sitting in the corner. Her interest level didn't seem to have risen much.

Did he know a man named Giles Templeton?

Why, yes, of course. Giles was a friend from university. No, he hadn't been on the stag weekend.

Did he know that Giles had been arrested that day in Lincoln in possession of a large quantity of illegal drugs?

No. That couldn't be right. Old Giles? Why, he never even smoked. Quite impossible!

Many drug smugglers weren't drug users, said the officer solemnly, or slightly pompously, depending on your point of view.

Giles! No, absolutely not. You must have the wrong man. Giles would never do anything like that.

Perhaps – in spite of himself Vince was beginning to enjoy himself – Mr Butcher would care to comment on the startling coincidence that Mr Templeton had been driving a blue Montego.

Well, Michael just openly laughed at that. Giles? In a ten-year-old Montego? No, this was clearly a different Giles Templeton. His friend Giles wouldn't be seen dead in a piece of junk like that.

Would Michael like to amend or clarify any of the answers he had given earlier? No, why on earth should he? Because – Vince couldn't help but to stray into the dramatic here – he had been seen in the town of Baarle Nassau on the Dutch-Belgian border.

Never heard of the place.

Seen in the company of known Dutch criminals.

Preposterous!

Perhaps he'd like to comment on the fact that Giles Templeton had confessed to being part of a drug-smuggling operation masterminded by Mr Michael Butcher?

Michael laughed.

And further Mr Templeton had alleged, according to Vincent, that he had been tricked into participating. That Michael Butcher had taken advantage of their friendship and his naivety.

Michael laughed again. "Look I have no idea what Giles, if it is Giles, which I doubt, has got himself into, but I can assure you that I am not the mastermind of a drug-smuggling ring and that I have never been to Baarle Nassau."

Vince turned and looked at the woman in the corner. She gave the tiniest shake of her head.

"Just wait there a moment, would you?" said the uniformed officer; he rose and the woman followed him out.

The moment turned out to be fifteen minutes. When the officer returned, he handed Michael his car keys and said, "Thank you for your time."

And that was it. He was free to go.

*

"Just because a knock has been called it doesn't mean that you have to go charging in like Custer with his arse on fire."

This message, or some version of it, had been delivered to every single Customs investigator on his or her basic training course. And in the right circumstances every single one would have agreed that it was correct and wise. Unfortunately, the right circumstances are not those where someone has screamed the knock into a microphone. They are not those where a team has spent months either sitting in parked cars or mooching about in a disused bomber station arguing about whose turn it was to buy the toilet rolls, and they are certainly not those when the opportunity to be the arresting officer for the principal target is up for grabs.

Engines screamed and wheels span as cars raced towards the row of lock-up garages. Pyke heard them coming before he saw them. His first reaction was to turn right, away from the cars that were fishtailing around the corner and towards the playing fields. But Lake was running towards him from that direction. Instead, he ran back into the garage, threw the rucksack through the small hole at the base of the wall and crawled after it.

Steve was first into the garage behind Pyke, Lake slightly behind him. Pyke tugged at the mechanism of the up-and-over door of garage number fourteen. It opened and he was through it. A car was arriving to his right. In front of him were the fences of the rear gardens of the houses beyond. He turned left towards the playing fields, mentally cursing the takeaways, the cigarettes and the gym sessions missed. He glanced over his shoulder; Steve was ten yards behind him and closing in. He couldn't possibly outrun him carrying the rucksack. He threw it high to his right over the garden fence, found another gear and sprinted for the playing fields.

Lake might have been able to catch Pyke, but he didn't think that he would overtake Steve, so he focussed instead on retrieving the orange rucksack. The fence was high, possibly too high to scale, possibly not. Lake never found out, full of adrenalin, his mind took in the height of the fence but also its state of repair. He dropped his right shoulder and simply charged through it. There was a tremendous crashing sound and splinters everywhere. He half stumbled, half fell and performed a graceless sort of sideways roll before coming to a halt at the foot of a bird table beside an orange rucksack. He fumbled in his pocket for the transmit button. "*From Joe. I've got the gear.*"

An elderly lady was standing in the garden. She stood stock-still, transfixed in shock and horror. In her right hand a watering can spilled its contents onto her feet. The absurdity of the situation dawned on Lake. "It's okay," he said, "I'm here on behalf of the Queen."

For a moment Pyke thought that he might somehow get away. He heard a curse and a thud behind him. His pursuer had perhaps fallen. He ignored the searing pain across his chest and forced his legs and arms to pump. But Kevin Cleary had spent three months at Scampton and seen *The Great Escape* at least four times. He steered his Yamaha past Pyke's Mercedes and was gathering speed across the playing fields. In his mind he was Steve McQueen. In the van Monster was laughing and trying to capture the scene on video. Not to be outdone, Carl was driving the Primera diagonally across the playing fields. He had always hated this car and part of him was hoping that he would have an excuse to wreck it.

Pyke heard the roar of the motorcycle. He looked over his right shoulder and saw it. Instinctively he veered away to his left but failed to see the waist-high rope guarding a patch of newly sown grass. More importantly he failed to see the iron spike holding it up. It caught him amidships, as the cricket commentators euphemistically call it, and he went down in agony. Steve slowed to a jog and then a walk as he tried to get his breath back.

"John Edward Pyke. My name is Bradford. I'm a Customs officer and I'm arresting you on suspicion of being involved in the illegal importation of controlled drugs."

Pyke grunted, rolled over and was sick.

*

Michael drove back to Rutland steadily. His mind was full of his interview at Dover. None of it made sense. The idea of Giles being

305

caught with a bagful of pills was simply preposterous. And if, by some miracle, he had been his grandfather would hardly have summoned him home with the 'hunky dory' codeword. Was it possible that the old man had been coerced? That idea was even more laughable. And, if any of it had been true. If, for example, he had been seen in Baarle Nassau they would hardly have just let him walk out, would they? Unless he had been released to lead Customs to his grandfather. He started to look for a tail. He pulled into Birchanger Green services and made a phone call from a public phone. Then he took up a position from which he could see a surveillance officer go and make a call themselves to mark his. Nothing. He ran through the full range of anti-surveillance techniques that his grandfather had taught him. Nothing.

*

When he arrived home, there was a black Range Rover parked outside the old vicarage. He parked the Montego in the ancient garage and closed the doors with difficulty. It had been a long day. Wearily he walked to the back door and into the kitchen. Giles was there, kneeling in front of the fridge and wrestling with the ice tray.

"Oh, hello!" said Giles, looking up, the light of the fridge illuminating just half of his face. Cast half in shadow, half in bright light, Giles' face looked different, not entirely different, just slightly…

Understanding dawned upon Michael. "Ah!" he said. "Oh, you sod! You bloody sod!"

"They're in the front room."

"Of course they are. Of course they are."

It wasn't really chilly enough for a fire, but old people feel the cold and besides, it seemed to somehow fit the circumstances. The brigadier was sitting in his usual place, nearest the hearth. Michael took the other armchair, where he could see both him and the young woman on the sofa. Alongside Giles the resemblance that had been nagging him was obvious.

"Philippa Templeton, I presume?"

"Good evening, Michael, you must be tired."

Michael turned to his grandfather. "Is this the something that was bound to turn up?"

The old man nodded. He tried not to appear smug, but he was out of practice.

"We can do this in the morning if you prefer," said Philippa.

Giles entered at this moment with a glass full of ice.

"Well played, Giles," said Michael. "Well played indeed."

Giles beamed.

Philippa extended a glass towards Giles, and he dropped two cubes of ice into it. "Am I correct in assuming that you have deduced who I am and why I am here?"

"Oh, I think I have a pretty good idea." He glanced again at his grandfather, who had given up all pretence now and was beaming like a pensioner who had produced an unfeasibly large marrow.

Phillipa went on. "It's all very irregular, of course, even for us. Normally there are candidate assessments, background checks, aptitude tests, interviews and so on."

"I imagine that normally the candidate actually knows he is a candidate throughout the process."

"Well, yes, as I say, it's irregular, but given your, er, pedigree, we dispensed with some of the more tedious stages."

"And proceeded directly to the aptitude test?"

"Quite."

"How did I do?"

"A narrow pass."

"Narrow?"

"Yes, quite good in parts, commendable discipline. Decent under interrogation. Fieldcraft a bit slack in places, but we can fix that. I liked the shameless manipulation of Giles here, enjoyed that."

"My manipulation of *him*?"

"Yes, well. But the thing that tipped the balance in your favour was your appetite for… how shall I put it?"

"Skulduggery and mischief?"

"Something like that."

"And Luise?"

"Who's Luise?"

Was there a very slight twinkle in Phillipa's eye? He decided to believe that there was. "So what is the next stage, of this selection process?"

"Oh, there are no more stages. The process is complete."

Michael looked once more at his grandfather. A tweed-clad old man, sitting in his favourite armchair, enjoying a quiet retirement in the heart of the country. A man he had barely known a couple of months ago. When had it begun? The pub quiz, probably. Or was it the extraordinary find under the grass clippings? He couldn't have arranged that, surely? And everything since then. When had he called his old friends? Was he even really retired?

THIRTY-TWO

The old man was pottering about in the kitchen when Michael made it downstairs at about nine o'clock.

"Ah, there you are, Mikey, would you like some tea?"

Unusually the radio was on. "Grandpa? I have a couple of questions…"

The old man raised a hand in a signal for Michael to be quiet.

"A Lincoln man will appear in court this morning charged with importing ten thousand ecstasy tablets. John Edward Pyke of Staunton Crescent was arrested by Customs officers in Newark on Thursday."

"And I suppose you wanted me in Germany in case anything went wrong?"

"Of course."

"Will he be convicted, do you think?"

"I imagine so. He was caught red-handed. He's been under surveillance for weeks. He's going to have trouble explaining why he's been visiting telephone kiosks and cathedrals, bowling alleys and graveyards. And why he has been placing adverts for the sale of puppies and golf clubs."

"And the other two jokers? The ones in that ridiculous car?"

"Also red-handed, as I understand it."

"And if any of them mention us?"

"What are they going to say? That they received instructions from someone they never met? Whose name they never knew, without even a telephone number? It couldn't possibly help them."

"But could Customs trace it back to us?"

"I doubt it, and there is nothing they could prove if they did. No, the exercise is complete. Mr Pyke and his friends will get their just deserts and you will have a career that I think you will rather enjoy."

"And what do you have?"

"Another successful mission to put in my mental scrapbook. At my age that's the most one can reasonably expect. And I've got a couple of cases of my favourite beer and Phillipa very kindly brought me back a packet of my favourite biscuits. I call that a more than satisfactory outcome."

*

McBride and Lake decided to take one last walk around Scampton before they left it for the final time. The video and radio links had been removed, the television and video. The maps and pictures were no longer on the wall, and their footsteps echoed slightly as they prowled the corridors checking for anything that might have been overlooked, but mostly just enjoying a companionable silence.

"I was thinking," began Lake, "perhaps our next target should be the brigadier."

McBride shook his head slowly and removed the pipe from his mouth. "I'm not sure that that would be particularly fruitful."

"You don't think he's a smuggler for hire?"

"I don't know what he is. Except this. He's a pro. And he didn't behave like one."

"What do you mean?"

"The last run. He took Pyke to places he had been before. Used methods he had used before. Left-handed golf clubs? Really? He was building a case against him. Sending him to buy an orange rucksack. Orange! And that nonsense with the hole in the back wall of the garage. He knew it was being watched. And he gave Pyke enough notice to give us time to respond, to be in position, to gain the evidence that he knew we needed. And finally, that last text. Had he ever sent a text before? No. But he knew it would be live on Pyke's phone when he was arrested. That makes it evidence. Admissible in court. The brigadier was building our case for us. He wanted Pyke caught, and not just that, he wanted him to be certain to be convicted."

"And so… what? He set him up?"

"No. Not that. Pyke is a drug smuggler. The evidence against him is overwhelming and legally obtained. There's no miscarriage of justice here."

"So, the brigadier was on our side?"

"I don't know. I don't know."

They had reached the door. McBride locked it for the last time.

"Are you going to miss it? All this? I mean, you know, retirement?"

"Times change. We all move on. Actually, your life is going to change far more profoundly than mine."

"What?"

"Ah, Joseph. I hope I have helped to make you a slightly better investigator. But under no circumstances should you seek to emulate me as a father."

"How? How?"

McBride chuckled. "Francis is a nice name, don't you think? Or Frances?"

"How?"

"I'll let you work that out. Now," he looked at his watch, "I retire in three hours. That's plenty of time for you to buy me a pint."

EPILOGUE

Winter had arrived right on cue. The brigadier shivered slightly inside his dressing gown. The heat from last night's fire had gone. He shuffled across the living room, he would have called it a drawing room, and pulled back the heavy velvet curtains. Outside frost had glazed the top of his privet hedge and there was a dusting on the war memorial opposite. The brigadier peered out and emitted a small noise that might have been exasperation or might have been the sound of the contentment that accompanies the fulfilment of a minor prediction. He decided that his morning cup of coffee could wait and that, in all conscience, he should get dressed and venture outside.

It was eight o'clock, but the clock set into the tower of St Cuthbert's no longer chimed on the hour. The brigadier glanced at it as he crossed the road to the bench opposite the war memorial. He sat down next to the other occupant.

"It's a bit cold for this, don't you think, Francis?"

"I didn't expect to have to wait for very long, Sir Bernard."

"Bernard will do, if you don't mind. I'd rather keep the K quiet."

"Of all the things I know about you, the one you want kept quiet is that!"

"Yes. Well, the difference is, you see, you can *prove* I'm a knight."

"Are you sure that's all I can prove?"

"Yes. As a matter of fact, I am sure."

Neither man said anything for a minute and a half.

McBride nodded at the names on the war memorial. "Relatives?"

"Uncles, my father's brothers."

"Somme?"

"One at the Somme, three at Ypres."

"Ah! Tell me, Bernard, did your family lose anyone at Waterloo?"

"Oh, very good, Francis, very good. Touché."

Another period of silence. This one lasted almost two minutes. McBride shivered.

"We're going to be neighbours."

"Yes, so I understand."

The two men sat in silence for a few more minutes.

"Francis?"

"Frank."

"Frank, are you any good at pub quizzes?"

"I'm bloody unbeatable."

"Oh, I think we should be able to do better than that."

ABOUT THE AUTHOR

Michael Dane spent over ten years as an officer in the Customs and Excise National Investigation Service investigating drug trafficking, VAT fraud and smuggling of all kinds. He later retrained as a lawyer and joined the private sector where he investigated fraud and corruption all over the world. He is retired and lives in the Vale of Belvoir.